Consider Sterry, John Sterry

The American Youth

being a new and complete course of introductory mathematics: designed for the

use of private students

Consider Sterry, John Sterry

The American Youth
being a new and complete course of introductory mathematics: designed for the use of private students

ISBN/EAN: 9783337398613

Printed in Europe, USA, Canada, Australia, Japan

Cover: Foto ©Andreas Hilbeck / pixelio.de

More available books at **www.hansebooks.com**

THE

AMERICAN YOUTH

BEING

A NEW AND COMPLETE COURSE

OF

Introductory Mathematics:

DESIGNED FOR THE USE OF

PRIVATE STUDENTS.

BY

CONSIDER and JOHN STERRY.

VOL. I.

—————*where the mind*
In endless growth and infinite ascent,
Rises from state to state, and world to world.
THOMSON.

PRINTED AT *PROVIDENCE,*
BY BENNETT WHEELER, FOR THE AUTHORS, 1790.

PREFACE.

TIME, *ever big with wonders to be unfolded to the human mind, has ush-ered in, through a series of the most important events, the rising Empire of America ; who hath established her own Independence, and the flame of her liberty has spread itself to the remotest parts of the earth ; the ef-fect of which great example has not yet spent its force, but must continue to operate throughout ages, and form a grand ingredient in the active fermentation, and in the history of nations.*

But the great object of true national dignity and grandeur, consists in the cultivation of the human mind, whereby the natural savage barbarity, rudeness and im-becility of human nature are eradicated, and those prin-ciples of knowledge and virtue engrafted in the soul, which are the foundation of that knowledge and pre-eminence of merit, which is the noblest of all distinctions.

As soon as we begin to exist, that savage and im-becile spirit takes root in the soul, and grows as the mind enlarges, till the seeds of knowledge by cultivation do take effectual root, and then like the tender bud it will burst its native bonds, expand and flourish in its own beauty : The veil will then disappear, and an

infinite

infinite diverſity of ſcenes, both pleaſing and inſtructing, will open themſelves to our view. But in order to prepare the mind for theſe pleaſing and enlarging views, we muſt early employ ourſelves in the ſtudy of ſomething which is noble and important, whereby our minds may be cultivated aud brought to maturity. " A juſt and perfect acquaintance with the ſimple elements of ſcience, is a neceſſary ſtep towards our future progreſs and advancement ; and this, aſſiſted by laborious inveſtigation, and habitual enquiry will conſtantly lead to eminence and perfection."

" But as the various modes, ſituations and circumſtances of life are various, ſo accident, habit and education, have each their predominante influence, and give to every mind its particular bias." It is, therefore, for this reaſon, we particularly admire thoſe things which are the moſt compatible with our genius and purſuits in life.

" Riches and honours are the gifts of fortune, caſually beſtowed, or hereditarily received, and are frequently abuſed by their poſſeſſors ; but the ſuperiority of wiſdom and knowledge, is a pre-eminence of merit, that originates with the man, and is the nobleſt of all diſtinctions."

Since, therefore, the cultivation of knowledge is a thing of the laſt importance, too many attempts cannot be made to render it univerſal, and ſince youth is the time therefor, we have therefore, " only to point out to them ſome valuable acquiſition, and the means of obtaining it. The active principles are immediately put in motion, and the certainty of the conqueſt is enſured from a determination to conquer." But of all the ſciences cultivated by mankind, none are more uſeful than the
Mathematics,

Mathematics, to call forth a spirit of enterprise and enquiry. The unbounded variety of their application, which is of universal utility to mankind, first prompts our curiosity to have in possession a treasure of such inestimable value. By their elegant and sublime manner of reasoning, our minds are enlightened and our understanding enlarged, and thereby we acquire a habit of reasoning, an elevation of thought, that determines the mind and fixes it for every other pursuit; and none but those who either from sordid views, or a gross ignorance of what they despise, will ever think their time misspent, or their labours useless in the pursuit of that, which is the guide of our youth, and the perfection of our reason.

The subject of the present performance, is Arithmetic and Algebra, the foundation of all our mathematical enquiries.

Although a great number of books has been published on the subject of Mathematics, yet few of them are adapted to the capacity of young and tender minds. Where is that simplicity, plainness and brevity, which is absolutely necessary for the young and unassisted beginner? That close and refined reasoning with which those Authors' writings are replete, renders them unfit for learners in general, and entirely useless to those unassisted by a Tutor: They have consulted more the elegance of their diction, and refined demonstrations, than the method of conveying their knowledge to their readers. Others again, in attempting to render their subjects attainable to the weakest minds, have been so prolix and voluminous, as even to discourage a learner at the sight of their works: Thus, we see that writers in general, aim at the extremes, while the true and proper medium is for the most part omitted. Propriety therefore, and

compatibility

compatibility ought always to be the grand text, while simplicity joined with brevity leads the chain of argument.

In all countries, where the sciences are cultivated, local interests have been particularly considered, which must therefore exclude those who neglect the cultivation of the Arts and Sciences, from many advantages of their works.

Taking into consideration the works of those who have gone before us on this subject, the utility of an alteration appeared manifest, while reason and convenience urged the practicability thereof.

In the prosecution of this plan, we have in the first Book of the present Volume, explained the rudiments and application of numbers; beginning with the properties of an unit, we have led the learner by easy and natural gradations to the most remote analogies of the science. In all the calculations relating to money, we have made use of the Federal Money, or Money of the United States, which is not only much more concise than the present practice by pounds, shillings, &c. but it is equally estimable for its simplicity and brevity. The denominations of this money being in a decimal ratio, are therefore above all other numbers, the most natural and easy to be managed, and which must consequently give it a preference to any other method whatever.

The subject of the second Book is Algebra, or the analytic art; which above all others is the most extensive and sublime. It was by this, with the consideration of motion, that one did in some measure do honour to human nature itself, by his almost divine invention; which succeeding ages will view with pleasing admiration.*   *Algebra*

---

* Alluding to Sir Isaac Newton's invention of Fluxions.

Algebra is a general method of discovering truth in all cases where proper data can be established, with the greatest expedition, elegance and ease.

In delivering the rudiments of this science, we have particularly consulted the ease and accomodation of the learner, by confining every thing within the sphere of the ingenious Student, and therefore, exploding those tedious and complicated explanations, which are commonly to be found in authors on this subject. The leading questions are short and simple, and the method of arguing brief and conspicuous ; which particular, although of the last importance to facilitate the progress of learners, is too much neglected by most writers, and consequently, deter many from becoming acquainted with this interesting and important acquirement. Great attention has been paid to render the doctrine of irrational quantities plain and intelligible, particularly the method of expanding quantities into infinite series, and noting their powers and roots, which is a matter of the last importance in the higher branches of the Mathematics. And finally, through the whole of the following sheets, simplicity and brevity has been our general aim, and at the same time to explode all foreign and provincial customs, and adapt the whole to the practice and convenience of the United States.

Thus far, for the satisfaction of the learner, we have explained the economy of the present performance, we shall now submit it to the candid public, and from the pains we have taken to render the subject useful to learners in general, are not without hopes of its meeting with their approbation.

THE AUTHORS.

Preston (Connecticut) July, 1790.

RECOMMENDATIONS.

Extract of a letter from Mr. NATHAN DABOLL, *Teacher of Mathematics and Aſtronomy, in the Academic School in Plainfield, to the Authors ; dated March* 1, 1787.

GENTLEMEN,

"I HAVE peruſed the firſt Volume of your new courſe of introductory Mathematics, entitled THE AMERICAN YOUTH ; and it appears to me a work well executed, and compatible with its deſign. You have given your rules and examples in a conciſe, plain and familiar manner, and conſequently well-adapted your matter to the capacities of learners : I therefore eſteem it a very valuable performance, and wiſh you ſucceſs in its publication, and that it may meet with an encouragement from the public equal to its merit."

From

RECOMMENDATIONS.

From

RECOMMENDATIONS.

From Col. SAMUEL MOTT *to the Authors, dated Preſton, April* 28, 1788.

GENTLEMEN,

"YOUR Manuſcript Treatiſe on Arithmetic and Algebra, entitled THE AMERICAN YOUTH, has been put into my hands. I have paid particular attention in its peruſal. I have heretofore been conſiderably engaged in the reading and ſtudy of authors upon the various branches of Mathematics, though of late I have been more diverted from that purſuit. It has however given me great pleaſure and ſatisfaction to obſerve the ingenuity, concifeneſs and perſpicuity which appears in your work, notwithſtanding the extenſive and finiſhed reſearches demonſtrated in all your rules and examples ; yet it appears to me exceedingly well accommodated to the capacity of a learner, and your method through the whole more eaſy than any I have before ſeen. If you ſhould publiſh your book (which my high eſteem for mathematical ſcience, and ſincere regard for the progreſs of literature among the youth of our country, induces me earneſtly to wiſh you may) juſtice obliges me to ſay, that I am clearly of opinion it will be found more uſeful among ſtudents than any other author now extant upon the ſubject. I ſincerely wiſh

you

RECOMMENDATIONS.

you fuccefs, and that you may meet with every encouragement which the merit of fo important a work
deferves."

From the Rev. JOSEPH HUNTINGTON, D. D. *one of
the Truftees of Dartmouth College, &c. to the Hon.*
JOHN DOUGLAS, *Efq. dated Coventry, May* 23,
1788.

"I HAVE with much pleafure perufed the mathematical compofition in which the two Meffrs.
STERRY's are united, and really think it worthy of
publication and encouragement : The fcience of
Arithmetic and Algebra has hitherto been extended
nearly to its bounds, but I efteem this work an ex-
cellent piece for the ftudy of youth, to lead them to
the knowledge of this ufeful fcience, fince it is more
eafy and intelligible to tender capacities than any
work of the kind preceding, and this, more efpecially
in the moft abftrufe part of the whole fcience, *i. e.*
Algebra. I could wifh that you, Sir, and many o-
ther gentlemen, eminent for their friendfhip to the
liberal fciences, might pay attention to the work I
have alluded to."

TABLE of CONTENTS.

PART I.

PART II.

PART III.

A

VII.

ALTHOUGH the Authors examined the Proof-Sheets, yet the following escaped their Notice.

ERRATA.

PAGE 28, last line, dele See the Example. P. 34, l. 12. read 69530000. l. 14, r. 720800. P. 35, l. 18, for 3, r. 4. P. 55, l. 4, r. content. l. 24, for 3 qr. 3 na. r. 1 qr. 3 na. l. 26, for 3 qr. 2 na. r. 1. qr. 2 na. P. 67, l. 4, r. 105 dol. P. 74, l. 9, r. 56388. l. 19, r. 15480 yards. P. 77, l. 20, for in, r. is. P. 80, l. 13, for 13, r. 15. P. 85, l. 1, for $20\frac{8}{20} \div 20$, r. $20\frac{8}{20} \div 24$. P. 100, l. 15, for .5, r. 5. P. 106, l. 20, r. preceding. P. 107, l. 27, r. $8 =$. P. 113, l. 12, r. 31.415, &c. P. 132, l. 25, r. numbers. P. 157, l. 13, r. operation. P. 169, l. 13, r. 49 cts. P. 193, l. 7, r. 51 dol. $72\frac{24}{38}$ cts. l. 15, r. fellowship. P. 322, l. 5, r. $6 \times 2 \times 6$. P. 245, l. 16, for $+2a$, r. $+2b$. P. 246, for ax, r. az. P. 249, for $\sqrt{aw} - yb$, r. $\overline{\sqrt{aw} - yb}$. P. 266, l. 16, r. $\overline{x+y}|^2 \div \overline{x+y}|^2$. P. 288, for $a^{\frac{3}{6}}$, r. $a^{\frac{2}{6}}$. P. 353, l. 16, for last, r. xvi. P. 357, l. 19, r. $v = -c$. P. 379, l. 9, read axiom 8. l. 10, r. axiom 8. l. 18, r. axiom 8. P. 380, l. 1, r. ax. 7. l. 2, r. ax. 9. l. 3, r. ax. 8. l. 5, r. ax. 8.

B O O K I.

OF ARITHMETIC.

PART I.

ARITHMETIC of WHOLE NUMBERS.

CHAP. I.

Of DEFINITIONS and ILLUSTRATIONS.

ARITHMETIC consists of three parts; two of which are natural, and the third artificial. The first part of natural Arithmetic, is wherein an unit or integer represents one whole quantity, of any kind or species; and is therefore stiled Arithmetic of whole numbers. The second part of natural Arithmetic, is wherein an unit is considered as broken or divided into parts, either even or uneven, which are considered either as pure parts of an unit, or as parts mixed with an unit; and is usually stiled the doctrine of vulgar fractions. The third part, or artificial Arithmetic, is an easy and elegant method of managing fractional, or broken quantities; the operations are nearly similar to those of whole numbers. This part is of general use in the various branches of the Mathematics.

C   THE

THE operations of common Arithmetic in all its parts, are performed by the various ordering and difposing of ten *Arabic* characters, or numeral figures ; which are thefe following, viz.

one	two	three	four	five	fix	feven	eight	nine	cypher
1	2	3	4	5	6	7	8	9	0

AN unit (by *Euclid*) is that by which every thing that is, is one ; and number is compofed of a multitude of units.

NINE of the aforefaid figures, are compofed of units ; each character reprefenting fo many units put together in one fum, as was intended they fhould denote ; nine of thofe units, being the greateft number which is thought beft for any one character to reprefent ; the laft of the before-mentioned characters, is a cypher, or as fome call it a nothing ; for of itfelf it is nothing ; becaufe, if ever fo many cyphers be added to, or fubtracted from an unit or number, they will neither increafe nor diminifh its value : confequently a cypher of itfelf is no affignable quantity ; but cyphers annexed or prefixed to an unit or number, will increafe, or diminifh that unit or number in a tenfold proportion.

THAT the learner may underftand the following fheets, it is abfolutely neceffary for him to be well acquainted with the following *Algebraic* figns.

SIGNS & NAMES.   SIGNIFICATIONS.

+ Plus, or more, { is the fign of Addition : as $4+6$, which denotes that 6 is to be added to 4, and is read thus,——— 4 more 6.

— Minus, or lefs, { is the fign of Subtraction : as $4-2$, which fignifies that 2 is to be taken from $\cdot4$; and is read thus, 4 lefs 2.

X into,

✕ into, or with,	is the sign of Multiplication: thus 4✕3 denotes, that 3 is to be multiplied into 4; and is read thus, 4 into, or with, 3.
÷ by,	is the sign of Division: thus 6÷3, is 6 divided by 3, or $\frac{6}{3}$, signifies the same thing; and is read thus, 6 by 3.
= equal,	is the sign of Equality: and whenever this sign is placed between any two quantities, it denotes that those quantities are equal: thus 9=9; that is, 9 equals 9; also 6+4=10, is read 6 more 4 equals 10.
:: so is,	is the sign of Proportionality; and is always placed between the second and third numbers that are in proportion: thus 2:4::4:8.
: to,	is also a sign of Proportion, and is placed between the first and second, third and fourth numbers in proportion: thus 2:4::3:6; is read thus, 2 to 4 so is 3 to 6.
$\overline{4+6}$✕2	denotes the sum of 4 & 6 multiplied with 2.
÷	is the sign of continued Proportion.

THE whole doctrine of Number is founded on the five following general rules, to wit, Notation, Addition, Subtraction, Multiplication and Division.

CHAP. II.

CHAP. II.

Of NOTATION or NUMERATION.

NOTATION or Numeration teaches us, how to exprefs the value of figures ; and confequently to note or write down any propofed number, according to its juft value ; in the operation of which, two things muft be obferved, viz. the order of writing down figures, and the method of valuing each in its proper place, as in the following Table ;

NUMERATION TABLE.	
Hundreds of Thoufands of Millions	3
Tens of Thoufands of Millions	2
Thoufands of Millions	1
Hundreds of Millions	9
Tens of Millions	8
Millions	7
Hundreds of Thoufands	6
Tens of Thoufands	5
Thoufands	4
Hundreds	3
Tens	2
Units	1

Here

'HERE the order of reckoning begins on the right hand, to wit, at unity, and fo on as the table directs. But to make the underftanding of this table plain, it is required to exprefs the value of the numeral figures 321. Firft, beginning at the firft figure on the right hand, viz. at 1, which ftands in the units' place, where it reprefents its own fimple value, which is an unit, or 1 ; the next to be confidered is the figure 2, which ftands in the tens' place, reprefenting fo many tens, as the figure 2 is compofed of units, which are two ; fo that the figure 2 ftanding in the place of tens reprefents 2 tens, or 20 ; the next figure, 3, ftands in the hundreds' place, and fignifies as many hundreds as the faid figure hath units, viz. 3, that is, three hundred : now, if the whole value of the figures 321 be expreffed, the expreffion will be three hundred twenty-one. Altho the figure 3, is in the laft place on the right, or the firft on the left, yet when we come to read or exprefs them, we begin with the figure 3 ; becaufe the method of reading figures is the fame as that of words. Hence the firft figure in numbering, is the firft figure on the right hand ; but in reading or expreffing the value of numbers, the firft figure in the expreffion is the firft figure on the left hand. Again, let it be required to read or exprefs 7645. Here as before, the firft figure of the propofed number, to wit. 5, ftands in the units' place, and is 5 units, or five, the fecond figure which is 4, is in the tens' place, and is four tens or 40, the third figure which is 6, in the hundreds' place, is called hundreds, and the fourth figure, which ftands in the thoufands' place, is for the fame reafon called thoufands ; and the expreffion for the whole value, beginning as before, is feven thoufand fix hundred forty-five.

IF

IF what has been faid concerning notation and valuation of figures, be thoroughly confidered, together with the following examples and their anfwers,
the whole bufinefs of Numeration will appear plain
to the meaneft capacity.

EXAMPLES.

What is the value of 56434 ?
Anfwer. *Fifty-fix thoufand four hundred thirty-four.*
What is the value of 7843217 ?
Anf. *Seven million eight hundred forty-three thou-
fand two hundred feventeen.*
What is the value of 640036 ?
Anf. *Six hundred forty thoufand thirty-fix.*
What is 891000002 ?
Anf. *Eight hundred ninety-one million two.*

C H A P. III.

Of ADDITION of SIMPLE WHOLE NUM-
BERS.

ADDITION is the collecting or putting together feveral quantities or numbers into one
fum, fo that their total amount may be known; and
in order to perform the operations of this rule, two
things muft be carefully obferved, which are, Firft,
the right placing or fetting each figure in its proper
place; that is, units muft ftand under units, tens under tens, hundreds under hundreds, and fo on, fetting
each denomination under that of the fame value:
thus 246 + 25 + 163, being fet as directed, will ftand
thus,

$$\text{thus,} \quad \begin{cases} 246 \\ 25 \\ 163 \end{cases}$$

The second thing to be obferved, is the right collecting or adding together each perpendicular row of figures, placed as before directed ; which is performed as in the following example, being the fame as made ufe of above, viz. 246+25+163 :

$$\text{or thus,} \quad \begin{cases} 246 \\ 25 \\ 163 \end{cases}$$

Then ftriking a line beneath the figures, as in the example ; begin on the right hand at the units' place, adding together all thofe figures which ftand in the units' place, and if their fum be under ten, fet it down underneath in the units' place ; but if their fum exceed ten, fet down the furplus, carrying one to the next place, viz. the tens' place : or, more generally, as many tens as the fum of thofe units amounts to, you muft carry to the next place of figures, to wit, the tens' place, adding them up with all the figures that ftand in that perpendicular line ; and fo on for the reft ; remembering to carry one for every ten of your aggregate : the whole of which will be illuftrated in the following

EXAMPLE.

Find the fum of the following numbers, viz. 392+466+256.

Those numbers being placed as the rule directs, will ftand

$$\text{thus,} \quad \begin{cases} 392 \\ 466 \\ 256 \end{cases}$$

1114=fum required.   Then

Then begin with the bottom figure, in the units' place ; faying 6 and 6 is 12, and 2 is 14; fetting down 4, carry 1 to the next, or place of tens, faying 5 and 1 that I carry make 6, and 6 is 12, and 9 is 21 ; here becaufe the aggregate or fum total is 21 units (or becaufe it ftands in the tens' place) 2 tens and one unit ; therefore fet down 1 and carry 2 to the next place, faying 2 and 2 that I carry make 4, and 4 is 8, and 3 is 11 ; which being the fum of the laft place of figures in the example, fet down the whole. [See the work at the bottom of the preceding page.]

THE reafon of fetting down the furplus, or odd figures, and carrying for the tens, as in the laft and all other examples in addition of fimple quantities, is to fhorten the work under confideration ; and to fave the trouble of ufing fuperfluous figures. To exemplify which, let us make ufe of the foregoing example, to wit, 392+466+256, which muft be placed

<table>
<tr><td rowspan="8">thus,</td><td>3</td><td>9</td><td>2</td><td></td></tr>
<tr><td>4</td><td>6</td><td>6</td><td></td></tr>
<tr><td>2</td><td>5</td><td>6</td><td></td></tr>
<tr><td></td><td>1</td><td>4</td><td>the fum of the row of units</td></tr>
<tr><td>2</td><td>0</td><td>0</td><td>the fum of the row of tens</td></tr>
<tr><td>9</td><td>0</td><td>0</td><td>the fum of the row of hundreds</td></tr>
<tr><td>1 1</td><td>1</td><td>4</td><td>the fum of the whole ;</td></tr>
</table>

then adding up each fingle row, fet down its fum in its proper place, in the fame manner as if there were but one fingle row ; fupplying the vacant places on the right hand with cyphers. Hence the refult of this operation is the fame as in the former method of carrying for the tens ; and hence alfo it appears, that, adding the cyphers, makes no alteration in the value of the fum of the other figures.

THE

THE manner of proving your work, flows as a natural confequent, from the following felf-evident propofition, on which the truth of the rule depends, viz. that every whole is equal to all its parts taken together. Wherefore if you divide, or feperate the given numbers into two, or more parcels, according to your propofition ; and by adding together each part fo feperated, if the fum of all thofe parts added together, is equal to the fum total of all the given numbers, found before feperation, your work is right.

THIS method will appear plain by the following example. Suppofe it were required to add together the following numbers, viz. $3489 + 6725 + 2324 + 6744$; which according to the rule of Notation muft ftand thus,

$$\begin{array}{r} 3489 \\ 6725 \\ 2324 \\ 6744 \\ \hline 19282 \end{array}$$

$19282 = $ *fum before feperation.*

First part $\left\{\begin{array}{l} 3489 \\ 6725 \end{array}\right.$

$10214 = $ *fum of firft part.*

Second part $\left\{\begin{array}{l} 2324 \\ 6744 \end{array}\right.$

$9068 = $ *fum of fecond part.*

The fum of the firft and fecond parts $\left\{\begin{array}{l} 9068 \\ 10214 \end{array}\right.$

Sum of all the parts 19282

which agrees with the fum total before feperation ; therefore the work is right. But the moft ufual methods of proving Addition, is either by beginning at the top, and reckoning downwards ; which fum, if equal to that found by cafting upwards, the work is right. Or, firft add together all the propofed num-

D

bers

bers into one fum; then feperate the upper number
from the reft, by a line, and add together the remaining numbers beneath; placing their fum under
the former, or fum total before feperation; which being done, add the fum laft found to the upper line in
your example; which fum, if equal to the fum total
or firft addition, the work is right: this is the fame
in effect, as the firft method of proof, though a little
different in mode, as will appear by the following
example.

$$34678$$

$$
\begin{aligned}
& 24532 \\
& 12760 \\
& 53865 \\
& 21671
\end{aligned}
$$

$147506 =$ *fum of the whole*
$112828 =$ *fum of all but the upper line*
$147506 = 34678 + 112828 =$ *fum of the whole* :
therefore the work is right.

TAKE the following examples, without their anfwers, for practice.

3457643	460039	2	6538764
4567012	914321	372	875623
2354123	675422	42734	43521
1678432	342310	8173456	6300
		37240	579
		421	84
		2	1

CHAP. IV.

Of SUBTRACTION of SIMPLE WHOLE NUM-BERS.

SUBTRACTION is the taking one number out of another; whereby the remainder, difference, or excefs may be known : thus 3 taken out or from 5, leaves 2, which is the difference between 3 and 5 ; and is alfo the excefs of 5 above 3.

HENCE it follows, that the number from which fubtraction is to be made, muft be equal to, or greater than the fubtrahend, or number to be fubtracted ; and alfo, that Subtraction is the reverfe of Addition ; for Subtraction is the taking of one number from another, but Addition is the collecting or putting them together.

HERE the Notation is the fame as in Addition, to wit, thofe numbers which are of like value, muft ftand directly beneath each other ; that is, units muft ftand under units, tens under tens, &c. After having thus placed your numbers, the lefs beneath the greater, you may proceed to fubtract them apart, by obferving the following

RULE.

BEGIN with the firft figure on the right-hand, which ftands in the units' place, and fubtract the lower figure from that which ftands directly over it, of the fame value ; fetting down the remainder (if any) beneath in the units' place : If the figure in your fubtrahend be equal to the figure which ftands directly over it, you muft fet a cypher for the remainder ; but if the lower, or figure in your fubtrahend, contains more units than your upper figure, you muft add 10 to the upper figure, or fuppofe it to be fo added

ed

ed in your mind; then fubtract your lower figure from your upper fo increafed, fetting down the remainder or difference in its proper place; then proceed to your next place of figures; now it is fuppofed that the 10 you before added was borrowed from your next fuperior place of figures, where you muft pay what you before borrowed, which is performed as the ufual method is, by calling the lower figure, ftanding in that place, one more than it really is; then fubtracting it fo augmented, from your upper figure, or figure ftanding directly over it, fet down the difference as before directed; and fo on, from one place of figures to another, until the whole be completed; the whole of which, is illuftrated in the following

EXAMPLES.

Suppose, that from 4567, you were to fubtract 3692; which numbers, being placed according to the rule, will ftand

thus, $\begin{cases} 4567 \\ 3692 \end{cases}$

Here begin with the 2, faying 2 from 7 and there remains 5, fetting it down as directed; then proceed to your next place of figures, faying 9 from 6 I cannot, becaufe my lower figure, to wit, 9, contains more units than my upper, or figure from which I would fubtract; therefore I fuppofe 10 to be added to the upper figure which makes 16; then faying 9 from 16 and there remains 7; then proceed to the next place, where you muft pay what you have borrowed, by faying 6 and 1 that I borrowed make 7; then 7 from 5 I cannot, but 7 from $5+10=15$, and there remains 8; then to the next place, faying 3 and 1 that I borrowed make 4, 4 from 5 and there remains 1; now there being no more places of figures, fet down the 1 and the work is done. (See the example.)

THE

THE truth of fubtraction is founded on the fame felf-evident propofition, or axiom, as that of Addition, viz. the whole is equal to all its parts taken together. From which propofition is deduced the following method of proving your work, to wit, by adding the fubtrahend, or number to be fubtracted, to the remainder : for the number from which fubtraction is made, is here confidered as the whole, and the fubtrahend, as a part of that whole ; confequently if that part be taken from the whole, the remainder will be the other part ; therefore if both parts when added together, be equal to the whole, the work is right.

HENCE it is manifeft that fubtraction may be proved by fubtraction ; for if from

$$67834 \text{ the whole,}$$
$$\text{is taken } 53723 \text{ a part of that whole,}$$

there will remain 14111 the other part;
and if from 67834 the whole, there is taken
the laft part 14111

there will remain 53723 the firft part, or fubtrahend: confequently, &c.

AGAIN, if from 27942 the whole,

$$\text{is taken } 13724 \text{ a part of that whole ;}$$

there will remain 14218 the other part,

$$27942 = \text{fum of the fubtrahend}$$

and remainder = the whole.

TAKE the following examples for practice.

From	37654	394076	2876955	7654109
take	28765	123468	423610	347472
Rem.				

CHAP. V.

CHAP. V.

Of SIMPLE MULTIPLICATION.

MULTIPLICATION is a rule by which a given number may be increafed any number of times propofed.

THERE are three requifites in Multiplication : firft, the multiplicand, or number to be multiplied : fecond, the multiplier, which denotes how many times the multiplicand is to be taken ; for by *Euclid*, as many units as there are in the multiplier, fo many times is the multiplicand to be added to itfelf : third, the product, or multiplicand increafed fo many times as there are units in the multiplier.

SUPPOSE for example, that 7 be increafed 4 times ; that is, to multiply 7 into or with 4 ; thefe numbers muft be placed as in Addition,

$$\text{thus,} \left\{ \begin{array}{l} 7 \ \textit{multiplicand} \\ 4 \ \textit{multiplier} \end{array} \right.$$

28 *product.*

Now that 4 times 7 make 28, will appear evident by fetting down the multiplicand 4 times, and adding up the whole, as in this,

$$\left\{ \begin{array}{l} 7 \\ 7 \\ 7 \\ 7 \end{array} \right.$$

28 = *fum or product.*

HENCE it is plain, that multiplication is a concife method of Addition.

BUT before you proceed any further on the fubject of multiplication, you muft learn the following Table :——

MUL-

MULTIPLICATION TABLE.

1	2	3	4	5	6	7	8	9	10	11	12
2	4	6	8	10	12	14	16	18	20	22	24
3	6	9	12	15	18	21	24	27	30	33	36
4	8	12	16	20	24	28	32	36	40	44	48
5	10	15	20	25	30	35	40	45	50	55	60
6	12	18	24	30	36	42	48	54	60	66	72
7	14	21	28	35	42	49	56	63	70	77	84
8	16	24	32	40	48	56	64	72	80	88	96
9	18	27	36	45	54	63	72	81	90	99	108
10	20	30	40	50	60	70	80	90	100	110	120
11	22	33	44	55	66	77	88	99	110	121	132
12	24	36	48	60	72	84	96	108	120	132	144

For an explanation of the foregoing Table, fuppofe that it were required to find the product of 3✕4. Firft, look in the left hand column for 3, and right oppofite with it in the column under 4 at the top, is 12, the product of 3✕4.

Again, to find the product of 9✕12. Look for 9 in the left hand column as before, and right oppofite to it, under 12 in the upper column, is 108, the product required; and the like is to be underftood of all the reft.

Having given you this fhort, but comprehenfive idea of the foregoing Table, we fhall now proceed to examples,

examples, with this caution, to wit, that in multiplying, care muſt be taken, that the product of the firſt
figures, ſtand directly under its multiplier; alſo remembering to carry 1 for every 10 of the product.

EXAMPLES.

It is required to multiply 120×94; which placed
as before directed will ſtand thus,

$$120 \; \textit{multiplicand}$$
$$94 \; \textit{multiplier}$$

$$480$$
$$1080$$

$$11280 \; \textit{product.}$$

Here you begin with that figure of your multiplier, which ſtands in the units' place, viz. 4, ſaying
4 times 0 is 0, which ſet down directly under the
figure you are multiplying with; then ſay 4 times 2
is 8, which ſet under the 9; then 4 times 1 is 4, which
alſo place as in the example; and the product of the
multiplicand with the firſt figure of your multiplier,
is 480: then begin with the next figure of your multiplier, ſaying 9 times 0 is 0, which place under your
multiplying figure, then ſay 9 times 2 is 18; here ſet
down 8 and carry 1 to the next place, ſaying 9 times
1 is 9, and 1 that I carry makes 10; now this being
the product of the laſt place of figures, ſet down the
whole, and the product of the multiplicand, with
the ſecond figure of your multiplier is 1080, or more
properly 10800: then adding up both products,
their ſum is 11280, the product required. (See the
example above.)

It is required to multiply 2439×421; theſe numbers placed as directed will ſtand

thus,

thus, $\left\{\begin{array}{c}2439\\421\end{array}\right\}$ *factors*

$2439 = product$ *of* 2439×1
$48780 = product$ *of* 2439×20
$975600 = product$ *of* 2439×400

$1026819 = product$ *of* 2439×421

THE annexing of cyphers, as in the laft example, is to fupply the vacant places; and to fhew the feveral products are increafed in a tenfold proportion, with regard to the places in which your multiplying figures ftand. Thus the product of the multiplicand with the fecond figure of your multiplier, is not the product of 2439×2, but the product of 2439×2 tens or 20; which product is 10 times more than it would have been, had the multiplying figure (2) ftood in the units' place; fo alfo the annexing of two cyphers, as in the product of the multiplicand with the third figure of the multiplier, to wit, 4, is becaufe that figure ftands in the hundreds' place; and therefore the product is not 2439×4, but really the product of 2439×400; yet thofe cyphers may be omitted, by obferving the direction in the beginning of this chapter, viz. that the firft figure of the feveral products ftand directly beneath its correfponding figure of the multiplier.

Find the product of 24354×32001

thus, $\left\{\begin{array}{c}24354\\32001\end{array}\right\}$ *factors*

24354
48708
73062

$779352354 = 24354 \times 32001 = product$ *required.*

E

HERE

HERE you may obferve that we pafs the cyphers, taking care only to place the next figure according to the foregoing directions.

WHEN there are cyphers on the right-hand of the multiplicand, or multiplier, or to both, you may multiply the figures as before, neglecting the cyphers, until you have found the product of the digets only ; to which annex fo many cyphers as there are in both factors: as in thefe,

$$21200 \atop 34 \Big\} \textit{factors} \qquad\qquad 347650 \atop 200 \Big\} \textit{factors}$$

$$848 \atop 636 \qquad\qquad 69530000 = 347650 \times 200$$

$$7208200 = 21200 \times 34$$

$$24000000 \atop 24000000 \Big\} \textit{factors}$$

$$96 \atop 48$$

$$576000000000000 = 24000000 \times 24000000$$

IF it be required to multiply any number with 10, 100, 1000, &c. you need only annex to your multiplicand fo many cyphers as are in the multiplier, and the work is done ; as in the following,

$$4647 \times 10 = 46470 \qquad\qquad 20 \times 100 = 2000$$
$$5224 \times 1000 = 5224000 \qquad 300 \times 1000 = 300000$$
$$26460 \times 10000 = 264600000$$

HERE it may perhaps be ufeful, to acquaint the learner of the method of performing Multiplication by Addition; which in fome cafes will be found ufeful :

ful : the method is as follows : firſt, ſet down the 9 digets, or numeral figures, in a ſmall column made for that purpoſe ; then againſt 1, place the multiplicand, againſt 2, double the multiplicand, againſt 3, three times the multiplicand, and ſo on to the laſt.

Find the product of 2439×421 by Addition.

1	2439	=multiplicand
2	4878	=2 times do.
3	7317	=3 do. do.
4	9756	=4 do. do.
5	12195	=5 do. do.
6	14634	=6 do. do.
7	17073	=7 do. do.
8	19512	=8 do. do.
9	21951	=9 do. do.

againſt $\begin{cases} 1 \ is & 2439 \\ 2 & 4878 \\ 4 & 9756 \end{cases}$

Sum 1026819=2439×421=prod. req.

HERE it is evident, that the foregoing table will ſerve let the multiplier be any number whatever ; for ſuppoſe it were required to find the product of 2439×6734.

OPERATION.

againſt $\begin{cases} 4 \ is & 9756 & =2439×4 \\ 3 & 7317 & =2439×30 \\ 7 & 17073 & =2439×700 \\ 6 & 14634 & =2439×6000 \end{cases}$

Sum 16424226=2439×6734=prod. req.

EXAM-

EXAMPLES.

$$691861 \times 26 = 17988386$$
$$346732 \times 652 = 226069264$$
$$7901375 \times 30000 = 237041250000$$
$$129186 \times 98 = 12660228$$
$$76001 \times 1302 = 98953302$$
$$3581 \times 2007 = 7187067$$

THE proof of Multiplication, is beſt done by Diviſion.

CHAP. VI.

Of DIVISION of SIMPLE NUMBERS.

DIVISION is a ſpeedy method of ſubtracting one number from another; to know how many times one number is contained in another; and alſo what remains.

THERE are three requiſites in Diviſion; the diviſor; the dividend, and the quotient; which ſhews how many times the diviſor is contained in the dividend.

WHEN any number meaſures another, the number ſo meaſured, is ſaid to be a multiple of the other: thus, 21 is meaſured by 7, for 7 is contained juſt 3 times in 21; conſequently 21 is a multiple of 7.

ONE number is ſaid to meaſure another, by a third number, when it either multiplies, or is multiplied by the meaſuring number, produces the number meaſured. (See *Euclid*'s 7th book, def. 23.)

HENCE it follows, that in Diviſion the quotient muſt be ſuch a number, which if multiplied with the diviſor, will produce the dividend; conſequently
Diviſion

Divifion is the reverfe of Multiplication ; and there-fore operations in Divifion, muft be performed directly reverfe of thofe in Multiplication; that is, the divifor muft be placed firft ; then make a ftroke on the right-hand of it, and fet down your dividend, on the right-hand of which, make another ftroke, to feperate the dividend from the quotient ; then begin on the left-hand, and decreafe the dividend by a repeated fubtraction of the products of the divifor and each quotient figure, as they become known.

EXAMPLES.

Required to divide 344 by 4; the operation of which will ftand in the following order,

<pre>
                  dividend
    divifor 4) 344 (86 quotient
                 32
                 ——
                 24
                 24
                 ——
                 00
                 —
</pre>

The explanation of the above is as follows : firft enquire how many times your divifor, which confifts of 1 figure, is contained in the firft figure of your dividend, which is 0 times ; becaufe your divifor (4) is greater than the firft figure of your dividend (3), as appears by infpection ; and therefore cannot meafure it; for a greater number to meafure a lefs is abfurd ; therefore you muft increafe the value of the firft figure of the dividend, by taking the annexed figure (4) into the expreffion ; which will then be 34 (for the reafons before given) ; then enquire how many times your divifor is contained in thofe two figures

of

of the dividend, to wit, 34; which is 8 times, for 8 times 4 is 32, and 32 being the greateſt multiple of the diviſor that can be made under 34; conſequently 8 muſt be the firſt figure of the quotient, which place as in the example; then multiplying the quotient figure (8) with your diviſor, as in Multiplication, ſubtract their product from thoſe two figures of the dividend, by which the ſaid quotient figure was obtained; and to the remainder (2) annex the next figure of your dividend (4), and the remainder ſo increaſed becomes 24; then enquire how many times 4 is contained in 24, which is 6 times; therefore place 6 in the quotient, and multiply it with your diviſor, ſubtracting their product as before, and the work is done. (See the example page 37.)

Now the quotient obtained in the example is 86; and there being no remainder, ſhews that 4 is contained in 344, juſt 86 times.

The greateſt difficulty in diviſion, is when your diviſor conſiſts of many places of figures, and does not exactly meaſure the figures of the dividend with which you compare it: therefore to find the right quotient figure, may be done by conſidering that the product of the quotient figure with your diviſor, muſt never be greater than that part of the dividend, with which you compare it; nor yet ſo ſmall, that the number remaining after ſubtracting the product of the quotient figure and diviſor from the aforeſaid part of the dividend, ſhall be greater than the diviſor. Therefore by ſuppoſing a figure for the quotient, and multiplying it with a figure or two on the left-hand of your diviſor, you may eaſily determine the right quotient figure; which may be obtained by ſuch mental operations, on the ſecond or third trial, at fartheſt.

By thoroughly obſerving the foregoing directions, you may proceed to the performance of the following
examples;

examples ; wherein we shall prove those operations, performed in the last chapter ; in order to which, we shall begin with the second example ; taking the product of the factors for a dividend, and the multiplier for a divisor ; and proceed as before.   (See the operation annexed.)

<pre>
                     dividend   -
        divisor 421) 1026819(2439 quotient
                      842···

                      ————
                      1848
                      1684   ·

                      ————
                       1641
                       1263

                       ————
                        3789
                        3789 ··

                        ————
                        ··00
                        ——
</pre>

Note, *It will be best to point the figures of the dividend, as they are annexed to the several remainders ; without which you may annex a wrong one.*

HERE you may see the quotient is the same as the multiplicand of the example before quoted ; which proves that the product of $2439 \times 421 = 1026819$.

Required to divide 779352354 by 32001.

O P E R-

OPERATION.

$$32001\,)\,7793522354\,(\,24354 = 7793522354 \div 32001$$
$$64002$$

$$139332$$
$$128004$$

$$113283$$
$$96003$$

$$172805$$
$$160005$$

$$128004$$
$$128004$$

$$\ldots\ldots 0$$

Again, divide 1798836 by 26.

OPERATION.

$$26\,)\,1798836\,(\,69186 = 1798836 \div 26$$
$$156$$

$$238$$
$$234$$

$$48$$
$$26$$

$$223$$
$$208$$

$$156$$
$$156$$

Once more, divide 12660228 by 98.

OPERATION.

98)12660228(129186=*quotient required.*
98
———
286
196
———
900
882
———
182
98
———
842
784
———
588
588
———

IF there be cyphers annexed to the divisor and dividend, expunge an equal number in both factors: as in the following example.

Divide 694000 by 2000.

OPERATION.

2(000)694(000(347=694000÷2000
6
———
9
8
———
14
14
———
0

F   IT

It will fometimes happen in Divifion, that the remainder, when augmented by annexing the next figure of the dividend, is lefs than the divifor, and confequently cannot be meafured by it; in which cafe, place o in the quotient, and annex the next figure of the dividend to the former number; but if this number be ftill lefs than the divifor, place o in the quotient and annex another figure of the dividend; and fo on, in like manner till the faid number be fo increafed, that it may be meafured by the divifor.   (See this illuftrated in the following.)

Divide 98953302 by 1302.

OPERATION.

$$1302 \,)\, 98953302 \,(\, 76001 = 98953302 \div 1302$$
$$9114$$

$$7813$$
$$7812$$

$$1302$$
$$1302$$

$$\ldots 0$$

The proof of the remaining examples in Multiplication, are left to the fagacity of the learner.

It is required to divide 32176432 by 3476.

OPER-

OPERATION.

3476) 32176432 (9256
       31284
       ‾‾‾‾‾‾‾
        8924
        6952
       ‾‾‾‾‾‾‾
        19723
        17380
       ‾‾‾‾‾‾‾
        23432
        20856
       ‾‾‾‾‾‾‾
        2576 *remainder.*

HERE follows fome examples and their anfwers without their work.

What is the quotient of 23884044718÷45007 ?
Anfwer. 530674.

What is the quotient of 34500000÷100000 ?
Anfwer. 345.

What is the quotient of 244572000÷356 ?
Anfwer. 687000.

What is the quotient of 1332250÷365 ?
Anfwer. 3650.

THAT Divifion is a fpeedy method of fubtraction, as before hinted, may be thus proved. Suppofe 18 were to be divided by 6 : firft fubtract the divifor from the dividend, and the divifor again from that remainder, and fo on till nothing remains. (See the operation in the next page.)

OPER-

OPERATION.

$$
\begin{array}{rl}
18 & dividend \\
-6 & divisor \\
\hline
12 & remainder \\
-6 & divisor \\
\hline
6 & remainder \\
-6 & divisor \\
\hline
0 &
\end{array}
$$

Hence it is manifeſt, that the diviſor is contained in the dividend, juſt 3 times; that is, 3 times 6 $=$ 18 : conſequently, &c. *Q. E. D.*

The next thing to be conſidered, is the proof of your work, i. e. whether the quotient found is a true one. The method is directly reverſe of that uſed for the proof of Multiplication; for, as the truth of Multiplication is known by Diviſion, ſo that of Diviſion is known by Multiplication; that is, by multiplying the quotient with the diviſor, which product muſt be equal to the dividend; therefore multiply the quotient with the diviſor, and to their product add what remains after diviſion; which aggregate will be equal to the dividend, if the work is right.

There is another method of proving Diviſion; which is much ſhorter than the former, and is no more than adding together the products of the ſeveral quotient figures with the diviſor, as they ſtand in your operation; which aggregate, together with the remainder, will be equal to the dividend. (See the following example.)

Required to divide 8765452 by 3463.

OPER-

OPERATION.

$$3463)8765452(2531$$
$$+6926 \cdots = 3463 \times 2000$$

$$18394$$
$$+17315 \quad = 3463 \times 500$$

$$10795$$
$$+10389 \quad = 3463 \times 30$$

$$4062$$
$$+3463 \quad = 3463 \times 1$$

$$+599 \; remainder$$

$$8765452 = dividend.$$

Or, $6926000 + 1731500 + 103890 + 3463 + 599 = 8765452$. Therefore, &c.

A SUPPLEMENT to CHAPTER VI.

NOTWITHSTANDING what hath been said on this subject, respecting the division of simple quantities, is universally true; yet there is another method of dividing quantities, which is very ready in practice; and is therefore called Short Division: this method is performed by the following Rules.

RULE I.

ARRANGE the factors as before in Division; then by comparing the divisor with the dividend, you
will

will obtain a quotient figure, which muſt be ſet in its proper place, under that part of the dividend by which your diviſor was compared ; valuing ſaid figure as though there were no other ; alſo obtain the difference (if any) of the product of the diviſor and quotient figure, and the aforeſaid part of the dividend ; prefixing that difference in your mind to the next figure of your dividend ; which forms an expreſſion for obtaining the next quotient figure, which muſt be ſet directly under that figure, to which the difference was prefixed ; and ſo on till the whole be completed.

EXAMPLES.

Divide 46782 by 3.

THOSE numbers being placed as directed will ſtand thus,

$$3\overline{)46782}$$

$$15594 = 46782 \div 3$$

Again, divide 68432 by 4:

thus, $4\overline{)68432}$

$$17108 = quotient\ required.$$

Note 1. *If there be a remainder after the laſt quotient figure is found, ſet it at a little diſtance on the right-hand of your quotient, making a dot with your pen, denoting the ſeperation; as in the following.*

Divide 23764 by 5: thus, $5\overline{)23764}$

$$4752 \cdot 4 = \frac{23764}{5} \quad rem.$$

Again,

Again, find the quotient of 73215÷6:

thus, 6)73215

12202 . 3 *rem.*

Alfo, divide 43206 by 8:

thus, 8)432106

54013 . 2 *rem.*

Note 2. *If your divifor be* 10, *feperate the firft fig-ure on the right-hand of your dividend for a re-mainder, and the work is done.*

thus, 10)76435(2 *rem.*

Find the quotient of 645384÷12:

thus, 12)645384

53782=*anfwer.*

R U L E   II.

1. Resolve your divifor into feveral parts fuch, that their continued product fhall be equal to the given divifor.

2. Substitute thofe parts fucceffively as divifors, in the following manner, viz. divide the given divi-dend by one of thofe parts, now called divifors, and the refulting quotient by another of thofe divifors, and fo on; the laft quotient arifing by fuch divifors, will be the quotient required.

EXAMPLE.

Divide 2904 by 24.

Your

Your divisor resolved into parts as above directed will be, either 8 and 3, 6 and 4, or 12 and 2; for $8\times3=24$, $6\times4=24$, or $12\times2=24$; therefore let the parts be 6 and 4; then $2904\div6=484$, and $484\div4=121=$ quotient required; and if the others be tryed they will equally succeed.

CHAP. VII.

ADDITION of COMPOUND QUANTITIES or NUMBERS.

ADDITION of compound quantities, is the adding together numbers of different denominations, so that their aggregate, or total amount may be known. The operations are performed by the following general

RULE.

1. WRITE down the several denominations so, that all those of the same name may stand directly under each other.

2. BEGIN on the right-hand, at the least of the given denominations, adding together the whole of that denomination, as in Simple Addition; then divide this sum by such a number, as it takes parts to make one of the next greater denomination; placing the remainder (if any) under its own denomination, and carrying the quotient to the said next greater denomination, add them up with the whole of that denomination, then divide as before; and so on, from one denomination to another, until the whole be completed.

SECT.

S E C T. I.

ADDITION of TROY WEIGHT.

TROY WEIGHT is that by which gold, filver, jewels, medical compofitions, and all liquors are weighed. It is divided into four denominations, to wit, ℔. pounds, *oz.* ounces. *dwt.* pennyweights and *gr.* grains, according to the following

TABLE.

24*gr.*=1*dwt.* 480*gr.*=20*dwt.*=1*oz.* 7560*gr.*=240*dwt.*=12 *oz.*=1 ℔.

EXAMPLES.

Find the fum of the following, 14℔. 11*oz.* 16*dwt.* 13*gr.*+19℔. 10*oz.* 17*dwt.* 17*gr.*+17℔. 11*oz.* 12*dwt.* 22*gr.*

THESE numbers being placed, according as the general rule directs, will ftand

	℔.	*oz.*	*dwt.*	*gr.*
thus,	14	11	16	13
	19	10	17	17
	17	11	12	22
	52	10	7	4 =*fum required.*

THEN begin at the leaft denomination, to wit, grains, and adding together all that denomination, we find the fum to be 52 : now becaufe 24 grains make one pennyweight, divide 52 by 24, and the quotient will be 2, leaving a remainder of 4, which write under grains, and carry the quotient 2, to the next place, and adding it up with that denomination, we find the fum to be 47, which divide by 20 (becaufe 20 pennyweights make one ounce) and the quotient will

G   *be*

be 2, leaving a remainder 7, which write in its proper place, and carry the quotient 2, to the next place ; this being added up with the denomination, we find the sum to be 34, which divided by 12 quotes 2, and 10 remaining ; write this under its own denomination, and carry the quotient 2 to the next place, which added up with that denomination, we find the sum to be 52 ; and becaufe this is the laft denomination, write the whole, and the work is done.   Hence we find the fum total to be 52 ℔. 10 *oz*. 7*dwt*. and 4 *gr*. as was required.   (See the example, page 49.)

℔.	oz.	dwt.	gr.		℔.	oz.	dwt.	gr.
37	10	17	19		47	11	19	24
12	7	12	17		27	8	17	20
17	10	17	12		19	7	12	17
18	9	19	23		10	5	15	17

S E C T.   II.

ADDITION of MONEY.

This is to find the aggregate, or fum total of feveral fums of money.

Every nation of the world has a particular method of reckoning their money.   Great-Britain makes ufe of pounds, fhillings, pence and farthings ; and the United States followed the fame method, until the prefent fyftem of government was eftablifhed; by which it is enacted, that all the monies of every nation or kingdom, fhall be reckoned or eftimated in America, in dollars and cents : fo that thefe two fpecies of money are to be made the ftandard money of the United States.

Note that 100 *cents make one dollar.*

EXAM-

EXAMPLES.

Find the sum of 174*dol.* 17*cts.*+197*dol.* 19*cts.*+ 375*dol.* 92*cts.*+275*dol.* 92*cts.* These being placed according to the general rule, will stand

	dol.	cts.
thus,	174	17
	197	19
	375	92
	275	92
	1023	20 *sum required.*

Note. *Since* 100 *cents make one dollar, we must divide the sum of the cents by* 100 ; *but to divide by* 100 *is no more than to seperate the two right-hand figures of the dividend for a remainder, the rest are the quotient. Therefore, after you have added up the last place of figures in the cents' place, proceed to the dollars' place as though the whole was but one denomination.*

Find the sum of 127*dol.* 19*cts.*+278*dol.* 19*cts.*+ 137*dol.* 19*cts.*+122*dol.* 92*cts.*+127*dol.* 90*cts.*

dol.	cts.
127	19
278	19
137	19
122	92
127	90.
793	39=*sum required.*

dol.

dol.	cts.	dol.	cts.	dol.	cts.
127	17	3787	19	2784	19
172	57	3729	72	1234	27
189	68	4229	91	3456	78

Total

HAVING thus explained the principles, and given a general rule for the Addition of all compounds in whole numbers; we shall leave the rest to the sagacity of the learner, who with the assistance of the following tables and examples, will be able to manage any such compounds as have relation therewith.

S E C T. III.

Of AVOIRDUPOIS WEIGHT.

BY Avoirdupois Weight are weighed, flesh, butter, cheese, salt; also all coarse and drossy commodities; as grocery wares; likewise pitch, tar, rosin, wax, iron, steel, copper, brass, tin, lead, hemp, flax, tobacco, &c.

THE characters in Avoirdupois Weight are *dr. oz. lb. qr. C. T.* that is drachm, ounce, pound, quarter, hundred, tun.

TABLE.

16 *dr.*=1 *oz.*   256 *dr.*=16 *oz.*=1 *lb.*   7168 *dr.*=448 *oz.*=28 *lb.*=1 *qr.*   28672 *dr.*=1792 *oz.*=112 *lb.*=4 *qr.*=1 *C.*   573440 *dr.*=35840 *oz.*=2240 *lb.*=80 *qr.*=20 *C.*=1 *T.*

EXAMPLES.

T.	C.	qr.	lb.	oz.	dr.	T.	C.	qr.	lb.	oz.	dr.
346	12	2	16	10	14	576	19	1	16	12	13
67	16	3	22	8	10	867	4	0	24	14	13
46	10	3	15	12	15	453	6	3	27	3	4

S E C T.

SECT. IV.

Of APOTHECARIES WEIGHT.

THE Apothecaries pound and ounce is the fame as the pound and ounce Troy, but differently divided, as in the following

TABLE.

20*gr.*=1℈. 60*gr.*=3℈.=1ʒ. 480*gr.*=24℈.
=8ʒ.=1℥. 5760*gr.*=288℈.=96ʒ.=12℥.=1℔.

APOTHECARIES make ufe of thefe-weights in the compofition or mixture of their medicines, but fell their drugs by Avoirdupois Weight.

EXAMPLES.

℔.	℥.	ʒ.	℈.	*gr.*	℔.	℥.	ʒ.	℈.	*gr.*
124	10	4	2	14	266	9	5	1	15
64	8	6	1	16	76	10	4	2	14
30	11	7	0	17	96	11	6	2	10
50	9	3	1	12		10	7	1	1

SECT. V.

BY Long Meafure, is eftimated length, where no regard is had to breadth : or in other words, it meafures the diftance of one thing from another : and the ufual method of dividing and fub-dividing of length, is into degrees, leagues, miles, furlongs, poles, yards, feet, inches, and barley-corns, as in the following

TABLE I.

3*bc.*=1*in.* 36*bc.*=12*in.*=1*f.* 108*bc.*=36*in.*=3*f.*
=1*yd.* 594*bc.*=198*in.*=16½*f.*=5½*yd.*=1*p.* 23760*bc.*
=7920*in.*=660*f.*=220*yd.*=40*p.*=1*fur.* 190080*bc.*
=63360*in.*

=63360 in.=5280 f.=1760 yd.=320 p.=8 fur.= 1 m.
570240 bc.=190080 in.=15840 f.=5280 yd.=960 p.=24 fur.=3 m.=1 le.

TABLE II.

3 bc.=1 in. 36 bc.=12 in.=1 f. 108 bc.=36 in.=3 f.=1 yd. 1188 bc.=396 in.=33 f.=16 yd.=1 ch. 23760 bc.=7820 in.=660 f.=220 yd.=20 ch.=1 fur. 190080 bc.=63360 in.=5280 f.=1760 yd.=160 ch.=8 fur.=1 m. 570240 bc.=190080 in.=15840 f.=5280 yd.=480 ch.=24 fur.=2 m.=1 le. 11404800 bc.=3801600 in.=316800 f.=105600 yd.=9600 ch.=480 fur.=60 m.=20 le.=1 deg.

THE length of a degree as laid down in table 2d. is not to be underſtood as the true one, but the length of a degree as commonly received and practiſed; for the length of the greateſt degree is $70\frac{1}{10}$ miles, and the leaſt $67\frac{3}{4}$ miles nearly; a mean degree is therefore $68\frac{92}{100}$ miles.

EXAMPLES.

deg.	le.	m.	fur.	ch.	yd.	f.	in.	bc.
120	14	2	6	14	5	2	10	1
87	12	0	7	12	3	1	5	0
90	19	1	5	18	2	2	4	2

deg.	le.	m.	fur.	ch.	yd.	f.	in.	bc.
332	15	1	7	12	8	1	10	2
	19	2	0	14	9	2	9	
		1	6	13	5	0		
			4	10	4			
				9				

S E C T.

SECT. VI.

Of LAND MEASURE.

The ufe of this meafure, is to find the area or fu-
perficial contents of any piece of land in acres, and
parts of an acre; which parts are as in the following

TABLE.

9 ſq. f. = 1 ſq. yd.   1089 ſq. f. = 121 ſq. yd. = 1 ſq. ch.
10890 ſq. f. = 1210 ſq. yd. = 10 ſq. ch. = 1 ſq. qr.   43560
ſq. f = 4840 ſq. yd. = 40 ſq. ch. = 4 ſq. qr. = 1 ſq. acre

EXAMPLES.

ac.	qr.	cb.	yd.	f.
24	2	3	104	8
37	3	7	111	7
47	2	4	90	7

ac.	qr.	cb.	yd.	f.
92	1	7	100	7
27	3	7	98	8
39	0	7	117	7

SECT. VII.

Of CLOTH MEASURE.

The divifions of Cloth Meafure are as in the
following

TABLE.

4 na. = 1 qr.   16 na. = 4 qr. = 1 yd.   Alſo, 3 qr. = 1 ell
Flem.   5 qr. = 1 ell Eng.   6 qr. = 1 ell Fr.

EXAMPLES.

yd.	qr.	na.
226	3	2
74	3	0
362	2	3

ell Fl.	qr.	na.
327	3	3
39	2	1
500	3	2

ell Eng.

ell Eng.	qr.	na.		ell Fr.	qr.	na.
327	4	3		529	5	3
90	3	2		468	2	2
264	2	1		436	4	3
354	3	3		43	3	1

S E C T. VIII.

Of DRY MEASURE.

DRY MEASURE is fo called becaufe it meafures all fuch dry commodities as corn, wheat, rye, oats, barley, peas, beans, and all kinds of grafs-feed; alfo all kinds of roots and fruits.

THE ftandard of this meafure, is a bufhel of a cylindrical form, of the following dimenfions, viz. $18\frac{1}{2}$ inches in diameter, and 8 inches in altitude; confequently a veffel of fuch form and dimenfions will contain $2150\frac{42}{100}$ cubic inches, which is the content of the Winchefter bufhel: Therefore the quart Dry Meafure, contains $67\frac{2}{10}$ cubic inches nearly; and the divifions are as in the following

TABLE.

67 . 2 *cu. in.*=1*qrt.*   268 . 8 *cu. in.*=4 *qrt.*=1 *gal.*
537 . 6 *cu. in.*=8 *qrt.*=2 *gal.*=1 *pc.*   2150 . 42 *cu. in.*
=32 *qrt.*=8 *gal.*=4 *pc.*=1 *bufh.*

EXAMPLES.

bufh.	pc.	gal.	qrt.		bufh.	pc.	gal.	qrt.		bufh.	pc.	gal.	qrt.
57	3	1	3		37	3	1	1		2	3	1	2
24	0	0	2		19	0	0	0				1	1
47	2	1	0		33	2	0	3		2	3	1	3

SECT.

S E C T. IX.

Of LIQUID MEASURES.

In Liquid Meaſures, the gallon is made the ſtand-ard, and from thence are deduced the other denominations made uſe of in ſuch meaſures. The wine gallon is ſuppoſed to contain 231 cubic inches, conſequently the quart muſt contain $57\frac{3}{4}$ cubic inches; from thence is deduced the following

TABLE of WINE MEASURE.

$57\frac{3}{4}$ *cu. in.*=1 *qrt.* 231 *cu. in.*=4 *qrt.*=1 *gal.* 9702 *cu. in.*=168 *qrt.*=42 *gal.*=1 *tr.* 14553 *cu. in.*=252 *qrt.* =63 *gal.*=$1\frac{1}{2}$ *tr.*=1 *hhd.* 19404 *cu. in.*=336 *qrt.*=84 *gal.*=2 *tr.*=$1\frac{1}{3}$ *hhd.*=1 *pun.* 29106 *cu. in.*=504 *qrt.* =126 *gal.*=3 *tr.*=2 *hhd.*=$1\frac{1}{2}$ *pun.*=1 *bt.* 58212 *cu. in.*=1008 *qrt.*=252 *gal.*=6 *tr.*=4 *hhd.*—3 *pun.*=2 *bt.* 1 *tun.*

EXAMPLES.

tun	hhd.	gal.	qrt.	tun.	hhd.	gal.	qrt.
237	2	62	3	279	2	57	2
234	1	27	0	273	0	39	0
72	2	25	3	99	2	47	3
34	0	59	0	93	1	24	2

Of ALE or BEER MEASURE.

The gallon of Ale or Beer Meaſure contains 282 cubic inches, as in the following

TABLE.

$70\frac{1}{2}$ *cu. in.*=1 *qrt.* 282 *cu. in.*=4. *qrt.*=1 *gal.* 2397 *cu. in.*=34 *qrt.*=$8\frac{1}{2}$ *gal.*=1 *fir.* 4794 *cu. in.*=68 *qrt.* =17 *gal.*=2 *fir.*=1 *kil.* 9588 *cu. in.*=136 *qrt.*=34 *gal.*

H

gal.=4 *fir.*=2 *kil.*=1 *bar.* 14382 *cu. in.*=204 *qrt.*=
51 *gal.*=6 *fir.*=3 *kil.*=1½ *bar.*=1 *bhd.*

EXAMPLES.

bhd.	kil.	fir.	gal.	qrt.	bhd.	kil.	fir.	gal.	qrt.
79	2	1	7	2	73	2	1	6	3
64	3	0	5	0	97	1	1	7	2
49	1	1	6	2	37	2	1	2	0

S E C T. X.

Of the MEASURE of TIME.

In the divifion of Time, a year is made the ftand-ard or integer, which is determined by the revolu-tion of fome celeftial body in its orbit; which body is either the fun or moon. The time meafured by the fun's revolution in the ecliptic (or imaginary circle in the heavens, fo called by aftronomers) from any equinox or foltice to the fame again, is 365 days, 5 hours, 48 minutes, 57 feconds, and is called the folar or tropical year.——Although the folar year before mentioned, is the only proper or natural year, yet the civil or Julian year is the one which the dif-ferent nations of the world make ufe of in the re-gulation of civil affairs.

The civil folar year contains 365 days, 6 hours; but in common mathematical computations, the odd hours are generally heglected, and the year taken only for 365 days; from which, the divifions in the following T A B L E are made, wherein a fecond is con-fidered (as it really is) the leaft part of time that can be truly meafured by any mechanical engine.

60″.=1′.   3600″.=60′.=1 *h.*   86400″.=1440′.=
24 *h.*=1 *d.*   31536000″.=525600′.=8760 *h.*=365 *d.*
=1 *year.*   EXAM-

EXAMPLES.

y.	d.	h.	'	"
167	272	14	42	29
234	173	22	58	59
39	290	19	19	19
43	222	22	22	22
99	99	20	57	21

y.	d.	h.	'	"
173	192	10	17	29
346	364	23	59	59
199	170	19	17	16
344	19	10	34	46
79	38	23	43	43

SECT. XI.

Of CIRCULAR MOTION.

WHAT is here meant by Circular Motion, is that of the heavenly bodies in their orbits; which are reckoned in figns, degrees, minutes, and feconds, as in the following

TABLE.

$60'' = 1'$. $3600'' = 60' = 1°$. $108000'' = 1800' = 30°$ $= 1 S$. $1296000'' = 21600' = 360° = 12 S. = great circle$ of the ecliptic.

EXAMPLES.

S.	°	'	"
10	12	30	10
9	11	47	47
8	4	37	4
7	24	42	36

S.	°	'	"
11	13	13	13
8	17	23	43
7	29	44	27
6	19	38	59

Note. *In the Addition of Circular Motion, when the fum of the figns exceed 12, or any multiple of it, write fuch excefs in the place of figns, rejecting the reft.*

Note.

Note. *In order to prevent a misconstruction of the abbreviations, in the nine preceding* TABLES, *we have subjoined the following explanation, viz. gr. stands for grains. ℈ scruples. ʒ drachms. ℥ ounces. ℔ pounds.—bc. barley-corns. in. inches. f. feet. yd. yards. ch. chains. p. poles. fur. furlongs. m. miles. le. leagues. deg. degrees.— sq. square. qr. quarters. ac. acres.—na. nails. Flem. Flemish. Eng. English. Fr. French.—cu. cubic.—qrt. quarts. gal. gallons. pc. pecks. bush. bushels.—tr. tierces. hhd. hogsheads. pun. puncheons. bt. butts.—fir. firkins. kil. kilderkins. bar. barrels.—″ seconds. ′ minutes. h. hours. d. days. y. years. ° degrees. S. Signs.*

C H A P. VIII.

SUBTRACTION of COMPOUNDS.

SUBTRACTION of Compounds is the taking one number from another: and is performed by the following general

R U L E.

1. RANGE the given denominations according to the directions in the last chapter.

2. BEGIN at the same place as in Addition, to wit, at the least of the given denominations, subtracting the lower number from the upper, as in Simple Subtraction, writing the difference under its own name; but if the number in the subtrahend or under number, be greater than that which stands directly over it (as it often happens) you must add to your upper number, so many units of that denomination as are equal to

one

one of the next greater; from which perform the intended fubtraction, writing the difference as before. Then proceed to the next place, where you muft pay what you before borrowed of this denomination, by adding one to the fubtrahend; and then perform fubtraction as before; and fo on to the laft place, where the fubtraction is performed as in fimple quantities.

EXAMPLES.

From 37 ℔ 10 *oz.* 17 *dwt.* 20 *gr.* take 27 ℔ 11 *oz.* 19 *dwt.* 17 *gr.*

Thefe numbers being placed according to the rule, will ftand

	℔	*oz.*	*dwt.*	*gr.*
thus,	37	10	17	20
	27	11	19	17
	9	10	18	3 *diff. required.*

HERE beginning at the leaft denomination, to wit, at grains, fubtract 17 from 20, and there remains 3, which write under its own name; then proceed to the next denomination; but here the under number is the greateft, and therefore cannot be taken from the upper; wherefore add 20 to the upper number (becaufe 20 pennyweights make one ounce) and the fum is 37, from which take 19, and their remains 18; or take 19 from 20, and then add 17, and the fum will be 18, as before. Then proceed to the next place; and here again, the under number is the greateft, therefore add 1 to 11 for what you before borrowed, and the fum will be 12, which taken from 22, leaves 10, which write in its proper place, and proceed to the laft denomination, where paying what you before borrowed, perform the fubtraction as in whole numbers,

bers, and the remainder will be 9. Hence we find the whole difference to be 9 pounds, 10 ounces, 18 pennyweights, and 3 grains.

	℔	oz.	dwt.	gr.		dol.	cts.		dol.	cts.
From	27	10	13	17		37	19		78	92
Take	22	8	19	19		21	18		27	75
Rem.	5	1	13	22		16	1		51	17

As the foregoing rule is general, the learner by duly obferving the application of it, to the above examples, may very readily perform the following ones without any further direction.

	T.	C.	qr.	lb.	oz.	dr.		yd.	qr.	na.
From	324	19	3	17	2	15		227	3	2
Take	233	17	2	20	13	14		204	1	3
Rem.										

	ell Flem.	qr.	na.	ell Eng.	qr.	na.	ell Fr.	qr.	na.
From	52	1	3	42	4	1	53	3	3
Take	35	2	1	36	2	3	49	5	0
Rem.									

	T.	hhd.	gal.	qrt.		bhd.	kil.	fir.	gal.	qrt.
From	37	3	36	2		33	2	1	7	3
Take	23	1	37	3		27	1	0	4	3
Rem.										

	y.	d.	h.	′	″		℔	℥	ʒ	϶	gr.
From	434	320	17	24	42		47	10	7	2	14
Take	329	370	19	47	29		45	8	5	1	17
Rem.											

THE

THE method of proving your work, is the fame as that of Simple Subtraction.

CHAP. IX.

MULTIPLICATION and DIVISION of COMPOUNDS.

SECT. I.

Of MULTIPLICATION.

MULTIPLICATION of Compound Numbers is the multiplying any fum compofed of divers denominations, with a fimple multiplier, according to the following

RULE.

BEGIN the operation as in all other compounds, multiplying that denomination with your multiplier, as in Simple Multiplication ; then divide this product by as many units as make one of the next greater denomination, writing the remainder as in Addition ; then note the quotient, and proceed to the next place, and multiply that denomination with your multiplier, to which add the aforefaid quotient ; then divide this product as before, and fo on, till you have multiplied your multiplier with every denomination in your multiplicand ; and the refult will be the product required.

EXAMPLES.

Multiply 120 ℔ 10 *oz.* 13 *dwt.* 17 *gr.* with 4.

OPER-

OPERATION.

lb	oz.	dwt.	gr.	
120	10	13	17	*multiplicand*
			4	*multiplier*
483	6	14	20	*product required.*

HERE we begin with 4×17=68; then 68÷24=2, and 20 remaining, which write in its proper place; then 4×13=52, to which add 2, the quotient juft found, and the fum will be 54; then 54÷20=2, and 14 remaining, which write in its proper place; then 4×10=40, to which add the laft quotient 2, and the fum is 42; now 42÷12=3, and 6 remaining, which write in its proper place. Laftly, 4×120=480, to which add 3, the laft found quotient, and the fum is 483. Hence we find the whole product to be 483 pounds, 6 ounces, 14 pennyweights, and 20 grains.

Multiply 127 *dol.* 17 *cts,* with 6.

OPERATION.

dol.	cts.	
127	17	
	6	
763	2	*product.*

S.	°	′	″		yd.	qr.	na.	
10	13	42	10		4	2	3	
			4				6	
5	24	48	40	*prod.*	28	0	2	*product.*

ell Flem.

ell Fl.	qr.	na.	ell Eng.	qr.	na.	ell Fr.	qr.	na.
17	2	1	10	4	2	13	5	3
		7		12				8
124	0	3	130	4	0	111	4	0 *prod.*

deg.	le.	m.	fur.	p.	f.	in.	bc.
12	10	2	5	10	10	1	2
							4
50	3	1	5	2	7	6	2 *product.*

Note. *You may resolve your multiplier into several parts, as in Short Division, and if those parts when multiplied together, do not exactly make the given multiplier, add as many times the multiplicand to the product, as the product of the said parts fall short of the given multiplier; as in these:*

Find the product of 127 *dol.* 19 *cts.* ×15.

HERE the parts of the multiplier are 3 and 5.

Therefore, $\begin{cases} \textit{dol.} & \textit{cts.} \\ 127 & 19 \end{cases}$

$$\begin{array}{r} 3 \\ \hline 381 \quad 57 \\ 5 \\ \hline 1907 \quad 85 \end{array}$$
(*because* 3×5=15)=127 *dol.* 19 *cts.* ×15.

Required the product of 197 *dol.* 87 *cts.* ×23.

I

Let

Let the parts be 3 and 7. Therefore,

$$
\begin{array}{rr}
dol. & cts. \\
197 & 87 \\
& 3 \\
\hline
593 & 61 \\
& 7 \\
\hline
4155 & 27 = 197 \; 87 \times 21. \\
\end{array}
$$

add 2 *times* 197 *dol.* 87 *cts.* or 395 74

$$
\begin{array}{rr}
4551 & 1 = product \; req.
\end{array}
$$

What is the product of 22 ℔ 6 *oz.* 10 *dwt.* 12 *gr.* ×32 ?
Anſwer. 721 ℔ 4 *oz.* 16 *dwt.*

What is the product of 13 *yd.* 3 *qr.* 2 *na.* ×48 ?
Anſwer. 666 *yd.*

S E C T. II.

DIVISION of COMPOUNDS.

DIVISION being directly the reverſe of Multiplication, needs no other explanation than the following examples; only obſerve, that when any denomination is not exactly meaſured by the diviſor, the remainder muſt be reduced to the next inferiour denomination, and added to it; then perform the diviſion.

EXAMPLES.

$$
\begin{array}{l}
℔ \;\; oz. \;\; dwt. \; gr. \\
2)375 \;\; 11 \;\; 13 \;\; 14 \\
\hline
187 \;\; 11 \;\; 16 \;\; 19
\end{array}
\qquad
\begin{array}{l}
dol. \; cts. \\
4)347 \;\; 12 \\
\hline
86 \;\; 78
\end{array}
\qquad
\begin{array}{l}
dol. \; cts. \\
7.)784 \;\; 49 \\
\hline
112 \;\; 7 \; quo. \\
\quad\quad\quad\quad 0 \; le.
\end{array}
$$

$$\begin{array}{ccccccccc} & \text{o} & le. & m. & fur. & ch. & yd. & f. & in. \\ 4\overline{)}47 & 14 & 2 & 6 & 12 & 5 & 1 & 7 \end{array}$$

$3165\,dol.\div 6=527\,dol.\;50\,cts.$ and $527\,dol.\;50\,cts.$ $\div 5=105\,dol.\;50\,cts.$

Likewise, $101\,dol.\;50\,cts.\div 5=20\,dol.\;30\,cts.$ (because $6\times 5\times 5=150)=3165\div 150$

Miscellaneous Questions for the Learner's Practice.

SIR Isaac Newton was born in the year 1642, and died in 1726: What was his age when he died?

There are two numbers, the greater 96, and the less 45: What is their sum and difference?

To find a number such, that 426 taken from it, will leave 127 remainder.

A certain number of merchants in trade, gained 19140 dollars, which being equally divided, a share was found to be 4785 dollars: How many merchants were there in that trade?

What is the quotient of 3276 divided by 3, and by 9?

What number is the divisor of 1530320, when the quotient is 470?

What is the cost of 51 yards of broadcloth, at 4 *dol.* 10 *cts.* per yard?

C H A P.

CHAP. X.

REDUCTION.

BY Reduction, numbers compofed of different de-nominations are brought into one, by unfolding the feveral denominations by the parts that compofe them. Or, from any number of homologous parts, to difcover the number of certain heterogeneous, or unlike denominations. The former is called Reduc-tion by Multiplication, and the latter Reduction by Divifion.————Reduction by Multiplication has the following general

RULE.

BEGIN at the greateft denomination mentioned, multiplying it with as many units as one of this de-nomination contains units of the next inferiour de-denomination; and to the product add the numbers in the lefs denomination; then multiply this fum as before, add as above, and fo on (multiplying with as many units as it takes thofe of the next lefs denomi-nation to make one of the prefent), until you have reduced the given parts to the denomination required.

EXAMPLES.

Required the number of cents equal to 1000 dollar.

OPERATION.

1000
100 = *number of cents in a dollar.*
──────────
100000 = *number of cents required.*
──────────

Reduce

Reduce 1057 *dol.* 90 *cts.* into cents.

OPERATION,

dol. cts.

1,057 90

100

——————

105790 = *number of cents required.*

——————

BUT to reduce the monies of foreign nations, to thofe of the United States, confult the following

TABLE.

	dol.	cts.
Pound Sterling of Great-Britain =	4	.44
Livre Tournois of France		$18\frac{1}{2}$
Guilder of the United Netherlands		39
Mark Banco of Hamburgh		$33\frac{1}{3}$
Rix Dollar of Denmark	1	
Rix Dollar of Sweden	1	
Real Plate of Spain		10
Milree of Portugal	1	24
Pound Sterling of Ireland	4	10
Tale of China	1	48
Pagoda of India	1	$94\frac{6}{10}$
Rupee of Bengal		$55\frac{1}{2}$
Mexican Dollar	1	
Crown of France	1	15
Crown of England	1	11

Note. *The gold coins of France, England, Spain, and Portugal, are valued at* 89 *cents per pennyweight.*

In

In 127 pounds sterling of Great-Britain, how many cents?

Here multiply the pounds with 444.

$$\begin{array}{r} 127 \\ 444 \\ \hline 508 \\ 508 \\ 508 \\ \hline 56388 \end{array}$$ *the answer.*

In 274 livres tournois of France, how many cents?

Multiply with 18, and add half the multiplicand to that product.

$$\begin{array}{r} 274 \\ 18 \\ \hline 2192 \\ 274 \\ \hline 4932 \\ 137 \\ \hline 5069 \end{array}$$ *the answer.*

In 540 marks banco of Hamburg : how many cents?

Multiply

Multiply with 33, and add one third of the multiplicand to that product.

$$540$$
$$33$$
$$1620$$
$$1620$$
$$17820$$
$$180$$
$$18000 \text{ the answer.}$$

In 424 rupees of Bengal: how many cents?

Multiply with 55, and proceed as in the livres tournois of France.

$$424$$
$$55$$
$$2120$$
$$2120$$
$$23320$$
$$212$$
$$23532 \text{ the answer.}$$

Note. *In reducing the following species of money to cents, take the following methods.*

For the Guilders of the United Netherlands, multiply

with	39
Real Plate of Spain	10
Milree of Portugal	124
Pound Sterling of Ireland	410

Tale

Tale of China	148
Pagoda of India	194
Crown of France	111
Crown of England	111

In 127 ℔, how many ounces, pennyweights and grains ?

$$127$$
$$12 = \text{\textit{number of ounces in 1 pound}}$$

$$1524 = \text{\textit{number of ounces in 127 pounds}}$$
$$20 = \text{\textit{number of pennyweights in 1 ounce}}$$

$$30480 = \text{\textit{number of pennyweights in 127 pounds}}$$
$$24 = \text{\textit{number of grains in 1 pennyweight}}$$

$$121920$$
$$60960$$

$$731520 = \text{\textit{number of grains in 127 pounds.}}$$

℔. oz. dwt. gr.

In 12   8   12   4 how many grains ?

$$12$$

$$152 = 12 \times 12 + 8$$
$$20$$

$$3052 = 152 \times 20 + 12$$
$$24$$

$$12212$$
$$6104$$

$$73252 = 3052 \times 24 + 4 = \text{\textit{number of grains req.}}$$

In

In 333 milrees of Portugal : how many cents ?
Anfwer. 41292.

In 555 tales of China : how many cents ?
Anfwer. 82140.

REDUCTION *by* DIVISION.

THIS method is directly reverfe of the former ; for where we before multiplied, here we muft divide with the fame number ; and therefore admits of the following

R U L E.

DIVIDE the numbers in each denomination, by the number of units that make one of the next fuperiour denomination ; and the quotients refulting, will be the numbers in the feveral denominations required.

EXAMPLES.

In 57200 cents : how many dollars ?

$$1(00 \overline{)572(00}$$

Therefore 572 *dollars is the anfwer.*

In 73252 grains Avoirdupois : how many penny-weights, ounces, and pounds ?

```
24)73252 | 20|3052
   72     |
  ----    | 12|152 . 12 rem.
   125    |
   120    |    12 . 8 rem.
  ----
    52
    48
   ----
     4
```

K   Therefore

Therefore in 73252 grains, there are 3052 penny-weights, 152 ounces, or 12 pounds.

Note. *The several remainders are of the same name of their dividends.*

In 41292 cents: how many milrees of Portugal?
41292 ÷ 124 = 333, *the answer.*

In 82140 cents: how many tales of China?
Answer. 555.

In 56388 cents: how many pounds sterling of England?
Answer. 127.

Note. *In reducing cents into livres tournois of France, you must multiply with 2, and divide that product by 37.——The mark banco of Hamburg, multiply with 3, and divide that product by 100.——The rupee of Bengal, multiply with 2, and divide by 111.*

In 752 nails: how many yards?
Answer. 47 yards.

In 15840 ~~barley-corns~~ yards : how many miles?
Answer. 3 miles.

In 469 gallons: how many hogsheads?
Answer. 7 hhd. 38 gal.

Miscellaneous Questions.

THE comet of 1680, at its greatest distance from the sun, was 11184768000 miles: now suppose a body had been projected from the sun, with a degree of swiftness equal to that of a cannon ball,

which

which is at the rate of 480 miles per hour : in what time would this body reach the aforesaid comet; allowing the year to consist of 365 days?

Answer. 2660 *years.*

How many times will a ship of 97 feet 6 inches long, sail her length, in the distance of ;2800 leagues and 10 yards:

Answer. 2079408.

A MERCHANT bought 4 tuns, 15 hundreds, and 24 pounds of sugar, and ordered it to be put up into parcels of 24 pounds, of 20, of 16, of 12, of 8, of 4, of 2, and of each a like number. How many parcels will be made of the sugar?

Answer. 124.

A GENTLEMAN had 15 dollars to pay among his labourers—to every boy he gave 10 cents—to every woman 20 cents, and to every man 45 cents: the number of men, women and boys was the same. I demand the number of each sort?

Answer. 20.

THERE are five tooth wheels placed in such order, that their teeth play directly into each other : the first wheel contains 500 teeth—the second 750—the third 1500—the fourth 2000, and the fifth 3000: how many times will the fifth wheel turn in 100 turns of the first?

Answer. 600.

THE velocity of light being at the rate of 10000000 miles per minute, takes up 6 years, 32 days, 5 hours, and 20 minutes in coming from the nearest fixed star to the earth : what is the distance of that star?

Answer. 32000000000000.

PART.

PART II.

CONTAINING THE DOCTRINE OF

VULGAR FRACTIONS.

CHAP. I.

DEFINITIONS and ILLUSTRATIONS.

A FRACTION is a broken quantity, or the parts of an unit, which are expreſſed like quantities in diviſion ; to wit, by writing two quantities, one above and the other below a ſmall line ;

$$\text{thus,} \begin{cases} \dfrac{3}{4} & \textit{numerator} \\ & \textit{denominator or diviſor} \end{cases} \quad \text{or} \begin{cases} \dfrac{1\times3}{4} = \dfrac{1}{4}\times3 \end{cases}$$

which is three times the quotient of unity divided by 4 : therefore in all Vulgar Fractions, unity is divided into ſuch parts, as are expreſſed by the denominator ; that is, the denominator expreſſes what kind of parts the unit is divided into, and the numerator the number of thoſe parts.

HENCE it follows, that all Vulgar Fractions whatſoever, repreſent the quotients of quantities, which are to unity, as the numerator to the denominator ; thus, if the fraction be $\frac{3}{4}$, it will be $\frac{3}{4} : 1 :: 3 : 4$; and ſo on for others.

ALL Vulgar Fractions whatſoever, fall under the five following forms, viz. proper, improper, ſingle, compounded, and mixed.

A

A PROPER fraction, is when the numerator is lefs then the denominator: thus $\frac{3}{4}$, $\frac{4}{5}$, and $\frac{7}{12}$, are proper factions.

AN improper fraction, is when the numerator is greater than the denominator: thus $\frac{5}{4}$, $\frac{7}{3}$, and $\frac{10}{5}$, are improper fractions.

A SINGLE fraction, is a fimple expreffion for the parts of an unit: thus $\frac{1}{2}$, $\frac{1}{3}$, and $\frac{3}{4}$, are fingle fractions.

A COMPOUND fraction, is a fraction of a fraction: thus, $\frac{1}{3}$ of $\frac{1}{2}$ and $\frac{2}{3}$ of $\frac{1}{4}$ of $\frac{5}{7}$, are compound fractions.

WHEN whole numbers are joined or connected with fractions, they are fometimes called mixed numbers; as $10\frac{1}{2}$, and $15\frac{9}{8}$.

A MIXED fraction, is when either or both the numerator and denominator, is a mixed number: thus, $\left\{\dfrac{12\frac{1}{2}}{17}\ \text{and}\ \dfrac{17\frac{11}{10}}{42\frac{12}{10}}\right.$, are mixed fractions.

ANY whole number may be expreffed in the form of a Vulgar Fraction, by writing unity, or 1 under it: thus, $120=\dfrac{120}{1}$ and $52=\dfrac{52}{1}$ &c.

THE common meafure of two numbers, is any number that will meafure both without a remainder: thus, 3 is the common meafure of 9 and 12; becaufe it meafures 9 by 3, and 12 by 4.

THE greateft common meafure of two numbers, is the greateft number that will meafure both without a remainder: thus, 7 is the greateft common meafure of 21 and 49; becaufe no number greater than 7 can meafure 21 and 49, without a remainder.

ANY number that can be meafured by feveral other numbers, the number meafured, is called their common multiple: thus, 24 is a common multiple of 4 and 6, for $2\times12=24$, $4\times6=24$, and $6\times4=24$: the leaft number that can be meafured in this manner, is

called.

called the leaſt common multiple: thus, 12 is the leaſt common multiple of 4 and 6 ; becauſe no number leſs than 12, can be divided by 4 and 6, without a remainder.

A PRIME number is that, which is meaſured only by unity: as 5, 7, 11, 19, &c.

NUMBERS prime to each other are ſuch, as no number except unity will meaſure both without a remainder: thus, 9 and 4 are numbers prime to each other; for although 2 will meaſure 4 without a remainder, yet it cannot divide 9 without a remainder: 3 may meaſure 9, but it cannot meaſure 4 : therefore, &c.

A COMPOSED number is that, which ſome certain number meaſures: thus, 6, 8 and 12, are compoſed numbers; for $3\times2=6$, $4\times2=8$, and $2\times6=12$.

CHAP. II.

REDUCTION of VULGAR FRACTIONS.

REDUCTION of Vulgar Fractions, is the changing of one fraction into another of equivalent value; and thereby fitting them for the purpoſe of Addition, Subtraction, &c.

THE whole buſineſs of Reduction, is compriſed in the following Problems.

PROBLEM I.

To find the leaſt common multiple of ſeveral numbers.

RULE.

1. RANGE the numbers in a direct line.

2. FIND what number will divide two or more of them, without a remainder; by which divide them,

and

and fet their quotients together with the undivided numbers, in a line beneath.

3. DIVIDE this line in the fame manner as the firft; and fo on, from line to line, until no number, except unity will divide two of them without a remainder; then the continued product of all the divifors, and the laft quotients, will be the leaft common multiple required.

EXAMPLES.

Find the leaft common multiple of 4, 8, and 12.

OPERATION.

$$4)\overline{\begin{array}{ccc} 4 & 8 & 12 \\ 1 & 2 & 3 \end{array}}$$

WHENCE, $4\times1\times2\times3=24$, the leaft common multiple required.

Find the leaft common multiple of 2, 4, 6, 7 and 20.

OPERATION.

$$\begin{array}{c|ccccc} 2 & 2 & 4 & 6 & 7 & 20 \\ 2 & 1 & 2 & 3 & 7 & 10 \\ & 1 & 1 & 3 & 7 & 5 \end{array}$$

WHENCE, $2\times2\times3\times7\times5=420$, the leaft common multiple required.

PROBLEM II.

To find the greateft common meafure of two or more quantities.

RULE.

1. FIND the greateft common meafure of any two of the quantities, by dividing the greater by the lefs, and the divifor by the remainder; and fo on, dividing the laft divifor, by the laft remainder, till noth-

ing

ing remains; and the laſt diviſor made uſe of, will be the greateſt common meaſure of theſe two quantities.

2. FIND the greateſt common meaſure of any one of the other quantities, and the common meaſure laſt found; and ſo on, from one number to another, thro' the whole; and the laſt common meaſure thus found, will be the greateſt common meaſure required.

EXAMPLES.

Find the greateſt common meaſure of 12 and 15.

OPERATION.

$$12 \overline{)15(1}$$
$$12$$

$$3 \overline{)12(4}$$
$$12$$

HENCE, 3 is the greateſt common meaſure required.

Find the greateſt common meaſure of 12, 18, 26, 36.

OPERATION.

Fïrſt find the greateſt common meaſure of 12 and 18.

thus, $\left\{ 12 \overline{)18(1} \right.$
$$12$$

$$6 \overline{)12(2}$$
$$12$$

HENCE, the greateſt common meaſure of 12 and 18 is 6.

Again, find the greateſt common meaſure of 6 and 26,

thus

thus, $\left\{\begin{array}{l}6 \overline{)26}(4 \\ \quad\; 24\end{array}\right.$

$2\overline{)6}(3$

Therefore the greateſt common meaſure is 2.

Laſtly, find the greateſt common meaſure of 2 and 36 :

thus, $\left\{\; 2\overline{)\begin{array}{l}36 \\ 18\end{array}}\right.$

Conſequently the greateſt common meaſure of 12, 18, 26, and 36, is 2 ; which was to be done.

PROBLEM III.

To abbreviate, or reduce a Vulgar Fraction to its leaſt or moſt ſimple terms.

RULE.

FIND the greateſt common meaſure of the numerator and denominator, by the laſt problem ; then divide them by their greateſt common meaſure, and the reſult will be the terms of the fraction required.   Or,

DIVIDE both the numerator and denominator of the given fraction, by ſuch a number, as will divide them without a remainder, and the reſulting fraction in the ſame manner ; and ſo on, till no number except unity, will divide both without a remainder ; and you will have the fraction required.

EXAMPLES.

Reduce $\dfrac{64}{384}$ to its moſt ſimple terms.

L

THE

THE greateſt common meaſure of 64 and 384, is 64. Therefore $64 \div 64 = 1$, and $384 \div 64 = 6$; conſequently $\frac{64}{384} = \frac{1}{6}$, *the fraction required.*

Or, $\frac{64 \div 8}{384 \div 8} = \frac{8}{48}$, and $\frac{8 \div 8}{48 \div 8} = \frac{1}{6}$, *the ſame as before.*

Find the value of $\frac{35}{45}$, in its moſt ſimple terms.

Thus, $\frac{35 \div 5}{45 \div 5} = \frac{7}{9}$, *the fraction required.*

Reduce $\frac{192}{480}$, to its moſt ſimple terms. *Anſ.* $\frac{2}{5}$

PROBLEM IV.

To write a mixed number, in the form of a Vulgar Fraction.

R U L E.

MULTIPLY the whole number with the denominator of the fraction, and to the product add its numerator; then under this, write the ſaid denominator; and you will have the fraction required.

EXAMPLES.

Write $4\frac{1}{2}$, in the form of a Vulgar Fraction. Thus, $4 \times 2 = 8$, and $8 + 1 = 9$ *the numerator;*

Whence $\frac{9}{2}$ *is the fraction required.*

$$12\frac{6}{10} = \frac{12 \times 10 + 6}{10} = \frac{126}{10}; \text{ and } 40\frac{20}{100} = \frac{40 \times 100 + 20}{100}$$

$$= \frac{4020}{100}; \text{ Alſo, } 20\frac{17}{20} = \frac{20 \times 20 + 17}{20} = \frac{417}{20}.$$

PROB-

PROBLEM V.

To find the value of an improper fraction.

RULE.

DIVIDE the numerator of the given fraction by the denominator; and the quotient will be the value sought.

EXAMPLES.

Find the value of $\frac{120}{12}$.

Thus, $\frac{120}{12} = 120 \div 12 = 10$; $\frac{126}{10} = 126 \div 10 = 12\frac{6}{10}$

$\frac{4020}{100} = 4020 \div 100 = 40\frac{20}{100}$; $\frac{417}{20} = 20\frac{17}{20}$.

PROBLEM VI.

To write a whole number in the form of a Vulgar Fraction, whose denominator is given.

RULE.

MULTIPLY the whole number with the given denominator; and under this product write the said denominator; and you will have the fraction required.

EXAMPLES.

Reduce 40 to its equivalent Vulgar Fraction, whose denominator is 10.

Thus, $40 \times 10 = 400 = $ *numerator.*

Whence, $\frac{400}{10}$ *is the fraction required.*

Change 304 into its equivalent Vulgar Fraction, having 5 for its denominator.

Thus,

Thus, $\dfrac{304 \times 5}{5} = \dfrac{1520}{5}$ *the fraction required.*

Change 3476 into its equvialent Vulgar Fraction, having 12 for its denominator.

Thus, $\dfrac{3476 \times 12}{12} = \dfrac{41712}{12}$ *the fraction required.*

PROBLEM VII.

To alter or change a Vulgar Fraction into another of equivalent value; whose denominator is given.

RULE.

MULTIPLY the given numerator with the propofed denominator; the product divided by the denominator of the given fraction, will give a new numerator; under which write the propofed denominator; and you will have the fraction required.

EXAMPLES.

Change $\dfrac{1}{2}$ into its equivalent Vulgar Fraction, whofe denominator is 20.

Thus, $\dfrac{20 \times 1}{2} = 10$ *the new numerator.*

Therefore, $\dfrac{10}{20}$ *is the fraction required.*

Change $\dfrac{15}{20}$ into its equivalent Vulgar Fraction, having 40 for its denominator.

Thus, $\dfrac{15 \times 40}{20} = 30$: *therefore* $\dfrac{30}{40}$ *is the fraction req.*

Change $\dfrac{17}{20}$ into its equivalent Vulgar Fraction, whofe denominator is 24.

Thus,

Thus, $\dfrac{17 \times 24}{20} = 20\frac{8}{20}$: therefore $\dfrac{20\frac{8}{20}}{20} = $ *fraction req.*

PROBLEM VIII.

To change a Vulgar Fraction into another of equivalent value, whose numerator is given.

RULE.

Multiply the given denominator with the proposed numerator; and the product divided by the numerator of the given fraction, will give a new denominator; over which write the proposed numerator; and you will have the fraction required.

EXAMPLES.

Change $\dfrac{5}{10}$ into its equivalent Vulgar Fraction, whose numerator is 20.

Thus, $\dfrac{10 \times 20}{5} = 40$: therefore, $\dfrac{20}{40}$, *is the fraction req.*

Change $\dfrac{7}{9}$ into its equivalent Vulgar Fraction, whose numerator is 8.

Thus, $\dfrac{9 \times 8}{7} = 10\frac{2}{7}$: therefore, $\dfrac{8}{10\frac{2}{7}}$, *is the fraction req.*

Change $\dfrac{24}{27}$ into its equivalent Vulgar Fraction, whose numerator is 37.	*Ans.* $\dfrac{37}{41\frac{15}{24}}$

PROBLEM IX.

To reduce a mixed fraction to simple terms.

RULE.

1. Reduce the numerator and denominator of the given fraction to improper fractions.

2. Multiply

2. MULTIPLY the numerator of the denominator, into the denominator of the numerator, for a new denominator; and multiply the numerator of the numerator, into the denominator of the denominator, for a new numerator; and you will have the terms of the fraction required.

EXAMPLES.

Reduce $\dfrac{4\frac{1}{4}}{7\frac{1}{3}}$ to simple terms.

First, $\dfrac{4\frac{1}{4}}{7\frac{1}{3}} =$ (by reducing to impr. fract.) $\dfrac{\frac{17}{4}}{\frac{22}{3}} = \dfrac{3\times 17}{4\times 22}$

$= \dfrac{51}{88}$ the fraction required.

Reduce $\dfrac{8\frac{1}{2}}{10}$ to simple terms.

Thus, $\dfrac{8\frac{1}{2}}{10} = \dfrac{\frac{17}{2}}{10} = \dfrac{17}{2\times 10} = \dfrac{17}{20}$; and $\dfrac{12\frac{1}{3}}{16} = \dfrac{\frac{37}{3}}{16} = \dfrac{37}{48}$.

Also, $\dfrac{20}{30\frac{1}{2}} = \dfrac{20}{\frac{61}{2}} = \dfrac{20\times 2}{61} = \dfrac{40}{61}$; $\dfrac{10}{20\frac{10}{20}} = \dfrac{10}{\frac{410}{20}} = \dfrac{10\times 20}{410}$

$= \dfrac{200}{410}$; $\dfrac{300}{640\frac{1}{4}} = \dfrac{300}{\frac{2561}{4}} = \dfrac{1200}{2561}$.

PROBLEM X.

To reduce a compound fraction to a simple one of equal value.

R U L E.

1. REDUCE all such parts of the given fraction as are whole numbers, mixed numbers, and mixed fractions; according to the foregoing rules; that is, whole and mixed numbers must be reduced to improper fractions, and mixed fractions to simple terms.

2. MUL.-

2. MULTIPLY all the numerators continually to-gether, for a new numerator, and all the denomina-tors continually together, for a new denominator; and the former product written above the latter, will give the fraction required.

Note. Any number that is found among the nume-rators and denominators, may be struck out of both.

EXAMPLES.

Reduce $\frac{2}{3}$ of $\frac{3}{4}$ of $\frac{5}{6}$, to a simple fraction.

Thus, $\frac{2\times3\times5}{3\times4\times6}=$ (by striking out the 3) $\frac{2\times5}{4\times6}=\frac{10}{24}$ *the fraction required.*

Reduce $\frac{3}{4}$ of $\frac{7}{9\frac{1}{2}}$, to a simple fraction.

First, $\frac{7}{9\frac{1}{2}}=\frac{14}{19}$; *then* $3\times14=42$ *the new numerator, and* $4\times19=76$ *the new denominator : therefore* $\frac{42}{76}$ *is the fraction required.*

$\frac{1}{2}$ of $\frac{4}{6}$ of $\frac{2}{4\frac{1}{2}}$ of $8=\frac{1}{2}$ of $\frac{4}{6}$ of $\frac{4}{9}$ of $\frac{8}{1}=\frac{128}{108}$.

$\frac{4}{3}$ of $\frac{2}{5}$ of $\frac{1\frac{7}{2}}{2\frac{2}{3}}=\frac{4}{3}$ of $\frac{2}{5}$ of $\frac{51}{88}=\frac{4\times2\times51}{3\times5\times88}=\frac{408}{1320}$.

PROBLEM XI.

To reduce several fractions of different denominators, to equivalent fractions, having a common denominator.

RULE.

1. REDUCE all fractions to simple terms.

2. MUL-

2. MULTIPLY each numerator into all the denominators except its own, for new numerators.

3. MULTIPLY all the denominators continually together, for a new and common denominator, and this written under the feveral new numerators, will give the fractions required.

EXAMPLES.

Reduce $\frac{1}{2}$, $\frac{3}{4}$, and $\frac{5}{6}$, to their equivalent fractions, having a common denominator.

$$\text{Firft,}\begin{cases} 1\times4\times6=24 \text{ the new numerator for } \tfrac{1}{2} \\ 2\times3\times6=36 \text{ the new numerator for } \tfrac{3}{4} \\ 5\times2\times4=40 \text{ the new numerator for } \tfrac{5}{6} \end{cases}$$

Then $2\times4\times6=48$ *the new and common denominator.*

Hence $\frac{24}{48}$, $\frac{36}{48}$, and $\frac{40}{48}$, *are the fractions required.*

$\frac{4}{7}$, $\frac{3}{4}$, and $\frac{1}{9}$, *reduced to a common denominator*$=\dfrac{4\times4\times9}{7\times4\times9}$, $\dfrac{3\times7\times9}{7\times4\times9}$, and $\dfrac{1\times7\times4}{7\times4\times9}=\dfrac{144}{252}$, $\dfrac{189}{252}$, and $\dfrac{28}{252}$.

$\frac{1}{3}$ and $\frac{1}{3}$ of $\frac{2}{5}$ of $4\frac{1}{4}$, *reduced to a common denominator*$=$ $\dfrac{1\times1320}{3\times1320}$, and $\dfrac{3\times408}{3\times1320}=\dfrac{1320}{3960}$, and $\dfrac{1224}{3960}$.

$2\frac{1}{7}$, $\frac{2\frac{1}{4}}{4}$, and $\frac{1}{3}$ of 4, *reduced to a common denominator*$=$ $\dfrac{720}{336}$, $\dfrac{189}{336}$, and $\dfrac{448}{336}$.

PROB-

PROBLEM XII.

To reduce several fractions of different denominators, to others of equivalent value, having the least possible common denominator,

R U L E.

1. REDUCE all the fractions to simple terms.

2. FIND the least common multiple of all the denominators; and you will have the least common denominator required.

3. DIVIDE the denominator thus found by the denominator of each fraction, and multiply the quotient with its numerator, and you will have new numerators, under which write the common denominator; and you will have the fractions required.

EXAMPLES.

Reduce $\frac{1}{8}$, $\frac{3}{4}$, and $\frac{1}{2}$ to equivalent fractions, that shall have the least possible common denominator.

First, the least common multiple of 8, 4, and 2, is 8:

Then, $\overline{8 \div 8} \times 1 = 1$, *the new numerator for* $\frac{1}{8}$

And, $\overline{8 \div 4} \times 3 = 6$, *the new numerator for* $\frac{3}{4}$

Also, $\overline{8 \div 2} \times 1 = 4$, *the new numerator for* $\frac{1}{2}$.

Hence the fractions required are $\frac{1}{8}$, $\frac{6}{8}$, and $\frac{4}{8}$.

Reduce $\frac{1}{3}$, $\frac{3}{4}$, $\frac{4}{5}$, and $\frac{5}{6}$, to equivalent fractions, having the least possible common denominator.

First, the least common multiple of the 3, 4, 5, and 6, is 60.

Then, $\overline{60 \div 3} \times 1 = 20$, *the new numerator for* $\frac{1}{3}$

And, $\overline{60 \div 4} \times 3 = 45$, *the new numerator for* $\frac{3}{4}$

M

Also,

Alſo, $\overline{60 \div 5} \times 4 = 48$ *the new numerator for* $\frac{4}{5}$

Laſtly, $\overline{60 \div 6} \times 5 = 50$ *the new numerator for* $\frac{5}{6}$.

Hence, $\frac{20}{60}$, $\frac{45}{60}$, $\frac{48}{60}$, and $\frac{50}{60}$, *are the fractions req.*

PROBLEM XIII.

To change the fraction of one denomination to the fraction of a greater one, retaining its ſame value.

RULE.

CHANGE the given fraction into a compound one, by writing its value in all the intermediate denominations up to the one wherein the value of the fraction is to be expreſſed ; and the value of this compound fraction, will be the fraction required.

EXAMPLES.

Change $\frac{1}{3}$ of a nail, to the fraction of an ell Eng.

Firſt, $\frac{1}{3}$ *of a nail* $= \frac{1}{3}$ *of a quarter, and* $\frac{1}{4} = \frac{1}{5}$ *of an ell.*

Therefore, $\frac{1}{3}$ *of a nail* $= \frac{1}{3}$ of $\frac{1}{4}$ of $\frac{1}{5} = \frac{1}{60}$, *the fraction req.*

2 pennyweights, reduced to the fraction of a pound $= \frac{2}{20}$ of $\frac{1}{12} = \frac{2}{240}$. 3 grains, reduced to fraction of an ounce $= \frac{3}{24}$ of $\frac{1}{20} = \frac{3}{480}$. $\frac{1}{3}$ of a cent, reduced to the fraction of a milree of Portugal $= \frac{1}{3}$ of $\frac{1}{124} = \frac{1}{372}$. 10 cents, reduced to the fraction of a pound ſterling of Ireland $= \frac{10}{410} = \frac{1}{41}$. $\frac{7}{8}$ of a cent, reduced to the frac-

tion

tion of a dollar $= \frac{7}{8}$ of $\frac{1}{100} = \frac{7}{800}$. 1 drachm Avoir-

dupois $= \frac{1}{16}$ of $\frac{1}{16}$ of $\frac{1}{112}$ of $\frac{1}{20}$ of a tun.

PROBLEM XIV.

To change the fraction of one denomination to the fraction of a lefs one, retaining its fame value.

RULE.

MULTIPLY the numerator of the given fraction into all the intermediate denominations down to the one wherein the value of the given fraction is to be expreffed, and under this product, write the given denominator, and you will have the fraction required.

EXAMPLES.

Reduce $\frac{1}{70}$ of an ell Eng. to the fraction of a nail.

Thus, $1 \times 5 \times 4 = 20$ *the numerator*

Therefore, $\frac{20}{70} = \frac{2}{7}$ *is the fraction required.*

Reduce $\frac{3}{1120}$ of a ℔ Troy to the fract. of a grain.

Thus, $\frac{3 \times 12 \times 20 \times 24}{1120} = \frac{17280}{1120}$ *is the fraction required.*

$\frac{2}{1240}$ of a pound Troy, reduced to the fraction of a

pennyweight $= \frac{2 \times 12 \times 20}{1240} = \frac{480}{1240}$; $\frac{8}{17920}$ of an hun-

dred weight, reduced to the fraction of an ounce $=$

$8 \times 112-$

$$\frac{8 \times 112 \times 16}{17920} = \frac{14336}{17920}. \qquad \frac{1}{372} \text{ of a milree of Portugal,}$$

reduced to the fraction of a cent $= \dfrac{1 \times 124}{372} = \dfrac{124}{372} = \dfrac{1}{3}.$

PROBLEM XV.

To find the value of a Vulgar Fraction in known parts of the integer.

RULE.

MULTIPLY the numerator of the given fraction with the parts in the next inferiour denomination, and divide the product by the denominator; then if there be any remainder, multiply it with the parts in the next inferiour denomination, and divide by the former divisor, and so on, and the several quotients resulting will exhibit the value sought.

EXAMPLES.

Find the value of $\dfrac{5}{24}$ of an ounce Troy.

OPERATION.

$$\begin{array}{r} 5 \\ 20 \\ \hline \end{array}$$

$$24\,)\,100\,(4 \text{ pennyweights,}$$
$$96$$

$$\begin{array}{r} 4 \\ 24 \\ \hline \end{array}$$

$$24\,)\,96\,(4 \text{ grains,}$$
$$96$$

Therefore,

Therefore, $\frac{5}{24}$ of an ounce$=$4 *dwt.* 4 *gr.* *the value sought.*

Find the value of $\frac{5}{7}$ of an ounce Troy.

OPERATION.

$$5$$
$$20$$

7)100(
14 2 *rem.*
— 24

7)48(
6 6 *rem.*

Therefore 14 *dwt.* $6\frac{6}{7}$ *gr. is the value sought.*

Find the value of $\frac{6}{7}$ of an hundred weight.

OPERATION.

$$6$$
$$4$$

7)24(
3 3 *rem.*
— 28

7)84(
12

Therefore 3 *qr.* 12 *lb. is the value sought.*

Find the value of $\frac{1}{41}$ of a pound sterl. of Ireland:

Thus,

Thus, $\dfrac{1 \times 410}{41} = 10$ cts. *the value sought.*

Find the value of $\dfrac{2}{97}$ of a pagoda of India.

Thus, $\dfrac{2 \times 194}{97} = 4$ cts. *the value sought.*

PROBLEM XVI.

To reduce the known parts of an integer to their equivalent Vulgar Fraction.

R U L E.

1. REDUCE the given parts to the least denomination mentioned.

2. REDUCE the integer to the same denomination; and the latter written beneath the former, will be the fraction required.

EXAMPLES.

Reduce 3 *dwt.* 7 *gr.* to the fraction of a pound.

OPERATION.

dwt.	gr.		oz.
3	7		12
24			20
—			—
79			240
—			24
			—
			960
			480
			—
			5760

Therefore, $\dfrac{79}{5760}$ *is the fraction required.*

Reduce

Reduce 10 *cts.* to the fraction of a pound sterling, of Ireland.

Thus, $\dfrac{10}{410}$ *is the fraction required.*

$10\frac{8}{10}$ *in.* reduced to the fraction of a foot $=\dfrac{10\frac{8}{10}}{12}=\dfrac{9}{10}$.

$5\frac{1}{3}\ p.$ reduced to the fract. of an acre $=\dfrac{5\frac{1}{3}}{160}=\dfrac{16}{480}=\dfrac{1}{30}$.

CHAP. III.

ADDITION, SUBTRACTION, MUL-TIPLICATION, AND DIVISION OF VULGAR FRACTIONS.

SECT. I.

Of ADDITION of VULGAR FRACTIONS.

RULE.

1. REDUCE all the fractions to a common denominator, by the rule to problem XI of the last chapter: those of different denominations to the same, by the rules to problem XIII or XIV.

2. ADD all the numerators together for a new numerator, under which write the common denominator; and you will have a fraction equal to the sum required.

EXAMPLES.

Find the sum of $\dfrac{1}{2}+\dfrac{1}{3}+\dfrac{1}{4}$.

Thus,

Thus, $\frac{1}{2}+\frac{1}{3}+\frac{1}{4}=$ (by reducing to a common denominator) $\frac{12}{24}+\frac{8}{24}+\frac{6}{24}=\frac{12+8+6}{24}=\frac{26}{24}$ *sum required.*

Required the sum of $2\frac{1}{7}+\frac{2\frac{1}{4}}{4}+\frac{1}{3}$ of 4.

Thus, $2\frac{1}{7}+\frac{2\frac{1}{4}}{4}+\frac{1}{3}$ of $4=\frac{15}{7}+\frac{9}{16}+\frac{4}{3}=$ (by reduction) $\frac{720}{336}+\frac{189}{336}+\frac{448}{336}=\frac{720+189+448}{336}=\frac{1357}{336}$ *sum req.*

Find the sum of $\frac{3}{4}$ of a grain $+\frac{5}{7}$ of an ounce.

First, $\frac{3}{4}$ *of a grain* $=\frac{3}{4}$ *of* $\frac{1}{24}$ *of* $\frac{1}{20}=\frac{3}{1920}$ *of an ounce;* then the sum becomes $\frac{3}{1920}+\frac{5}{7}=\frac{9621}{13440}$ the sum req.

S E C T. II.

Of SUBTRACTION of VULGAR FRACTIONS.

R U L E.

1. PREPARE the fractions as in Addition.

2. SUBTRACT the numerator of one fraction from the numerator of the other, and the result placed above the common denominator will be the difference required.

EXAMPLES.

From $\frac{1}{3}$ take $\frac{1}{4}$.

Thus, $\frac{1}{3}-\frac{1}{4}=\frac{4}{12}-\frac{3}{12}=\frac{4-3}{12}=\frac{1}{12}$ the difference req.

From

From $\frac{4}{5}$ take $\frac{1}{3}$ of $\frac{1}{3}$.

Thus, $\frac{4}{5} - \frac{1}{3}$ of $\frac{1}{3} = \frac{4}{5} - \frac{1}{9} = \frac{36}{45} - \frac{5}{45} = \frac{36-5}{45} = \frac{31}{45}$ *the* *difference required.*

$3\frac{1}{3} - \frac{3}{4}$ of $\frac{1}{9}$ of $\frac{2}{3} = \frac{10}{3} - \frac{6}{108} = \frac{1080}{324} - \frac{18}{324} = \frac{1080-18}{324}$

$= \frac{1062}{324}$; $1\frac{1}{4} - \frac{\frac{7}{4}}{\frac{22}{3}} = \frac{5}{4} - \frac{51}{88} = \frac{440}{352} - \frac{204}{352} = \frac{236}{352}$.

From $\frac{5}{7}$ of an ounce take $\frac{3}{4}$ of a grain Troy.

First, $\frac{3}{4}$ *of a grain* $= \frac{3}{1920}$ of and ounce : Therefore,

$\frac{5}{7} - \frac{3}{1920} = \frac{9589}{13440}$ *is the difference required.*

S E C T.   III.

Of MULTIPLICATION of VULGAR FRACTIONS.

R U L E.

1. Reduce all whole and mixed numbers to improper fractions, mixed fractions to simple terms, and fractions of different denominations to the same.

2. Multiply all the numerators together for a new numerator, and all the denominators together for a new denominator; and you will have the terms of the fraction required.

EXAMPLES.

Required the product of $\frac{1}{3} \times \frac{3}{4}$.

Thus, $\frac{1 \times 3}{3 \times 4} = \frac{3}{12}$ *the product required.*

$6\frac{1}{7} \times$

$$6\tfrac{1}{3} \times \tfrac{1}{4} \text{ of } \tfrac{2}{9} = \text{(by reduction)} \ \tfrac{19}{3} \times \tfrac{2}{36} = \tfrac{19 \times 2}{3 \times 36} = \tfrac{38}{108};$$

$$\tfrac{4}{3\tfrac{1}{3}} \times \tfrac{3\tfrac{1}{3}}{4} = \text{(by reduction)} \ \tfrac{12}{10} \times \tfrac{10}{12} = \tfrac{12 \times 10}{10 \times 12} = \tfrac{120}{120} = 1;$$

$$\tfrac{1}{3}\,\text{lb} \times \tfrac{1}{4}\,dr. = \tfrac{1}{3} \times \frac{1}{4 \times 16 \times 16} = \frac{1 \times 1}{3 \times 4 \times 16 \times 16} = \frac{1}{3072}\,\text{lb}$$

S E C T.   IV.

Of DIVISION of VULGAR FRACTIONS.

R U L E.

Prepare the numbers as in Addition, then multiply the numerator of the divisor into the denominator of the dividend, and the numerator of the dividend into the denominator of the divisor; then the latter written above the former, will give the quotient required.   Or,

Invert the divisor, that is, write the denominator in the place of the numerator, and the numerator in the place of the denominator; then proceed as in Multiplication, and the result will give the quotient required.

EXAMPLES.

Required the quotient of $\tfrac{1}{2} \div \tfrac{1}{4}$.

Thus, $1 \times 4 = 4$ *the numerator;* and $1 \times 2 = 2$ *the denom.*

Therefore, $\tfrac{4}{2} = 2$ *is the quotient required.*

Or, $\tfrac{4}{1} \times \tfrac{1}{2} = \tfrac{4}{2}$ *the same as before.*

$$\tfrac{2}{3} \div \tfrac{8}{27} = \tfrac{27}{8} \times \tfrac{2}{3} = \tfrac{27 \times 2}{8 \times 3} = \tfrac{54}{24}; \quad \tfrac{4}{7} \div \tfrac{4}{28} = \tfrac{28}{4} \times \tfrac{4}{7} = \tfrac{28 \times 4}{}$$

$$\frac{28\times4}{4\times7}=\frac{112}{28}=4;\quad \frac{1\frac{1}{3}}{8}\div\frac{3\frac{1}{2}}{1}=\text{(by reduction)}\frac{4}{24}\div\frac{7}{2}=$$

$$\frac{4\times2}{7\times24}=\frac{8}{168};\quad \frac{1}{4}\text{ of }\frac{1}{2}\div\frac{1}{3}\text{ of }1=\frac{1}{8}\div\frac{1}{3}=\frac{3\times1}{1\times8}=\frac{3}{8}.$$

Miscellaneous Questions.

A MAN at hazard won the firſt throw $2\frac{1}{2}$ dol-lars—the ſecond throw he won as much as he then had in his pocket—the third throw he won 4 dollars, and the fourth throw he won double of all that he then had, at which time he found that he had in all 45 dollars. How many had he at firſt.

Anſwer. *3 dollars.*

THERE is a certain club, whereof $\frac{1}{4}$ are merchants, $\frac{1}{3}$ mathematicians, $\frac{1}{5}$ mechanics, and 13 phyſicians. How many were there in the whole ?

Anſwer. 60.

REQUIRED the difference between three times thir-ty-three and a third ; and three times three and thir-ty and a third.

Anſwer. $60\frac{2}{3}$.

A MAN who was driving ſome ſheep to market, was met by another who demanded the number of ſheep in his drove : the drover to evade a direct anſ-wer replies, that if I had as many more, and half as many more, and $12\frac{1}{2}$ ſheep, I ſhould have 100. What number had he ?

Anſwer. 35.

PART

PART III.

CONTAINING THE DOCTRINE OF

DECIMAL FRACTIONS.

CHAP. I.

DEFINITIONS and ILLUSTRATIONS.

A DECIMAL Fraction is formed from a proper Vulgar Fraction, by dividing the numerator with cyphers annexed to it, by the denominator; that is, the equivalent Decimal of any Vulgar Fraction is found by multiplying the numerator with 10, 100, or 1000, &c. till it be so increased, that it may be exactly measured by its denominator; and this quotient will be the decimal required:

Thus, $\frac{1}{4} \times 100 = \frac{1 \times 100}{4} = \frac{100}{4} = 25$; and $\frac{1}{2} \times 10 = \frac{1 \times 10}{2} = \frac{10}{2} = .5$; Also, $\frac{3}{4} \times 100 = \frac{3 \times 100}{4} = \frac{300}{4} = 75$: which quotients are expressed by writing them with a point on the left-hand: Thus, $\frac{1}{4} = .25$, $\frac{1}{2} = .5$, and $\frac{3}{4} = .75$; which are respectively equal to $\frac{25}{100}$, $\frac{5}{10}$, and $\frac{75}{100}$; but these denominators are always omitted, and the numerators written as above, where the point distinguishes them from whole numbers: Thus, $2.3 = 2\frac{3}{10}$, $4.25 = 4\frac{25}{100}$, &c.

HENCE

HENCE it appears that every Decimal Fraction, is equal to a Vulgar one, whofe numerator is the decimal, and the denominator unity, with as many cyphers annexed to it as there are places of figures in the numerator: Thus, .1, .44, and .127, are refpectively equal to $\frac{1}{10}$, $\frac{44}{100}$, and $\frac{127}{1000}$.

THEREFORE it follows, that in decimals, unity is divided in 10, 100, or 1000, &c. equal parts; and the given decimal reprefents the number of thofe parts: Thus, $.1 = \frac{1}{10}$ reprefents one tenth part of an unit, .44 reprefents forty-four hundred parts of an unit, &c. Therefore, in decimals, cyphers annexed neither increafe nor diminifh their value; but cyphers prefixed, diminifh their value in a ten fold proportion: Thus, $.440 = \frac{440}{1000} = $ (by the nature of Divifion) $\frac{44}{100} = .44$; but $.04 = \frac{4}{100} = \frac{1}{10}$ of $(\frac{4}{10})$ .4, and fo on for any other decimal.

WHENCE it follows, that the farther any diget or numeral figure ftands from the units' place, or decimal point towards the right-hand, the lefs will be its value, to wit, in a tenfold proportion. Thus in the decimal .1111, the figure next to the decimal point is $\frac{1}{10}$, the fecond is $\frac{1}{100}$, the third $\frac{1}{1000}$, and the fourth $\frac{1}{10000}$, that is, $.1111 = \frac{1}{10} + \frac{1}{100} + \frac{1}{1000} + \frac{1}{10000}$, which is plainly a feries of numbers in geometrical proportion, decreafing by the common divifor 10. Again $.0123 = \frac{1}{100} + \frac{2}{1000} + \frac{3}{10000}$; and the like to be underftood of all others.

HENCE, the notation of decimals, or the valuation of the feveral places from unity downwards, is the fame among themfelves as that of integers or whole numbers; therefore every figure is to be valued according to the diftance it ftands from unity downwards.

CHAP. II.

ADDITION, SUBTRACTION, MUL-TIPLICATION, and *DIVISION* of *DECIMAL FRACTIONS.*

SECT. I.

Of ADDITION of DECIMALS.

RULE.

1. WRITE the given decimals in such order, that those places of equal distance from unity or the decimal point, may stand directly under each other.

2. Find their sum as in whole numbers, then distinguish with a point as many places of figures on the right-hand, as are equal to the greatest number found in any given decimal; and you will have the sum required.

EXAMPLES.

Find the sum of .176+.1264+.34+.994

These numbers being placed according to the rule will stand

$$\text{thus,}\begin{cases} .176 \\ .1264 \\ .34 \\ .994 \end{cases}$$

1.6364=*sum required.*

Find the sum of 34.123+6437.27+347.2+1.347634+347634.1.

thus,

$$\text{thus,}\begin{cases} 34.123 \\ 6437.27 \\ 347.2 \\ 1.347634 \\ 347634.1 \end{cases}$$

$$354454.040634 = \textit{sum required.}$$

Required the sum of $25.124 + 12.247 + 24.3485 + 352.1 + 4578.74$

$$\text{thus,}\begin{cases} 25.124 \\ 12.247 \\ 24.3485 \\ 352.1 \\ 4578.74 \end{cases}$$

$$4992.5595 = \textit{sum required.}$$

$$17.45 + .42 + 345.284 + 34 + 4232.425 = 4629.579$$

S E C T. II.

Of SUBTRACTION of DECIMALS.

R U L E.

WRITE down the numbers as in Addition, then subtract the less from the greater as in whole numbers, remembering to point off in the remainder as in Addition; and you will have the difference sought.

EXAMPLES.

Required the difference between 12.19, and 8.9

$$\text{thus,}\begin{cases} 12.19 \\ 8.9 \end{cases}$$

$$3.29 = \textit{difference required.}$$

Required

Required the difference between 342.364, and 299.2437

$$\text{thus,}\begin{cases} 342.364 \\ 299.2437 \end{cases}$$

$$43.1203 = \textit{difference required.}$$

2473.0024—1999.99998=473.00242 ;

2479.3777—930.00004$=1549.377655 ;

9999.8888—8888.9999=1110.8889

S E C T.   III.

Of MULTIPLICATION of DECIMALS.

R U L E.

WRITE the numbers and multiply them as in common Multiplication; then diftinguifh with a point as many places of decimals in the product, as are equal to the number in both factors; and you will have the product required.

Note. *If the number of places in the product, are lefs than the number of decimal places in both factors, you muft fupply the deficiency by prefixing cyphers.*

THAT the number of decimal places in the product, ought to be equal to the number in both factors, may be thus demonftrated.

SUPPOSE .34 were to be multiplied with .27; the product of thefe two numbers by common Multiplication is 918; but $.34 = \frac{34}{100}$ and $.27 = \frac{27}{100}$; therefore, $.34 \times .27 = \frac{34}{100} \times \frac{27}{100} = \frac{918}{10000} =$ (by the nature of decimal notation) .0918, confifting of as many places of figures as there were in both factors; and the fame will hold true in any others. *Q. E. D.*

EXAM

EXAMPLES.

Required the product of 2.438 × .005.

OPERATION.

$$2.438$$
$$.005$$

.012190 = *product required.*

Required the product of 34.38×24.7

OPERATION.

$$34.38$$
$$24.7$$

$$24066$$
$$13752$$
$$6876$$

849.186=*product required.*

Required the product of 384.02×.01

thus, $\begin{cases} 384.02 \\ .01 \end{cases}$

3.8402= *product required.*

Required the product of 2.7122×3.2121

thus, $\begin{cases} 3.2121 \\ 2.7122 \end{cases}$

$$64242$$
$$64242$$
$$32121$$
$$224847$$
$$64242$$

8.71185762=*product required.*

O

IN the multiplication of decimals, where the factors consist of a great number of decimal places, the operation becomes very prolix, and besides, a great part of it is entirely useless, since that four or five places of decimals in the product, is sufficient for common purposes. Therefore to abridge the work by obtaining the product true to any designed number of places of decimals, you must observe the following

RULE.

1. WRITE the multiplier inverted, so that the units' place may stand under that figure of the multiplicand, to whose place the product is to be found true.

2. IN multiplying with the several figures of the multiplier, you must reject all the figures of the multiplicand, that are to the right-hand of the figure you are multiplying with ; placing the first figure of the several products directly under each other, increased by adding 1 from 5 to 15, 2 from 15 to 25, &c. of the product of the multiplying figure with the proceeding figure of the multiplicand, when you begin to multiply ; and the sum of all the products will be the product required.

EXAMPLES.

Required the product of 3.2121 × 2.712, to three places of decimals.

3.2121

3.2121
2172
___

6424=*product of* 3.212×2 .
2248=*product of* 3.21×7, *increased by adding* 1 *for*
  32=*product of* 3.2×1   [*the prod. of* 7×2
   6=*product of* 3×2
___

8.710=*product required.*

Required the product of 3.24211×2.34634, to four places of decimals.

  3.24211
  436432
___

  64842=3.2421×2
   9726=3.242×3
   1297=3.24×4, *increased by adding* 1 *for* 4×2
    194=3.2×6, *increased by adding* 2 *for* 6×4
     10=3×3, *increased by adding* 1 *for* 3×2
___

  7.6069=*product required.*

Required the product of 2.13214×2.21134, to five places of decimals.

2.13214
431122
___

 426428=2.13214×2
  42643=2.1321×2, *increased by adding* 1 *for* 2×4
   2132=2.132×1
    213=2.13×1
     64=2.1×3, *increased by adding* 1 *for* 3×3
      2=2×4
___

 4.71488=*product required.*

Required

Required the product of 27.17$\times$19.14, in integers only.

$$27.17$$
$$4191$$

$272 = 27.1 \times 1$, *increased by adding* 1 *for* 1$\times$7
$244 = 27 \times 9$, *increased by adding* 1 *for* 9$\times$1
$3 = 2 \times 1$, *increased by adding* 1 *for* 1$\times$7
$1 = 4 \times 0$, *increased by adding* 1 *for* 4$\times$2

$520 = product \; required.$

SECT. IV.

Of DIVISION of DECIMALS.

In division of decimals, it may at first appear difficult to determine the number of decimal places the quotient must consist of; but this difficulty will vanish, when we consider that the quotient must be such a number that when multiplied with the divisor will produce the dividend; therefore it follows, that the number of decimal places in the divisor and quotient taken together, must be equal to the number in the dividend, by the nature of Multiplication; consequently the difference between those in the divisor and dividend, must be equal to the number in the quotient; which affords the following

RULE.

RANGE the numbers and divide them as in common Division, then point off as many places of decimals in the quotient, as are equal to the difference between those in the divisor and dividend; and you will have the quotient required.

Note

Note 1. *If there are not so many places of figures in the quotient, as are equal to the difference between those in the divisor and dividend, you must supply the defect by prefixing cyphers.*

2. *If the places of figures in the dividend, are less in number than those in the divisor, you must annex cyphers to the dividend.*

EXAMPLES.

Required the quotient of 849.186 divided by 24.7

OPERATION.

$$24.7 \overline{)849.186} (34.38 = quotient\ required.$$

$$741$$

$$1081$$
$$988$$

$$938$$
$$741$$

$$1976$$
$$1976$$

$$0$$

Note. If the divisor be 10, or 100, &c. the quotient may be found by removing the decimal point in the dividend, as many places towards the left-hand as there are cyphers in the divisor : thus, the quotient of $1000 \overline{)2737.45}$ *is* 2.73745 *and* $.0234 \div 100 = .000234.$

Required the quotient of $.012190 \div 2.438$

OPERATION.

$$2.438 \,\overline{)\,.012190\,(\,5}$$
$$12190$$

0

Here, the quotient found by divifion is 5 ; but the difference between the decimal places in the divifor and dividend are three ; therefore .005 is the quotient required.

Required the quotient of 2÷42.

OPERATION.

$$42 \,\overline{)\,200000\,(\,.04761}\; \&c. = quotient\; required.$$
$$168$$

320
294

260
252

80
42

38 *&c.*

Required the quotient of 165.6995001296÷ 52.7438

OPER-

OPERATION.

52.7438) 165.6995001296 (3.141592 = *quotient req.*
    1582314

746810
527438

2193720
2109752

839681
527438

3122432
2637190

4852429
4746942

1054876
1054876

0

HERE, as in Multiplication, the work may be greatly contracted, by finding the quotient true to any determinate number of decimal places : The method is as follows.

R U L E.

1. RANGE the numbers as in common Division.

2. TAKE the figures of the given divisor, to as many places of decimals as you intend the quotient shall consist of, for your first divisor, and find a quotient figure by comparing this divisor as in common
Division ;

Divifion ; then fubtract its product with the divifor, from the dividend as ufual, calling the remainder a new dividend.

3. REJECT the right hand figure of your former divifor, and call the refult a new divifor ; then find a quotient figure by comparing the new divifor and dividend together, and place it in the former quotient, fubtracting as before ; and fo on, making each remainder a new dividend, and rejecting the right-hand figure of the laft divifor for a new one ; alfo remembering to add for the figures rejected as in Multiplication.

Note 1. If there are not fo many places of decimals in the divifor, as you intend there fhall be in the quotient, fupply the defect by annexing cyphers.

2. You may determine how many places of whole numbers there will be in the quotient, by confidering that the firft figure of the quotient, is always of the fame denomination of that figure of the dividend, which ftands directly over the units' place of the product of the firft quotient figure and divifor.

EXAMPLES.

Required the quotient of 10.1934÷4.2, to three places of decimals.

OPER-

4.200)10.1934(2.427 = *quotient required.*
   8400

420)1793
  1680

42)113
  84

4)29
 28

 1

Required the quotient of 165.6995001296 ÷ 52.7438, to five places of decimals.

52.74380)165.6995001296(3.141592 = *quotient req.*
  15823140

52.7438)746810
  527438

52.743)219372
  210975 = 52.743 × 4, *encreased by add-*
              [*ing* 3 *for* 4 × 8

52.74)8397
  5274

52.7)3123
  2637 = 527 × 5, *encreased by adding*
            [2 *for* 5 × 4

52)486
  473 = 52 × 9, *increased by adding* 5
            [*for* 9 × 7

5)13
 10

Required the quotient of 780.516 ÷ 24.3, in integers only.

OPERATION.

$$24 \overline{)780.516} (32 = quotient\ required.$$
$$73 = 24 \times 3,\ increased\ by\ adding\ 1\ for\ 3 \times 3$$

$$2 \overline{)5}$$
$$5 = 2 \times 2,\ increased\ by\ adding\ 1\ for\ 2 \times 4$$

$$0$$

CHAP. III.

Of REDUCTION of DECIMALS.

PROBLEM I.

To reduce a Vulgar Fraction to its equivalent decimal.

RULE.

ANNEX cyphers to the numerator, and divide by the denominator till nothing remains, and the quotient will be the decimal required.

EXAMPLES.

Reduce $\dfrac{3}{20}$ to its equivalent decimal.

Thus, $20 \overline{)3.00} (.15 = the\ decimal\ required.$
$$20$$

$$100$$
$$100$$

$$0$$

Reduce

Reduce $\dfrac{18}{20}$ to its equivalent decimal.

Thus, $20\,)\,18.0\,(.9 =$ *the decimal required.*
$\,180$
$\,0$

Reduce $\dfrac{6}{15}$ to its equivalent decimal.

Thus, $15\,)\,6.0\,(.4 =$ *the decimal required.*
$\,60$
$\,0$

Required the equivalent decimal of $\dfrac{8}{9}$.

OPERATION.

$9\,)\,8.00000\,(.8888$ *&c. ad infinitum.*
72

80
72

80
72

8 *&c.*

Here, we have what is called a circulating decimal for the quotient, that is, a continual repetition
of the fame figure without any poffibility of ever
coming to an end, as is evident from the example.
Therefore it follows, that the equivalent decimal of
$\frac{1}{9}$ can never be found in finite terms ; but may be
obtained to any degree of exactnefs you pleafe.

Note.

Note. *When a vulgar fraction is annexed to any number of cents, reduce the fraction to its equivalent decimal, and annex it to the cents, and the whole will become a decimal: Thus,* .37¼ *cents* = .3775

PROBLEM II.

To reduce numbers of different denominations to their equivalent decimal.

RULE.

REDUCE the given numbers to their equivalent vulgar fraction, by problem XVI. of vulgar fractions, then proceed as in the laft problem.

EXAMPLES.

REDUCE 3 qr. 2 na. to their equivalent decimal of a yard.

Firft, 3 qr. 2 na. $= \frac{14}{16}$ of a yard;

Then 16) 14.000 (.875 = *the decimal required.*
      128

      120
      112

        80
        80

         0

4 b. 30′ 10″, reduced to the decimal of a day = .187615 &c.

8 S. reduced to the decimal of the ecliptic = .666 &c. *ad infinitum.*

10$\frac{8}{10}$ *in.* reduced to the decimal of a foot = .9

5⅓

5¼*p.* reduced to the decimal of an acre=.0333 *&c. ad infinitum.*

PROBLEM III.

To find the value of a decimal in known parts of the integer.

RULE.

1. MULTIPLY the given decimal with the parts in the next inferiour denomination, and point off as in common multiplication of decimals; and the whole numbers will be the value of the given decimal in that denomination.

2. MULTIPLY the remaining decimal with the parts in the next inferiour denomination, and point off as before, and so on, thro all the inferiour denomination, if need be ; and you will have the value sought.

EXAMPLES.

Find the value of .875 of a yard.

OPERATION.

```
 .875
    4
 ─────
3.500
    4
 ─────
```
       qr. na.
:2.000 *therefore,* .875=3 2, *the value sought.*

Find the value of .426 of a pound troy.

OPER-

OPERATION.

$$
\begin{array}{r}
.426 \\
12 \\
\hline
5.112 \\
20 \\
\hline
2.240 \\
24 \\
\hline
960 \\
480 \\
\hline
\end{array}
$$

        ℔ oz. dwt. gr.

5.760 *therefore* .426 = 5 2 5.76

Find the value of .75 of a pound sterling of Great-Britain.

OPERATION.

$$
\begin{array}{r}
.75 \\
444 \\
\hline
300 \\
300 \\
300 \\
\hline
\end{array}
$$

        £. cts. dol. cts.

333.00 *therefore* .75 = 333 = 3 33.

Find the value of .37752 of a pound sterling of Great-Britain.

        cts. dol. cts.

Thus .37752 × 444 = 167.61888 = 1 6761888.

Note. *There never can be more than two places of cents, and where there are other figures annexed, they are the parts of another cent : thus, in the last example, the 6761888 cts. is 67 cents, and .61888 of another.*   A

A Supplement to Part III,

CONTAINING THE DOCTRINE OF
CIRCULATING DECIMALS.

CHAP. I.

DEFINITIONS and ILLUSTRATIONS.

A CIRCULATING decimal is generated or produced from a vulgar fraction, whose numerator and denominator are incommensurable to each other ; and therefore if the numerator with cyphers annexed, be divided by the denominator, there will always be a remainder, or the quotient will run on sempiternally ; consequently the true and adequate decimal of every such vulgar fraction, must consist of an infinite number of decimal places, which is therefore not assignable in finite terms, and consequently the true and complete decimal impossible.

NOTWITHSTANDING the equivalent decimal of every vulgar fraction of the kind above described, if actually completed, would then consist of an infinite number of decimal places ; yet from a few of the first, we obtain some certain law by which the figures ever after circulate or return again ; and it is for this reason they are called circulating decimals : the circulating figures are called repetends, of which there are four kinds, viz. single, compound, mixed-single, and mixed compound.

A SINGLE repetend is a continual repetition of the same figure : Thus .666 &c. and .2222 &c. are single repetends, which are expressed by writing the re-

peating

peating figure with a point over it : thus, for .666 *&c.*

write .6 for .2222 *&c.* we write .2 ; and so on for others.

A compound repetend is when the same figures circulate or return alternately : thus .9595 *&c.* and .321321 *&c.* are compound repetends, which are expressed by writing the combination of figures that circulate or return together, with a point over the first and last figure : thus, instead of .9595 *&c.* we write .95 for .321321 *&c.* we write .321 ; and so on for others.

A mixed single repetend is when one or more figures occur before the repeating ones : thus .172444 *&c.* and .1942777 *&c.* are mixed single repetends.

A mixed compound repetend is when several figures stand before those that circulate alternately : thus .1724747 *&c.* and .41972972 *&c.* are mixed compound repetends,

Those combinations of figures, which circulate or return together, are called circulates, of which there are three kinds, viz. similar, dissimilar, similar and conterminous.

Similar circulates are those that consist of the same number of repeating figures, beginning either before or after the decimal point : thus 42.7 and 9.19 are similar circulates.

Dissimilar circulates are those that consist of an unequal number of repeating figures, beginning at different places : thus 1.77 and 217.4 are dissimilar circulates.

Similar

Similar and conterminous circulates, are thofe which confift of an equal number of repeating figures, beginning and ending together : thus, 27.47 and 4.73 are fimilar and conterminous circulates.

CHAP. II.

Of REDUCTION of CIRCULATING DECIMALS.

PROBLEM I.

To reduce a fingle repetend to its equivalent Vulgar Fraction.

RULE.

UNDER the given repetend, with as many cyphers annexed to it, as there are places of whole numbers, write as many 9's as there are places of figures in the repetend ; and you will have the Vulgar Fraction required.

The reafon of this rule will appear obvious, when we confider, that $.\dot{9}=1$; for $\frac{1}{9}=.\dot{1}11$ &c.$=.\dot{1}$; confequently $.\dot{1}\times9=\frac{1}{9}\times9$; that is, $.\dot{9}=\frac{9}{9}=1$; whence it follows, that each figure of the repetend is equal to that figure divided by 9 : thus $.\dot{3}=\frac{3}{9}=\frac{1}{3}$ $.\dot{5}=\frac{5}{9}$,&c.

EXAMPLES.

Required the leaft Vulgar Fraction equivalent to $.\dot{7}\dot{2}$

          Thus,

Thus, $\frac{72}{99} = \frac{8}{11} =$ *fraction required.*

$\dot{2}1.\dot{3} = \dfrac{21300}{999}.$ $6\dot{4}3.2\dot{5} = \dfrac{64325000}{99999}.$ $\dot{1}.742\dot{1} = \dfrac{174210}{99999}.$ $1\dot{2}7.000\dot{2} = \dfrac{1270002000}{9999999}.$

PROBLEM II.

To reduce a mixed compound repetend to its equivalent Vulgar Fraction.

R U L E.

WRITE down as many 9's as there are places of figures in the repetend, to which annex as many cyphers as are equal to the number of occurring places of figures in the finite part, (i. e. the figures occurring before the alternate circulates) for a denominator; then multiply the 9's in the denominator, with the finite part, to which product, add the infinite or circulating part for a numerator; and you will have the fraction required.

Note. *When the circulate begins any where in the integral part, omit the cyphers in the denominator, and annex as many to the numerator as there are places of whole numbers included in the circulate.*

THE reason of this rule will appear plain from the following. Suppose the decimal whose equivalent VulgarFraction is required, to be .5̇3̇ : Conceive it to be divided into finite and infinite parts; that is, conceive it to be made of the finite part .5 and the infinite or circulating part .0̇3̇ ; then .5̇3̇ = .5 + .0̇3̇; but .3̇ = $\frac{1}{3}$; consequently .0̇3̇ = $\frac{1}{10}$ of $\frac{1}{3}$ = $\frac{1}{30}$; wherefore

.5̇3̇

$$\cdot 5\overset{\cdot}{3} = \frac{5}{10} + \frac{3}{90} = \frac{450}{900} + \frac{30}{900} = \frac{9\times 5 + 3}{90},$$ which is the same as the rule.

EXAMPLES.

Required the Vulgar Fraction equivalent to .4$\overset{\cdot}{7}3\overset{\cdot}{9}$
First, 9990 = *denominator.*
Then 999 $\times$ 4 = 3996 = *product of the 9's in the denominator and finite part ; and* 3996 + 739 = 4735 = *numerator.*
Wherefore $\frac{4735}{9990}$ *is the fraction required.*

Required the equivalent Vulgar Fraction of 5.2$\overset{\cdot}{7}$:
Thus, $\overline{52\times 9 + 7} \div 900 = 468 + 7 \div 900 = \frac{475}{900}$ *the fraction required.*

Required the equivalent Vulgar Fraction of 4$\overset{\cdot}{2}.\overset{\cdot}{3}$:
Thus, $\overline{990\times 4 + 230} \div 99 = \frac{4190}{99}$ *the fraction required.*

Required the equivalent Vulgar Fraction of 32$\overset{\cdot}{1}.\overset{\cdot}{7}$:
Thus, $\overline{999\times 3 + 217} \div 999 = 3214 \div 999$; then $\frac{321400}{999} =$ *fraction required.*

PROBLEM III.

To determine whether the decimal equivalent to any Vulgar Fraction be finite, or infinite ; and if infinite, to find the number of places of figures that constitute the circulate.

RULE.

1. Reduce the given fraction to its least terms.
2. Divide the denominator of the resulting fraction

tion by 2, 5 or 10, as often as you can without a remainder, making the refult a divifor, and 999 &c. a dividend, divide till nothing remains, then will the circulate confift of as many places of figures as you ufed places of 9's.

> Note. 1. *The circulate will begin, after as many places of figures as you made divifions of the denominator.*
>
> 2. *In dividing the denominator as above, if the quotient become equal to unity, then the decimal is finite, confifting of as many places of figures as you made divifions of the denominator.*

The principles on which this rule is inveftigated, may be fhewn in the following manner.

Firft, let it be premifed, that if unity with cyphers annexed, be divided by any prime number, except 2, or 5, the figures in the quotient will begin to repeat when the remainder becomes unity; confequently 999 &c. divided by any prime number, except 2, or 5, will leave no remainder.

Now if the places of figures in the circulate are any number, when the dividend is unity, they will remain the fame, let the dividend be any other number whatever; for it is plain, that if the decimal be multiplied with any number, every circulate will be equally multiplied, and what one is increafed will be carried to another, and fo on through the whole; confequently, the places of figures will remain the fame: But to multiply the decimal or quotient with any number, is the fame thing, as to divide the divifor by the fame number before divifion is made; whence, &c.

EXAMPLES.

EXAMPLES.

Required to know, whether the equivalent decimal, of $\frac{158}{557}$ is infinite or finite, and if infinite, how many places of figures there will be in the circulate.

First, $\frac{158}{557}$ reduced to its least terms$=\frac{2}{7}$; then $999999\div7=142857$, and therefore the decimal is infinite, whose circulate consists of 6 places of figures, beginning at the tenth's place.

Required to know whether the equivalent dicimal of $\frac{2100}{11120}$ is infinite, or finite; and if infinite, how many places of figures there will be in the circulate.

First, $\frac{2100}{11120}=$ (by reducing to its least terms) $\frac{3}{16}$; then, $16\div2=8$, $8\div2=4$, $4\div2=2$, and $2\div2=1$: Consequently the decimal is finite, consisting of 4 places of figures.

Required to know whether the equivalent decimal of $\frac{364}{490}$ is infinite, or finite; and if infinite, to know how many places of figures there will be in the circulate.

First, $\frac{364}{490}=$ (by reducing to its least terms) $\frac{52}{70}$; then $70\div10=7$, and $999999\div7=142857$: Consequently the dicimal is infinite, and the circulate consists of 6 places of figures, beginning at the hundredth's place.

PROBLEM IV.

To make dissimilar circulates, similar and conterminous.

R U L E.

1. Find the least possible common multiple of the several numbers expressing the number of places of figures in the given circulates.

2. Change the given circulates into others, confifting each of as many places of figures as the leaft
common multiple found as above, and the work will
be done.

EXAMPLES.

Make .7̇2̇7, .1̇7̇9, .1̇2̇ and .1̇9̇ fimilar and conterminous.

Firft the leaft common multiple of 3, 3, 2 and 2,
is 6.

Diffimilar. Similar and conterminous.

$$\text{Then,} \begin{cases} .7̇2̇7 = .7̇27727 \\ .1̇7̇9 = .1̇79179 \\ .1̇2̇ = .1̇21212 \\ .1̇9̇ = .1̇91919 \end{cases}$$

Make 24.3̇, .4̇76̇2, 32.6̇ and .5̇76̇ fimilar and
conterminous.

Diffimilar. Similar and conterminous.

$$\text{Thus,} \begin{cases} 24.3̇ = 24.3̇33333333333 \\ .4̇76̇2 = .4̇762476̇24762 \\ 32.6̇ = 32.6̇66666666666 \\ .5̇76̇ = .5̇765765̇76576 \end{cases}$$

C H A P.

CHAP. III.

ADDITION, SUBTRACTION, MULTIPLICATION AND DIVISION OF CIRCULATING DECIMALS.

SECT. I.

Of ADDITION of CIRCULATING DECIMALS.

RULE.

MAKE the given circulates similar and conterminous, by problem IV, of the last chapter; then add them together as in common Addition, and because each figure of the circulate is equal to that figure divided by 9, you must divide the sum of the circulates, by as many places of 9's as there are places of figures in the circulate, and writing the remainder (if any) directly beneath the figures of the circulate, carry the above quotient to the next place; then proceed as in common decimals, and you will have the sum required.

Note. *When the remainder consists of a less number of places than the circulate, you must supply the defect by prefixing cyphers.*

EXAMPLES.

EXAMPLES.

Required the sum of $3.\dot{3}+4.\dot{2}7\dot{1}+3.\dot{7}2\dot{5}$:

Diffimilar.   Similar and conterminous.

$$\text{Thus,} \begin{cases} 3.\dot{3} & =3.\dot{3}3\dot{3} \\ 4.\dot{2}7\dot{1} =4.\dot{2}7\dot{1} \\ 3.\dot{7}2\dot{5}=3.\dot{7}2\dot{5} \end{cases}$$

$11.33\dot{0}=$ *fum required.*

Required the sum of $24,32742\dot{5}+37.27\dot{4}+27.\dot{3}\dot{5}+34.\dot{2}\dot{7}$:

Diffimilar.   Similar and conterminous.

$$\text{Thus,} \begin{cases} 24.32742\dot{5}=24.327\dot{4}2542\dot{5} \\ 37.27\dot{4} & =37.274444444 \\ 27.\dot{3}\dot{5} & =27.35353535\dot{3} \\ 34.\dot{2}\dot{7} & =34.277777777 \end{cases}$$

$123.23318300\dot{1}=$ *fum req.*

S E C T. II.

Of SUBTRACTION of CIRCULATING DECI-MALS.

R U L E.

PREPARE the given numbers, as in Addition, and then fubtract them as in common Subtraction, only with this difference, viz. when the circulate to be fub-tracted, is greater than the one from which Subtraction is to be made, you muft make the right-hand

figure

figure of the difference lefs by unity, than as found by common Subtraction. The reafon of this rule will appear plain from the following.

Suppose $1.8\dot{1}$ were to be taken from $2.7\dot{2}$; the difference by common Subtraction would be $.91$; but $2.7\dot{2} = \frac{2\dot{7}\dot{0}}{9\dot{9}}$ and $1.8\dot{1} = \frac{1\dot{8}\dot{0}}{9\dot{9}}$, then $2.7\dot{2} - 1.8\dot{1} = \frac{2\dot{7}\dot{0}}{9\dot{9}} - \frac{1\dot{8}\dot{0}}{9\dot{9}} = \frac{\dot{9}\dot{0}}{9\dot{9}} = .\dot{9}\dot{0}$; whence, &c.

EXAMPLES.

Required the difference between $6.47\dot{2}\dot{9}$ and $3.4\dot{9}$:

Diffimilar. Similar and conterminous.

Thus, $\begin{cases} 6.47\dot{2}\dot{9} = 6.47\dot{2}972\dot{9} \\ 3.4\dot{9} = 3.4949494 \end{cases}$

$2.97\dot{8}023\dot{4} = $ *difference required.*

Required the difference between $4.37\dot{5}\dot{2}$ and $1.1\dot{2}1\dot{0}$:

Diffimilar. Similar and conterminous.

Thus, $\begin{cases} 4.37\dot{5}\dot{2} = 4.37\dot{5}25\dot{2} \\ 1.1\dot{2}1\dot{0} = 1.1\dot{2}101\dot{0} \end{cases}$

$3.25\dot{4}2404\dot{1} = $ *difference required.*

S E C T.   III.

Of MULTIPLICATION of CIRCULATING DE-CIMALS.

R U L E.

Instead of the given circulates, write their equivalent Vulgar Fractions, and find their product as usual ;

ufual; then this product thrown into a decimal, will give the product required.

EXAMPLES.

Required the product of $3.\dot{2}\times.\dot{7}$

Firft, $.\dot{3}\dot{2}=\frac{29}{90}$ and $.\dot{7}=\frac{7}{9}$; wherefore $.\dot{3}\dot{2}\times.\dot{7}=\frac{29}{90}\times\frac{7}{9}=\frac{203}{810}$, which thrown into a decimal is, $.\dot{2}5061\dot{7}39=$ *product required.*

Required the product of $1.\dot{8}\times2.\dot{7}$:

Thus, $1.\dot{8}\times2.\dot{7}=\frac{17}{9}\times\frac{25}{9}=\frac{425}{81}=5.\dot{2}46913580$ *the product required.*

Required the product of $.20\times.\dot{3}\dot{6}$:

Thus, $.20\times.\dot{3}\dot{6}=\frac{20}{100}\times\frac{36}{99}=\frac{720}{9900}=\frac{8}{110}=.0\dot{7}\dot{2}=$ *product required.*

SECT. IV.

Of DIVISION of CIRCULATING DE-CIMALS.

RULE.

CHANGE the given decimals into their equivalent Vulgar Fractions, and find their quotient as ufual; then this quotient thrown into a decimal, will give the quotient required.

EXAMPLES.

Required the quotient of $.2\dot{6}$ divided by $.\dot{3}$:

Firft, $.2\dot{6}=\frac{24}{90}$ and $.\dot{3}=\frac{3}{9}$:

Wherefore,

Wherefore, $.2\dot{6} \div .\dot{3} = \frac{24}{90} \div \frac{3}{9} = \frac{216}{270} = .8$ *the quotient required.*

Required the quotient of $.\dot{9} \div .10\dot{8}$:

Thus, $.\dot{9} \div .10\dot{8} = \frac{9}{9} \div \frac{108}{999} = \frac{1}{1} \div \frac{12}{111} = \frac{111}{12} = 9.25$ = *quotient required.*

Required the quotient of $2.\dot{9} \div .\dot{2}\dot{7}$:

Thus, $2.\dot{9} \div .\dot{2}\dot{7} = \frac{27}{9} \div \frac{27}{99} = \frac{99}{9} = 11$ *the quotient required.*

A

A Supplement to Part I,

CONTAINING THE DOCTRINE AND APPLICATION OF RATIOS, OR PROPORTION, EXTRACTION OF ROOTS, &c.

CHAP. I.

Of PROPORTION or ANALOGY.

PROPORTION is a degree of likeneſs which quantities bear to each other, by a ſimilitude of ratios.

RATIO is the mutual reſpect of two quantities of the ſame kind ; but they form no Analogy, becauſe there can be no ſimilitude of ratios between two quantities, and therefore Analogy conſiſts of three quantities at leaſt, whereof the ſecond ſupplies the place of two : Thus the reſpect of 2 to 6, being compared with 18, it will be, 2:6::6:18.

SECT. I.

Of CONTINUED PROPORTION ARITHMETICAL,

OR

ARITHMETICAL PROGRESSION.

WHEN quantities increaſe or decreaſe by an equal difference, thoſe quantities are in Arithmetical Proportion continued : Thus, the number 1, 2, 3, &c, are a ſeries of quantities in Arithmetical Proportion continued,

continued, increasing by unity, or 1, which is called the common difference of the series.

ALSO, the numbers 2, 4, 6, 8, are numbers in Arithmetical Progression, whose common difference is 2; but the numbers 9, 7, 5, 3, 1, are a series of quantities in Arithmetical Progression, decreasing by the common difference, 2.

LEMMA I.

If three numbers are in Arithmetical Progression, the sum of the two extreme numbers will be double the mean or middle number.

THUS, let 1, 3, 5, be the numbers in progression; Then, $1 + 5$, the sum of the two extremes $= 3 + 3$ the double of the mean. Again, in the numbers 14, 10, 6, the sum of the two extremes are $14 + 6 = 20$, and the double of the mean $10 + 10 = 20$; and the like will hold in any other numbers.

LEMMA II.

If four numbers are in Arithmetical Progression, the sum of the two extremes will be equal to the sum of the two means.

LET the number be 4, 7, 10, 13; then $4 + 13 = 17$, the sum of the two extremes, and $7 + 10 = 17$, the sum of the two means: Again, in the numbers 16, 13, 10, 7; $16 + 7 = 13 + 10$.

AND since in four numbers as above, the sum of the two extremes, is equal to the sum of the two means, we have no reason to doubt of the like, let the terms be any number whatever: Whence it follows, that in any Arithmetical series, of any assignable number of terms whatever, the sum of any two terms equidistant from the mean, will be equal to

the

the fum of any other two terms, equidiftant from the mean ; as in thefe, 2, 4, 6, 8, 10, 12, 14, 16, 18, 20 ; where $2+20=4+18=6+16=8+14=10+12$: Therefore, &c.

LEMMA III.

In any feries of numbers in Arithmetical Progreffion, the feveral terms are formed or made up by the addition of the common difference to the firft term, fo often repeated, as there are number of terms to the feveral places, except the firft.

LET the feries be, 1, 4, 7, 10, 13, 16, 19, 22, &c. wherein the common difference is 3.

Now $1+3=4$ *the fecond term,* $1+3+3=7,$ *the third term ;* $1+3+3+3=10,$ *the fourth term ;* $1+3+3+3+3=13,$ *the fifth term ;* and $1+3\times7=22,$ *the 8th term, &c.* Confequently the difference of the two extremes, is equal to the common difference multiplied with the number of terms lefs 1 : Thus in the above feries, the common difference is 3, and number of terms 8 ; therefore $\overline{8-1}\times3=7\times3=21=$ difference of the two extremes.

PROBLEM I.

To find the fum of a feries of numbers in Arithmetical Progreffion.

THERE are feveral ways of deducing a rule for the folution of this problem, but perhaps none more fimple and natural than the following.

LET the feries whofe fum is required, be $2+4+6+8+10+12.$

Or,

Or,   2+2+2+2+2+2
         + + + + +
        2 2 2 2 2
          + + + +
          2 2 2 2
           + + +
           2 2 2
            + +
            2 2
             +
             2

which is the fame as the former, though differently
expreffed : Now under the given feries place the
fame inverted and add up the whole.

Thus,

1 term.	2 term.	3 term.	4 term.	5 term.	6 term.
2	2	2	2	2	2
2	2	2	2	2	2
2	2	2	2	2	2
2	2	2	2	2	2
2	2	2	2	2	2
2	2	2	2	2	2
2	2	2	2	2	2
2	2	2	2	2	2

$$14 + 14 + 14 + 14 + 14 + 14 = fum.$$

By this means the terms of the feries are reduced
to an equality, to wit, equal to the fum of the firft
and laft term ; but the fum above found, is evidently double the fum of the propofed feries : Whence
it

it follows, that the fum of an Arithmetical feries, is equal to half the product of the firft and laft term, with the number of terms; wherefore if the firft term, laft term, and number of terms of an Arithmetical Progreffion be given, the fum of the feries may be found by the following

RULE.

MULTIPLY the fum of the firft and laft terms, or two extremes, with the number of terms, and half of that product will be the fum required.

EXAMPLES.

Let the firft term of a feries of numbers in Arithmetical Progreffion, $=1$, laft term $=37$, and number of terms 19; required the fum of the feries.

OPERATION.

Firft, $1+37=38=$ *fum of the firft and laft terms:* Then $38\times19\div2=722\div2=361$ *the fum required.*

A MAN bought 20 yards of broad-cloth; for the firft yard he gave 2 dol. and for the laft 80 dol. what did the whole coft?

The fum of the two extremes, is $2+80$, then

$2+80\times20\div2=820$ dol. *the anfwer.*

A MAN travelled 12 days, the firft day 4 miles, and the laft day 40 miles; what was the diftance travelled in the 12 days?   Anfwer. 264 *miles.*

PROBLEM II.

To find the common difference of an Arithmetical feries, when the two extremes and number of terms are given.   A

A RULE for the folution of this problem, is eafily deduced from the inference to Lemma III ; for fince the difference of the two extremes, is equal to the common difference multiplied with the number of terms lefs 1, it follows, that if that difference, be divided by the number of terms lefs 1, the quotient muft be the common difference of the feries ; whence the following rule is evident.

R U L E.

DIVIDE the difference of the two extremes by the number of terms lefs 1, and the quotient will be. the common difference required.

EXAMPLES.

In an Arithmetical feries, there is given the firft term $= 3$, laft term $= 60$, and number of terms 20: Required the common difference.

OPERATION.

The difference of the two extremes, is $60 - 3$; therefore (pr. rule) $\dfrac{60 - 3}{20 - 1} = \dfrac{57}{19} = $ *the common difference required.*

Four men differing in their ages by an equal interval : The age of the firft, is 19 years, and the fourth 40 : What are their feveral ages ?

OPERATION.

Firft, find the common difference of their ages : Thus, $40 - 19 \div 4 - 1 = 21 \div 3 = 7$ *years* ; therefore

19+7=26 *years, the age of the second,* and 26+7=33 *years, the age of the third;* laftly, 33+7=40 *years, the age of the fourth, as given above.*

A man owes a certain debt, to be difcharged at 8 feveral payments; all of which are to be made in Arithmetical Progreffion, the firft payment to be 4 dol. and the laft 32 dol. Query, the whole debt and each payment.

OPERATION.

$$\frac{\overline{32+4}\times 8}{2}=144 \text{ dol. } \textit{the whole debt,} \text{ and } \overline{32-4}\div$$

$\overline{8-1}=4$ dol. *the common difference;* wherefore 4+4 =8 dol. *the fecond payment,* and 8+4=12 dol. *the third payment;* alfo, 12+4=16 dol. ; *for the fourth;* moreover 16+4=20 dol. *for the 5th,* in like manner 20+4=24 dol. *for the 6th,* and 24+4=28 dol. *for the 7th;* laftly 28+4=32 dol. *for the laft payment as before.*

PROBLEM III.

To find the number of terms of an Arithmetical feries, when the firft term, laft term and common difference are given.

FROM the laft rule, it is eafy to conceive how a rule for the folution of this problem may be obtained; for fince the difference of the two extremes, divided by the number of terms lefs 1, gives the common difference; it follows, that the difference of the two extremes, divided by the common difference, muft quote the number of terms lefs 1.

Whence is deduced the following

RULE.

R U L E.

DIVIDE the difference of the two extremes, by the common difference, the quotient increased by unity or 1, will be the number of terms.

EXAMPLES.

Given the firft term of an Arithmetical feries=2, laft term=167, and common difference 3, to find the number of terms.

OPERATION.

$$\frac{167-2}{3}+1=\frac{165}{3}+1=55+1=56 \text{ the number of}$$

terms required.

A man bought a quantity of broad-cloth ; for the firft yard he gave 6 dol. for the fecond, 10 dol. and fo on, in Arithmetical Progreffion, to the laft yard, for which he gave 246 dol. ; what was the quantity of cloth bought ?

OPERATION.

$$\frac{246-6}{4}+1=\frac{240}{4}+1=61, \text{ the number of yards bought.}$$

A man travels from Bofton, to a certain place, in the following manner, viz. the firft day 10 miles ; the fecond day 15 miles, and fo on, till a day's journey is 55 miles : In how many days will he perform the whole journey ; alfo, how many miles is the place he goes to, diftant from Bofton ?

Anfwer. He will perform the whole in eleven days. The place diftant from Bofton, 330 miles.

S E C T.

SECT. II.

Of CONTINUED PROPORTION GEOMETRICAL,
Or
GEOMETRICAL PROGRESSION.

GEOMETRICAL Progreſſion continued, differs from Arithmetical Progreſſion in this ; in Arithmetical Progreſſion, each following term of the ſeries is formed or made up by the Addition or Subtraction of the common difference, (as we have before ſhewn) : Whereas in Geometrical Progreſſion, each ſucceſſive term of the ſeries, is produced by the Multiplication or Diviſion of the preceeding term, with a common multiplier or diviſor : Or in other words, Arithmetical Progreſſion, is the effect of a conſtant Addition or Subtraction ; but Geometrical Progreſſion, of a conſtant Multiplication or Diviſion.

THUS, 2, 4, 8, 16, 32, 64, 128, &c. are a ſeries of numbers in Geometrical Proportion continued ; whoſe reſpective terms are compoſed by the Multiplication of the Ratio or common multiplier, (2) : thus, $2 \times 2 = 4$, *the ſecond term*, $4 \times 2 = 8$, *the third term* ; $8 \times 2 = 16$, *the fourth term*, and ſo on.

ALSO, 16, 8, 4, 2, are a ſeries of numbers in Geometrical Proportion, continually decreaſing by the diviſion of the Ratio, or common diviſor, (2) : Thus, $\frac{16}{2} = 8$, *the ſecond term*, $\frac{8}{2} = 4$, *the third term*, $\frac{4}{2} = 2$, *the fourth term*, and $\frac{2}{2} = 1$, *the fifth term*.

LEMMA I.

If three numbers are in Geometrical Progreſſion, the product of the two extremes, will be equal to the product of the mean with itſelf. LET

LET the numbers be 2, 8, 32; where $2 \times 32 = 64$, and $8 \times 8 = 64$; confequently $2 \times 32 = 8 \times 8$.

L E M M A II.

In any Geometrical Proportion confifting of four terms, the product of the two extremes, is equal to the product of the two means.

IF the numbers are, 2, 8, 32, 128, it will be $2 \times 128 = 8 \times 32$; therefore $2 : 8 :: 32 : 128$.

CONSEQUENTLY, if the product of any two numbers, be equal to the product of any other two numbers, thofe four numbers are proportional.

HENCE it may be eafily underftood, that if any number of terms are in $\div\div$ the product of the two extremes, will be equal to the product of any other two terms, equidiftant from thofe extremes.

LET the feries be 3, 6, 12, 24, 48, 96; where $3 \times 96 = 6 \times 48 = 12 \times 24$.

WHEN numbers are compared together, in order to difcover their relation to each other, the number compared is writen firft, and called the antecedent, and the number by which you compare the other, being written next, is called the confequent : Thus if you would compare 2 with 4, the numbers muft be wrote thus, 2, 4; where 2 is the antecedent, and 4 the confequent : Again in thefe, $3 : 6 :: 6 : 12$; where 3 is antecedent, and 6 its confequent ; alfo, 6 the middle term, is an antecedent to 12, its confequent. Therefore in every feries of numbers in Geometrical Proportion continued, all the terms except the laft, are antecedents, and all except the firft are confequents.

THUS in the feries 3, 9, 27, 81, 243, 729, the numbers 3, 9, 27, 81, 243, are all antecedents, and

9, 27, 81, 243, 729, are all consequents; therefore
$3 : 9 :: 9 : 27 :: 27 : 81 :: 81 : 243 :: 243 : 729$.

THE Ratio is had by dividing any consequent by
its antecedent.

LEMMA III.

*If any numbers are proportional, it will be, as any
one of the antecedents, is to its consequent; so is the sum
of all the antecedents, to to the sum of all the consequents, (Vid. Euclid's fifth book, Proposition 12.)*

LET the numbers be these, 4, 8, 16, 32, 64, then
$4 : 8 :: \overline{4+8+16+32} : \overline{8+16+32+64}$, that is,
$4 : 8 :: 60 : 120$; for $\overline{4\times120 = 8\times60}$; therefore,
&c.

PROBLEM I.

To find the sum of any Geometrical series increasing.

SUPPOSE the sum of the following series, 1, 4, 16,
64, 256, is required : Multiply this series with the
Ratio, which is 4, and the product will be a new series, 4, 16, 64, 256, 1024 : Now it is plain, that
the sum of the produced series, is as many times the
sum of the former, as the Ratio hath units ; or the
produced series, is to the proposed, as the Ratio to
unity, or 1 : Subtract the first series from the second.

Thus, $\begin{cases} 4, \ 16, 64, \ 256, \ 1024 \\ 1, 4, \ 16, \ 64, \ 256. \end{cases}$

$-1, \ * \ * \ * \ +1024,$ or, $1024-1,$
which is evidently equal to the sum of the first series
multiplied with the Ratio, less 1, by what has been
said ; consequently the same divided by the Ratio,
less 1, must give the sum of the proposed series ; that
is,

is, $\dfrac{\overline{256\times4-1}}{4-1} = \dfrac{\overline{1024-1}}{4-1} = $ *sum of the series re-*

quired.

THEREFORE, when the firſt term, laſt term, and Ratio of a Geometrical ſeries are given, we may find the ſum of all the terms by the following

R U L E.

MULTIPLY the laſt term with the Ratio, from which product, ſubtract the firſt term, divide the remainder by the Ratio leſs 1, and the quotient reſulting will be the ſum of the ſeries.

MR. WARD, in his introduction to the Mathematics, page 78, has given an analytical inveſtigation of a rule for finding the ſum of any ſeries in ÷ increaſing ; which is after the manner following.

LET a Geometrical ſeries be given, ſuppoſe the following, 2, 4, 8, 16, 32, 64.

Put $x =$ *ſum of the ſeries* :

Then, $x - 64 =$ *ſum of all the antecedents* :

And $x - 2 =$ *ſum of all the conſequents* :

Therefore, $2 : 4 :: x - 64 : x - 2$; per Lemma III.

Conſequently, $\overline{x - 2} \times 2 = \overline{x - 64} \times 4$;

That is, $2x - 4 = 4x - 256$:

Then, $4x - 2x = 256 - 4$:

Therefore, (by diviſion) $2x - x = 128 - 2$:

Whence, $x = \overline{128 - 2} \div \overline{2 - 1}$, *which affords the ſame rule as that above.*

Or finding the value of x in the equation $4x - 2x = 256 - 4$, *to wit,* $x = \overline{256 - 4} \div \overline{4 - 1}$ *which admits of the following*

R U L E.

R U L E.

FROM the product of the second and last terms, subtract the square of the first, divide the remainder by the second term less the first ; and the quotient will be the sum of the series.

EXAMPLES.

In a Geometrical series, there is given, the first term=3, last term=243, and Ratio 3; to find the sum of the series, per Rule first.

OPERATION.

First, $243 \times 3 = 729 = $ *product of the last term with the Ratio ; then* $729 - 3 \div 3 - 1 = 726 \div 2 = 363$ *the sum required.*

A man bought a quantity of cloth ; for the first yard he gave 2 dol. for the second 4 ; and so on, in continued proportion Geometrical to the last yard, for which he gave 256 dol. what did the whole cost ?

Here, is given the first, second, and last terms, to find the sum of the series, per Rule second.

$256 \times 4 - 4 = 1024 - 4 = 1020 = $ *product of the second and last terms, less the square of the first ;* then $\dfrac{1020}{4-2} = \dfrac{1020}{2} = 510$ dol. $=$ *the aforesaid difference divided by the second term less the first $=$ sum that the whole cloth cost.*

BUT in finding the sum of the series by the foregoing rules, it is necessary to have the last term given : therefore the next thing in order, is, to shew how the last term of the series, when it is not given in the question, may be obtained.

PROBLEM

PROBLEM II.

The first term, Ratio, and number of terms of a Geometrical series being given, to find the last term.

I. WHEN the first term and Ratio are alike.

RULE I.

1. WRITE down an Arithmetical series of a convenient number of terms, whose first term, and common difference is unity or 1.

2. WRITE a few of the leading terms of the Geometrical series, under the first terms of the Arithmetical one.

Thus, $\left\{ \begin{array}{llllll} 1, & 2, & 3, & 4, & 5, & \textit{Indices, or exponents.} \\ 2, & 4, & 8, & 16, & 32, & \textit{Geometrical series.} \end{array} \right.$

3. ADD together any two of the indices, and multiply the terms in the Geometrical series, which belong to those indices, together, and their product will be that term of the Geometrical series, which the sum of those two corresponding indices point out.

4. CONTINUE the addition of the indices, and multiply their corresponding terms, of the Geometrical series, respectively as before, until the sum of the indices is equal to the number of terms, the product answering thereunto, will be the last term required.

II. WHEN the first term is either greater or less than the Ratio, (unity excepted.)

RULE II.

1. WRITE down an Arithmetical series, beginning with a cypher, the common difference, the same as in the last rule.

T

2.

2. PLACE the leading terms of the Geometrical feries, under the Arithmetical, fo that the cypher may ftand over the firft term of the Geometrical feries; then add the indices, and multiply their correfponding terms as before.

3. DIVIDE that product by the firft term, and the quotient will be that term of the feries, which is denominated by the fum of thofe indices : The reft the fame as before.

III. WHEN the firft term is unity or 1.

RULE III.

WRITE down the terms, and place their indices as in the laft rule ; then add the indices, and multiply the terms which they denominate, together, till the fum of the indices is one lefs than the number of terms, and the refult will be the laft term, as required.

AN example in each of the foregoing rules, will make their application eafy.

In a Geometrical feries, there is given, the firft term=2, Ratio 2, and number of terms 12, to find the laft term, per rule 1.

OPERATION.

Thus, $\begin{cases} 1, & 2, 3, 4, 5, 6, \textit{Indices.} \\ 2, & 4, 8, 16, 32, 64, \div. \end{cases}$

Here, $4+2=6$, *the index of the fixth term ; confequently* $4\times16=64$, *the fixth term. Again,* $6+6=12$, *and* $64\times64=4096=twelfth$ *term, as required.*

Suppofe the firft term of a feries in $\div$, is 3, Ratio 2, and number of terms 15 ; required the laft term, per rule 2.

OPERATION.

OPERATION.

First, $\begin{cases} 0, & 1, & 2, & 3, & 4, & 5, & \textit{Indices.} \\ 3, & 6, & 12, & 24, & 48, & 96, & \div. \end{cases}$

Then, $3+5=8$, and $24\times96=2304$; therefore, $2304\div3=768=eighth\ term$. Again, $3+4=7$, and $24\times48=1152$; therefore, $1152\div3=384=seventh$ term. Lastly, $7+8=15$; whence $\dfrac{384\times768}{3}=98304$ $=15th$, and last term which was to be done.

Given first term$=1$, Ratio 4, and number of terms 11, to find the last term, per rule 3.

OPERATION.

Thus, $\begin{cases} 0, & 1, & 2 & 3, & 4, & \textit{Indices.} \\ 1, & 4, & 16, & 64, & 256, & \div. \end{cases}$

Then, $4+3+3=10=number\ of\ terms\ less\ one= index\ to\ the\ 11th\ term$; therefore, $256\times64\times64= 1048576=11th\ term\ as\ was\ required.$

Miscellaneous Questions.

A MAN hired himself to a farmer, for 28 weeks upon these considerations; that for the first week to have 1 *ct.*; for the second 2 *cts.*; and the third 4 *cts.*; and so on, in $\div$: What did his 28 weeks wages amount to ?

The last term by the foregoing rules, is, 134217728, which multiplied with the Ratio (2) produces 268435456; therefore, $\dfrac{268435456-1}{2-1}=268435455$ *cts.*$=2684354$ *dol.* 55 *cts. the answer.*　　　A

A MAN bought 20 yards of velvet, at the following prices, viz. for the firſt yard he gave 2 *cts.* ; for the ſecond, 4 *cts.* ; for the third, 8 *cts.* and ſo on, in Geometrical Proportion : How much did the whole coſt ?

Anſwer. 20971 *dol.* 50 *cts.*

A MERCHANT ſold 24 yards of lace ; the firſt yard for 3 pins, the ſecond for 9, the third for 27 ; and ſo on, in triple Proportion Geometrical : Now ſuppoſe he afterwards ſold his pins 120 for a cent : What did his lace amount to, and what was his gain in the whole, when he gave 50 *cts.* per yard for his lace ?

Anſ. { *Lace come to,* 4236443047 *dol.* 20 *cts.*
{ *Gain in the whole,* 4236443035 *dol.* 20 *cts.*

A THRESHER agreed with a farmer to work for him 25 days, for no other conſideration than 2 barley-corns for the firſt day 8 ; for the ſecond 32 ; for the third ; and ſo on, in quadruple proportion Geometrical : How much did his wages amount to, allowing 7680 barley-corns to make one pint, and the barley to be ſold for 25 *cts.* per buſhel ?

Anſwer. 381774870 *dol.* 75 *cts.*

SUPPOSE a wheat-corn had been ſowed at the creation, and continued to increaſe in a ten-fold proportion every year, down to the preſent time ; now allowing 5000 years for the elapſe of time : What would be the number of wheat-corns produced ?

Here the firſt term being 1, the Ratio 10, and the number of terms 5000, it is therefore plain, that the laſt term will be 1, having as many cyphers annexed, as there are number of terms leſs one ; conſequently its value is 1(4999)0's, where the numeral figures included in the parentheſis, expreſs the number of cyphers annexed to the 1 : Next to find the ſum of the ſeries.

Firſt,

First, 1(4999) 0'*s* × 10 = 1(5000) 0'*s, then* 1(5000) 0'*s* — 1 = (5000) 9'*s* = *the number of* 9'*s therefore*

$$\frac{5000 \ 9's}{10 - 1} = 11111111111111111 \ \&c. \ \text{to} \ 5000$$

places of figures = *number of wheat-corns produced;* which number far exceeds all human imagination; for the whole space occupied by our solar system, which is at least twenty thousand million of miles in diameter, is by much too small, to contain the aforesaid quantity of wheat: Nay, such a quantity would take up more space, than is contained in the whole heavens on this side the fixed stars. Hence we may learn the great power of progressive numbers, and that small portion of space, necessary to express a number by the help of numeral figures contrived for that purpose, which so far exceeds all our imagination.

CHAP. II.

DISJUNCT PROPORTION,
OR
The RULE *of* THREE.

WHEN of four numbers, the first has the same Ratio to the second, as the third has to the fourth: Or when the second is the same multiple or quotient of the first, as the fourth is of the third; then are those numbers said to be in Disjunct Proportion.

IF four numbers are proportional directly, as the first to the second; so is the third to the fourth; then will they also be proportional; Inversely, Alternate-

ly,

ly, Compoundedly, Dividedly, and Mixtly. (*Vid*
Book 11. *Chap.* XII.)

SECT. I.

DIRECT PROPORTION,
OR
The RULE *of* THREE DIRECT.

THIS is fometimes called the golden rule, from the
great benefit people in all kinds of bufinefs receive
from it, as well the farmer and mechanic as the merchant, &c. It confifts of four numbers, which are
proportional, as the firft to the fecond; fo is the third
to the fourth, as above: The two firft are a fuppofition, the third a demand, and the fourth the anfwer.
The two fuppofitions and the demand are always giv-
en, and the fourth required.

Let the four numbers be, a, b, c, d. *Then* $a : b :: c : d$, *directly; therefore,* $a \times d = b \times c$, *or* $ad = bc$, per
Lemma 11, of the laft Section.

Whence by the nature of divifion $bc \div a = d$, that is,
if the product of the fecond and third terms, be divided by the firft, the quotient will be the fourth. Or
fince the Ratio of the firft to the fecond, is the fame
as that of the third to the fourth; it follows, that
$b \div a \times c = d$, that is, if the fecond term be divided by
the firft, and that quotient multiplied into the third,
it will produce the fourth.

Now, in order to prepare your numbers for obtaining a fourth proportional, according to the foregoing rules, you muft obferve the following

R U L E.

R U L E.

WRITE that number which is of the same name with the number sought, in the middle place, and the other two so, that the expression may read according to the nature of the question.

Let the following conditions be expressed in numbers.

What is the cost of 24lb. of cheese, when the price of 3lb. is 20 *cts.* ?

Here the middle number must be cost, because the fourth, or number required, is always of the same name and denomination of the second, by the nature of the proportion : Hence the above conditions in numbers, is,

Thus, 3lb. 20*cts.* 24bl. ; that is, if 3 pounds cost 20 *cts.* what will 24 pounds cost ? Then to find a fourth number, proceed as before directed.

Note. *If the first and third numbers are not of the same name, they must be made so by the rules of reduction : Also, if any of the numbers are compounds, they must be reduced to the least denomination mentioned.*

EXAMPLES.

If 4lb. of cheese cost 32 *cts.* ; what will 320lb. cost at the same rate ?

OPERATION.

OPERATION.

These numbers being placed according to the
rule, will stand thus,

$$\begin{array}{c} \text{lb.} \quad cts. \quad \text{lb.} \\ 4 : 32 :: 320 \\ 32 \\ \hline 640 \\ 960 \\ \hline 4)\,10240 \\ 1(00).25(60 = 25\;dol.\;60 \\ \qquad\qquad [cts.\;the\;answer. \end{array}$$

Or, $32 \div 4 = 8$; therefore, $320 \times 8 = 2560$ cts. $= 25$
dol. 60 cts. the same as before.

What will 6 yards of holland cost, when the price
of 40 yards, is 24 *dol.* 40 *cts.* ?

OPERATION.

$$\begin{array}{c} \text{yd.} \quad dol.\;cts. \quad \text{yd.} \\ As\;40 : 24\;40 :: 6\;stated. \end{array}$$

Then, $24.40 \div 40 = .61$, and $6 \times .61 = 366$ cts. $=$
3 dol. 66 cts. the answer.

Find the value of 100lb. of flax, when the price of
1lb. is 12 *cts* ?

OPERATION.

$$\begin{array}{c} \text{lb.} \quad cts. \quad \text{lb.} \\ As\;1 : 12 :: 100 \\ 12 \\ \hline 12.00 = 12\;dol.\;the\;answer. \end{array}$$

What

What is the coft of 40lb. of cheefe, when the price of 3lb. is 15 *cts.*

OPERATION.

Firft, $15 \div 3 = 5$, *the ratio of the firft term to the* *fecond.*

Then, $40 \times 5 = 200$ *cts.* $= 2$ *dol. the anfwer.*

What is the coft of 87lb. of tobacco, at $8\frac{1}{2}$ *cts.* per lb. ?

OPERATION.

$$\begin{array}{cccc} \text{lb.} & \text{\textit{cts.}} & \text{\textit{cts.}} & \text{lb.} \\ \textit{As } 1 : & 8\frac{1}{2} = & 8.5 :: & 87 \\ & & & 8.5 \\ \hline & & & 435 \\ & & & 696 \\ \hline \end{array}$$

$$739.5 = 739\frac{1}{2} \text{ cts.} = 7 \text{ dol.}$$
$$[39\frac{1}{2} \text{ cts. the anfwer.}$$

A goldfmith fold a tankard for 29 *dol.* 97 *cts.* at the rate of 1 *dol.* 11 *cts.* per oz. : What was the weight of it ?

Anfwer. 27 *oz.*

A man bought fheep at 1 *dol.* 11 *cts.* per head, to the amount of 51 *dol.* 6 *cts.* : How many fheep did he buy ? *Anfwer.* 46.

S E C T. II.

RECIPROCAL, *or* INVERTED PROPORTION,
OR
The RULE *of* THREE INDIRECT.

THIS kind of proportion, is the reverfe of the former, as to the performance ; for the greater the

U

third

third term is, in refpect of the firft, the lefs will be the fourth, in refpect of the fecond ; whereas in direct proportion, the greater or lefs the third term is, in refpect of the firft, the greater or lefs will be the fourth term, in refpect of the fecond ; but to illuftrate the former. If two men can produce a certain effect in 12 days : In how many days would 6 men produce the fame ? Here it is manifeft, that 6 men would produce the effect in lefs time than 2 ; and therefore the greater the third term is, the lefs will be the fourth. Again, if 10 men can produce a certain effect in 6 days : In how many days would 4 men do the fame ? Here it is evident, that 10 men would produce the effect in lefs time than 4 men ; and therefore the lefs the third term is, the greater will be the fourth : Confequently, more requires lefs, and lefs requires more, in indirect proportion.

HERE the fame rule is to be obferved, in ftating your queftion, as in the former proportion, and the refults in refpect of names and denominations are the fame alfo : Then to find a fourth proportional, proceed with the following rules.

R U L E I.

MULTIPLY the firft and fecond numbers together, and divide that product by the third ; the quotient refulting will be the fourth proportional required.

R U L E II.

DIVIDE the fecond number by the third, and that quotient multiplied into the firft, will produce the fourth.

R U L E

R U L E III.

DIVIDE the third term by the firſt, and the ſecond
term by this quotient ; and the reſulting quotient
will be the fourth number.

EXAMPLES.

If 5 men can perform a certain piece of work in
8 days : How long will four men be in doing the
ſame ?

OPERATION.

```
Men. D. Men.              Or,
  5  8  4          ⌠        4   40
     5             ⎮    8 ÷ --- = ---
 ________          ⎨        5    4
 4) 40  D.         ⎮     = 10 days  as before.
    10 = 10 the an.⌡
```

If 20 buſhels of grain, at 50 *cents* per buſhel, will
pay a debt : How many buſhels at 60 *cents* per buſhel will pay the ſame ?

OPERATION.

OPERATION.

cts. Bush. cts.
50 20 60
20

6(o)100(o
16⅘

Answer. 16 ⅘ *bushels.*

If 2 yards of cloth, 1 yard and 3 quarters wide, is sufficient to make a coat; how many yards of 1 yard wide, will make the same?

OPERATION.

y. q. y. y.
1   3 : 2 :: 1
4   4
------   ------
7   4
2
------
4)14
3²⁄₄ = 3½ *yards the answer.*

A man being desirous to draw off a cask of brandy into bottles, finds that if he makes use of three quart bottles, it will require 60 : How many five-pint bottles will it require, to draw off the aforesaid cask of brandy.   *Answer.* 72 *bottles.*

A man bought a piece of cloth 9 quarters wide, and 11 quarters long : How many yards of 3 quarters cloth will line it?   *Answer.* 8¼ *yards.*

If 3½ yards of yard-wide cloth will make a coat : How many yards of 7 quarters cloth, will make the same?   *Answer.* 2 *yards.*

S E C T.

SECT. III.

COMPOUNDED RATIO.

COMPOUNDED Ratio is when the antecedent and confequent taken together, is compared to the confequent itfelf: thus, $a : b :: c : d$, directly, therefore by compofition; as $a+b : b :: c+d : d$.

Note. *The fame Rule is to be obferved here, as in direct proportion.*

EXAMPLES.

If A can produce a certain effect in 5 days, B can do the fame in 7 days; fet them both about it together, in what time will it be finifhed?

ORERATION.

$$As \; \overline{5+7} : 7 :: 5$$

$$5$$

$$12)35(2 \; days.$$
$$24$$

$$11$$
$$24$$

$$44$$
$$22$$

$$12)264($$
22 *hours. Anf.* 2 *days* 22 *h.*

If A in in 5 hours, can make 1000 nails, B in 8 hours, can make 2000: In what time would they jointly make 50000 nails?

Here

Here you muft firft find in what time each perfon would make 50000 nails, and then proceed as in the laft example.

OPERATION.

$$\text{n.} \qquad \text{h.} \qquad \text{n.}$$
As $1000 : 5 :: 50000 : \overline{50000 \times 5 \div 1000} = 250$ *bours, the time it would take A to make* 50000 nails.

$$\text{n.} \qquad \text{h.} \qquad \text{n.}$$
As $2000 : 8 :: 5000 : \overline{50000 \times 8 \div 2000} = 200$ *bours, the time it would take B to make* 50000 *nails.*

Therefore, as $\overline{250 + 200} : 200 :: 250 : \overline{200 \times 250 \div}$ $450 = 111\frac{1}{9}$ *bours, the time it would take them jointly to make* 50000 *nails, as was required.*

Note. *From this operation, we have the following general theorem for folving all queftions of a fimilar nature, let the perfons or agents employed, be any number whatever.*

T H E O R E M.

MULTIPLY the joint effect with the time each one would produce his particular effect, and divide the product by the faid particular effect; then multiply all the refulting quotients together for a dividend, and make the fum of them a divifor; then divide, and the refulting quotient will be the time required.

S E C T.

S E C T. IV.

DIVIDED RATIO.

DIVIDED Ratio is when the excefs wherein the antecedent exceeds the confequent, is compared with the confequent : *Thus, a : b :: c : d, directly ; therefore by divifion as a—b : b :: c—d : d.*

EXAMPLES.

If A can do a piece of work in 8 days, A and B can do it in 5 days : In what time can B do the fame work ?

OPERATION.

$$\text{As } 8-5=3 : 5 :: 8 : \overline{5\times8}\div3=40\div3=13 \overset{d. \quad h.}{} 8, \; the$$
time required.

Two fhips, one in chafe of the other, the headmoft fhip is 48 miles diftant from the other, and fails at the rate of 4 miles per hour, and the fternmoft fhip at the rate of 7 miles per hour : How long before the fternmoft fhip will overtake the other ?

OPERATION.

$$\text{As } 7-4=3 : 1 :: 48 : \overline{48\times1}\div3=16 \; hours, \; the$$
time required.

A hare is is 50 leaps before a grey-hound, and takes 4 leaps to the grey-hound's three ; but 2 of the grey-hound's leaps are as much as three of the hare's : How many leaps muft the grey-hound take to catch the hare ?

Here you muft firft find how many leaps of the hare, anfwers to three of the grey-hound's : Thus, 2 : 3 :: 3

$$: \overline{3\times3}\div2=4\tfrac{1}{2}=4.5 : \qquad\qquad Then,$$

Then, as $4.5-4=.5 : 3 :: 50 : \overline{3\times50}\div.5 = 300$ *the answer.*

The hour and minute-hand of a clock are exactly together at 12 o'clock; when are they next together?

Here the proportion of the velosities of the hour and minute-hand, is as 1 to 12. Therefore, $12-1=11 : 1$ $:: 12 : \overline{12\times1}\div11 = 1h. 5\frac{5}{11}',$ *the answer.*

If A, B and C, can produce a certain effect in 12 days, A can do it in 30 days and C in 50 days, in what time will B do the same work?

First find the time in which A and C, would produce the effect jointly, by Ratio of composition. Thus, $\overline{30+50} : 50 :: 30 : \overline{50\times30}\div70 = 21\frac{3}{7}$ *days. Then, as* $21\frac{3}{7}-12=9\frac{1}{7} : 12 :: 21\frac{3}{7} : 25\frac{49}{62},$ *the time required.*

There is an island 100 miles in circumference, and two footmen, A and B, set out together, to travel the same way round it, A travels 15 miles per day, and B 17 miles: When will they come together again?

First, find how many miles B must travel to overtake A, after their departure : Thus, as $17-15=2 : 17$ $:: 100 : 850,$ *the number of miles B must travel, which is 50 days journey; therefore they will be together again 50 days after their departure.*

There is three pendulums of unequal lengths; the first of which vibrates once in 12 seconds, the second in 18 seconds, and the third in 24 seconds : Now supposing them all to move from a line of conjunction, at the same moment of time : When will they come into the same situation again, and move on together?

First

First, find the time when the two first pendulums will move on together, as in the last example : Thus, 18—12 : 18 :: 1 : 18×1÷6=3, the number of vibrations of the first, which is performed in 36 seconds=2 vibrations of the second. Therefore, after the first has vibrated 3 times, and the second 2, they will move on together again.

In the next place, we must examine into the situation of the third pendulum, at the conjunction of the two first. In 36 seconds, there is 1.5 vibration of the third pendulum, which is therefore, .5 of a vibration, distant from the conjunction of the other two ; wherefore, .5 : 1 :: 3 : 6, the number of vibrations of the first, at which time, they all come into a line of conjunction, and move on together. Consequently, when the first has made 6 vibrations, the second will have performed 4, and the third three=24×3=72 seconds, the time required.

If A can do a piece of work in 20 days ; A and B in 13 days ; A and C in 11 days ; and B and C in 10 days : How many days will it take each person to perform the same work ?

OPERATION.

As 20—13 : 13 :: 20 : 37¼ *the time that B would do it.*

As 20—11 : 11 :: 20 : 24⁴⁄₉ *the time that C would do it.*

CHAP. III.

SIMPLE INTEREST.

SIMPLE intereſt is a premium of a certain ſum paid for the loan of money borrowed for a particular term of time, at any rate per cent or hundred, as the borrower and lender ſhall agree.

Thus, if 100 dollars be lent at 6 per cent per annum, the premium for 1 year will be 6 dollars, for 2 years 12 dollars, for 3 years 18 dollars; and ſo on.

The ſum lent is called the principal, and the premium per 100, the Ratio or rate per cent; and the amount is the principal and intereſt added together.

All the varieties of ſimple intereſt, are compriſed in the following caſes.

C A S E I.

When the ſum lent, is for any number of years, and the rate per cent, any number of dollars.

R U L E.

Multiply the principal with the number of years, and that product with the Ratio, and divide by 100; the quotient reſulting, will be the intereſt required.

EXAMPLES.

Required the intereſt of 700 dollars, for 4 years, at 6 per cent per annum?

OPERATION.

OPERATION.

700
4
———
2800
6
———

1(oo)168)oo

Anfwer. 168 dollars, the intereft required.

Required the intereft of 3520 dollars, for 7 years, at 6 per cent per annum.

OPERATION.

3520
7
———
24640
6
———

1(oo)1478(40=1478 *dol. 40 cts. the*
[*anfwer.*

What is the intereft of 57821 dollars, for 5 years, at 5 per cent per annum?   *Anf.* 2891 *dol. 5 cts.*

What is the intereft of 5972 dollars, for 12 years, at 3 per cent per annum?   *Anf.* 716 *dol. 64 cts.*

CASE II.

When the fum is lent for years and months; the Ratio the fame as before.

RULE.

REDUCE the number of months into the decimal of a year, then multiply the principal with the time, and

and that product with the Ratio, then divide by 100 and you will have the interest required.

Or,

MULTIPLY the principal with the number of years, and take parts of the principal for the rest part of the time, and add them to the rest ; then proceed as before directed.

Required the interest of 735 dollars, for 5 years, 4 months, at 5 per cent per annum.

OPERATION.

4 months$=\frac{1}{3}$ of a year, 3)735
 5

3675
245$=$735$\div$3

3920
5 *ratio.*

1(00)196)00$=$196 *dollars, the*
[*interest required.*

Required the interest of 52374 dollars, for 7 years 8 months, at 6 per cent per annum.

OPERATION.

OPERATION.

8 months $=\frac{2}{3}$ *of a year,* 3)52374
                                          7

                                      366618
                                       17458 $=\frac{1}{3}$ *of* 52374
                                       17458

                                      401534
                                          6 $=ratio.$
                                      ——————   *dol.   cts.*
                    1(00)24092)04 $=$ 24092   4, *the in-*
                                      [*terest required.*

What is the interest of 32104 dollars, for 4 years, 3. months, at 5 per cent per annum ?
Anf. 6827 *dol.* 10 *cts.*

C A S E III.

When the Ratio is dollars and parts of a dollar, the reft the fame as before.

R U L E.

1. Reduce the number of months into the decimal of a year, and multiply the principal with the whole time.

2. Reduce the fractional parts of the Ratio into the decimal of a dollar.

3. Multiply the former refult with the latter, and divide by 100, and you will have the intereft required :   Or,

Multiply the principal with the number of years, and take parts of the principal for the reft part of the time, and add them to the former product ; then

multiply

multiply this product with the dollar's part of the rate, and take parts of the multiplicand for the reft part of the rate, and add them to the latter product; then divide them by 100, and you will have the intereft required.

EXAMPLES.

Required the intereft of 700 dollars, for 3 years 6 months, at $6\frac{1}{2}$ per cent per annum.

OPERATION.

$$700$$
$$3.5 = time.$$

$$3500$$
$$2100$$

$$2450.0$$
$$6.5 = ratio.$$

$$122500$$
$$147000$$

dol.   cts.

1(00)159)25.00 = 159   25, *the anfwer.*

Or.   6 months $= \frac{1}{2}$ *a year*   2)700

$$3$$

$$\cdot 2100$$
$$350 = 700 \div 2$$

for the $\frac{1}{2}$ *per cent*   2)2450

$$6$$

$$14700$$
$$1225$$

dol. cts.

1(00)159(25 = 159 25 *as before.*

Required

Required the intereſt of 3520 dollars 17 cents, for 2 years 6 months, at $5\frac{1}{4}$ per cent.

OPERATION.

2)3520.17
   2
____

 704034
 176003.5=3520.17÷2
____

4)8800.375
   5
____

 44001875
 2200.093
_______________ *dol. cts.*
1(00)462(01.968=462 1. 968 *the*
          [*anſ.*

C A S E IV.

When the ſum is lent for any number of weeks.

R U L E.

REDUCE the number of weeks into the decimal of a year, and proceed as in the laſt caſe.
Or,

FIND the intereſt of the given ſum, according to the foregoing rules for one year ; then ſay, as 52, the number of weeks in a year, is to the intereſt thus found ; ſo is the given number of weeks, to the intereſt required.

EXAMPLES.

Required the intereſt of 720 dollars, for 10 weeks, at $5\frac{1}{2}$ per cent per annum.

OPERATION.

OPERATION.

720
.192=*time nearly.*

1440
6480
720

138.240
5.5=*ratio.*

691200
691200

dol. cts.
7.60.3200=7 60.32 *the answer.*

| | *w.* | *dol. cts.* | *w.* |

Or, 720   As 52 : 39 60 :: 10
   5.5   10

3600   52)396.00(7.61=7 *dol.* 61 *cts.*
3600   364

1)00)39)60.0   320
                    312

                     80
                     52

                     28

Note. *The reason why the two methods of operation a-
bove, do not bring out the same answer, is because the
decimal of* 10 *weeks can never be exactly found;
yet the errour arising from any such computation,
will be inconsiderable.*

Required

dol. cts.

Required the intereſt of 527 2, for 13 weeks, at ¹⁄₃ per cent per annum.

OPERATION.

$$527.2$$
$$.25 = time.$$
___
$$26360$$
$$10544$$
___
$$1318.00$$
$$5.5$$
___
$$659000$$
$$659000$$
___

1(00)72(49.000 = 72 *dol.* 46 *cts. the anſ.*

C A S E V.

When the ſum is lent for any number of days.

R U L E.

REDUCE the days into the decimal of a year, and proceed as in the laſt caſe.

Or,

1. MULTIPLY the given ſum with the number of days, and that product with the Ratio for a dividend.

2. MULTIPLY 365, the number of days in a year, with 100 for a diviſor ; then divide, and the quotient will be the intereſt required.

Or,

As 365 days, is to the intereſt of the principal for one year ; ſo is the time propoſed, to the intereſt required.

Y   *EXAMPLES.*

EXAMPLES.

Required the interest of 300 dollars, for 219 day!
at 6 per cent per annum.

OPERATION.

                        Or, 219   365
        300   300   100
         .6=*time,*   ______   ______
        ______   65700   36500
        180.0   6
          6=*ratio,*   ______ *dol. cts.*
        ______   *d.* 365(00)3942(00)1080 *as before*
1(00)10)80.0=1080 *ct. anf.* 365
                                ______
                                292.0
                                2920
                                ______
                                  o

Required the interest of 1000 dollars, for 35 days
at 6 per cent per annum.

OPERATION.

              d.   dol.   d.
    1000   *As* 365 : 60 :: 35
      6   60
    ______   ______
    60.00   365)2100 (5 *dol.* 75 *cts.*
)1825
                        ______
                         275.0
                         2555
                        ______
                         1950
                         1825
        dol. cts.   ______
    Anf. 5 75¹²⁵⁄₃₆₅   125

                                C A S E

C A S E VI.

When the principal, Ratio, and interest are given to find the time.

R U L E.

1. FIND the interest of the principal for one year, at the given rate.

2. SAY as the interest thus found, is to one year ; so is the given interest, to the time required.

EXAMPLES.

Required the time in which 500 dollars will gain 150 dollars, at 6 per cent per annum.

OPERATION.

$$
\begin{array}{ll}
500 & \text{dol.} \quad y. \quad \text{dol.} \\
6 & As\ 30 : 1 :: 150 \\
& \qquad\qquad\quad 1 \\
\hline
30.00 & 30)15\overset{.}{0}(5 = 5\ years\ the\ time \\
& \qquad 150 \qquad\quad [required.
\end{array}
$$

Find in what time 700 dollars will gain 159 dol. 25 cts. at $6\frac{1}{2}$ per cent per annum.

OPERATION.

$$
\begin{array}{ll}
700 & \text{dol. cts. } y. \quad \text{dol. cts.} \\
6.5 = time. & As\ 45\ 50 : 1 :: 159\ 25 \\
\hline
3500 & \qquad\qquad\qquad\qquad 1 \\
4200 & \hline \qquad\qquad\qquad\qquad\qquad\qquad y. \\
\hline & 45.50)15925(3.5 = 3.5 \\
45.500 & \qquad\quad 13650 \qquad [the\ an. \\
& \hline \\
& \qquad\quad 2275.0 \\
& \qquad\quad 22750 \\
& \hline \qquad\qquad\qquad Req.
\end{array}
$$

———————— *dol. cts.*

Required the time in which 283 33⅓ will amount
to 370 dol. 50 cts. at 6 per cent per annum.

OPERATION.

dol. cts.   *dol. y. dol. cts.*

283 33⅓   As 17 1 87 16⅔

6   1

———————   ———————

17.0000   87 16 ⅔

                        3

              ———————

17×3=51)261.50(5.12 *years, the*

            255   [*answer.*

            ———

             65

             51

            ———

            140

            102

            ———

             38

C A S E   VII.

*When the Ratio, time, and amount are given to
find the principal.*

R U L E.

As the amount of 100 dollars, at the rate per
cent and time given, is to 100 dollars; so is the giv-
en amount, to the principal required.

EXAMPLES.

Required the principal that will amount to 3766
dol. 40 *cts.* in 7 years, at 6 per cent per annum.

OPERATION.

OPERATION.

$$100$$
$$6$$

$$6.00$$
$$7$$

$$42.00$$

dol.   *dol. cts.*   *dol. cts.*

As $100 + 42 = 142 : 100 :: 3766 \ 40 : 2793 \ 23 \ \frac{134}{142}$ *the answer.*

Required the principal that will amount to 868 dollars in 4 years, at 6 per cent per annum.

OPERATION.

$$100 \qquad 100 + 24 = 124 : 100 :: 868$$
$$4 \qquad\qquad\qquad\qquad\qquad 100$$

$$400 \qquad\qquad\qquad 124)86800(700$$
$$6 \qquad\qquad\qquad\qquad 868$$

$$24.00 \qquad\qquad\qquad\qquad 000.$$

Therefore 700 dol. is the principal required.

Required the principal that will amount to 270 dollars, in 2 years at 6 per cent per annum.

OPERATION.

OPERATION.

$$\text{As } 100 + 12 = 112 : 100 :: 270$$

$$
\begin{array}{r}
100 \\
2 \\
\hline
200 \\
6 \\
\hline
12.00
\end{array}
\qquad
\begin{array}{r}
270 \\
100 \\
\hline
112)27000(241.07 \\
224 \\
\hline
460 \\
448 \\
\hline
120 \\
112 \\
\hline
8.00 \\
784 \\
\hline
16
\end{array}
$$

Therefore, 241 *dol.* $7\frac{16}{112}$ *cts. is the principal required.*

Admit I have a legacy of 196 dol. $66\frac{2}{3}$ cts. to pay, but is not due till the end of 3 years, and the legatee being in want of money, defires I would lend him fome : What fum muft he have to amount to his legacy in 3 years, at 6 per cent per annum ?

Anfwer. 166 *dol.* $66\frac{2}{3}$ *cts.*

C A S E   VIII.

When the principal, amount, and time are given to find the Ratio.

R U L E.

1. SUBTRACT the principal from the amount, and the remainder is the intereft.

2.

2. SAY as the given principal, is to its intereſt ; ſo is 100 dollars, to the intereſt of 100 dollars for the given time.

3. DIVIDE the intereſt of 100 dollars thus found by the given time, and the quotient will be the ratio required.

EXAMPLES.

Required the rate per cent per annum ſuch, that 1240 dollars may amount to 1400 in 3 years.

OPERATION.

```
1400      1240 : 200 :: 100
1200                  100
————      ——————————————————
 200      124)0) 2000(0(16.12
                 124
                 ———
                  760
                  744
                  ———
                   16.0
                   124
                   ———
                    360
                    248
                    ———
            dol. cts. 112
```

Then, 16,12 ÷ 3 = 5.37 *the Ratio required.*

Required

Required the rate per cent per annum, that 100 dollars in 7 years will amount to 135 dollars.

OPERATION.

$$135 \qquad As\ 100 : 35 :: 100$$
$$100 \qquad\qquad\qquad 100$$

$$35 = interest, \qquad 1)00(00(35$$
$$7(35\ dol.$$
$$5 = ratio\ req.$$

At what Ratio will 3333 dollars 33⅓ cents amount to 4000 dollars in 20 years. *Answer*, 6 *dol.*

C A S E IX.

COMMISSION *or* PROVISION.

THIS is a premium allowed to factors for buying or felling goods, wares, or merchandize, at fo much per cent, without any regard to time ; which rate is governed according to the cuftoms of particular places.

THE method of proceeding, is the fame as in cafe III, except no regard is had to time.

EXAMPLES.

If I buy goods for my correfpondent in Philadelphia, to the value of 4000 dollars : What may I demand for my commiffion, at 4½ per cent ?

OPERATION.

OPERATION.

$$4000$$
$$4.5 = ratio,$$

$$20000$$
$$16000$$

$$1(00)180(00.0 = 180 \; dol. \; the \; anfwer.$$

Required the commiffion for felling 5720 dollars worth of goods, at $2\frac{1}{2}$ per cenr.

OPERATION.

$$5720$$
$$2.5 = ratio,$$

$$28600$$
$$11440$$

$$143.000 = 143 \; dol. \; the \; anf.$$

My correfpondent fends me word, that he has dif-burfed goods on my account, to the value of 13333 dollars $33\frac{1}{3}$ cents : What is his commiffion at $2\frac{1}{2}$ per cent ? *Anfwer.* 333 *dol.* $33\frac{1}{4}$ *cts.*

CASE X.

BROKERAGE.

BROKERAGE is an allowance of fo much per cent, made to perfons called brokers, for finding cuftom-ers, and felling to them goods, wares, &c. which be-long to other men.

Z

R U L E.

FIND the intereſt of the given ſum, at one per cent ; or which is the ſame thing ; divide the given ſum by 100, and take parts of the quotient, agreeing with the rate per cent.

Or,

REDUCE the rate per cent to a decimal, and multiply it with the given ſum ; then divide by 100, and the quotient will be the anſwer.

EXAMPLES.

Required the Brokerage of 1000 dollars, at 25 cents per cent.

OPERATION.

1(00)10(00

25 cents$=\frac{1}{4}$ *of a dollar, therefore,* $10 \div 4 = 2$ *dollars 50 cents = Brokerage of 1000 dollars divided by* $4=$ *Brokerage required.*

Or,

1000
.25*=ratio,*

5000
2000

2.5000*=2 dol. 50 cts. as be-*
[*fore.*

Required the Brokerage of 324 dollars 40 cents, at $\frac{1}{7}$ of a dollar per cent.

OPERATION.

OPERATION.

$$324.40$$
$$.20 = \tfrac{1}{5} \text{ of a dollar,}$$

$$1(00)64.8800 = 64.88 \text{ cts. } \textit{the Brokerage}$$
required.

What is the Brokerage of 15600 dollars, at 77 cents per cent ?   *Anf.* 120 *dol.* 12 *cts.*

CHAP. IV.

COMPOUND INTEREST.

COMPOUND Intereft arifes from the computation of the intereft of any principal added o its intereft, when the payment fhould be made ; vhich forms a new principal at every time when he payments become due ; and is for this reafon, ometimes called intereft upon intereft.

THUS, if 100 dollars be put to intereft at 6 dollars ɔer cent per annum ; at the end of the firft year, the ntereft will be 6 dollars as in fimple intereft, which f added to its principal will be 106 dollars, for a new ɔrincipal the fecond year, which principal at the nd of the fecond year, will amount to 112 dollars 36 cents ; which is 36 cents more than if 100 ɔollars had been put out at fimple intereft only.

THE Compound Intereft of any fum may be found ɔy the following

R U L E.

1. FIND the intereft of the propofed fum for thē irft year at the given rate per cent, as in fimple intereft.   2.

2. ADD this interest to its principal, which amouu makes the principal for the second year.

3. FIND the interest of the second year's principal in the same manner as you did the first, and add it to its principal, for the third year's principal, which must be computed as before; and so on, for the time required.

4. SUBTRACT the given principal from the last amount, and the remainder will be the Compound Interest required. Or,

FIND the amount of one dollar for one year, at the given rate per cent, and multiply it continually with the principal, as many times as the given number of years, and the resulting product will be the amount; from which subtract the principal, and the remainder will be the Compound Interest.

EXAMPLES.

Required the Compound Interest of 100 dollars for 3 years, at 6 per cent per annum.

OPERATION.

100	100	106	112.36
6	6	6.36	6.7416
6.00	106	112.36	119.1016
	6	6	
	6.36	6.7416	

Then, 119 dol. 10.16 cts.—100 dol. = 19 dol. 10.16 cts. = interest required.

Or,

Or,

As 100 : 106 :: 1 : 1.06 ⎰ 100 × 1.06 × 1.06 ×
the amount of 1 *dollar for* 1 ⎱ 1.06 = 119.1016 = 119
year, at 6 *per cent.* ⎰ *dol.* 10.16 *cts.*

Then, 119 *dol.* 10.16 *cts.* — 100 *dol.* = 19 *dol.* 10.16 *cts. the same as before.*

THE following is a Table of the amount of 1 dollar, from 1 to 30 years ; for the more ready computing Compound Intereſt at 6 per cent per annum.

Years.	The amount of 1 dol. at 6 per cent, &c. comp. intereſt.	Years.	The amount of 1 dol. at 6 per cent, &c. comp. intereſt.	Years.	The amount of 1 dol. at 6 per cent, &c. comp. intereſt.
1	1.06	11	1.898298558	21	3.399563600
2	1.1236	12	2.012196471	22	3.603537416
3	1.191016	13	2.132928260	23	3.819749661
4	1.26247696	14	2.260903955	24	4.048934641
5	1.338225577	15	2.396558193	25	4.291870719
6	1.418519112	16	2.540351684	26	4.549382962
7	1.503630259	17	2.692772785	27	4.822345940
8	1.593848074	18	2.854339152	28	5.116686697
9	1.689478959	19	3.025599502	29	5.418387899
10	1.790847696	20	3.207135472	30	5.743491729

BY the above table, the amount of any ſum may be computed from 1 to 30 years, by only multiplying the principal with the numbers ſtanding againſt the number of years in the table, and the product will be the amount required.

EXAMPLES.

Required the amount of 127 dollars, for 7 years, at 6 per cent per annum.

OPERATION.

OPERATION.

Against 7 *in the table is* 1.503630 *&c.*

                    127
                    ———————
                10525410
                3007260
                1503630
                ——————— *dol. cts.*
                190.961010 = 190 96.1 *&c.*
the answer.

Required the Compound Interest of 555 dollars, for 30 years, at 6 per cent per annum.

OPERATION.

Against 30 *in the table is* 5.743491 *&c.*

                    .555
                ———————
                28717455
                28717455
                28717455
                ——————————
                3187.637505 = *amount.*

Then, 3187 *dol.* 63.7505 *cts.* — 555 *dol,* = 2632 *dol.* 63.7505 *cts. the interest required.*

C H A P.

CHAP. V.

REBATE or DISCOUNT.

REBATE or Difcount is when any fum of money is due at a certain time to come, and the debtor is ready to make prefent payment, provided he can have allowance made him at a certain rate per cent per annum, which allowance is called the Rebate or Difcount, and the prefent payment, a fum of money, which if put to intereft, would amount to the given fum, at the rate per cent and time given.

THE Rebate of any fum is found by the following

RULE.

As the amount of 100 dollars, at the rate per cent and time given, is to the intereft of 100 dollars, at the fame rate and time ; fo is the given fum, to the Rebate : And from the given fum fubtract the Rebate, and the remainder will be the prefent payment.

EXAMPLES.

A, hath 100 dollars due to him, to be paid at the end of 2 years ; but his debtor agrees to make prefent payment, provided A will make a Rebate at 6 dollars per cent per annum : Required the Rebate.

OPERATION.

OPERATION.

First, 100
　　　　　6 = *ratio,*
　　　────
　　　600
　　　　2 = *time,*
　　　────
　12.00

　　　　Then, as 100 + 12 = 112　12 :: 100
　　　　　　　　　　　　　　　　　　　12
　　　　　　　　　　　　　　　　────
　　　　　　　　　　112)1200(10.71 =
　　　　　　　　　　112 [*rebate*
　　　　　　　　　────
　　　　　　　　　　80.0
　　　　　　　　　　784
　　　　　　　　　────
　　　　　　　　　　160
　　　　　　　　　　112
　　　　　　　　　────
　　　　　　　　　　48

　　Required the Rebate of 720 dollars, for 2½ years, at 6 per cent per annum.

OPERATION.

OPERATION.

Then, as 100 + 15 = 115 : 15 :: 720

```
        100                          15
          6                    ____________
     ___________                     3600
     2)600                            720
          2                    ____________
     ___________            115)10800(93.91 = re-
        1200                      1035        [bate req.
         300                    ____________
     ___________                      450
       15.00                          345
                               ____________
                                     105.0
                                     1035
                               ____________
                                      150
                                      115
                               ____________
                                       35
```

Find what sum ought to be paid down for a debt of 1000 dollars due 3¼ years hence, discounting at 5 per cent per annum.

OPERATION.

```
              100
                5
         ____________
         2)500
                3
         ____________
             1500
              250
         ____________
            17.50
```


As

As 100+17.50=117.50 : 17.50 :: 1000
1000

117.50)1750000(148.93= *reb.*
11750

57500
47000

105000
94000

11000.0
105750

42500
35250

7250

And, 1000—148.93=851 *dol.* 7 *cts. the answer.*

Suppose I have a legacy due to me of 4000 dollars, whereof 800 dollars is to be paid in 8 months, and the rest at the end of 16 months : How much ought I to receive for present payment, allowing 6 per cent, &c. discount ? *Answer.* 3732 *dol.* 21 *cts.*

A owes B 15000 dollars, one half of which is to be paid in 4 months, and the rest at the end of 8 months : What ought B to receive in present payment, allowing 6 per cent discount ? *Ans.* 14564 *dol.* 58 *cts.*

CHAP.

CHAP. VI.

EQUATION of PAYMENTS The COMMON WAY.

EQUATION of payments, is when feveral fums of money are due at different times, to find a certain time when the whole may be paid without lofs to either party

RULE.

MULTIPLY each payment with its refpective time, and divide the fum of the products by the fum of the payments ; the quotient refulting, will be the time required.

THIS rule will give the equated time near enough for common practice in matters of this nature ; but not accurately true, becaufe the rule is founded on a fuppofition that the fum of the interefts of the debts due before the equated time, computed from the times they become due to that time, is equal to the fum of the intereft of the debts, payable after the equated time, computed from that time to their refpective terms of payment ; that is, the gain made by the debtor's keeping thofe debts which become due before the equated time, until that time, is equal to the lofs fuftained by paying thofe debts at the equated time, which are not due till afterwards ; but it is manifeft, that the gain made by keeping a debt any time after it is due, is equal to the intereft of that debt for that time; but the lofs fuftained by paying a debt any time before it becomes due, is plainly no more than the rebate of the debt for that time ; and fince the rebate is always lefs than the intereft of the fame

fum,

ſum, it follows that the ſuppoſition is not true, and conſequently the rule falſe.

Examples in equation of payments the common way.

A owes B 100 dollars, whereof 50 dollars is to be paid at the end of 4 months and the reſt at the end of 8 months : Required the time when the whole may be paid without loſs to either party.

OPERATION.

Firſt, $50 \times 4 = 200$ *the firſt payment with its time :*
Secondly, $50 \times 8 = 400$ *the ſecond payment with its time :*
Then, $400 + 200 = 600$ *the ſum of the products.*
And, $50 + 50 = 100$ *the ſum of the payments :*
Conſequently, $600 \div 100 = 6$ *months, the time required.*

W owes X 865 dollars, whereof 50 dollars is to be paid preſent, 195 dollars to be paid in 8 months, and the reſt at the end of 12 months : Required the equated time to pay the whole.

OPERATION.

$50 \times 1 = 50$ *the firſt payment with its time :*
$195 \times 8 = 1560$ *the ſecond payment with its time :*
$620 \times 12 = 7440$ *the laſt payment with its time :*
And $50 + 1560 + 7440 = 9050$ *the ſum of the products.*
Conſequently, $\frac{9050}{865} = 10$ *months* $13 \frac{755}{865}$ *days the time required.*

P owes a debt to be paid at 5 ſeveral payments, in the following manner, to wit, $\frac{1}{5}$ in 4 months, $\frac{1}{5}$ at 8 months, $\frac{1}{5}$ at 12 months, $\frac{1}{5}$ at 16 months, and $\frac{1}{5}$ at

20 months : Required the equated time to pay the whole.

OPERATION.

Suppose the debt $=25$ *dollars, one fifth of which is* 5 *dollars, then* $5\times4+5\times8+5\times12+5\times16+5\times20=20+40+60+80+100=300$. *Therefore,* $\frac{300}{25}=$ 12 *months, the time required.*

In the solution of the above queſtion, we made uſe of 25 dollars to repreſent the whole debt ; but any other number would have equally ſucceeded, as may be thus analytically demonſtrated.

Let $x=$ *any ſum whatever, to be paid in manner as above.*

Then, $\frac{1}{5}x$ *is* $\frac{x}{5}$, *and* $\frac{x}{5}\times4+\frac{x}{5}\times8+\frac{x}{5}\times12+\frac{x}{5}\times16+\frac{x}{5}\times20=\frac{4x}{5}+\frac{8x}{5}+\frac{12x}{5}+\frac{16x}{5}+\frac{20x}{5}=\frac{60x}{5}=$ ſum of the products of the ſeveral payments with their reſpect- ive times : *Therefore,* $\frac{60x}{5}\div x=\frac{60x}{5x}=\frac{12x}{x}=12$ months *the ſame as before.*

$$Q. E. D.$$

CHAP. VII.

BARTER.

BARTER is the exchanging one commodity for another in ſuch a manner, that the parties bartering, may neither of them ſuſtain loſs. Thus, ſuppoſe A hath 50lb. of ginger, at 30 cents per lb. and would Barter with B for pepper at 70 cents per lb.

lb. What quantity of pepper muſt, B give A for his 50 lb. of ginger ?

In the ſolution of this queſtion, and all others of the like nature, you muſt firſt find the value of the given quantity at the given price, and then find how much of the quantity ſought at its price, will amount to the value of the given quantity, and the reſult will be the anſwer to the queſtion.

Thus, in the above queſtion, the quantity given, is 50 lb. of ginger, at 30 cents per lb. and the quantity ſought is pepper, at 70 cents per lb. Therefore, as 70 cts. : 1 lb. :: 15 dol. (the price of the ginger) : 21⅖ lb. the quantity of pepper required. Conſequently in Barter, the method of operation is the ſame as in the rule of three direct.

EXAMPLES.

Required the quantity of flax, at 8 cents per lb. that muſt be given in Barter, for 12 lb. of indigo, at 2 dol. 50 cts. per lb.

OPERATION.

> lb. dol. cts. lb. dol.
>
> *Firſt, as* 1 : 2 50 :: 12 : 30, *the value of the indigo.*
>
> cts. lb. dol. lb.
>
> *Then,* 8 : 1 :: 30 : 375, *the anſwer.*

A hath rum at 70 cents per gallon ready money, but in Barter he muſt have 80 cents ; B hath raiſins at 12 cents per lb. ready money : How many lb. of raiſins muſt A have for 60 gallons of rum.

Here you muſt firſt find what B's raiſins ought to be per lb. in Barter, which muſt be as much more in proportion, as A's price in ready money, is to his price in

Barter ;

Barter ; which to obtain, say as 70 cts. : 80 cts. :: 12 cts. : 13.71 cts.=price of B's raisins per lb. in Barter ; then proceed as before directed, and the quantity of raisins that B must give A will be found=350.11lb.

How much wheat at $91\frac{2}{3}$ cts. per bushel, must be given for 8 cwt. of sugar at $8\frac{1}{3}$ cts. per lb. ?

Answer. $81\frac{5}{1\,1\,1}$ *bushels.*

A hath rum at 70 cents per gallon ready money, but in Barter he must have 84 cents ; B hath corn at 50 cents per bushel ready money : How much must B have per bushel in Barter for his corn ; also, how many bushel of corn B must give A for a hogshead of rum containing 120 gallons ?

Answer. B must have $57\frac{1}{7}$ *cts. per bushel in Barter, and must give A* 168 *bushel of corn for the* 120 *gallons of rum.*

D hath 12 cwt. of sugar, which he will sell to H for 8 dollars $33\frac{1}{3}$ cents per cwt. ready money, but in Barter he must have $8\frac{1}{3}$ cents per lb. H hath a horse which he would sell for 90 dollars ready money, but in Barter he must have 20 per cent advance : They Barter, D takes the horse, and H the sugar : Query which is in debt, and how much ?

Answer. H is in debt 3 *dol.* $37\frac{1}{7}$ *cts. ready money.*

CHAP. VIII.

LOSS and GAIN.

LOSS and gain is a rule by which merchants are instructed how to raise or fall in the prices of their goods, so as to gain or loose so much per lb. bag, or barrel, &c.

The

The operations are performed by the rule of three direct.

EXAMPLES.

Suppose I buy cheese at 6 dollars per 100lb. and sell it again at 8 cents per lb. What do I gain in buying and selling 600lb. ?

Here you must first find what 600lb. comes to, at 6 dollars per 100lb. and 600lb. at 8 cents per lb. then subtract one sum from the other, and the result will be the answer.

OPERATION.

First, 6×6=36 dol. the value of 600lb. at 6 dol. per 100lb.

Then, 600×8 cts. = 48 dol. the price of 600lb. at 8 cts. per lb.

And, 48—36=12 dol. the answer.

When butter cost 7 dollars per firkin of 56lb. To find how it must be sold per lb. to gain 25 per cent.

OPERATION.

As 56lb. : 7 dol. :: 1lb. : $12\frac{1}{2}$ cts. the price that the butter cost per lb.

As 100lb. : $12\frac{1}{2}$ cts. :: 100+25=125 : 15.625 cts. the answer.

When tea cost 75 cts. per lb. To find how it must be sold per lb. to gain 25 per cent.

OPERATION.

As 100 : 75 :: 100+25=125 : 93.75 cts. the answer.

At

At $12\frac{1}{2}$ *cts. profit in a dollar : How much per cent ?*
As 1 *dol.* : 12.5 *cts.* :: 100 *dol.* : $12\frac{1}{2}$ *per cent the*
answer.

Bought rum at 50 cents per gallon, and paid impost, at 8 cents per gallon, and afterwards sold it at 53 cents per gallon : What do I loose in laying out 600 dollars.   *Answer.*   86 *dol.* 21 *cts.*

If I buy tallow at $12\frac{1}{2}$ cents per lb. and give $2\frac{7}{8}$ cents per lb. to a chandler to make it into candles, and 14oz. of tallow make a dozen of candles, which I sell at $19\frac{5\,2}{7\,2}$ cents per dozen : What do I gain in buying and selling 180lb. of tallow.

     Answer.   12 *dol.* 50 *cts.*

CHAP. IX.

FELLOWSHIP.

FELLOWSHIP is a rule, when several persons as merchants, &c. trade in company with a joint stock, to ascertain each man's proportional part of the gain or loss, which arises from the employment of the joint stock, according to the quantity of goods, sum of money, &c. each man puts into the said stock ; which admits of a two-fold consideration.

SECT. I.

FELLOWSHIP SINGLE.

SINGLE Fellowship is when all the several stocks are employed in the common stock, an equal term of time. Therefore, since the times of the several

stocks

ftocks employed in the joint ftock, are all equal ; it follows, that each partner's fhare of the gain or lofs, is as his fhare of that ftock : Wherefore it is mani-feft ; if I put in $\frac{1}{4}$ of the whole ftock, I ought to have $\frac{1}{4}$ of the whole gain, or fuffer $\frac{1}{4}$ of the whole lofs : Hence we have the following

RULE.

MULTIPLY each partner's part of the joint ftock, with the whole gain or lofs, and divide the feveral products by the whole ftock, and the quotients re-fulting will be the anfwer to the queftion. Or, as the whole ftock is to the whole gain or lofs ; fo is each man's particular part of that ftock, to his particular part of the gain or lofs.

EXAMPLES.

Two partners, A and B, conftitute a joint, ftock of 300 dollars, whereof A put in 200 dollars, and B 100 dollars, and they trade and gain 150 dollars : Required each man's part of the gain.

OPERATION.

150		150
200		100

3)oo)300)oo   3)oo)150)oo
100= *A's gain.*   50= *B's gain.*

Or,

As 300 : 150 :: 200 : 150×200÷300=100 *dol. A's part of the gain.*

As 300 : 150 :: 100 : 150×100÷ 300=50 *dol. B's part of the gain ;*

Or,

Or, $150 \div 300 = .5$ *the ratio of the first term to the second :*

Therefore, $200 \times .5 = 100$ *A's part, and* $100 \times .5 = 50$ *B's part as before.* (Vid. Chap. 11.)

Three merchants, A, B, and C, make a joint stock of 2000 dollars, whereof A put in 500 dollars, B 800 dollars, and C 700 dollars; and by trading gain 400 dollars : Required each man's part of the gain ?

OPERATION.

First, $400 \div 2000 = .2$ *the ratio of the first term to the second.*

$$\text{Therefore,} \left\{ \begin{array}{l} 500 \times .2 = 100 \ dol. \ A's \\ 800 \times .2 = 160 \text{------} B's \\ 700 \times .2 = 140 \text{------} C's \end{array} \right\} gain.$$

Four merchants enter into partnership, and constitute a joint stock of 60000 dollars, whereof A put in 15000 dollars 24 cents, B 20000 dollars 76 cents, C 21000 dollars, and D 3999 dollars, and in trade they gain 24000 dollars : Required each partner's share of the gain ?

OPERATION.

First, $24000 \div 60000 = .4$ *the ratio of gain :* There-fore, $15000.24 \times .4 = 6000$ *dol.* 9.6 *cts.* *A's part of the gain ; and* $20000.76 \times .4 = 8000$ *dol.* 30.4 *cts. B's part of the gain ; also,* $21000 \times .4 = 8400$ *dol. C's part ; lastly,* $3999 \times .4 = 1599$ *dol.* 60 *cts. D's part.*

Six farmers, A, B, C, D, E, and F, hired a farm for 300 dollars ; A paid 20 dollars, B 30, C 40, D 60, E 80, and F 70 dollars ; and they gained 60 dollars : What is each man's part of the gain ?

Answer.

Anſwer. *A's* 4 *dol.* *B's* 6, *C's* 8, *D's* 12, *E's* 16,
and *F's* 14 *dol.*

SECT. II.

COMPOUND FELLOWSHIP.

THE only difference between Fellowſhip ſingle and
compound, is, that in the latter regard muſt be had
to the time each partner's ſtock continues in company ; whereas in ſingle Fellowſhip the times of con-
tinuance are all ſuppoſed equal, and when the times
are equal, the ſhares of gain or loſs, are as their
ſtocks, as we have before ſhewn : Therefore when
the ſtocks are equal, the ſhares muſt be as the times.
Conſequently, when neither the ſtocks nor times are
equal, the ſhares muſt be as their products ; which
affords the following

RULE.

1. MULTIPLY each man's ſtock with the time it
is employed, and find the ſum of all the products.

2. As the ſum of the products thus found, is to
the whole gain or loſs ; ſo is the product of each
man's ſtock with its time, to its proportional part
of the gain or loſs.

Or,

FIND the ratio between the two firſt terms, and
proceed as in the laſt rule.

EXAMPLES.

Two men, A and B, made a joint ſtock of 600
dollars, whereof A put in 200 dollars for 2 months,
and B put in 400 dollars for 4 months ; at the expir-
ation

ation of which, they find they have loſt 200 dollars?
Required each man's part of the loſs?.

OPERATION.

Firſt, 200×2=400= *A's ſtock with its time :*
And, 400×4=1600= *B's ſtock with its time :*
Then, 400+1600=2000 *the ſum of the products of
each man's ſtock, with its time : Therefore, as* 2000 :
200 :: 400 : 200×400÷2000=40 *dol. A's part of the
loſs ; and as* 2000 : 200 :: 1600 : 200×1600÷2000
=160 *dol. B's part of the loſs.*

Or, 200÷2000 = .1 *the ratio of loſs ; then,*
400×.1=40 *A's part, and* 1600×.1=160 *B's part,
the ſame as before.*

Three merchants made a joint ſtock of 8000 dollars in the following manner, viz. A put in 1200 dollars for 3 years, B 2000 dollars for 7 years, and C 4800 dollars for 8 years ; and at the end thereof, they find they have gained 6720 dollars : Required each man's part of the gain ?

OPERATION.

Firſt, 1200×3=3600=*A's ſtock with its time :*
And, 2000×7=14000=*B's ſtock with its time :*
Alſo, 4800×8=38400=*C's ſtock with its time :*
Then, 3600+14000+38400=56000 *the ſum of the
products :*
And, 6720÷56000=.12 *the ratio of gain : -*
Therefore, 3600×.12=432 *dol. A's part of the
gain ; and* 14000×.12=1680 *dol. B's part ; Alſo,*
38400×.12=4608 *dol. C's part.*

Two.

Two merchants, A and B, made a joint ſtock ; A put in at firſt, 300 dollars for 7 months, and 4 months after put in 500 dollars more : B put in at firſt, 700 dollars, and 3 months after put in 200 dollars more. Now at the end of 7 months, they make a ſettlement of their accounts, and find they have gained 1860 dollars : Required each man's part of the gain, according to his ſtock and time ?

Firſt, $300 \times 4 = 1200$ *the product of A's firſt ſtock with its time, and* $\overline{300 + 500} \times 3 = 800 \times 3 = 2400$ *the product of A's increaſed ſtock, with the remainder of the time : Therefore,* $1200 + 2400 = 3600$ *the product of A's ſtock with the whole time, according to the queſtion.*

Secondly, $700 \times 3 = 2100$ *the product of B's firſt ſtock with its time, and* $\overline{700 + 200} \times 4 = 900 \times 4 = 3600$ *the product of B's augmented ſtock, with the remainder of the time : Therefore,* $2100 + 3600 = 5700$ *the product of B's whole ſtock, with the whole time, and* $3600 + 5700 = 9300$ *the ſum of the products.*

Hence, $1860 \div 9300 = .2$ *the ratio of gain : Therefore,* $3600 \times .2 = 720$ *dol.* $= A$*'s part of the gain, and* $5700 \times .2 = 1140 = B$*'s part of the gain.*

Four merchants, A, B, C and D, enter into partnerſhip for 12 months : A put into the common ſtock at firſt, 300 dollars, B 400, C 500, and D 800 dollars, and at the end of four months, A took out 200 dollars, and 3 months after that, he put in 100 dollars more ; B at the end of 2 months took out 200 dollars, and 2 months after that, put in 200 dollars more : C at the end of 6 months, took out 300 dollars, and two months after that, put in 200 dollars more : D at the end of 8 months, took out 400 dollars, and 2 months after that, put in 200 dollars

more :

more : Now at the end of 12 months, they find they have gained 406 dollars : Required each man's part of the gain ?

OPERATION.

First, $300 \times 4 = 1200$ *the product of A's first stock with its time, and* $\overline{300-200} \times 3 = 100 \times 3 = 300$ *the product of A's remaining stock for 3 months after the taking out of the 200 dol. Again,* $\overline{100+100} \times 5 = 200 \times 5 = 1000$ *the product of A's stock with the remainder of the time according to the question ; then,* $\overline{1200+300+1000} = 2500$ *the product of A's stock for the whole time.*

Secondly, to obtain the product of B's stock with its time, proceed as before : Thus $400 \times 2 = 800$; *then,* $\overline{400-200} \times 2 = 200 \times 2 = 400$; *and* $\overline{200+200} \times 8 = 400 \times 8 = 3200$. *Hence,* $\overline{800+400+3200} = 4400$ *the product of B's stock with its time.*

Thirdly, $500 \times 6 = 3000$; *then* $\overline{500-300} \times 2 = 200 \times 2 = 400$; *and* $\overline{200+200} \times 4 = 400 \times 4 = 1600$; *wherefore* $3000+400+1600 = 5000$ *the product of C's stock with its time.*

Fourthly, $800 \times 8 = 6400$; *then* $\overline{800-400} \times 2 = 400 \times 2 = 800$; *and* $\overline{400+200} \times 2 = 600 \times 2 = 1200$; *therefore* $6400+800+1200 = 8400$ *the product of D's stock with its time.*

Consequently,

Consequently, 2500+4400+5000+8400=20300 *the sum of all the products according to the question.*

Therefore, 406÷20300=.02 *the ratio of gain ; and* 2500×.02=50 *dol. A's part of the gain ; also,* 4400×.02=88 *dol. B's part ; likewise,* 5000×.02=100 *dol. C's part ; lastly,* 8400×.02=168 *dol. D's part.*

CHAP X.

COMPOUND PROPORTION.

COMPOUND Proportion, is used in the solution of questions that require several operations in simple proportion, whether direct or reciprocal.

For instance : Suppose a footman performs a journey of 240 miles in 8 days, when the days are 16 hours long : In what time would he perform a journey of 540 miles, when the days are but 12 hours long. This question resolved by simple proportion is thus,

$$\text{As } 240 : 8 :: 540 : \frac{540\times8}{240}=18 \ days.$$

THAT is it would require 18 days to perform a journey of 540 miles, when the days are 18 hours long; but it is required to know how many days it will take to perform the said journey of 540 miles when the days are but 12 hours long; which is thus :

$$\text{As } 16 \, h. : \overline{540\times8\div240} \, (18d.) :: 12 : \overline{540\times8\times12\div}$$

$$240\times12 = 24 \ days, \ by \ inverse \ proportion.$$

Now

Now from the laſt analogy, is deduced the following rule, for ſtating and working all queſtions in compound proportion, at one operation.

R U L E.

1. PLACE that term which is of the ſame name of the term ſought, ſo that it may ſtand in the middle place:

$$\text{Thus,} \begin{cases} * : 8 :: * \\ * : \text{------} :: * \end{cases} \text{d.} \quad See\ the\ aforeſaid\ queſtion.$$

2. WRITE the remaining terms of ſuppoſition, one above the other in the firſt places, and the terms of demand in like manner in the third places, ſo that the firſt and third terms in each row, may be of the ſame name and denomination :

$$\text{Thus,} \begin{cases} \text{m.} \quad \text{d.} \quad \text{m.} \\ 240 : 8 :: 540 \\ \text{h.} \qquad \quad \text{h,} \\ 16 : \text{------} :: 12 \end{cases}$$

3. HAVING thus ſtated your queſtion, find your diviſor by comparing the terms in each row : Thus if the firſt term gives the ſecond, does the third term require more or leſs ? If more, diſtinguiſh the leſs extreme with a point over it ; but if the third term require leſs, point the greater extreme :

$$\text{Thus,} \begin{cases} .\text{m.} \quad \text{d.} \quad \text{m.} \\ 240 : 8 :: 540 \\ \text{h.} \qquad \quad .\text{h.} \\ 16 : \text{------} :: 12 \end{cases}$$

4. MULTIPLY together the terms which are pointed for a diviſor, and the remaining terms for a dividend, and the quotient reſulting will be the anſwer :

Thus, $540 \times 8 \times 16 \div 240 \times 12 = 24$ days as before.

C c   *EXAMPLES.*

EXAMPLES.

If 12 bushels of corn are sufficient for a family of 9 persons 12 months : How many bushels will be sufficient for a family of 16 persons, 20 months ?

OPERATION.

Here bushels are sought ; therefore the question stated will stand

Thus,
$$\begin{cases} \text{.per. b. per.} \\ 9 : 12 :: 16 \\ \text{. m. \qquad m.} \\ 12 : \underline{\quad\quad} :: 20 \end{cases}$$

Then say, if 9 persons eat 12 bushels in 12 months, 16 persons will eat more ; therefore point the less extreme, which is 9. Again, say, if 12 months require 12 bushels for 9 persons, 20 months will require more ; therefore point the less extreme, which is 12.

Therefore, $\overline{12 \times 20 \times 16} \div \overline{12 \times 9} = 3840 \div 108 = 35\frac{5}{9}$ *bushels, the quantity of corn required.*

Note. *If the same quantity is found both in the divisor and dividend, it may be expunged from both :*

Thus in the above expression, $\overline{12 \times 20} \times \overline{16} \div \overline{12 \times 9}$, *the 12 may be struck out of the divisor and dividend : thus,*

$\overline{20 \times 16} \div 9 = 35\frac{5}{9}$ *the same as before.*

If 15 dollars be the hire of 8 men 5 days : What time will 40 dollars hire 20 men ?

OEERATION.

OPERATION.

.dol. d. *dol.*
15 : 5 :: 40
m.   .m.
8 :——— :: 20

Whence $\overline{8 \times 5 \times 40} \div \overline{15 \times 20} = 1600 \div 300 = 5\frac{1}{3}$ *days,
the time required.*

If 200 dollars in 2 years, gain 15 dollars : What will 150 dollars gain in half a year ?

Thus, $\overline{15 \times 150 \times 26} \div \overline{200 \times 104} = 2\frac{69}{208}$ *dol.* the *answer.*

If 1500 lb. of bread ferve 400 men 14 days : How many pounds of bread will ferve 140 men 9 days ?

Thus, $\overline{1500 \times 140 \times 9} \div \overline{400 \times 14} = 337 lb.$ *8oz.* the *answer.* -

If 12 Clerks will write 72 fheets of paper in 3 days : How many Clerks will write 140 fheets in 8 days ?

Anfwer. $\overline{12 \times 3 \times 140} \div \overline{72 \times 8} = 8\frac{432}{576}$ *Clerks.*

If 5000 bricks are fufficient to make a wall 4 feet high and 5 feet long : How many bricks of the fame fize will make 7 feet of wall 2 feet high ?

Anfwer. 3500.

CHAP.

CHAP. XI.

CONJOINED PROPORTION.

CONJOINED Proportion is when, in a rank of numbers, the firft term is compared with the fecond, and the fecond term being increafed or diminifhed, is compared with the third, and fo on ; from thence to determine the equality of any of the terms : Thus, if $3a = 4b$, and $8b = 12c$, then will $3a = 6c$; becaufe, as $4b : 3a :: 8b : 6a = 12c$, or $3a = 6c$ as before. Again, if $24a = 32b$, $48b = 30c$, and $10c = 9d$, then will $24a = 20c = 18d$; becaufe, as $32b : 24a :: 48b :$

$$\overline{24a \times 48b} \div 32b = 36a,$$ that is, $48b = 36a = 30c$, and

$24a = 20c$. Again as $30c : \overline{24a \times 48b} \div 32b :: 10c :$

$$\overline{24a \times 48b \times 10c} \div \overline{32b \times 30c} = 12a = 9d,$$ or $24a = 18d$. Hence from the foregoing analogy we have the following

RULE.

1. BEGIN with that term whofe equality with any other term is required, which call A and write out all the terms up to the one B, by which the aforefaid term is to be compared.

2. MULTIPLY all the alternate numbers together, beginning with the firft, for a dividend, and all the remaining ones together for a divifor.

3. Divide, and the quotient will be the anfwer.

EXAMPLES.

EXAMPLES.

If G in 48 days can produce a certain effect, which will require H 64 days to perform ; H can produce an effect in 80 days, which will take L 50 days to perform : Which is the moſt profitable to hire, G or L, and what is the difference ?

OPERATION.

Firſt, 48, 64, 80, *are the numbers written out according to the rule :*

Then, $\overline{48\times80\div64}=60=50$ *days of L, that is, 60 days of G are equal to 50 days of L ; and therefore it is the moſt profitable to hire L, to wit, in the proportion of 60 to 50, or as 6 to 5.*

If D in 24 days can do as much as E can in 32 days, E can do as much in 48 days, as F can in 30 days, and F can do as much in 10 days, as G can in 9 days : Which is the moſt profitable to hire, D, F, or G ?

OPERATION.

Firſt, find which is the moſt profitable to hire, D or F:

Thus, $\overline{24\times48\div32}=36=30$ *days of F, that is, 36 days of D are equal to 30 days of F ; and therefore F is more profitable to hire than D.*

Again, $\overline{24\times48\times10\div\overline{32\times30}}=12=9$ *days of G ; that is, 12 days of D are equal to 9 days of G, and therefore G is more profitable to hire than D ; and ſince F is more profitable to hire than D, and G more profitable than F ; it follows, that G is the moſt profitable to hire of the three.*   CHAP.

CHAP. XII.

ALLEGATION.

BY Allegation we are taught how to mix quantities of different quality, so that any quantity collectively taken, may be of a mean or middle quality ; that is, it shews us the value of any part of a composition, made of things all of a different quality.

WE shall consider Allegation, under the two following general heads, viz. Allegation Medial, and Allegation Alternate.

SECT. I.

ALLEGATION MEDIAL.

THIS is when any number of things are given, and the price of each : To find the price of any quantity of a mixture compounded of the whole.

RULE.

1. MULTIPLY each quantity with its price, and find the sum of all the products.

2. DIVIDE the sum of the products by the sum of all the quantities, and the quotient resulting will be the mean price required.

EXAMPLES.

A man is minded to mix 20 bushels of wheat, at 100 cents per bushel, with 10 bushels of rye, at 50 cents per bushel : Required the price of a bushel of this mixture. *OPERATION.*

OPERATION.

First, 20×100=2000 *cts.* = *price of all the wheat, and* 10×50=500 *cts.* = *price of the rye ; then* 2000+500=2500 *the fum of the products, and* 20+10=30 *the fum of the quantities : Therefore,* 2500÷30=83⅓ *cts. the price of a bufhel, as was required.*

A man would mix 27 bufhels of wheat, at 75 cents per bufhel, with 40 bufhels of rye, at 60 cents per bufhel, and 24 bufhels of oats, at 24 cents per bufhel : Required the price of a bufhel of this mixture.

OPERATION.

First, 27×75=1885 *cts.* = *price of the wheat, and* 40×60=2400 *cts.* = *price of the rye, alfo,* 24×24=576 *cts.* = *the price of the oats ; then* 1885+2400+576=4861 *the fum of the products, and* 27+40+24=91 *the fum of the quantities.*

Whence 4861 *cts.*÷91= *price of a bufhel, as was required.*

A maltfter would mix 70 gallons of one fort of beer, worth 12 cents per gallon, with 20 gallons of another fort, worth 24 cents per gallon, and 20 gallons of a third fort, worth 22 cents per gallon : How may this mixture be fold per gallon without gain or lofs ?

Anfwer. 16 *cts.*

Required what a gallon of the following mixture is worth, viz. 60 gallons of malaga, at .5 dollars per gallon, 40 gallons at .7 dollars per gallon, and 12 gallons at .3 dollars per gallon.

Anfwer. .55 *dol.*

A Goldfmith melts 18 ℔. of gold bullion, of 12 carats fine, with 10 ℔. of 16 carats fine, and 20 ℔. of

10 carats fine : How many carats fine is a pound of this mixture. *Anſwer.* 12 *carats.*

Note. *Goldſmiths ſuppoſe every quantity of gold to conſiſt of 24 parts, which they call carats ; but gold is generally mixed with ſome other metals, ſuch as copper, braſs, &c. which is called alloy, and the quality of the gold is eſtimated according to the quantity of alloy in it : Thus if 20 carats of pure gold, and 4 of alloy are mixed together, the gold is called 20 carats fine.*

SECT. II.

ALLEGATION ALTERNATE.

ALLEGATION Alternate conſiſts of 3 caſes.

CASE I.

When the prices of the ſeveral quantities to be mixed are given, to find what number of each ſort muſt be taken, to compoſe a mixture whoſe mean price ſhall be as given in the queſtion.

RULE.

1. WRITE all the particular rates or prices directly under each other, and the mean price on the left hand.

Thus, mean price, 4 $\begin{cases} 1 \\ 6 \\ 2 \\ 5 \end{cases}$ particular prices.

2. COUPLE or connect the particular prices with lines, ſo that one or more of thoſe greater than the mean price, may be coupled with one or more of thoſe leſs.   Thus,

Thus, 4 {1 6 2 5}   Or thus, 4 {1 6 2 5}

3. WRITE the difference between the mean price and every particular price, directly againſt the one with which it is coupled.

Thus, 4 {1 6 2 5} 1 2 2 3   Or thus, 4 {1 6 2 5} 1 2 2+1=3 3+2=5

4. THE difference ſtanding againſt each particular price, is the quantity that muſt be taken of that kind ; and where two or more differences are found ſtanding againſt any one particular price, their ſum is the quantity.

A maltſter has the following ſorts of beer, viz. at 12 cents, 22 cents, and 24 cents per gallon : Required the quantity of each ſort that muſt be taken to make a compoſition worth 20 cents per gallon.

OPERATION.

20 {12 22 24} 2+4=6 8 8

Therefore, there muſt be taken 6 gallons at 12 cts. 8 gallons at 22 cts. and 8 gallons at 24 cts. which may be proved by Allegation Medial.

To find how much wheat at 100 cents per buſhel, rye at 75 cents, corn at 40 cents, and oats at 30 cents per buſhel, may be mixed together, ſo that the mixture may be ſold for 50 cents per buſhel, without gain

OPERATION.

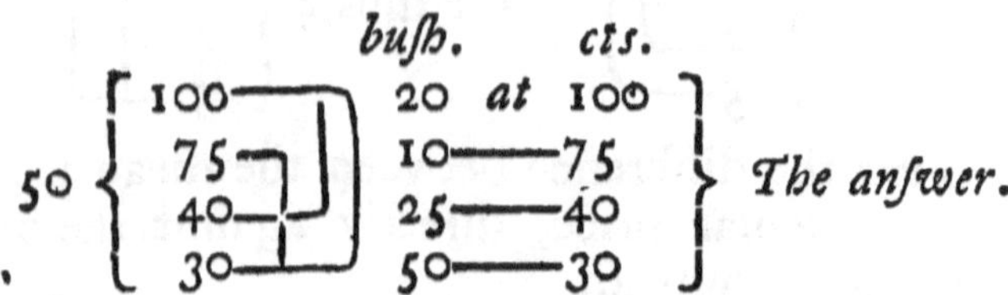

A merchant has coffee worth 12, 15, 16, and 1c
cents per lb. and would make a mixture worth 14
cents per lb. What quantity of each fort muft be
taken ?

OPERATION.

*Proceeding in this manner, by varying the order of link-
ing the particulars, you will difcover five more anfwer:
to this queftion, in whole numbers.*

How thefe kind of queftions can admit of variou:
anfwers, is eafy to conceive ; for if any two of the
particular prices make a balance by their increment
and decrement, in refpect of the mean price, then
will any multiple or quotient of the fame, make a
balance alfo : Therefore all numbers which are in
the fame proportion, equally anfwer the queftion
Confequently, there are fome queftions which wil
admit of an infinite variety of anfwers : Hence it is
that thefe queftions are fometimes called indetermin
ate or unlimited problems ; yet by an analytical pro
cefs

cefs, we can difcover all the poffible anfwers in whole numbers, when thofe anfwers are limited to finite terms. *(Vid. Book* ii, *Chap.* xxiii.*)*

CASE II.

When the quantity of one of the particulars is limited or given, thence to proportion all the others in the compofition by it.

RULE.

1. OBTAIN the difference between the mean price and every particular price, as in the laft rule.

2. As the difference found againft the fimple whofe quantity is given, is to the quantity itfelf; fo is each difference, to its refpectiye quantity of the compofition.

EXAMPLES.

A farmer would mix 12 bufhels of wheat at 72 cents per bufhel, with rye at 48 cents, corn at 36 cents, and barley at 30 cents per bufhel, fo that the whole compofition may be fold for 38 cents per bufhel : Required the quantity of each fort that muft be taken.

OPERATION.

$$38 \begin{cases} 72 \\ 48 \\ 36 \\ 30 \end{cases} \qquad \begin{matrix} 8 \\ 2 \\ 10 \\ 34 \end{matrix}$$

Whence, as 8 : 12 :: 2 : 3, *the quantity of rye, and, as* 8 : 12 :: 10 : 15, *the quantity of corn ; alfo, as* 8 : 12 :: 34 : 51, *the quantity of barley.*

To

To find how many gallons of frontenaic at 81 cents, claret at 60 cents, and port at 51 cents per gallon, muſt be mixed with 42 gallons of madeira at 90 cents per gallon, ſo that the whole compoſition may be ſold for 72 cents per gallon, without profit or loſs.

$$\textit{Firſt, } 72 \begin{cases} 90 \\ 81 \\ 60 \\ 51 \end{cases} \quad \begin{matrix} 21 \\ 12 \\ 9 \\ 18 \end{matrix}$$

Then, 42 ÷ 21 = 2 ; therefore, 12 × 2 = 24, the quantity of the claret, and 9 × 2 = 18, the quantity of the frontinaic ; alſo, 18 × 2 = 36, the quantity of port.

A tobacconiſt would mix 6 lb. of tobacco worth 6 cents per lb. with another ſort at 11 cents, and a third ſort at 12 cents : What quantity muſt be taken of each ſort, to make a mixture worth 10 cents per lb ?　　　　　　*Anſwer. 8 lb. of each ſort.*

C A S E III.

When the whole compoſition is equal to a given quantity ; that is, when the ſum of all the quantities which make up the compoſition, collectively taken, amount to the given quantity : To find the ſeveral quantities themſelves.

R U L E.

1. Link or couple the ſeveral particulars, and find their differences, as in the laſt caſe.

2. As the ſum of the differences, is to the ſum of the whole compoſition or given quantity ; ſo is each difference, to its reſpective quantity of the compoſition.

EXAMPLES.

EXAMPLES.

A grocer having fugars at 4 cents, 8 cents, and 12 cents per lb. would make a compofition of 240 lb. worth 10 cents per lb. Required the quantity of each fort that muft be taken.

OPERATION.

$$\textit{Firft, } 10 \begin{cases} 4 \\ 8 \\ 12 \end{cases} \begin{matrix} 2 \\ 2 \\ 6+2=8 \end{matrix}$$

$12=$ *fum of the differences.*

Then, as 12 : 240 :: 2 : 40, *and, as* 12:240 :: 2 : 40; *alfo, as* 12 : 240 :: 8 : 160. *Therefore, there muft be taken,* 40 *lb. at* 4 *cts.* 40 *lb. at* 8 *cts. and* 160 *lb. at* 12 *cts.*

A merchant would mix brandy of the following prices, viz. at 60 cents, 72 cents, and 84 cents per gallon, together with water at 0 cents per gallon, fo that a compofition of 846 gallons, may be fold for 48 cents per gallon, without gain or lofs : Required the quantity of each fort that muft be taken.

OPERATION.

$$\textit{Firft, } 48 \begin{cases} 72 \\ 60 \\ 84 \\ 0 \end{cases} \begin{matrix} 48 \\ 48 \\ 48 \\ 24+12+36=72 \end{matrix}$$

$216=$*fum of the differences.*

$$\textit{Then, as } 216 : 846 :: \begin{cases} 48 : 188 \textit{ at } 72 \textit{ cts.} \\ 48 : 188 \textit{ at } 60 \textit{ cts.} \\ 48 : 188 \textit{ at } 84 \textit{ cts.} \\ 72 : 282 \textit{ of water.} \end{cases}$$

In

In this cafe might be ftarted, a variety of very curious queftions about the fpecific gravities of metals ; but as they would require the knowledge of fome things which are not treated of in this volume, we defift.

CHAP. XIII.

Of POSITION, or the GUESSING RULE.

POSITION is a method of folving queftions, by fuppofing numbers, and then adding them, fubtracting, multiplying, &c. according as the refult or number given in the queftion is produced by addition, fubtraction, multiplication, &c, of the number required.

Position is diftinguifhed into two kinds, fingle and double.

SECT. I.

Of SINGLE POSITION.

Single Pofition is when one quantity is required, the propertics of which are given in the queftion.

RULE.

Suppose a number for the quantity required, and multiply or divide it, &c. according as the quantity required was multiplied, divided, &c. then ; as the refult of the fuppofition, is to the fuppofition, fo is the refult given in the queftion, to the number required.

EXAMPLES.

EXAMPLES.

To find such a number, that being divided by 2, 4, and 8, respectively, the sum of the quotients shall be 7.

OPERATION.

Suppose the number to be 24, *then,* $\frac{24}{2}+\frac{24}{4}+\frac{24}{8}=$ 12+6+3=21.

Whence, 21 : 24 :: 7 : 24×7÷21=8, *the number required.*

For, $\frac{8}{2}+\frac{8}{4}+\frac{8}{8}$=4+2+1=7 ; *therefore,* &c.

A man having a certain sum of money, said one half, one third, and one fourth of it being added together, made 13 dollars : What sum had he ?

Suppose he had 36 *dol. then* $\frac{36}{2}+\frac{36}{3}+\frac{36}{4}$=18+12 +9=39, *which ought to be* 13, *by the question.*

Therefore, 39 : 36 :: 13 : 12, *the answer.*

Three men found a purse of dollars, disputed how it should be divided between them. A said he would have one third ; B said he would have one third and one quarter ; well says C, I shall have but 2 dollars left for my part : How many dollars were there in the purse, and how many did each one take ?

Suppose the purse contained 12 *dollars* :
Then, $\frac{12}{3}+\frac{12}{3}+\frac{12}{4}$=4+4+3=11 :
And, 12−11=1, *which ought to be* 2.
Wherefore, 1 : 2 :: 12 : 24, *the number of dollars in the purse ; whence,* $\frac{24}{3}$=8, *the number of dollars that A took ; and* $\frac{24}{3}+\frac{24}{4}$=8+6=14, *the number that B took.*

Delivered to a banker, a certain sum of money, to receive interest for the same, at the annual rate of 6 dollars per cent ; at the end of 7 years, received

for

for intereſt and principal, 2495 dollars $27\frac{7}{9}$ cents : What was the ſum lent ?

Anſwer. 1736 *dol.* $11\frac{1}{9}$ *cts.*

S E C T. II.

Of DOUBLE POSITION.

DOUBLE Poſition is when there are ſeveral unknown numbers in the queſtion, analogous to each other; ſo that when one or more are found, the reſt may be had, either by addition, ſubtraction, or multiplication, &c. according as the queſtion requires.

R U L E.

1. ASSUME two convenient numbers, and work with them as the queſtion directs, finding their reſults.

2. FIND the difference between theſe reſults and the reſult given in the queſtion, and call thoſe differences errors, which place under their reſpective ſuppoſitions. Thus, $\begin{cases} x, y, \textit{ſuppoſitions.} \\ a, b, \textit{errors.} \end{cases}$

3. MULTIPLY the firſt error with the ſecond ſuppoſition; and the ſecond error with the firſt ſuppoſition. *Thus,* $a \times y$, *and* $b \times x$.

4. IF the errors are alike, that is, both too great, or both too ſmall, or more properly, the numbers from whence they were deduced, are both either greater or leſs than the true ones, you muſt divide the difference of the products, by the difference of the errors, that is, $a \times y - b \times x \div a - b$; but if the errors are unlike, that is, one too great and the other too ſmall, divide the ſum of the products by the ſum of

the

the errors : Thus, $a \times y + b \times x \div a + b$ and the quotient in either cafe, will be the number fought.

EXAMPLES.

A, B, and C, difcourfing of their money : Says B, I have 6 dollars more than A : Says C, I have 7 dollars more than B : Well fays A, the fum of all our money is 100 dollars : How much had each one ?

Suppofe A had 20 dol. then B muft have 20+6=26 *dol. and C* 26+7=33 *. dol. but* 20+26+33=79, *which fhould be* 100 *by the queftion.*

Therefore, 100—79=21, *the firft error, too fmall.*

Again, fuppofe A had 24 dol. then B muft have 24+6 =30, *and C* 30+7=37, *but* 24+30+37=91, *which fhould be* 100. *Therefore,* 100—91=9, *the fecond error, too fmall.*

Whence, 24×21=504=*produ&ct of the fecond fuppofition and firft error ;*

And, 20×9=180=*produ&ct of the firft fuppofition and fecond error ;*

Wherefore, 504—180÷21—9=27 *dol. A's money ;*

Then, 27+6=33 *dol.=B's money, and* 33+7=40, *C's money.*

A man having been to market with hogs, pigs and geefe ; received for them all 190 dollars, for every hog he received 4 dollars, for every pig 75 cents, and for every goofe 25 cents ; there were for every pig two hogs and three geefe : What was the number of each fort ?

Suppofe he had 12 *pigs, then he muft have* 24 *hogs, and* 36 *geefe, by the queftion; and* 12 *pigs at* 75 *cts. each, is* 9 *dol.* 24 *hogs at* 4 *dol. each, is* 96 *dol. and* 36 *geefe at* 25 *cts. each, is* 9 *dol. but* 9+96+9=114, *which fhould*

be

be 190: Therefore, 190—114=76, the first error, too small.

Again, suppose he had 16 pigs, then he must have 32 hogs, and 48 geese; and 16 pigs at 75 cts. is 12 dol. 32 hogs at 4 dol. is 128 dol. and 48 geese at 25 cts. is 12 dol. but 12+128+12=152 which should be 190. Therefore, 190—152= 38, the second error, too small.

Whence we have 16×76—12×38÷76—38=760 ÷38=20, the number of pigs, and 20×2=40, the number of hogs; also, 20×3=60, the number of geese.

CHAP. XIV.

CONCERNING PERMUTATION

AND

COMBINATION.

SECT. I.

Of PERMUTATION.

PERMUTATION is the changing or varying the order of things; and is when any number of quantities are given; to find how many ways it is possible to range them, so that no two parcels shall have the same quantities standing in the same place, with respect to each other.

PROBLEM I.

To find all the variations or changes that can be made of any number of things, all different one from another.

FIRST it is evident, that any one thing is capable of one position only, and therefore cannot possibly have any change or variation; but any two quantities; as *a* and *b*, are capable of change or variation; as *a b*, and *b a*, that is, the number of variations is 1×2. Again, if there be 3 quantities; as *a, b, c*, their variations are *a b c, a c b, b a c, b c a, c a b, c b a*; for taking only the two firſt, *a* and *b*, the number of their variations is 1×2; therefore taking in *c*, the number of changes is 1×2×3=6; and ſo on for any number of quantities. Hence we have the following

R U L E.

MULTIPLY together the natural ſeries of numbers, 1, 2, 3, 4, &c. continually, till your multiplier is equal to the number of things propoſed, and the laſt product will be the number of variations required.

EXAMPLES.

In how many different poſitions may a company of 8 perſons ſtand ?
 Anſwer. 1×2×3×4×5×6×7×8=40320 *poſitions.*

How many changes may be rung with 12 bells ?
 Anſwer. 1×2×3×4×5×6×7×8×9×10×11×12=479001600, *the number of changes required.*

PROBLEM II.

To find all the poſſible alternations or changes that can be made of any given number of different quantities, by taking any given number of them at a time.

THE manner in which this problem is ſolved, is directly the reverſe of the laſt; for it is manifeſt, that let the number of quantities be ever ſo many, and we take one of them at a time, the number of alternations will be equal to the number of quantities. Therefore
it

it follows, that the operation muſt begin at the number of things propoſed, and then decreaſe by unity, till the number of multiplications are one leſs than the number of things propoſed. Hence we get the following

R U L E.

MULTIPLY continually together, the terms of the ſeries, beginning at the number of things propoſed; and decreaſing by unity or 1, until the number of multiplications, are one leſs than the number of things to be taken at a time, and the laſt product will be the number of alternations required.

EXAMPLES.

How many different poſitions may a company of 9 men be placed in, taking 3 at a time?

Here the number of multiplications muſt be 2, and the ſeries 9, 8, 7, 6, &c. Therefore, $9 \times 8 \times 7 = 504$, the number of poſitions required.

How many alternations will the letters *a b b* admit of, taking 2 at a time?

Anſwer. $3 \times 2 = 6$, *the number of alternations required, and the letters will ſtand thus,* a b, b a, a b, b a, b b, b b.

How many alternations or changes can be made with the letters *a b c d*, taken 3 at a time?

Anſwer. $4 \times 3 \times 2 = 24$, *the number of alternations required; and the letters will ſtand*

$$
\text{Thus,} \begin{cases} a\,b\,c,\ a\,c\,b,\ b\,a\,c,\ b\,c\,a,\ c\,a\,b,\ c\,b\,a = alter.\ of\ a\,b\,c \\ a\,c\,d,\ a\,d\,c,\ c\,a\,d,\ c\,d\,a,\ d\,a\,c,\ d\,c\,a = do.\ of\ a\,c\,d \\ b\,c\,d,\ b\,d\,c,\ c\,b\,d,\ c\,d\,b,\ d\,c\,b,\ d\,b\,c = do.\ of\ b\,c\,d \\ d\,a\,b,\ d\,b\,a,\ a\,b\,d,\ a\,d\,b,\ b\,d\,a,\ b\,a\,d = do.\ of\ d\,a\,b. \end{cases}
$$

How

How many alternations or changes can be made with the letters of the word Algebra, taking 4 at a time?

Anſwer. $7 \times 6 \times 5 \times 4 = 840$.

PROBLEM III.

To find all the alternations or changes that can be made of any given number of quantities, which confiſt of ſeveral of one ſort, and ſeveral of another.

R U L E.

1. FIND the product of the ſeries, $1 \times 2 \times 3 \times 4$, &c. to the number of things to be changed, which call your dividend.

2. FIND all the alternations that can be made of each of thoſe things which are of the ſame ſort, by problem 1, and multiply them continually together for your diviſor.

3. DIVIDE, and the quotient reſulting will be the anſwer.

EXAMPLES.

Find all the variations that can be made of the following letters, *a a b c c c*.

OPERATION.

Firſt, $1 \times 2 \times 3 \times 4 \times 5 \times 6 = 720 = number\ of\ variations\ that\ can\ be\ made\ of\ 6\ different\ things,\ and$ $1 \times 2 = 2,\ the\ variations\ of\ the\ a's\ ;\ alſo,\ 1 \times 2 \times 3 = 6$ *the variations of the c's.*

Whence, $720 \div 6 \times 2 = 60,\ the\ number\ of\ variations$ *required.*

Find all the different numbers that can be made of the following numeral figures, 11122777.

OPERATION.

OPERATION.

First, $1 \times 2 \times 3 = 6 =$ *variations of the 1's, and* 1×2 $= 2 =$ *variations of the 2's ; also,* $1 \times 2 \times 3 = 6 =$ *variations of the 7's.*

Whence, $1 \times 2 \times 3 \times 4 \times 5 \times 6 \times 7 \times 8 \div 6 \times 2 \times 7$ $= 40320 \div 72 = 560,$ *the answer.*

S E C T. II.

Of COMBINATION.

COMBINATION of quantities, is, when any number of things are given, to find all the different forms in which those quantities can be possibly ordered, and from thence, all the different combinations in those forms, without any regard to the order in which the several quantities stand in those combinations. That is, by combination we determine how many ways it is possible to combine any number of things, so that no two combinations shall have the same things in both. Combinations of the same form, are those that have a like number of quantities which repeat in the same manner in both : Thus, *a a c d,* and *y y x z,* are of the same form; but *a a a b c,* and *s m n r y,* are of different forms.

P R O B L E M I.

To find all the different combinations that can be made of any number of quantities all different one from another, by taking any number of them at a time.

, THE rule for the solution of this problem, is easily deduced from the rule to Problem 11, of permutation. For it is plain, that the number of combinations

tions multiplied with the changes in the number of things taken at a time, gives the number of alternations in the whole. Therefore it follows, that the number of alternations in the whole, divided by the changes in a number of things equal to thofe taken at a time, gives the number of all the different combinations. Hence we have the following

R U L E.

1. FIND all the alternations or changes of the given quantities, taken as many at a time, as are equal to the number of things to be combined at a time; and call the refult your dividend.

2. FIND all the changes in as many quantities, as are equal to thofe to be taken at a time; and call the refult your divifor.

3. DIVIDE, and the refulting quotient will be the number of combinations required.

EXAMPLES.

Find all the different combinations that can be made with the following numeral figures, 1, 2, 3, 4, 5, 6, taken 2 at a time.

Here the number of given quantities are 6; and the number to be taken at a time are 2; therefore, $6 \times 5 = 30 = $ dividend; and $1 \times 2 = 2 = $ divifor.

Whence $30 \div 2 = 15$, the number of combinations required; and the figures will ftand as follows:

$$12, \ 13, \ 14, \ 15, \ 16$$
$$23, \ 24, \ 25, \ 26$$
$$34, \ 35, \ 36$$
$$45, \ 46$$
$$56.$$

FIND

FIND all the different combinations that can be made, with the following letters, *a b c d b*, taken 3 at a time.

Here the number of quantities are 5, and the number to be taken at a time are 3 ; therefore, $5 \times 4 \times 3 = 60 =$ dividend ; and $1 \times 2 \times 3 = 6 =$ divisor.

Whence, $60 \div 6 = 10$, the number of combinations required : and the letters will stand as follows :

$$a\,b\,c, \quad a\,b\,d, \quad b\,b\,b, \quad a\,c\,d$$
$$a\,c\,b, \quad a\,d\,b, \quad b\,c\,d$$
$$b\,c\,b, \quad b\,a\,b$$
$$c\,a\,b$$

How many different combinations may be made with the following numeral figures, 1, 2, 3, 4, 5, 6, 7, 8, 9, taken 5 at a time ?

Anſwer. 126 combinations.

PROBLEM II.

To find the number of different combinations that may be made from any number of ſets, by taking one out of each ſet and combining them together ; the things in every ſet being all different one from another.

RULE.

MULTIPLY the number of things in each ſet continually together, and the product reſulting, will be the number of combinations required.

EXAMPLES.

How many different combinations of two letters, may be made of theſe two ſets *a n w* and *s x y* ?

Here

Here the number of things in each set are 3:
Therefore, $3 \times 3 = 9$, the number of combinations required.

The method of making the combinations, may be shewn in the following manner.

Write down the two sets one beneath the other, and join those letters that are to be combined, with a straight line,

Thus,

Then drawing lines from *s* to *a*, from *x* to *n*, and from *y* to *w*, you will have three of the required combinations, to wit, *s a*, *x n*, and *y w*.

Again, let the sets be placed as before :

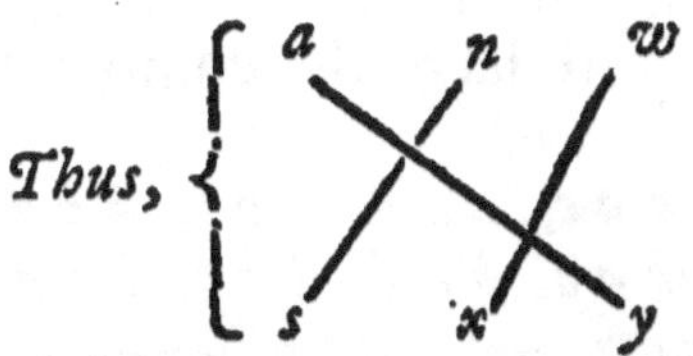

Thus,

Then joining *s* and *w*, *x* and *a*, and *y* to *n*, we get *s w*, *x a* and *y n*. Once more, place the sets as above.

Thus,

Then joining *s* and *n*, *x* and *w*, and *y* to *a*, we get *s n*, *x w*, and *y a*.

Hence, all the combinations are as follows,

$$s\,a, \quad s\,n, \quad s\,w,$$
$$x\,a, \quad x\,n, \quad x\,w,$$
$$y\,a, \quad y\,n, \quad y\,w,$$

Suppose

Suppofe there are three flocks of fheep ; in one of which there is 10, and in the other two, 20 each : To find how many ways it is poffible to choofe 3 fheep, one out of each flock.

Thus, 10 × 20 × 20 = 4000, *the anfwer.*

PROBLEM III.

To find the number of forms in which any given number of quantities may be combined, by taking any number at a time ; wherein there are feveral of one fort, and feveral of another.

RULE.

1. WRITE the quantities according to the order of the letters. *Thus, a, a, b, c, d.*

2. JOIN the firft letter to the fecond, third, fourth, &c. to the laft ; and the fecond letter to the third, fourth, &c. to the laft ; alfo, the third letter to the fourth, fifth, &c. to the laft : Proceeding in like manner through the whole, taking care to rejeƈt all combinations that have before accrued ; and you will have the combinations of all the twos.

3. JOIN the firft letter to every one of the twos, and the fecond, third, fourth, &c. in like manner to the laft ; and you will have the combinations of all the threes.

Thus, a a a, a a b, a a c, a a d, a b c, a b d, a c d,
b a a, a b b, b a c, b a d, b b c, b b d, b c d,
c a a, —— c c a, —— c c b, —— c c d,
d a a, —— —— d d a, —— —— d d c,

And proceed in this manner, till the number of things in the combination, are equal to the number to be taken at a time.

Note. *All thofe combinations which contain more things of the fame fort, than are given of the like kind in the queftion, muft be rejeƈted.* EXAM.

EXAMPLES.

Find all the different forms of combination, that can be made of the letters *a a b b c c*, taken 4 at a time,

OPERATION.

a a, a b, a c, b b, b c, c c = combinations of the twos.
a a b, a a c, b b a, b a c, b b c, b c c, a c c, = combinations of the threes.
a a b b, a a b c, b b c a, c c a b, a a c c, b b c c, = combinations of the fours.
Whence, a a b b, b b c c, a a c c, and a a c b, b b a c, c c a b, are the two forms required.

Find all the different forms of combination that can be made of the following figures, 22334455, taken 3 at a time.

OPERATION.

Thus, 22, 23, 24, 25, 33, 34, 35, 44, 45, 55 = combinations of the twos.
223, 224, 225, 234, 235, 245, 233, 334, 335, 345, 244, 344, 445, 255, 355, 455 = combinations of the threes.
Whence, 223, 224, 225, 233, 433, 533, 244, 344, 544, 255, 355, 455, and 234, 235, 245, 345, are the forms required.

Thus far, concerning Permutation and Combination.

CHAP.

CHAP. XV.

Of INVOLUTION.

WHEN any number is multiplied into itself, and that product multiplied with the same number; and so on, it is what is called Involution, and the several products resulting, are called the powers of the multiplying quantity, or root. Thus, $\overline{3\times3}$, $\overline{3\times3\times3}$, $\overline{3\times3\times3\times3}$, &c. are the powers of 3. And generally, $\overline{a\times a}$, $\overline{a\times a\times a}$, and $\overline{a\times a\times a\times a}$ &c. are the powers of a; whose height is denominated by the number of multiplications more one.

HENCE, the 2d power of 10, is $10\times10=100$
      the 3d ——————— $10\times10\times10=1000$
      the 4th ——————— $10\times10\times10\times10=10000$.

Therefore it follows, that the powers of any quantity, are a series of numbers in Geometrical Proportion continued, whose first term and ratio is the same, to wit, the root of the power: Consequently the height of the power at any particular term, will be expressed by the exponent of that term : As in these,

	1	2	3	4 &c. Expon.
	10,	10×10,	$10\times10\times10$,	$10\times10\times10\times10$,

&c. ÷.

HERE it is evident, that the index, or exponent of each term of the Geometrical series, is equal to the number of multiplications of the first term with itself, to that place, more one, and is therefore called the index, or exponent of the power.

Thus, $\begin{cases} 1+1+1+1+1=5. \\ 5\times5\times5\times5\times5=3125=5th\ power\ of\ 5. \end{cases}$
and so on for others.

WHENCE

WHENCE it follows, that to raise any number to any given power, is no more than to multiply the given number into itself, so often as there are units in the index of the power—1.

EXAMPLES.

Required the 5th power of 9.

OPERATION.

$$9$$
$$9$$

$81 = $ *2d power of 9*

$$9$$

$729 = $ *3d power of 9*

$$9$$

$6561 = $ *4th power of 9*

$$9$$

$59049 = $ *5th power of 9, as requir.*

Required the 7th power of 8.

Thus, $8 \times 8 \times 8 \times 8 \times 8 \times 8 \times 8 = 2097152 = $ *7th power of 8.*

CHAP. XVI.

Of EVOLUTION.

EVOLUTION is the converse of Involution ; and is when any power is given, to find
the

the number from whence fuch power was produced, which number (as we before faid) is called the root of the power; and the bufinefs of finding it, is called extraction of roots.

ALL powers whatever, are produced by the continual multiplication of their roots into themfelves, as is evident from what has been faid; yet there are many powers which have no finite root, that is, whofe true and adequate root cannot be expreffed in finite terms; but by approximation may be determined to any affigned degree of exactnefs.

THESE powers are called furds, or irrational powers.

PROBLEM I.

To extract the root of the fquare or fecond power of any number.

RULE.

1. PREPARE the given number for extraction, *i. e.* diftinguifh it into periods of two figures each, by beginning at the unit's place and placing a point over the firft, third, fifth, &c. figures of the given number, and if there are decimals, point them in the fame manner, from unity towards the right hand.

2. FIND a number by the help of a table of powers, whofe fquare is equal to, or lefs than the firft period on the left hand, and this number will be the firft figure of the root, which place in the form of a quotient; then fubftract its fquare from the aforefaid period; and to the remainder annex the next period for a dividend.

3. DOUBLE the firft figure of the root for a divifor.

4. FIND fuch a quotient figure, that when annexed

ed to the divisor and the result multiplied with the same number, the product will be equal to, or less than the dividend ; and this will be the second figure of the root.

5. To the remainder annex the third period for a new dividend, and add the figure in the root last found to your former divisor for a new one.

6. FIND the third figure of the root as you found the second ; and so on, till all be done.

Note 1.. *If there is a remainder after all the periods are annexed, the given number is a surd, and you must approximate to the root, by annexing cyphers two at a time, to the remainder.*

2. *If the given number consists of integers and decimals, you must ponit off as many places in the root, as there were periods of decimals in the given number.*

EXAMPLES.

Required the square root of 58081.

OPERATION.

```
              58081(241
               4
1st divisor=44)180
            4  176
               ___
2d divisor=481)  481
                 481
                 ___
                   0
```

Therefore, 241 *is the root required, as may be proved by involution : Thus,* 241×241=58081, *which is the same as the given number : Whence, &c.*

Required

Required the fquare root of 1000.

OPERATION.

1000(31.622 &c. = root required.
9

61)100
1 61

626)39.00
6 3756

6322)14400
2 12644

63242)175600
2 126484
&c.
49116 &c.

Required the fquare root of 105462.5625 :

OPERATION.

OPERATION.

$$105462.5625(324.75 = \text{root requir.}$$

$$
\begin{array}{r}
9 \\
\hline
62)154 \\
2\ 124 \\
\hline
644)3062 \\
4\ 2576 \\
\hline
6487)48656 \\
7\ 45409 \\
\hline
64945)324725 \\
324725 \\
\hline
0
\end{array}
$$

PROBLEM II.

To extract the square root of a Vulgar Fraction.

RULE.

Extract the root of the numerator, for the nume‑
rator of the root ; and the root of the denominator,
for the denominator of the root.

EXAMPLE.

Required the square root of $\frac{225}{1024}$.

OPERATION.

OPERATION.

$$\dot{2}2\dot{5}(15 = \textit{numerator of the root.}$$
$$1$$

$$25)\overline{125}$$
$$125$$
$$\overline{}$$
$$0$$

$$1\dot{0}2\dot{4}(32 = \textit{denominator of the root.}$$
$$9$$
$$\overline{}$$
$$62)124$$
$$124$$

Whence, $\frac{15}{32}$ is the root required.

PROBLEM III.

To find the root of the third power or cube, by approximation.

RULE.

1. DISTINGUISH the given number into periods of three figures each, by beginning at the unit's place, and placing a point over the firſt, fourth, feventh, figures, &c. and if there are decimals, point them from the unit's place towards the right hand, in the fame manner.

2. FIND the root of the firſt period on the left hand, by the help of the table of powers, and annex to it, as many cyphers as there are remaining periods, then involve this number to the fame power as the given number, and call the reſult the ſuppoſed cube; then : As twice the ſuppoſed cube + the given cube; is to twice the given cube + the ſuppoſed cube; ſo is the root of the ſuppoſed cube; to the root required, nearly.

3. IF a greater degree of exactneſs is required, involve the root already found, to the third power, and

call

call the result the supposed cube, with which proceed as as before, and so on, to any degree of exactness.

 Note. *When the root is finite, you may sometimes
 save the trouble of repeating an operation, by increasing the right hand figure of the root found, by
 unity.*

EXAMPLES.

Find the cube root of 1367631.

OPERATION.

First, 1367631 *is the given number prepared for extraction, the root of whose first period* (1) *is* 1 ; *then*
100 × 100 × 100 = 1000000 = *supposed cube* ; *and,*

as 1000000 × 2 + 1367631 : 1367631 × 2 + 1000000 ::
100, *i. e.* 3367631 : 3735262 :: 100
          100

   3367631)373526200(110
    3367631 +1

      3676310 111 = *root requir.*
      3367631

      3086790

Required the cube root of 729001101.

First, 729001101 *is the given number pointed, and
the root of the first period* (729) = 9 ; *therefore* 900 ×
900 × 900 = 729000000 = *supposed cube* ; *then,*

as 729000000 × 2 + 729001101 : 729001101 × 2 +
72900000.0 :: 900.

           That

That is, 2187001101 : 2187002202 :: 900
                                          900
                                    ____

. 2187001101)1968301981800(900.0004=
                1968300990<del>9</del>   [*root nearly.*
         ____

                        9909000000.

THE cube root of a Vulgar Fraction, is found by extracting the root of the numerator and denominator.

PROBLEM IV.

To extract the roots of powers in general.

RULE.

1. LET the index of the power whofe root is to be extracted, be denoted by *n*.

2. POINT the given number into periods of as many figures each, as there are units in *n*, beginning at the unit's place ; and if there are integers and decimals together, let them be pointed both ways from unity.

3. FIND the root of the firft period, by the help of the table of powers, and this will be the firft figure of the root.

4. SUBTRACT the *n* power of the firft figure of the root, from the firft period, and to the remainder annex the firft figure of the next period, which refult call your dividend.

5 INVOLVE the root now found to the *n*—1 power, and multiply the refult with *n* for your divifor.

6. DIVIDE, and the quotient will be the fecond figure of the root.

7. INVOLVE all the root now found to the *n* power, and fubtract it (always) from as many periods, as
                                                    you

you have found figures of the root : But if the number to be subtracted, is greater than the aforesaid periods, the last figure of the root is too great, which must therefore be diminished, so that the *n* power of the root now found, may be taken from the aforesaid periods.

8. To the remainder annex the first figure of the next period for a new dividend, then find a new divisor as before; and so on, till the whole be done.

EXAMPLES.

Required the cube root of 61209.566621 :

OPERATION.

Here n $=3$, *therefore the given number pointed is* 61209.566621, *and the nearest root of the first period* (61) *is* 3, *which is the first figure of the root, the* n *power of which is* $3\times3\times3=27$; *and* $61-27=34$, *which having the first figure of the next period annexed to it, becomes* $342=$ *first dividend, and* $3\times3\times3=27=$ *first divisor: Whence,* 27)342(9$=$ *second figure of the root, and the whole of the root now found is* 39; *therefore,* $39\times39\times39=59319=$ n *power of* 39, *which being subtracted from the two first periods, leaves* 1890, *and* 18905$=$ *second dividend; also,* $39\times39\times3=4563=$ *second divisor; whence,* 4563)18905(4$=$ *third figure of the root. Again,* $394\times394\times394=61162984$, *which subtracted from the three first periods, leaves* 46582, *then,* 465826$=$ *third dividend, and* $394\times394\times3=$ 465708$=$ *third divisor; whence,* 465708)465826(1 $=$*fourth and last figure of the root, and because there are two periods of decimals in the given number, the root required is* 39.41; *for* $39.41\times39.41\times39.41=$ 61209.566621$=$ *the number whose root was required: Whence, &c.*

Required the 6th root of 148035889.

OPERATION.

*First, extract the square root, and then the cube root
of that result will give the root required:*

Thus, 148035889(12167
      1
      ——

22) 48
 2 44
 ————————

241) 403
  1 241
 ————————

2426) 16258
   6 14556
 ————————

24327)170289
      170289
     ————————
            0

Again, 12167(23 = *root required.*
2×2×2=8
——

2×2×3=12)41
23×23×23=12167
     ————————
            0

The same at one operation :

Thus, 148035889(23 *as before.*
2×2×2×2×2×2=64
        ————

2×2×2×2×2×3=96)840
23×23×23×23×23×23=148035889
            ————————

In

In extracting the roots of heigher powers, it will be beſt to extract ſquare root out of ſquare root ſucceſſively, as often as the index of the given power is diviſible by 2 : Thus, in the 16th power, the index (16) is diviſible by 2, four times; for $16 \div 2 = 8$, $8 \div 2 = 4$, $4 \div 2 = 2$, and $2 \div 2 = 1$: Whence it follows, that the root of the 16th power may be obtained by four ſeveral extractions of the ſquare root; and the like may be ſhewn of all the even powers.

THE END OF BOOK FIRST.

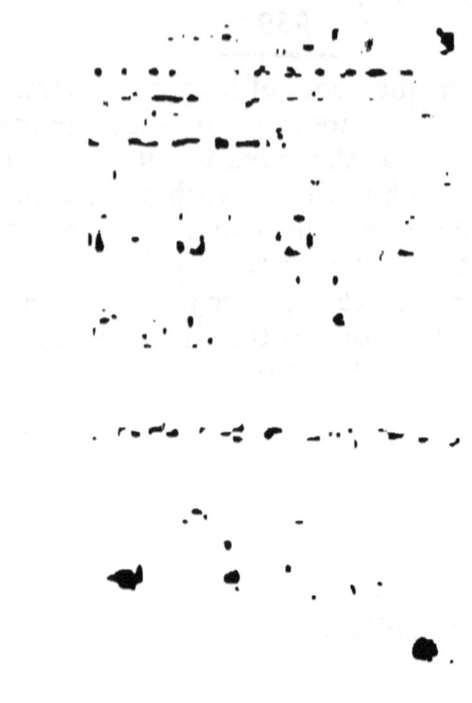

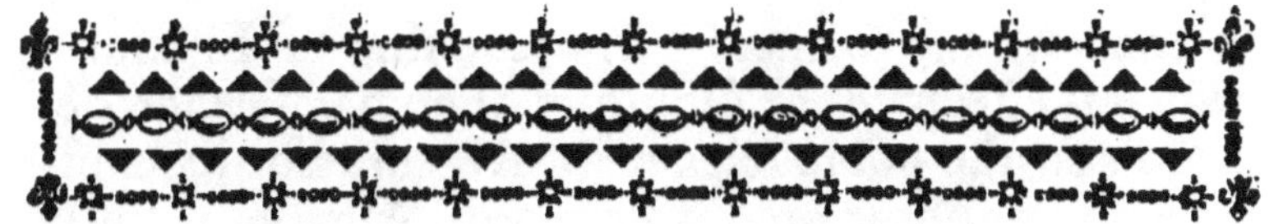

BOOK II.

OF ALGEBRA.

CHAP. I.

Of DEFFINITIONS

AND

ILLUSTRATIONS.

ALGEBRA, one of the moſt important branches of mathematical ſcience, is a method of computation by ſigns and ſymbols, which have been invented and found uſeful for that purpoſe. Its invention is of the higheſt antiquity, and has juſtly challanged the praiſe and admiration of the learned in all ages. Arithmetic is indeed uſeful, and is not to be the leſs valued, becauſe it is allowed to be the moſt clear and evident of the ſciences; yet it is confined in its object, and partial in its application. Geometry for clearneſs of principles, and elegance of demonſtration, no leſs deſerves, than commands our eſteem; but the many beautiful theories, that ariſe from the application of Algebra and Geometry to each other, fully evince the excellency and exten-

H h

ſiveneſs

livenefs of the former. The doctrine of Fluxions, which is efteemed the fublimity of human fcience, depends on the noble fcience of Algebra for its exiftance and application. In a word, Algebra is juftly efteemed the key to all our mathematical inquiries.

In Algebra, like quantities are thofe which have the fame letters : Thus, ax and ax are like quantities; but ax and dx are unlike quantities.

Given or abfolute numbers, are thofe whofe values are known : Thus, 6, 7, &c. are given numbers, becaufe their refpective values are known ; but the quantities x, y, &c. are not given quantities, becaufe their values are not known, and are therefore called unknown quantities.

Simple quantities are fuch as have but one term : Thus, b, axb, and xyz, are fimple whole quantities, and $\frac{eb}{b}$ and $\frac{ab}{cd}$ are fimple fractional quantities.

Compound quantities are fuch as confift of feveral terms connected by the figns $+$ and $-$: Thus, $a+b+c-d$ and $ax-xy$ are compound whole quantities, and $\frac{a}{b}+\frac{c}{d}-\frac{dx}{b}$; $\frac{a+b}{c-d}$ are compound fractional quantities. Compound quantities have fometimes a line drawn over them; as $\overline{a+b+c-d}$.

Co-efficients are numbers prefixed to quantities, denoting how many times the quantity to which they are prefixed, ought to be taken : Thus, $3a$ denotes that the quantity a is to be taken 3 times ; alfo, na fhews that the quantity a is to be taken as many times as there are units in n : Therfore, co-efficients multiply the quantities to which they are prefixed ; and quantities which have no co-efficient prefixed to them, are always underftood to have an unit for their co-efficient : Thus, a is $1a$, x $1x$, &c.

A

A POSITIVE, or an affirmative quantity, is a quantity having the sign + before it; as + a : Also, all quantities that have no signs set before them, as the leading quantity generally hath none, are underftood to have the sign +, and are therefore called positive quantities.

WHEN quantities have the sign — before them, they are called negative quantities : As — a, — x; and when any quantity is to be diftinguifhed, as a quantity to be fubtracted, the sign — muft be placed immediately before it.

QUANTITIES are faid to have like signs, when they are all + or all —.

UNLIKE signs is when the signs are + and —.

A QUANTITY confifting of two terms, as, $\overline{a+b}$, is called a binominal; $\overline{a+b+c}$, a trinominal ; $\overline{a+b+c+d}$, a quadrinominal, &c.

A RESIDUAL quantity, is the difference of two quntities. Thus, $\overline{a-b}$, is a refidual quantity.

THE letters made ufe of to reprefent the unknown quantities, are thofe of the laft part of the alphabet, and the letters of the firft part, reprefent thofe that are known.

THE principal signs by which quantities are managed in Algebra, are the following, in addition to thofe made ufe of in the firft book of this treatife.

Signs, and Explanations.

$\sqrt{}$ is the fign of the fquare root.

$\sqrt[3]{}$ ——————— of the cube root.

$\sqrt[n]{}$ ——————— of the n root.

$\pm$ ——————— of more or lefs.

$\sqrt{x}$

$\sqrt{x}$ or $x^{\frac{1}{2}}$ denotes the square root of x.

$\sqrt[3]{x}$ or $x^{\frac{1}{3}}$ the cube root of x.

$\sqrt{\overline{a+b}}$ or $\overline{a+b}|^{\frac{1}{2}}$ the square root of $\overline{a+b}$.

$\sqrt[n]{\overline{a+b}}$ or $\overline{a+b}|^{\frac{1}{n}}$ the n root of $\overline{a+b}$.

$\dfrac{1}{a}$ the reciprocal of a.

$\dfrac{y}{x}$ the reciprocal of $\dfrac{x}{y}$.

$a \pm b$ the sum or difference of a and b.

A X I O M S.

1. If to those quantities that are equal, there be added the same quantity, their sum will be equal.

2. If from those quantities that are equal, there be taken the same quantity, the remainders will be equal.

3. If those quantities which are equal, be multiplied with the same quantity, their products will be equal.

4. If those quantities that are equal, be divided by the same quantity, the quotients will also be equal.

5. Two quantities respectively equal to a third, are equal to each other.

6. Equal powers, or roots of equal quantities, are equal to each other.

7. If to any whole number, there be added any other whole number, the sum will be a whole number.

8. If from any whole number, there be taken any other whole number, what remains will also be a whole number.

9. IF any whole number be multiplied with any other whole number, the product will also be a whole number.

CHAP. II.

ADDITION of WHOLE QUANTITIES.

ADDITION confifts of three cafes.

CASE I.

When the quantities are alike, and have like figns.

RULE.

ADD the co-efficients together, and to their fum annex the common quantity, prefixing the common fign.

EXAMPLES.

$2ab$	$-2x$	$-3xy$	$3x-4a$	$3x^2+\ b$
$2ab$	$-6x$	$-2xy$	$2x-2a$	$2x^2+3b$
$6ab$	$-\ x$	$-10xy$	$6x-4a$	$6x^2+2b$
$3ab$	$-5x$	$-2xy$	$2x-\ a$	$1x^2+3b$
$4ab$	$-4x$	$-\ xy$	$x-\ a$	$3x^2+\ b$
$17ab$	$-18x$	$-18xy$	$14x-12a$	$15x^2+10b$

$$2\,av - 3\,xy^2 + 2\,az - b - 4\,w^{\frac{1}{2}} - 6\,a + 3 - 2\,d$$

$$10\,av - xy^2 + 3\,az - 3\,b - 6\,w^{\frac{1}{2}} - 2\,a + 1 - 8\,d$$

$$av - 6\,xy^2 + 9\,az - b - w^{\frac{1}{2}} - a + 0 - d$$

$$13\,av - 10\,xy^2 + 14\,az - 5\,b - 11\,w^{\frac{1}{2}} - 9a + 4 - 11\,d\ \textit{sum.}$$

C A S E II.

When the quantities are alike, but have unlike signs.

R U L E.

1. ADD all the affirmative quantities into one sum by the last rule, and the negative into another.

2. SUBTRACT their co-efficients, the less from the greater, and to their difference, prefix the sign of the greater, annexing the common quantity.

THE reason of the foregoing rule will appear evident, if you put $a =$ debt due to B, and $- a$ the want of a debt, or a debt due from B; then the balance is evidently equal o, or $+ a - a = 0$: Whence, &c.

EXAMPLES.

$$- ay$$
$$+ ay$$
$$+ 4\,ay$$
$$- 3\,ay$$
$$- 6\,ay$$

$- 10\,ay =$ *sum of the negative.*
$+ 5\,ay =$ *sum of the affirmative.*

$- 5\,ay =$ *sum required.*

$$+ 4\,a - 2\,y$$
$$+ 3\,a + 6\,y$$
$$- 8\,a + 2\,y$$
$$- 10\,a - 9\,y$$

$- 18\,a - 11\,y$
$+ 7\,a + 8\,y$

$-11\,a - 3\,y$
$$3\,d^2$$

$$3 d^2 + 8 d \sqrt{x^2 + yy}$$
$$-4 d^2 - 2 d \sqrt{x^2 + yy}$$
$$-7 d^2 - 8 d \sqrt{x^2 + yy}$$

$$-8 d^2 - 2 d \sqrt{x^2 + yy}$$

$$-3 a + 4 d - w^2$$
$$- a - 9 d + w^2$$

$$-4 a - 5 d \qquad *$$

CASE III.

When the quantities are unlike, and have unlike signs.

RULE.

WRITE the quantities one after another with their proper figns, and they will be the fum required.

Note. *If there be like quantities given, you muft collect them by the preceding rules.*

EXAMPLES.

$$-3 a$$
$$+4 b$$
$$-2 c$$
$$-8 d$$

$$-3 a + 4 b - 2 c - 8 d = fum.$$

$$7 cy + 99 y$$
$$-4 d + 7 c - y$$

$$7 cy + 99 y - 4 d + 7 c - y = fum.$$

$$3 w^2 + 27 y^3$$
$$-2 y^{\frac{1}{2}} - 2 dc + 2 y^{\frac{1}{2}}$$

$$3 w^2 + 27 y^3 - 2 dc$$

$$4 abv + 4 \sqrt{av^2}$$
$$- cb^2 + 96 - ^3 \sqrt{a^2} - 4 abv$$

$$4 \sqrt{av^2} - cb^2 - ^3 \sqrt{a^2} + 96$$

CHAP.

CHAP. III.

SUBTRACTION of WHOLE QUANTITIES.

ALGEBRAIC Subtraction is performed by the following general

RULE.

CHANGE the figns of the quantities in the fubtrahend (or fuppofe them in your mind to be changed) then add the quantities with their figns changed, to the number from which fubtraction is to be made, by the rules of the laft chapter, and their fum will be the remainder required.

THE reafon of this rule will appear obvious, when we confider that fubtraction is the revrfe of addition; and therefore, to fubtract an affirmative or negative quantity, is the fame thing as to add its oppofite kind: Whence, if $-a$ is to be taken from $+a$, the difference will be $+2a$, for if the remainder $2a$ be added to the fubtrahend $-a$, their fum will be $=a$ $=$ the number from which fubtraction was made: Whence, &c.

EXAMPLES.

From	$4a$	$4bu-3b^2$	$3zy+6a-5$
Take	$3a$	$2bu-2b^2$	$4zy+\ a+4+6$
Remains	a	$2bu-\ b^2$	$-zy+5a-9-6$

34 v^t

$$34\,v^{\frac{1}{3}}+6\,bc+7\,c^2b^2 \qquad 3^3\,\sqrt{}\;aw-yb+6\,dy$$
$$-16\,v^{\frac{1}{3}}+16\;-4\,c^2b^2 \qquad -2^3\,\sqrt{}\;aw-yb+6\,dy$$
$$\overline{50\,v^{\frac{1}{3}}+6\,bc-16+11\,c^2b^2 \quad 5^3\,\sqrt{}\;aw-yb \qquad *}$$

If any doubt arife, refpecting the truth of the peration, add the remainder to the fubtrahend, ʃhich fum muft be equal to the other number.

CHAP. IV.

Of MULTIPLICATION.

ALGEBRAIC Multiplication confifts of three cafes.

CASE I.

When both the factors are fimple quantities.

RULE.

MULTIPLY the co-efficients together, and to their roduct annex all the letters in both factors, as in a ʼord; this expreffion being wrote with its proper gn, will give the product required.

Note. *Like figns give* +, *and unlike figns* — *for the product.*

I i   *EXAMPLES,*

EXAMPLES.

$$+ 3\,a \qquad 3\,abc \qquad -21\,yy \qquad -3\,wyy$$
$$+ 4\,v \qquad -\ 6\,a \qquad\ \ 2\,y \qquad -2\,a$$
$$\overline{+12\,av \quad -18\,aabc \quad -42\,yyy \quad +6\,awyy\ \textit{product.}}$$

CASE II.

When one of the factors is a compound quantity.

RULE.

1. Write the compound quantity for the multiplicand, and the simple quantity for the multiplier.

2. Obtain the product of the multiplier with every particular term of the multiplicand, by the last rule, and place the terms of the product one after another, with their proper signs, found as in the last rule, and you will have the product required.

EXAMPLES.

$$a + b \qquad 3\,ab + cd \qquad 2\,aa + 2\,ab + bb$$
$$a \qquad\quad d \qquad\qquad 2\,a$$
$$\overline{aa + ab \quad 3\,abd + cdd \quad 4\,aaa + 4\,aab + 2\,abb}$$

$$au - 4\,cv + 34 \qquad 27\,ddd - aaa$$
$$-3y \qquad\qquad\qquad 3\,w$$
$$\overline{-3\,auy + 12\,cvy - 102\,y \quad 81\,dddw - 3\,aaaw.}$$

CASE III.

When both the factors are compound quantities.
RULE.

R U L E.

MULTIPLY every particular term of the multiplier, with all the several terms of the multiplicand, as in the last rule, the several products collected into one sum by the rules of addition, will give the whole product required.

EXAMPLES.

$$
\begin{array}{l}
v + y \\
v + y \\
\hline
vv + vy \\
\quad + vy + yy \\
\hline
vv + 2\,vy + yy
\end{array}
\qquad
\begin{array}{l}
a - b \\
a + b \\
\hline
aa - ab \\
\quad + ab - bb \\
\hline
aa \;\ast\; - bb
\end{array}
\qquad
\begin{array}{l}
v - 2z \\
v + 2z \\
\hline
vv - 2\,vz \\
\quad + 2\,vz - 4\,zz \\
\hline
vv \;\ast\; - 4\,zz
\end{array}
$$

$$
\begin{array}{l}
yy + xx \\
yy - xx \\
\hline
yyyy + yyxx \\
\quad - yyxx - xxxx \\
\hline
yyyy \;\ast\; - xxxx
\end{array}
\qquad
\begin{array}{l}
2xy + x - 4 \\
2x - 1 \\
\hline
4xxy + 2xx - 8x \\
\quad - 2xy - x + 4 \\
\hline
4xxy + 2xx - 2xy - 9x + 4
\end{array}
$$

THAT $+ \times -$ or $- \times +$ gives $-$, and $- \times -$ gives $+$ for the product, is demonstrable several ways, but none more simple than the following. Suppose $a = b$; then $a - b = 0$: Now it is plain, that if this expression be multiplied with any number whatever, the product will be $= 0$: Therefore, suppose $a - b = 0$, is to be multiplied with $+ n$; now it is manifest, the first term of the product $a \times n$ will be positive; or $+ na$, because both the factors are positive;

tive ; confequently the other term of the product $+ n$ $\times - b$ muft be negative, or $- nb$; for both terms of the product taken together, muft deftroy each other, and their amount $= 0$; that is, $na - nb = 0$: Confequently $+ \times -$, or $- \times +$ gives $-$ for the product.

Again, fuppofe $a - b = 0$, be multiplied with $- n$; the firft term of the product $- n \times a$ will be negative, or $- na$, by what has been proved : Confequently, the other term $- n \times - b$ will be pofitive, or $+ nb$; for both terms taken together muft $= 0$; thus, $- na + nb = 0$: Confequently, $- \times -$ gives $+$ for the product.   *Q. E. D.*

CHAP. V.

Of DIVISION.

DIVISION being the converfe of multiplication ; it follows, that the quotient muft be fuch a quantity, that if multiplied with the divifor, will produce the dividend ; confequently, like figns in divifion give $+$, and unlike figns $-$ for the quotient.

CASE I.

When the divifor is a fimple quantity.

RULE.

1. WRITE down the quantities, in form of a vulgar fraction, having the divifor for the denominator.

2. EXPUNGE all thofe quantities in the dividend and divifor, that are alike ; and divide the co-efficients

cients of the quantities by any number that will divide them without a remainder; the refult will be the quotient fought.

EXAMPLES.

$$\frac{8\,au}{2\,a}=4\,u \text{ the quotient}; \quad \frac{24\,zy-4\,z}{2\,z}=12y-2; \quad \frac{az}{a}=z$$

$$\frac{ab+bd}{-b}=-a-d; \quad \frac{12\,adz-8\,dcz}{-4\,z}=-3\,ad+2\,dc$$

$$\frac{16\,bcu}{12\,c}=\frac{4\,bu}{3}; \quad \frac{8\,uzy}{12\,dcu}=\frac{2\,yz}{3\,dc}.$$

IF you divide any quantity by itfelf, the quotient will be unity or 1 : Thus, $\frac{x}{x}=1$; for if the quotient be multiplied with the divifor, the product will be the dividend ; thus, $x \times 1 = x$: Confequently, if any term of the dividend be like that of your divifor, the quotient of that term will be 1 :   As in

$$\text{Thefe, } \frac{av+bv+v}{v}=a+b+1; \quad \frac{2\,ab+2\,bc-2}{2}=ab$$

$$+bc-1; \text{ alfo, } \frac{3\,vyz-3\,vyz}{3\,vyz}=1-1=0.$$

C A S E II.

When the divifor and dividend are both compound quantities.

R U L E.

1. RANGE the quantities in the divifor and dividend, according to the order of the letters.

2. FIND how often the firft term of the divifor is contained in the firft term of the dividend, and place the refult in the quotient.   3.

3. MULTIPLY the quotient term thus found, with the whole divisor, subtract the product from the dividend, and to the remainder bring down the next term of the dividend ; which forms a new dividend.

4. DIVIDE the firſt term of your new dividend, by the firſt term of your diviſor, as before ; and ſo on, until nothing remains, as in common Arithmetic, and you will have the quotient required.

EXAMPLES.

Suppoſe it is required to divide $2yyy + 8yy + 8y$ by $yy + 2y$; which being ranged as directed in the rule, the operation will ſtand

Thus, $yy + 2y$) $2yyy + 8yy + 8y$ ($2y + 4$
$$2yyy + 4yy$$

$$* \quad +4yy +8y$$
$$+4yy +8y$$

$$* \quad *$$

Here the firſt term of the dividend, which is $2yyy$, being divided by the firſt term of the diviſor yy, the quotient is $2y$; which being placed in the quotient as in vulgar Arithmetic, and multiplied with all the terms of the diviſor, the product is $2yyy + 4yy$, which ſubtracted from the dividend, the remainder is $4yy$, to which annex the next term of the dividend $8y$, the new dividend becomes $4yy + 8y$, and dividing $4yy$ by yy, the quotient is 4 ; which being annexed to the quotient term before found, and multiplied with every term of the diviſor, produces $4yy + 8y$, which ſubtracted from the laſt dividend, the remainder is nothing ; and having brought down all the terms of the propoſed dividend, the work is done ; therefore, $2y + 4$ is the true quotient, for $2y + 4 \times yy + 2y = 2yyy + 8yy + 8y =$ the given dividend.

Divide

Divide $6\,avv - 3\,av - 2\,vy + 2\,v + 2y - 1$ by $2\,v - 1$.

OPERATION.

$$2v - 1) \; 6\,avv - 3\,av - 4\,vy + 2\,v + 2y - 1 \; (3\,av - $$
$$6\,avv - 3\,av \qquad\qquad\qquad [2y + 1$$
$$\rule{4cm}{0.4pt}$$
$$* \qquad * \quad -4\,vy$$
$$-4\,vy \qquad\qquad +2y$$
$$\rule{5cm}{0.4pt}$$
$$* \quad +2\,v \quad * \quad -1$$
$$2\,v \qquad\qquad -1$$
$$\rule{5cm}{0.4pt}$$
$$* \qquad\qquad *$$

Divide $vvv - yyy$ by $v - y$.

OPERATION.

$$v - y) \; vvv - yyy \, (vv + vy + yy$$
$$vvv - vvy$$
$$\rule{3.5cm}{0.4pt}$$
$$* \quad + vvy - yyy$$
$$+ vvy - vyy$$
$$\rule{3.5cm}{0.4pt}$$
$$* \quad + vyy - yyy$$
$$+ vyy - yyy$$
$$\rule{3.5cm}{0.4pt}$$
$$* \qquad *$$

Divide 1 by $1 - v$

OPERATION.

OPERATION.

$$1 - v) \; 1 \qquad (.1 + v + vv + \text{\&c.}$$
$$\underline{1 - v}$$
$$* + v$$
$$+ v - vv$$
$$\overline{\qquad\qquad}$$
$$* + vv$$
$$+ vv - vvv$$
$$\overline{\qquad\qquad}$$
$$* \qquad + vvv$$

In this example, the divisor cannot exactly be found in the dividend, without a remainder; and you have what is called an infinite series for the quotient; that is, if the division could be carried on *ad infinitum*, you would have a series of terms for the quotient, that would come infinitely near to an equality with the true quotient, and therefore might be confidered as fuch; for when ratios from that of equality, are but indefinitely little, or lefs than can be affigned, they may be confidered as equal; but as it is impoffible to carry on the divifion *ad infinitum*, or take in a fufficient number of terms to exprefs the true quotient: Therefore, in general you need only take a few of the leading terms for the quotient, which will be fufficiently near for moft purpofes. : But more of this in its proper place, fince the knowledge of Algebraic fractions, is in moft cafes, abfolutely neceffary, in order to obtain an infinite feries by divifion.

CASE III.

When the quantities in the divifor cannot be found in the dividend.

RULE.

R U L E.

PLACE the dividend above, and the divisor below a fmall line, in form of a vulgar fraction; and the expreffion will be the quotient required.

EXAMPLES.

The quotient of a divided by b, is $\frac{a}{b}$.

The quotient of 21 bx $\div$ d $= \frac{21\ bx}{d}$.

The quotient of 8 ac + dc $\div$ zx + ab $= \frac{8\ ac + dc}{zx + ab}$

CHAP. VI.

INVOLUTION of WHOLE QUAN-TITIES.

INVOLUTION is the raifing of powers from quantities called roots, and differs from multiplication in this, viz. that in involution the multiplier is conftant, or the fame; therefore when any quantity is drawn into itfelf, and afterwards into that product, and fo on, the mode of operation is called involution, and the number produced, the power, whofe height is ufually denominated by plac-ing numeral figures over the right hand of the root, or quantity to be involved, and are called indices or exponents of the powers which they denominate: Thus, $a^2 = aa$ denominates the fquare of a, $a^3 = aaa$

aaa the cube of a, a^4 the fourth power of a; and generally, a^n the n power of a.

INVOLUTION of fimple quantities is performed by the following

R U L E.

MULTIPLY the index or exponent of the given quantity or root, with the exponent which denominates the power required, making the product the exponent of the power fought.

> Note. *If the quantities to be involved, have co-efficients, the co-efficients muft be involved as in vulgar Arithmetic, to the fame height as the index of the power required denotes.*

EXAMPLES.

The fquare of $a = a^{1 \times 2} = a^2$; *the cube of* $a = a^{1 \times 3} = a^3$; *the fquare of* $a^2 = a^{2 \times 2} = a^4$; *the cube of* $3a^2 = 3 \times 3 \times 3 \times a^{2 \times 3} = 27 a^6$; *the 4th power of* $4x^3y^2 = 4 \times 4 \times 4 \times 4 \times x^{3 \times 4} \times y^{2 \times 4} = 256 x^{12}y^8$; *the n power of* $x = x^{1 \times n} = x^n$.

IF the quantity propofed to be involved is pofitive, all its powers will be pofitive: Alfo, if the quantity propofed be negative, all its powers whofe exponents are even numbers, will likewife be pofitive; becaufe any even number of multiplications of a negative quantity, gives a pofitive one for the product, fince $- \times -$ gives $+$; confequently $- \times - \times - = + \times +$ for the product; therefore, that power of the negative quantity, only is negative, when its exponent

nent is an odd number: As may be feen in the following form,

$$
—a \text{ the root, } \left\{
\begin{array}{l}
—a \\
—a \\
\hline
a^2 = \text{\textit{square}} \\
—a \text{ the root} \\
\hline
—a^3 = \text{\textit{cube}} \\
—a \text{ the root} \\
\hline
a^4 = \text{\textit{4th power}} \\
—a \text{ the root} \\
\hline
—a^5 = \text{\textit{5th power.}}
\end{array}
\right.
$$

INVOLUTION of compound quantities, is performed by the following

RULE.

MULTIPLY the root into itfelf, and then into that
product, and fo on, until the number of multiplications are one lefs than the exponent of the power required; the refult will be the power fought.

EXAMPLES.

Let the binomial $a + b$ be involved to the 5th
power.

OPERATION.

OPERATION.

$a+b$ the root
$a+b$

$aa+ab$
$\quad +ab+bb$

$aa+2ab+bb=$ square
$a+b$

$aaa+2aab+abb$
$\quad +aab+2abb+bbb$

$aaa+3aab+3abb+bbb=$ cube
$a+b$

$aaaa+3aaab+3aabb+abbb$
$\quad +aaab+3aabb+3abbb+bbbb$

$aaaa+4aaab+6aabb+4abbb+bbbb=$ 4th power
$a+b$

$aaaaa+4aaaab+6aaabb+4aabbb+abbbb$
$\quad +aaaab+4aaabb+6aabbb+4abbbb+bbbbb$

$a^5+5a^4b+10a^3b^2+10a^2b^3+5ab^4+b^5=$ 5th do.

Involve

Involve $a - b$ to the 3d power.

OPERATION.

$$a - b$$
$$a - b$$

$$a^2 - ab$$
$$\quad - ab + b^2$$

$$a^2 - 2ab + b^2 = 2d \ power$$
$$a - b$$

$$a^3 - 2a^2b + ab^2$$
$$\quad - a^2b + 2ab^2 - b^3$$

$$a^3 - 3a^2b + 3ab^2 - b^3 = 3d \ power.$$

IT is to be obferved in the foregoing examples.

1. THAT all the terms in the feveral powers, raifed from the binomial $a + b$, are affirmative.

2. THE terms in the feveral powers raifed from the refidual $a - b$, have the figns $+$ and $-$, alternately; the firft term being a pure power of a, is confequently affirmative; the fecond term hath a negative fign, and fo on, alternately; but b is no where found negative, only where its exponent is an odd number; as in $a^3 - 3a^2b + 3ab^2 - b^3$; where the fecond and fourth terms are negative, becaufe the exponent of b in thofe terms, is an odd number.

3. THAT the firft term of any power, either of the binomial or refidual, hath the exponent of the power: That is, the index of the firft term, is equal to the index of the power; but in the reft of the terms following, the exponents of the leading quantity, decreafe in arithmetical progreffion, unity or 1, being the common difference; fo that the quantity a is

never

never found in the laft term ; but the exponents of *b*, on the contrary, increafe in the fame progreffion that the exponents of *a* decreafe ; that is, the quantity *b*, is not to be found in the firft term ; but in the fecond term, its exponent is unity or 1 ; in the third term 2, and fo on in the faid arithmetical progreffion, to the laft term, where its exponent is equal to the exponent of the power.

4. That the number of terms in any power, is one more than the number which denominates that power.

Hence from the foregoing obfervations it follows.

1. That the fum of the exponents of both quantities in any term, are equal to the exponent of the power in which thofe terms belong : Thus, the 6th power of $a + b = a^6 + 6a^5b + 15a^4b^2 + 20a^3b^3 + 15a^2b^4 + 6ab^5 + b^6$, where you will pleafe to obferve, that the fum of the exponents of *a* and *b*, in any term, are equal to the exponent of the power : Thus in the third term, the exponents of *a* and *b*, are 4 and 2, whofe fum $= 6 =$ exponent of the power.

2. The method of writing without a continual involution, the terms in any power of a binomial, or refidual quantity, without their co-efficients : Thus the terms of the 4th power of $x + y$ without their co-efficients, will ftand thus : $x^4 + x^3y + x^2y^2 + xy^3 + y^4$; and the terms of the 4th power of $x - y = x^4 - x^3y + x^2y^2 - xy^3 + y^4$.

In order to find the co-efficients of the feveral terms, it is neceffary to have the co-efficient of one of the terms given : And becaufe the firft term or leading quantity is a pure power, having its index equal to the index of the given power ; its co-efficient is therefore unity or 1 : Confequently, you

have

have the co-efficient of the firſt term given ; thence to find the co-efficients of the reſt of the terms by the following

R U L E.

DIVIDE the co-efficient of the preceding term, by the exponent of y in the given term ; the quotient multiplied with the exponent of x, in the ſame term, increaſed by 1, will give the co-efficient required.
Or,
MULTIPLY the co-efficient of any term, with the exponent of the leading quantity, in the ſame term ; the product divided by the number of terms to that place, will give the co-efficient of the next ſubſequent term.

EXAMPLES.

Given $x^4 + x^3y + x^2y^2 + xy^3 + y^4$, to find the co-efficients of the ſeveral terms.

Firſt, the co-efficient of x^4 is 1 ; thence to find the co-efficient of x^3y : And becauſe the exponent of y in the given term, is unity or 1 ; then per rule, $\frac{1}{1}$ $\times 3 + 1 = 1 \times 4 = 4$, the co-efficient required : Again, $\frac{4}{2} \times 2 + 1 = \frac{4}{2} \times 3 = \frac{12}{2} = 6$, the co-efficient of the third term ; and $\frac{6}{3} \times 1 + 1 = \frac{6}{3} \times 2 = \frac{12}{3} = 4$, the co-efficient of the fourth term ; but the next term hath the exponent of the power, being the laſt term of the 4th power of $x + y$, and conſequently, its co-efficient an unit or 1. Therefore, the co-efficients of the ſeveral terms of the 4th power of $x + y$, are 1, 4, 6, 4, 1.

HENCE

Hence you may obferve, that the co-efficients of the feveral terms increafe, until the exponents of x and y become equal to each other, and then decreafe in the fame order in which they increafed. And generally, the co-efficients of the terms increafe, until the exponents of the two quantities become equal in one term, if the exponent of the power is an even number; and when the exponent is odd, two of the terms will have equal co-efficients, and then decreafe in the fame order. Therefore, in finding the co-efficients, you need only obtain the co-efficients, until they decreafe; the reft of the terms having the fame co-efficients decreafing.

The n power of $x + a = x^n + nx^{n-1}a + n \times \dfrac{n-1}{2}x^{n-2}a^2 + n \times \dfrac{n-1}{2} \times \dfrac{n-2}{3}x^{n-3}a^3$ &c. to $n + 1$, terms.

Let $a + b + c$ be involved to the fecond power.

OPERATION.

$$
\begin{array}{l}
a + b + c \\
a + b + c \\
\hline
a^2 + ab + ac \\
\quad + ab + b^2 + bc \\
\quad\quad + ca + bc + c^2 \\
\hline
a^2 + 2ab + 2ac + b^2 + 2bc + c^2 = \text{2d power.}
\end{array}
$$

CHAP. VII.

Of *MULTIPLICATION* and *DIVISION* of *POWERS* of the *same ROOT.*

MULTIPLICATION of powers of the same root, is performed by the following

RULE.

ADD the exponents of the powers together, and make their sum the exponent of the product.

EXAMPLES.

$$a^3 \times a^2 = a^{3+2} = a^5 \; ; \; 6^2 \times 6^3 = 6^{2+3} = 6^5 =$$
$$7776 \; ; \; 6\,x^3 \times 4\,x^4 = 6 \times 4 \times x^{3+4} = 24\,x^7 \; ; \; -a^4 \times$$
$$a^6 = -a^{10} \; ; \; alfo, \; -a^1 \times -a^2 = a^3 \; ; \; in \; like \; man-$$
$$ner, \; \overline{a-b}|^2 \times \overline{a-b}|^6 = \overline{a-b}|^{2+6} = \overline{a-b}|^8 \; ; \; and$$
$$univerfally, \; a^m \times a^n = a^{m+n}.$$

DIVISION of powers that have the fame root, is effected by the following

RULE.

FROM the exponent of the dividend, fubtract the exponent of the divifor, and the remainder will be the exponent of the quotient.

EXAMPLES.

$$\frac{a^8}{a^6} = a^{8-6} = a^2 \; ; \; \frac{a^3}{a^2} = a^{3-2} = a^1 \; ; \; \frac{a^6 b^4}{a b^2} = a^{6-1}$$

$$b^{4-2} = a^5 b^2 \; ;$$

Alſo, $\dfrac{\overline{a+x}\,|^6}{\overline{a+x}\,|^2} = \overline{a+x}\,|^{6-2} = \overline{a+x}\,|^4 \; ; \; \dfrac{\overline{a+b+c}\,|^{12}}{\overline{a+b+c}\,|^8}$

$= \overline{a+b+c}\,|^4$

HENCE it follows, that in diviſion of powers which have the ſame root, if you divide a leſs power by a greater, the exponent of the quotient will be negative; for we have ſhewn, that to divide any power of a by a, is to ſubtract one from the exponent of the power of a: Thus, $\dfrac{a^2}{a} = a^1$; therefore, $\dfrac{a}{a} = a^{1-1}$

$= a^0$; but $\dfrac{a}{a} = 1$ by the nature of diviſion ; conſequently, $a^0 = 1$ by equality ; and therefore, $\dfrac{1}{a} = \dfrac{a^0}{a}$

$= a^{0-1} = a^{-1}$; and $\dfrac{1}{a^2} = \dfrac{a^0}{a^2} = a^{0-2} = a^{-2}$; and

ſo on for any power of $\dfrac{1}{a}$: Likewiſe, $\dfrac{\overline{x+y}\,|^2}{\overline{x+y}\,|^2} =$

$\overline{x+y}\,|^{2-2} = \overline{x+y}\,|^0 = $ (becauſe, $\dfrac{\overline{x \times y}\,|^2}{\overline{x+y}\,|^2} = 1,$) 1 ;

conſequently, $\dfrac{1}{\overline{x+y}\,|^1} = \dfrac{\overline{x+y}\,|^0}{\overline{x+y}\,|^1} = \overline{x+y}\,|^{-1}$; therefore,

$\dfrac{1}{\overline{x+y}\,|^2} = \dfrac{\overline{x+y}\,|^0}{\overline{x+y}\,|^2} = \overline{x+y}\,|^{0-2} = \overline{x+y}\,|^{-2}$; and $\dfrac{1}{\overline{x+y}\,|^3}$

$= \overline{x+y}\,|^{-3}$. And generally, $\dfrac{1}{\overline{x+y}\,|^{n}} = \dfrac{\overline{x+y}\,|^{0}}{\overline{x+y}\,|^{n}} = \overline{x+y}\,|^{-n}$. Therefore, a^{0}, a^{-1}, a^{-2}, a^{-3}, and, $\overline{x+y}\,|^{0}$, $\overline{x+y}\,|^{-1}$, $\overline{x+y}\,|^{-2}$, $\overline{x+y}\,|^{-3}$, and $\overline{x+y}\,|^{-n}$ respectively $= 1, \dfrac{1}{a}, \dfrac{1}{a^{2}}, \dfrac{1}{a^{3}}, 1, \dfrac{1}{x+y}, \dfrac{1}{\overline{x+y}\,|^{2}}, \dfrac{1}{\overline{x+y}\,|^{3}}, \dfrac{1}{\overline{x+y}\,|^{n}}$, and of which they are positive pow-ers.

HENCE the propriety of using negative exponents.

THE multiplication, and division of powers which have the same root, having negative exponents, is performed by the same rule as those powers which have affirmative ones; that is, add the exponents of the factors in multiplication, and in division subtract them.

EXAMPLES.

a^{-2} multiplied with $a^{-4} = a^{-2-4} = a^{-6}$; $a^{-3} \times a^{-1} = a^{-1-3} = a^{-4}$; $a^{-2} \times a^{2} = a^{-2+2} = a^{0} = 1 = a \div a$, and $\sqrt[-4]{a} \times \sqrt[+2]{a} = \sqrt[-2]{a}$.

$a^{-6} \div a^{-3} =$ (by the nature of subtraction) $a^{-6+3} = a^{-3} = 1 \div a^{3}$; and $a^{-3} \div a^{-6} = a^{-3+6} = a^{3}$; but by the nature of multiplication and division, $a^{-3} \div a^{-6} = a^{-3} \div a^{-3} \times a^{-3} = 1 \div a^{-3} = a^{0} \div a^{-3} = a^{0+3} = a^{3}$; likewise,

$$\sqrt[-4]{z+y}$$

$$-4\sqrt{z+y} \div\, -2\sqrt{z+y} = -4 + 2\sqrt{z+y} =$$
$$-2\sqrt{z+y}.$$

CHAP. VIII.

EVOLUTION of WHOLE QUANTI-TIES.

EVOLUTION is the unfolding of powers produced by involution; thereby difcovering the roots with which they are compofed, and is therefore the reverfe of involution.

THE rule for evolution of powers, whofe roots are fimple quantities, flows from this confideration ; that to involve any fimple quantity to any power, is to multiply the exponent of the quantity, with the exponent of the power ; making the product the exponent of the required power ; confequently, if the exponent of the power, be divided by the index which denominates the root required, the quotient will be the exponent of the root. Therefore, when the exponent of the power whofe root is required, is not a multiple of the number which denominates the kind of root required ; it follows, that the root will be expreffed by a fractional exponent : Thus, the fquare root of $a^5 = a^{\frac{5}{2}}$, and the cube root of $a^4 = a^{\frac{4}{3}}$. Whence, we have the following rule for evolution of fimple quantities.

RULE.

EXTRACT the root of the co-efficient, as in vulgar arithmetic, and divide the exponent of the power,

by

by the index of the root rquired; making the root of the co-efficient, the co-efficient of the root.

EXAMPLES.

The cube root of $a^9 = a^{\frac{9}{3}} = a^3$: The square root of $4a^4 = 2a^{\frac{4}{2}} = 2a^2$: The cube root of $64\,x^9 a^3 = {}^3\sqrt{64} \times x^{\frac{9}{3}} a^{\frac{3}{3}} = 4x^3 a$: The 4th root of $256\,a^4 b^{12} = {}^4\sqrt{256} \times a^{\frac{4}{4}} b^{\frac{12}{4}} = 4\,ab^3$: The cube root of $-27\,a^3 = -3a^3$. But the fquare root of a negative quantity; as $-x^2$, cannot be affigned, becaufe no even number of multiplications, either of a pofitive or negative quantity, can give a negative one for the product, as was fully explained in chapter VI; therefore, the fquare root of $-x^2$ is an imaginary quantitiy: And fince the fquare of any negative or pofitive quantity, is always pofitive; it follows, that the fquare root of x^2 may be $+x$, or $-x$. Therefore, when the number which denominates the root to be extracted, is odd, the fign of the root will the fame as the fign of the power; and when the number which denominates the root, is even, the fign of the root may be either $+$ or $-$: Thus, the cube root of $-27\,a^{15} b^9 = -3\,a^5 b^3$, and the 4th root of $16\,a^8 x^4 = 2\,a^2 x$ or $-2\,a^2 x$; the the n power of $x^m = x^{\frac{m}{n}}$

Evolution of compound quantities, requires a different method of proceeding from that of fimple ones.

To extract the fquare root of a compound quantity we have the following

RULE.

R U L E.

1. RANGE the quantities according to the order of the letters, fo that the firft term fhall have the index of the power.

2. FIND the root of the firft term, as in evolution of fimple quantities, and place it in the quotient.

3. SUBTRACT the fquare of the root thus found, from the firft term of the power propofed, and to the remainder bring down the reft of the terms for a dividend.

4. DIVIDE the firft term of the dividend, by double the root, and write the refult in the quotient, for the fecond term of the root,

5. ADD the laft term of the quotient to your divifor, and multiply their fum with the faid quotient term, fubtracting the product from the dividend; and fo on, to obtain the next term of the root, by the help of thofe already found, in the fame manner as the fecond term was obtained by the help of the firft.

EXAMPLE.

Extract the fquare root of $a^2 + 2ay + y^2 + 2za +2yz + z^2$.

The fquare root of the firft term viz. a^2, is a, which being placed in the quotient, is the firft term of the root, (fee the operation annexed) which fquared and fubtracted from the firft term of the propofed power, leaves no remainder ; the reft of the terms being brought down for a dividend, the firft term, viz. $2ay$ divided by $2a$ (the double of the root) gives y for the fecond term of the root ; which with the divifor, being multiplied with y, and the product fubtracted from the firft terms of the

dividend,

dividend, the remainder is nothing; the remaining terms being brought down as before and divided by the double of the two firſt terms of the root, gives z for the third term of the root, which added to the diviſor and multiplied with z, the product ſubtracted as before, leaves no remainder: Therefore, the root ſought, is $\overline{a+y+z}$, for $\overline{a+y+z} \times \overline{a+y+z} = a^2 + 2ay + y^2 + 2az + 2yz + z^2.$

OPERATION.

$$a^2 + 2ay + y^2 + 2az + 2yz + z^2 (a+y+z = root$$
$$a^2$$
$$2a+y)^* + 2ay + y^2 + 2az + 2yz + z^2$$
$$2ay + y^2$$
$$\overline{\qquad\qquad}$$
$$* \qquad *$$
$$2a+2y+z) + 2az + 2yz + z^2$$
$$2az + 2yz + z^2$$
$$\overline{\qquad\qquad}$$
$$* \qquad * \qquad *$$

And univerſally, to extract any root.

RULE.

1. Range the terms of the given power, as in the laſt rule.

2. Extract the root of the firſt term as before, and place it in the quotient for the firſt term of the root.

3. Subtract the power of the root thus found, and to the remainder bring down the next term for a dividend.

4. Involve the root to a dimenſion lower by unity than the number which denominates the root required, and multiply the reſult with the index of the

root

root to be extracted, which product call your divisor.

5. FIND how often the divisor is contained in the dividend, and write the result in the quotient for the second term of the root.

6. INVOLVE the whole of the root thus found, to the dimension of the given power, and subtract the result from the given power; and call the remainder a new dividend.

7. INVOLVE the whole of the root in the same manner as you did the first term, and multiply the result as before for a new divisor.

8. DIVIDE as before, and the result will be the third term of the root; and so on, till the whole be finished.

EXAMPLES.

Required the square root of $16y^6 - 48y^5 + 36y^4 + 96y^2 + 64.$

OPERATION.

$$16y^6 - 48y^5 + 36y^4 - 64y^3 + 96y^2 + 64 \,(\, 4y^3$$
$$16y^6$$

$$\times 2 = 8y^3 \,)\, -48y^5 \,(\, -6y^2$$

$$16y^6 - 48y^5 + 36y^4 = \overline{4y^3 - 6y^2}|^2$$

$$\overline{4y^3 - 6y^2}|^1 \times 2 = 8y^3 - 12y^2 \,)\, -64y^3 + 96y^2 + 64 \,(\, -8$$

$$16y^6 - 48y^5 + 36y^4 - 64y^3 + 96y^2 + 64$$

$$*\qquad*\qquad*\qquad*\qquad*\qquad*$$

Therefore, $4y^3 - 6y^2 - 8$ is the root required.

Required

Required the cube root of $8a^3 + 12a^2b + 6ab^2 + b^3$.

OPERATION.

$$8a^3 + 12a^2b + 6ab^2 + b^3 \ (2a$$
$$8a^3$$

$$\overline{2a}|^2 \times 3 = 12a^2) \ 12a^2b \ (b$$

$$\overline{2a+b}|^3 = 8a^3 + 12a^2 + b6ab^2 + b^3$$

* * * *

Whence, $2a+b$, *is the root required.*

C H A P. IX.

Of ALGEBRAIC FRACTIONS or BROKEN QUANTITIES.

ALGEBRAIC fractions are formed by the division of quantities incommenfurable to each other : Thus, if x is to be divided by y, it will be (by cafe III, of algebraic divifion) $\frac{x}{y}$, which is an algebraic fraction ; wherein x is the numerator and y the denominator. When fractions are connected with undivided quantities, as $a + \frac{x}{y}$, and $a + \frac{cx \mp z}{a+b}$. they are called mixed quantities ; alfo, if the denominator is lefs than the numerator, the fraction is called improper.

THE various operations, neceffary in managing algebraic fractions, arc comprifed in the following problems.

PROB.

PROBLEM I.

To reduce a mixed quantity to an improper fraction of equal value.

RULE.

MULTIPLY the denominator of the fraction with the integral part, to which product add the numerator, and under their sum, subscribe the denominator, for the fraction required.

EXAMPLES.

$$a + \frac{a}{y} = \frac{a \times y + a}{y} = \frac{ya + a}{y} \; ; \quad au + \frac{a+b}{c} = \frac{au \times c + \overline{a+b}}{c} =$$

$$\frac{cau + a + b}{c} \; ; \quad v + z + \frac{v+z}{a-2} = \frac{\overline{v+z} \times \overline{a-2} + v + z}{a-2} =$$

$$\frac{av + az - 2v - 2z + v + z}{a-2} = \frac{av + az - v - z}{a-2} \; .$$

PROBLEM II.

To reduce an improper fraction to a whole or mixed quantity.

RULE.

DIVIDE the numerator by the denominator for the integral part, and write the denominator under the remainder for the fractional part; and you will have the number required.

EXAMPLES.

EXAMPLES.

$$\frac{ac+ab}{c}=a+\frac{ab}{c}; \quad \frac{ay+2y^2}{a+y}=y+\frac{y}{a+y}; \quad \frac{a^2-y^2}{a}=a+$$

$$\frac{-y^2}{a}; \quad \frac{a^2+b^2}{a-b}=a+b+\frac{2b^2}{a-b}.$$

PROBLEM III.

To reduce fractions of different denominations, to fractions of the same value, that shall have a common denominator.

RULE.

1. REDUCE all mixed quantities to improper fractions.

2. MULTIPLY every numerator separately taken, into all the denominators except its own, for the several numerators, and all the denominators together for the common denominator, which being wrote under the several numerators, will give the fractions required.

EXAMPLES.

Reduce $\frac{x}{2}$ and $\frac{y}{4}$ to fractions of the same value, having a common denominator. First, $x\times4=4x$ and $y\times2=2y$ for the numerators : Then, $2\times4=8$, the common denominator. Therefore, $\frac{4x}{8}$ and $\frac{2y}{8}$ are the fractions required.

Reduce $\frac{v}{y}$, $\frac{z}{v}$, and $\frac{a}{c}$ to equivalent fractions, having a common denominator.

$$v\times v$$

$$v \times v \times c = cv^2$$
$$z \times y \times c = cyz$$
$$a \times y \times v = ayv$$
$\Big\} = $ *numerators.*

$c \times v \times y = cvy =$ *common denominator.*

Therefore, $\dfrac{cv^2}{cvy}$, $\dfrac{cyz}{cvy}$ and $\dfrac{ayv}{cvy}$ are the fractions re-

quired; which are respectively equal to $\dfrac{v}{y}$, $\dfrac{z}{v}$, $\dfrac{a}{c}$;

for $\dfrac{cv^2}{cvy} = $ (by the nature of division) $\dfrac{v}{y}$; and the like

for the reft. Whence, &c.

Reduce, $\dfrac{a-v}{2v}$, $\dfrac{vb}{2}$, and $\dfrac{ay}{v}$ to a common de-

nominator, retaining their refpective values.

$$\overline{a-v} \times 2 \times v = 2av - 2v^2$$
$$vb \times 2v \times v = 2v^3 b$$
$$ay \times 2v \times 2 = 4avy$$
$\Big\} = $ *numerators.*

$2v \times 2 \times v = 4v^2 =$ *common denominator.*

Therefore, $\dfrac{2av - 2v^2}{4v^2}$, $\dfrac{2v^3 b}{4v^2}$, and $\dfrac{4avy}{4v^2}$ are the

fractions required.

$a + \dfrac{b}{x}$, $\dfrac{cx}{ba}$, and $\dfrac{bc}{ax}$ reduced to a common denomin-

ator, are $\dfrac{bx^2 a^3 + b^2 a^2 x}{ba^2 x^2}$, $\dfrac{cax^3}{ba^2 x^2}$, and $\dfrac{b^2 acx}{ba^2 x^2}$.

PROBLEM IV.

To find the greateft common meafure of algebraic fractions.

R U L E.

R U L E.

1. Range the quantities as in divifion.

2. Divide the greater quantity by the lefs, and the laft divifor by the laft remainder, until nothing remains; taking care to expunge thofe quantities that are common to each divifor; and the laft divifor will be the greateft common meafure required.

EXAMPLES.

Find the greateft common meafure of $\dfrac{va - a^2}{vy^2 - y^2 a}$.

OPERATION.

$$va - a^2)\ vy^2 - y^2 a$$
$$\text{Or, } v - a\ )\ vy^2 - y^2 a\ (\ y^2$$
$$vy^2 - y^2 a$$
$$\text{*} \qquad \text{*}$$

Therefore, $v - a$, is the greateft common meafure required.

Find the greateft common meafure of $\dfrac{a^2 - b^2}{a^2 - 2ab + b^2}$.

OPERATION.

OPERATION.

$$a^2 - 2ab + b^2)\; a^2 - b^2\; (\; 1$$
$$a^2 - 2ab + b^2$$

$$*\qquad 2ab - 2b^2)a^2 - 2ab + b^2$$
$$Or,\;(by\;casting\;out\;2b)\;\; a - b)\; a^2 - 2ab + b^2\; (\; a$$
$$a^2 - ab$$

$$* - ab + b^2)\; a - b$$
$$Or,\;\; a - b)\; a - b\; (\; 1$$
$$a - b$$

$$*\qquad *$$

Therefore, a — b, is the greatest common measure required.

PROBLEM V.

To reduce fractions to their least terms.

RULE.

1. FIND their greatest common measure by the last problem.

2. DIVIDE both terms of the proposed fraction by their greatest common measure, and the quotients will be the respective terms of the fraction, reduced to its least terms.

EXAMPLES.

EXAMPLES.

Reduce $\dfrac{xa + a^2}{xy^2 + y^2a}$ to its leaft terms.

Firft, $xa + a^2) \; xy^2 + y^2a$

  Or, $x + a) \; xy^2 + y^2a (y^2$
$$xy^2 + y^2a$$
$$* \qquad *$$

Then, $x + a) \; xa + a^2 \; (a ==$ *numerator.*
$$xa + a^2$$
$$* \qquad *$$

And, $x + a) \; xy^2 + y^2a \; (y^2 =$ *denominator.*
$$xy^2 + y^2a$$
$$* \qquad *$$

  Therefore, $\dfrac{a}{y^2}$ *is the propofed fraction in its leaft*
terms.

Reduce $\dfrac{y^4 - x^4}{y^5 - x^2y^3}$ to its leaft terms.

Firft, the greateft common meafure is $y^2 - x^2$:

Then, $y^2 - x^2) \dfrac{y^4 - x^4}{y^5 - x^2y^3} = \dfrac{y^2 + x^2}{y^3} =$ *frac. req.*

PROBLEM VI.

To add algebraic fractions.

RULE.

1. PREPARE the given fractions by reduction ;
that is, mixed quantities muft be reduced to improper

er fractions, and all fractions to a common denominator.

2. ADD all the numerators together, under which write the common denominator; and you will have the fum required.

FOR, put $\frac{v}{y} = a$, and $\frac{z}{y} = b$; then will $v = ya$ and $z = yb$ by the nature of divifion; confequently $ya + yb = v + z$, and therefore by divifion $a + b = \frac{v + z}{y}$.

But, $a + b = \frac{v}{y} + \frac{z}{y}$; confequently, $\frac{v}{y} + \frac{z}{y} = \frac{v + z}{y}$; which is the fame as the rule.

EXAMPLES.

Given $\frac{u}{6}$, $\frac{u}{6}$ and $\frac{4z}{6}$ to find their fum.

$u + u + 4z = 2u + 4z$ and $\frac{2u + 4z}{6} = $ fum requir.

Having $\frac{u}{2}$, $\frac{3u}{y}$ and $\frac{3}{u}$ given to find their fum.

Firſt, $u \times y \times u = u^2 y$, and $3u \times 2 \times u = 6u^2$, alſo, $3 \times 2 \times y = 6y$; then, $2 \times y \times u = 2uy$, and $u^2 y + 6u^2 + 6y \div 2uy = $ fum required.

$\frac{4x}{2a} + x + \frac{2x}{3} = \frac{4x}{2a} + \frac{5x}{3} = \frac{12x + 10ax}{6a}$

PROBLEM VII.

To fubtract one fraction from another.

RULE.

1. PREPARE the quantities as in the laſt problem.

2.

2. Subtract the numerator of the fubtrahend from the numerator of the other fraction, and write the common denominator under their difference; and you will have the fraction required.

For put $\dfrac{v}{y} = m$ and $\dfrac{a}{y} = n$; then $v = ym$ and $a = yn$; alfo, $yn - ym = a - v$ by equality; and dividing the whole by y, it will be $n - m = \dfrac{a-v}{y}$; but the difference of m and n, is manifeftly equal to the difference of $\dfrac{a}{y}$ and $\dfrac{v}{y}$; confequently, $\dfrac{a}{y} - \dfrac{v}{y} = \dfrac{a-v}{y}$. Hence, &c.

EXAMPLES.

From $\dfrac{a}{b}$ take $\dfrac{cx}{ab}$. *Firft,* $a \times ab = a^2 b$, *and* $cx \times b = cbx$; *alfo,* $b \times ab = ab^2$. *Therefore,* $\dfrac{a^2 b}{ab^2}$ *and* $\dfrac{cbx}{ab^2}$ *are the fractions reduced; and* $\dfrac{a^2 b - cbx}{ab^2} =$ *difference required.* *From* $\dfrac{c^2 - x^2}{a^2}$ *take* $\dfrac{c^2 + x^2}{2}$, *and it will be* $\dfrac{c^2 - x^2}{a^2} - \dfrac{c^2 + x^2}{2} = \dfrac{2c^2 - 2x^2}{2a^2} - \dfrac{c^2 a^2 + x^2 a^2}{2a^2} = \dfrac{2c^2 - 2x^2 - c^2 a^2 - x^2 a^2}{2a^2}$. *From* $-x + \dfrac{x}{2}$ *take* $-\dfrac{3x}{4}$. *The fractions reduced are* $\dfrac{-4x}{8}$ *and* $\dfrac{-6x}{8}$, *therefore,* $\dfrac{-4x + 6x}{8} = \dfrac{2x}{8} =$ *difference required, by the nature of fubtraction.*

PROB.

PROBLEM. VIII.

To multiply fractional quantities together.

RULE.

MULTIPLY the numerators together for the numerator of the product, and the denominators together for the denominator of the product; and you will have the product required.

For put $\frac{v}{z} = m$ and $\frac{a}{b} = n$; then $v = zm$ and $a = bn$; also, $bn \times zm = a \times v$; that is, $bznm = av$, and dividing by bz, $nm = \frac{av}{bz}$; but $m \times n = \frac{v}{z} \times \frac{a}{b}$; consequently, $\frac{v}{z} \times \frac{a}{b} = \frac{av}{bz}$: Therefore, &c.

EXAMPLES.

$$\frac{3y}{6} \times \frac{4x}{3y} = \frac{12xy}{18y} = \frac{2x}{3}, \text{ or } \tfrac{2}{3}x; \quad \frac{a+b}{2x} \times \frac{a-b}{a-1} = \frac{a^2-b^2}{2ax-2x};$$

$$\text{and } a + \frac{d}{c} \times v = \frac{ca+d}{c} \times \frac{v}{1} = \frac{cav+dv}{c}; \text{ also, } \frac{vy}{4} \times$$

$$-v + \frac{6v}{3} = \frac{vy}{4} \times \frac{-3v+6v}{3} = \frac{vy}{4} \times \frac{3v}{3} = \frac{3v^2y}{12} = \frac{v^2y}{4},$$

$$\text{or, } \tfrac{1}{4}v^2y.$$

PROBLEM IX.

To divide one fraction by another.

RULE.

MULTIPLY the denominator of the divisor, with the numerator of the dividend, for the numerator of

the

the required quotient, and the numerator of the divisor, with the denominator of the dividend, for the denominator of the quotient.   Or,

INVERT the terms of the divisor, and proceed as in multiplication.

For put $\frac{x}{y} = m$ and $\frac{z}{d} = n$; then $x = ym$ and $z = dn$. Multiply $z = dn$ by y, and it will be $yz = ydn$; in like manner, $dx = dym$; therefore, $\frac{ydn}{dym} = \frac{yz}{dx}$; but $\frac{ydn}{ydm} =$ (by division) $\frac{n}{m}$, and therefore by restitution $\frac{z}{d} \div \frac{x}{y} = \frac{yz}{dx}$: Confequently, &c.

EXAMPLES.

$$\frac{a}{b} \div \frac{c}{d} = \frac{a \times d}{c \times d} = \frac{ad}{cb}.$$ Or, $\frac{a}{b} \div \frac{c}{d} = \frac{d}{c} \times \frac{a}{b} = \frac{ad}{cb}$ as before;

$$\frac{a-u}{v} \div \frac{a+u}{v} = \frac{a-u \times v}{a+u \times v} = \frac{va-uv}{va+uv} = \frac{a-u}{a+u}$$: Therefore, in divifion of fractions that have the fame denominator, caft off the denominators, and divide the numerator of the dividend, by the numerator of the divifor, for the quotient.

Thus, $\frac{4a^2}{3} \div \frac{6y^2}{4} \times a = \frac{4a^2}{3} \div \frac{6y^2 a}{4} = \frac{16a^2}{18y^2 a}$; $\frac{6a}{3} \div \frac{ay}{3} = \frac{6a}{ay}$.

PROBLEM X.

To find the powers of fractional quantities.

RULE.

R U L E.

1. PREPARE the given fraction, if need be, by the rules of reduction.

2. INVOLVE the numerator to the height of the power proposed, as in involution of whole quantities, for the numerator of the power required.

3. INVOLVE the denominator in like manner, for the denominator of the aforesaid power.

EXAMPLES.

Find the square of $\dfrac{cy-y}{y+1}$.

$\overline{cy-y} \times \overline{cy-y} = c^2y^2 - 2cy^2 + y^2$, and $\overline{y+1} \times \overline{y+1} = y^2 + 2y + 1$; therefore, $\dfrac{c^2y^2 - 2cy^2 + y^2}{y^2 + 2y + 1} = $ power required.

The 4th power of $\dfrac{za}{zy} = \dfrac{az \times az \times az \times az}{zy \times zy \times zy \times zy} = \dfrac{z^4 a^4}{z^4 y^4}$.

P R O B L E M XI.

To find the roots of fractional quantities.

R U L E.

1. EXTRACT the root of the numerator, by the rules for extracting the roots of whole quantities, for the numerator of the root required.

2. EATRACT the root of the denominator in like manner, for the denominator of the required root.

EXAMPLES.

EXAMPLES.

Find the square root of $\frac{a^6}{x^8}$.

Here, $a^{6 \div 2} = a^3$, *for the numerator of the root,* *and* $x^{8 \div 2} = x^4$ *for the denominator of the root; there-fore,* $\frac{a^3}{x^4}$ *is the root required.* The cube root of $\frac{a^3}{z^3 y^6}$

$= \frac{a}{zy^2}$. $\quad \sqrt{\frac{a^2 b^4}{z^2 c^6}} = \frac{ab^2}{zc^3}$.

The square root of $\frac{x^2 - 4x + 4}{y^2 + 6y + 9} = \frac{x - 2}{y + 3}$.

But if the proposed quantity hath not a true root of the kind required, it must be distinguished by the sign of the root: Thus, the square root of $\frac{a^2 - x^2}{a^2 + x^2}$

$= \sqrt{\frac{a^2 - x^2}{a^2 + x^2}}$, *or* $\overline{\frac{a^2 - x^2}{a^2 + x^2}}\Big|^{\frac{1}{2}}$.

CHAP. X.

CONCERNING SURDS *or* IRRA-TIONAL QUANTITIES.

IF the whole doctrine of surds, with every thing therein, which might be of use, were to be explained according to the methods used by some writers on the subject, it would become very complex, and by far the most intricate and difficult part of all Algebra; and necessarily swell this volume beyond

its

its defigned limit: And befides, there are many things in the explanation and management of furd quantities, as was taught by many writers on Algebra, which were then thought neceffary, are now at moft, confidered as ufeful. We fhall therefore, endevour on the one hand, to avoid all fuch tedious reductions, and complicated explanations, as would ferve rather to puzzle, than inftruct the learner: And on the other hand, not to omit any thing which is neceffary, either in the explanation or management of fuch furds as generally arife in algebraic operations.

A Surd quantity is that which has no exact root: Thus, the fquare root of 5 cannot exactly be found in fiinite terms, but is expreffed by $5^{\frac{1}{2}}$, or $\sqrt{5}$; the cube root of a by $a^{\frac{1}{3}}$, or $\overline{a}|^{\frac{1}{3}} = \sqrt[3]{a}$: The reciprocal of the fquare root of $a + y$, or 1 divided by the fquare root of $a + y$, is expreffed by $\overline{a+y}|^{-\frac{1}{2}} = \dfrac{1}{\sqrt{a+y}}$.

Therefore, the roots of irrational or furd quantities, may be confidered as powers having fractional exponents; that is, the index fhewing the height of the power, is here placed as the numerator of a fraction, whofe denominator is the radical fign.

S E C T. I.

Of REDUCTION of SURD QUANTITIES.

Reduction of furds has the following problems.

P R O B.

PROBLEM I.

To reduce a rational quantity to the form of an irrational, or surd quantity.

RULE.

Involve the rational quantity to the height of the proposed radical sign, or index shewing the root to be extracted ; the power distinguished by the radical sign, will be the form required.

EXAMPLES.

a, reduced to the form of the $\sqrt[3]{x}$, is $\sqrt[3]{a^{1\times3}} = \sqrt[3]{a^3}$; 6 reduced to the form of the square root of 2, $= \sqrt{6^{1\times2}} = \sqrt{6^2} = \sqrt{36}$.

Reduce $\frac{3}{4}$ to the form of a cube root. $\overline{\frac{3}{4}}\Big|^{1\times3|\frac{1}{3}}$

$= \overline{\frac{3^3}{4^3}}\Big|^{\frac{1}{3}} = \sqrt[3]{\frac{27}{64}} =$ form required ; $u+y$ reduced to the

form of a fourth root, is $\sqrt[4]{\overline{u+y}^{1\times4}} = \sqrt[4]{\overline{u+y}^4}$ $= \sqrt[4]{u^4+4u^3y+6u^2y^2+4uy^3+y^4}$. Also, $u = \sqrt{u^2} = \sqrt[3]{u^3} = \sqrt[4]{u^4} = \sqrt[5]{u^5} = \sqrt[n]{u^n}$.

PROBLEM II.

To reduce surds of different radical signs to the same.

RULE.

Reduce the indices of the surds to a common denominator, and the surds will have the same radical sign as required.   *EXAMPLES.*

The $\sqrt[3]{}$ of a, and the $\sqrt{}$ of b, reduced to the same radical sign $= a^{\frac{1\times2}{6}}$ and $b^{\frac{1\times3}{6}} = a^{\frac{2}{6}}$ and $b^{\frac{3}{6}}$, or $\sqrt[6]{a^2}$ and $\sqrt[6]{b^3}$. $z^{\frac{1}{4}}$ and $y^{\frac{2}{3}}$ reduced to the same sign $= z^{\frac{1\times3}{12}}$ and $y^{\frac{2\times4}{12}} = z^{\frac{3}{12}}$ and $y^{\frac{8}{12}}$, or $\sqrt[12]{z^3}$ and $\sqrt[12]{y^8}$.

$z^{\frac{3}{4}}\sqrt{ay+by}$ and $z^{\frac{1}{2}}\sqrt{a+y}$ reduced to a common radical sign, are $\frac{3\times2}{4}\sqrt{ay+by}$, $\frac{1\times2}{4}\sqrt{a+y} = \sqrt[4]{\overline{ay+by}\rvert^6}$ $\sqrt[4]{\overline{a+y}\rvert^2}$: Also, $y^{-\frac{1}{2}}$ and $y^{-\frac{2}{3}} = y^{-\frac{3}{6}}$ and $y^{-\frac{4}{6}}$

PROBLEM III.

To reduce surds to their most simple terms.

RULE.

1. Divide the quantity under the radical sign, by such a rational divisor, as will quote the greatest rational power contained in the proposed surd without a remainder.

2. Extract the root of the rational power, and place it before the surd, with the sign of multiplication, and the proposed surd will be in its most simple terms.

Reduce $\sqrt{32}$ to its most simple terms.

Here

Here $\frac{32}{2} = 16$ *the greatest rational power contained in*
$\sqrt{32}$; *therefore, the* $\sqrt{32} = \sqrt{16 \times 2} = \sqrt{16} \times \sqrt{2} =$
$4 \times \sqrt{2} = 4\sqrt{2}$. *The* $\sqrt{\frac{27}{28}} = \sqrt{\frac{9 \times 3}{4 \times 7}} = \frac{3}{2} \times \sqrt{\frac{3}{7}}$;
$\sqrt{a^3 x} = \sqrt{a^2 \times ax} = a \times \sqrt{ax} = a\sqrt{ax}$; $\overline{a^3 x - a^2 y}|^{\frac{1}{2}}$
$= \overline{a^2 \times ax - y}|^{\frac{1}{2}} = a \times \overline{ax - y}|^{\frac{1}{2}}$.
$\overline{\frac{64\,a^3 x}{54 y}}|^{\frac{1}{3}} = \frac{4a}{3} \times \overline{\frac{x}{2y}}|^{\frac{1}{3}}$.

S E C T. II.

Of ADDITION of SURD QUANTITIES.

ADDITION of surd or irrational quantities, consists
of the following cases.

C A S E I.

*When the proposed surds are of the same irrational
quantity (or can be made so by reduction) and the radical sign the same in all.*

R U L E.

ADD the rational to the rational, and to their sum
annex the irrational part with its radical sign.

EXAMPLES.

$3\sqrt{20} + 6\sqrt{20} = \overline{3 + 6} \times \sqrt{20} = 9\sqrt{20}$; $\sqrt{3a^2 x} +$
$\sqrt{27x} = \sqrt{a^2 \times 3x} + \sqrt{9 \times 3x} = \overline{a + 3}\sqrt{3x}$; $\overline{\frac{27}{5}}|^{\frac{1}{2}} +$

$\overline{\frac{48}{5}}|^{\frac{1}{2}}$

$$\overline{\tfrac{48}{5}}\Big\rvert^{\frac12} = \overline{\tfrac{9\times3}{5}}\Big\rvert^{\frac12} + \overline{\tfrac{16\times3}{5}}\Big\rvert^{\frac12} = 3\times\overline{\tfrac35}\Big\rvert^{\frac12} + 4\times\overline{\tfrac35}\Big\rvert^{\frac12} = 7\times\overline{\tfrac35}\Big\rvert^{\frac12} ;$$

$$\overline{ax^3 - x^3}\Big\rvert^{-\frac13} + \overline{8a-8}\Big\rvert^{-\frac13} = \overline{x^3\times a-1}\Big\rvert^{-\frac13} +$$

$$\overline{8\times a-1}\Big\rvert^{-\frac13} = x^{-1}\times\overline{a-1}\Big\rvert^{-\frac13} + \tfrac12\times\overline{a-1}\Big\rvert^{-\frac13} = \tfrac1x$$

$$+\tfrac12\times\overline{a-1}\Big\rvert^{-\frac13} = \frac{x+2}{2x}\times\frac{1}{\overline{a-1}\rvert^{\frac13}}.$$

CASE II.

When the irrational or surd quantity, and the radical sign are not the same in all.

RULE.

CONNECT the surds with their proper signs $+$ or $-$; and you will have the sum required.

Note. *If the sum consists of two terms, it is called a binomial, or residual surd, as the sign is $+$ or $-$.*

EXAMPLES.

$$\sqrt{a} + \sqrt{x} = \sqrt{a} + \sqrt{x} = \text{sum} ; \quad \sqrt[3]{16} + \sqrt{27}$$
$$= \sqrt[3]{8\times2} + \sqrt{9\times3} = 2\sqrt[3]{2} + 3\sqrt{3} :$$

$$\tfrac34\times\overline{\tfrac{81}{16}}\Big\rvert^{\frac13} + \tfrac23\times\overline{\tfrac{27}{36}}\Big\rvert^{\frac12} = \tfrac34\times\overline{\tfrac{27\times3}{8\times2}}\Big\rvert^{\frac13} + \tfrac23\times\overline{\tfrac{9\times3}{36\times1}}\Big\rvert^{\frac12} =$$

$$\tfrac34\times\tfrac32\times\overline{\tfrac32}\Big\rvert^{\frac13} + \tfrac23\times\tfrac36\times3^{\frac12} = \tfrac98\times\overline{\tfrac32}\Big\rvert^{\frac13} + \tfrac{6}{18}\times3^{\frac12} :$$

$$\sqrt{ax} \text{ added to } -\sqrt{xy-y^2} = \sqrt{ax} - \sqrt{xy-y^2}.$$

SECT. III.

"Of SUBTRACTION of SURD QUANTITIES.

CASE

C A S E I.

When the radical sign and quantity are the same in all.

R U L E.

FIND the difference of the rational parts, to which annex the common irrational or surd quantity, with the sign of multiplication.

EXAMPLES.

$$80^{\frac{1}{2}} - 45^{\frac{1}{2}} = \sqrt{16 \times 5} - \sqrt{9 \times 5} = 4 \times 5^{\frac{1}{2}} - 3 \times 5^{\frac{1}{2}}$$

$$= \overline{4 - 3}\sqrt{5} = \sqrt{5}; \quad \sqrt[3]{40a^3y^2} - \sqrt[3]{135y^2} =$$

$$\sqrt[3]{8a^3 \times 5y^2} - \sqrt[3]{27 \times 5y^2} = 2a\sqrt[3]{5y^2} -$$

$$3\sqrt[3]{5y^2} = \overline{2a - 3}\sqrt[3]{5y^2}:$$

$$\overline{\frac{54y^3}{20}}\Big|^{\frac{1}{2}} - \overline{\frac{150y^3}{80}}\Big|^{\frac{1}{2}} = \overline{\frac{9y^2 \times 6y}{4 \times 5}}\Big|^{\frac{1}{2}} - \overline{\frac{25y^2 \times 6y}{16 \times 5}}\Big|^{\frac{1}{2}} =$$

$$\frac{3y}{2} \times \overline{\frac{6y}{5}}\Big|^{\frac{1}{2}} - \frac{5y}{4} \times \overline{\frac{6y}{5}}\Big|^{\frac{1}{2}} = \frac{12y - 10y}{8} \times \overline{\frac{6y}{5}}\Big|^{\frac{1}{2}} = \frac{y}{4} \times$$

$$\overline{\frac{6y}{5}}\Big|^{\frac{1}{2}}; \quad 4 \times \overline{a^2y - a^2}\Big|^{-\frac{1}{2}} - 2 \times \overline{a^2y - a^2}\Big|^{-\frac{1}{2}} = -\frac{1}{4}$$

$$\times \overline{y - 1}\Big|^{-\frac{1}{2}}.$$

C A S E II.

When the irrational parts are not the same in all.

R U L E.

CHANGE the sign of the quantity to be subtracted, the expression connected, is the difference required.

EXAMPLES.

EXAMPLES.

$$27^{\frac{2}{2}} \text{ \textit{subtracted from} } 80^{\frac{1}{2}}, = \sqrt{16 \times 5} - \sqrt{9 \times 3} =$$
$$4\sqrt{5} - 3\sqrt{3}; \quad 48^{\frac{1}{2}} - 16^{\frac{1}{3}} = 48^{\frac{3}{6}} - 16^{\frac{2}{6}} = {}^{6}\sqrt{48^{3}} -$$
$${}^{6}\sqrt{16^{2}}; \quad 3^{4}\sqrt{ab - z} \text{ \textit{subtracted from} } {}^{4}\sqrt{z^{2} - y^{2}},$$
$$= {}^{4}\sqrt{z^{2} - y^{2}} - 3^{4}\sqrt{ab - z}.$$

S E C T. IV.

Of MULTIPLICATION of SURD QUANTITIES.

Surds being confidered as powers having fractional exponents; it therefore follows, that to multiply one furd with another, is to add their fractional exponents together, making the denominator of their fum the radical fign, and the numerator the index of the root.

Hence is deduced the following rule for multiplication of furds.

RULE.

1. Reduce the indices of the furds to a common denominator.

2. Annex the product of the furds, to the product of the rational parts with the fign of multiplication; and it will give the product required.

EXAMPLES.

EXAMPLES.

$$\sqrt[6]{16} \times \sqrt{8} = \sqrt[3]{8 \times 2} \times \sqrt{4 \times 2} = 2 \sqrt[3]{2} \times 2\sqrt{2} = 2 \times 2^{\frac{1}{3}} \times 2 \times 2^{\frac{1}{2}} = 2 \times 2^{\frac{2}{6}} \times 2 \times 2^{\frac{3}{6}} = 4 \sqrt[6]{2^3 2^2}$$

$$= 4 \sqrt[6]{32}; \quad \overline{z^2 + y^2}\big|^{\frac{1}{2}} \times \overline{z^2 + y^2}\big|^{\frac{1}{2}} = \overline{z^2 + y^2}\big|^{\frac{1}{2} + \frac{1}{2}} = z^2 + y^2;$$

$$z^{\frac{1}{2}} \times y^{\frac{1}{2}} = \overline{zy}\big|^{\frac{1}{2}}; \quad \overline{a+y}\big|^{-\frac{1}{2}} \times \overline{a+y}\big|^{-\frac{1}{2}} = \overline{a+y}\big|^{-\frac{1}{2} - \frac{1}{2}} = \overline{a+y}\big|^{-\frac{2}{2}} = \overline{a+y}\big|^{-1};$$

$$a^{\frac{1}{m}} \times b^{\frac{1}{n}} = a^{\frac{n}{nm}} \times b^{\frac{m}{nm}} = \sqrt[nm]{a^n b^m}.$$

S E C T. V.

Of DIVISION of SURD QUANTI-TIES.

R U L E.

1. REDUCE the surds to the same index.

2. DIVIDE the rational by the rational, and to the quotient annex the quotient of the surd quantities; and it will be the quotient required.

Note. If the quantity is the same in both factors, they are divided by subtracting their exponents.

EXAMPLES.

$$a^{\frac{1}{2}} \div a^{\frac{1}{3}} = a^{\frac{3}{6}} \div a^{\frac{2}{6}} = a^{\frac{3-2}{6}} = a^{\frac{1}{6}} = \sqrt[6]{a}; \quad \sqrt{32} \div \sqrt{18}$$

$$= \sqrt{16 \times 2} \div \sqrt{9 \times 2} = 4\sqrt{2} \div 3\sqrt{2} = \frac{4}{3} \times \sqrt{\frac{2}{2}} =$$

$$\frac{4}{3} \sqrt{1} = \sqrt{\frac{16}{9}} = \frac{4}{3}; \quad \overline{xa + ya}\big|^{\frac{1}{2}} \div \sqrt{a} = \frac{\overline{xa + ya}}{a}\Big|^{\frac{1}{2}} = \overline{x+y}\big|^{\frac{1}{2}}$$

$$\overline{x+y}|^{\frac{1}{2}} \; ; \quad x^{\frac{1}{2}} \div y^{\frac{1}{3}} = x^{\frac{3}{6}} \div y^{\frac{2}{6}} = \overline{\frac{x^3}{y^2}}\Big|^{\frac{1}{6}} \; ; \quad \frac{x^{\frac{1}{2}}}{y^{\frac{1}{3}}} \div$$

$$\frac{x^{\frac{1}{3}}}{y^{\frac{1}{2}}} = \frac{x^{\frac{3}{6}}}{y^{\frac{2}{6}}} \div \frac{x^{\frac{2}{6}}}{y^{\frac{3}{6}}} = \frac{y^{\frac{3}{6}} x^{\frac{3}{6}}}{x^{\frac{2}{6}} y^{\frac{2}{3}}} = \overline{\frac{y^3 x^3}{x^2 y^2}}\Big|^{\frac{1}{6}} = \overline{yx}\,|^{\frac{1}{6}} \; ;$$

$$a^{\frac{1}{n}} \div a^{\frac{1}{m}} = a^{\frac{m-n}{mn}}.$$

S E C T. VI.

Of *INVOLUTION* of *SURD QUAN-TITIES.*

THE powers of furds are found by the following

R U L E.

INVOLVE the rational part, as in involution of num-bers ; and to the refult annex the power of the furd, found by multiplying its exponent with the expo-nent of the power required.

EXAMPLES.

The fquare of $\sqrt[3]{6} = 6^{\frac{1}{3} \times 2} = 6^{\frac{2}{3}} = \sqrt[3]{6^2} = \sqrt[3]{36}$. The cube of $\sqrt{3} = 3^{\frac{1}{2} \times 3} = 3^{\frac{3}{2}} = \sqrt{3^3} = \sqrt{27}$. The fquare of $2\sqrt[3]{x^2} = 2 \times 2 \times x^{\frac{2}{3} \times 2} = 4 \times x^{\frac{4}{3}} = 4\sqrt[3]{x^4}$. The cube of $\sqrt[3]{ax-bx} = \overline{ax-bx}|^{\frac{1}{3} \times 3} = ax-bx$: Therefore, when the in-dex of the power required, is equal to, or a multiple of the exponent of the root ; the power of the furd be-

comes

comes rational. *The cube of* $\overline{a-x}|^{-\frac{2}{3}} = \overline{a-x}|^{-\frac{2}{3}} \times 3$
$= \overline{a-x}|^{-\frac{6}{3}} = \overline{a-x}|^{-2}$. *The* n *power of* $y^{\frac{1}{m}} =$
$y^{\frac{1}{m}} \times {}^{n} = y^{\frac{n}{m}} = {}^{m}\sqrt{y^{n}}$.

IF the propofed furd is a binomial 'or refidual one, involve it as in chapter VII.

Thus, the fquare of $\sqrt{6} + 2\sqrt{x} = 6 + 4x + 4\sqrt{6x}$.
(See the operation annexed.)

OPERATION.

$\sqrt{6} + 2\sqrt{x}$
$\sqrt{6} + 2\sqrt{x}$

$6 + 2\sqrt{6x}$
$+ 2\sqrt{6x} + 4x$

$6 + 4x + 4\sqrt{6x}$.

S E C T. VII.

Of EVOLUTION of SURDS.

THE powers of furds are found by multiplying their exponents with the index or exponent of the power to which they are to be involved; as we have fhewn; confequently, if thofe exponents be divided by the index of the root to be extracted, the quotient will be the exponent of the root; which gives the following

R U L E..

EXTRACT the root of the rational part, as in common extraction of roots; and annex the root of the furd, found by dividing the index of the furd, by the index of the root required.

EXAMPLES.

EXAMPLES.

The cube root of $\sqrt{a} = a^{\frac{1}{2}} \div 3 = a^{\frac{1}{6}} = \sqrt[6]{a}$. *The cube root of* $\frac{8}{27}\sqrt{3} = \sqrt[3]{\frac{8}{27}} \times 3^{\frac{1}{2}} \div 3 = \frac{2}{3} \times 3^{\frac{1}{6}} = \frac{2}{3}\sqrt[6]{3}$. *The square root of* $\sqrt[3]{\frac{a}{x}} = \sqrt[6]{\frac{a}{x}}$. *The square root of* $\sqrt[3]{a^3 + b^3} = \overline{a^3 + b^3}|^{\frac{1}{3}} \div 2 = \overline{a^3 + b^3}|^{\frac{1}{6}}$. *The cube root of* $x^{-\frac{2}{3}} = x^{-\frac{2}{9}} = \frac{1}{\sqrt[9]{x^2}}$. If the proposed furds are binomial, refidual, or trinomial, &c. find their roots as in Chap. VIII.

The square root of $x^8 + 6x^4\sqrt{y} + 9y = x^4 + 3\sqrt{y}$.

The n *root of* $20 + 2\sqrt{x} + z = \overline{20 + 2\sqrt{x + z}}|^{\frac{1}{n}}$.

C H A P. XI.

Of INFINITE SERIES.

AN infinite feries, is formed from a fraction whofe denominator is a compound quantity, by dividing the numerator by the denominator; or the extracting the root of a furd quantity, which if continued in either cafe, would run on fempiternally; that is, the number of terms in the feries would be infinite; but by obtaining a few of the firft terms of the feries, you will eafily perceive, what law the feries obferve in their progreffion; by which means you may continue the feries by notation as far as you pleafe, without an actual performance of the whole operation at large.　　　　　PROB.

PROBLEM I.

To find an infinite series by division; that is, to throw a compound fractional expression into such a series, whose sum, if the number of terms were continued ad infinitum, would be equal to the given fractional expression.

RULE.

DIVIDE the numerator by the denominator until you have 3, 4, 5, or more terms in the quotient.

EXAMPLES.

Throw $\dfrac{1}{y+v}$ into an infinite series.

OPERATION.

OPERATION.

$$y+v)\ 1\qquad\left(\frac{1}{y}-\frac{v}{y^2}+\frac{v^2}{y^3}-\frac{v^3}{y^4}+\&c.\right.$$

$$1+\frac{v}{y}$$

$$\overline{}$$

$$0-\frac{v}{y}$$

$$-\frac{v}{y}-\frac{v^2}{y^2}$$

$$\overline{}$$

$$*+\frac{v^2}{y^2}$$

$$+\frac{v^2}{y^2}+\frac{v^3}{y^3}$$

$$\overline{}$$

$$*-\frac{v^3}{y^3}$$

$$-\frac{v^3}{y^3}-\frac{v^4}{y^4}$$

$$\overline{}$$

$$*+\frac{v^4}{y^4}$$

$$\&c.$$

HERE the law of the progreſſion which the ſeries obſerve, is plain ; for each ſucceeding term is produced, by multiplying the preceding one with $-\frac{v}{y}$: Thus, the firſt term of the ſeries is $\frac{1}{y}$, which being multiplied with $-\frac{v}{y}$, gives $-\frac{v}{y^2}$ for the ſe-

cond

cond term, and $-\dfrac{v}{y^2} \times -\dfrac{v}{y} = \dfrac{v^2}{y^3} =$ third term; also, $\dfrac{v^2}{y^3} \times -\dfrac{v}{y} = -\dfrac{v^3}{y^4}$ the 4th term, which multiplied with $-\dfrac{v}{y}$ will give the 5th term; and so on, multiplying the preceding term by the common ratio $-\dfrac{v}{y}$, you may find any number of terms at pleasure.

But in order to have a converging series, or a series wherein the terms continually decrease, the greatest term of the divisor must stand first in the order of arrangement; for suppose in the above example, that y is very great in respect of v; then will $\dfrac{v}{y^2}$ be very great in respect of $\dfrac{v^2}{y^3}$; so that in this supposition, the terms being multiplied with the powers of v, and divided by those of y; it follows, that each succeeding term is very little in respect of the preceding one, and consequently the series, a converging series. Again, put v for the first term of the divisor (the supposition the same as before) and the series will be $\dfrac{1}{v} - \dfrac{y}{v^2} + \dfrac{y^2}{v^3}$, &c. and since y is very great in respect of v; it follows, that $\dfrac{1}{v}$ is very little in respect of $\dfrac{y}{v^2}$, and $\dfrac{y}{v^2}$ very little in respect of $\dfrac{y^2}{v^3}$; consequently, the series is a diverging one; that is, a series whose terms continually increase, and therefore, the farther you proceed in them, the farther you will be from the truth. Hence, &c.

And

AND fince it is impoffible to affign an infinite number; it follows, that the number of terms expreffing the true value of fuch a feries, is not affignable; yet the taking of a few of the firft terms will be fufficient for any practical purpofe.

Throw $\dfrac{a^2}{v-d}$ into an infinite feries.

OPERATION.

$$v-d)\,a^2 \qquad \left(\dfrac{a^2}{v}+\dfrac{a^2 d}{v^2}+\dfrac{a^2 d^2}{v^3}+, \&c.\right.$$

$$a^2-\dfrac{a^2 d}{v}$$

$$\ast+\dfrac{a^2 d}{v}$$

$$+\dfrac{a^2 d}{v}-\dfrac{a^2 d^2}{v^2}$$

$$\ast+\dfrac{a^2 d^2}{v^2}$$

$$+\dfrac{a^2 d^2}{v^2}-\dfrac{a^2 d^3}{v^3}$$

$$\ast+\dfrac{a^2 d^3}{v^3}, \&c.$$

HERE, each preceding term, after the firft, is multiplied with $\dfrac{d}{v}$, and the product is the next term following; therefore, the law of the progreffion is manifeft.

Throw $\dfrac{1}{1+b^2}$ into an infinite feries.

OPERATION.

OPERATION.

$$1 + b^2) \; 1 \qquad\qquad (1 - b^2 + b^4 - b^6, \text{\&c.}$$
$$\underline{1 + b^2}$$
$$0 - b^2$$
$$\underline{\; - b^2 - b^4}$$
$$\ast \quad + b^4$$
$$\underline{\quad + b^4 + b_6}$$
$$\ast \quad - b^6$$
$$\underline{\quad - b^6 - b^8}$$
$$\ast \quad + b^8$$
$$\text{\&c.}$$

HERE the law of the continuation is the preceding terms multiplied with $- b^2$.

PROBLEM II.

To extract the root of a compound surd in an infinite series; that is, to throw a compound surd quantity into a converging series, whose sum, if the terms were infinitely continued would be equal to the root required.

RULE.

EXTRACT the root of the quantity, as in common algebraic extraction; the operation continued as far as is thought neceffary, will give the feries required.

EXAMPLES.

Throw $\sqrt{a^2 + y^2}$ into an infinite feries.

Qq   *OPERATION.*

OPERATION.

$$a^2 + y^2 \ (a + \frac{y^2}{2a} - \frac{y^4}{8a^3} +, \&c.$$

$$\underline{a^2}$$

$$2a + \frac{y^2}{2a}) \ * \ + y^2$$

$$+ y^2 + \frac{y^4}{4a^2}$$

$$2a + \frac{y^2}{2a} - \frac{y^4}{8a^3}) - \frac{y^4}{4a^2}$$

$$- \frac{y^4}{4a^2} - \frac{y^6}{8a^4} + \frac{y^8}{64a^6}$$

$$+ \frac{y^6}{8a^4} - \frac{y^8}{64a^6}$$

$$\&c.$$

That is, $\overline{a^2 + x^2}|^{\frac{1}{2}} = a + \frac{x^2}{2a} + \frac{x^4}{8a^3} + \&c.$

Find

Find the value of $\overline{1 - x^2}|^{\frac{1}{2}}$ in an infinite series.

OPERATION.

$$1 - x^2 \left(1 - \frac{x^2}{2} - \frac{x^4}{8} - \frac{x^6}{16}, \&c. \right.$$

$$\underline{1}$$

$$2 - \frac{x^2}{2} \Big) \; 0 - x^2$$

$$- x^2 + \frac{x^4}{4}$$

$$\overline{\phantom{-x^2+\frac{x^4}{4}}}$$

$$2 - x^2 - \frac{x^4}{8} \Big) \; * \; - \frac{x^4}{4}$$

$$- \frac{x^4}{4} + \frac{x^6}{8} + \frac{x^8}{64}$$

$$\overline{\phantom{-\frac{x^4}{4}+\frac{x^6}{8}+\frac{x^8}{64}}}$$

$$2 - x^2 - \frac{x^4}{4} - \frac{x^6}{16} \Big) \; * \; - \frac{x^6}{8} - \frac{x^8}{64}$$

$$- \frac{x^6}{8} + \frac{x^8}{16} + \frac{x^{10}}{64} + \frac{x^{12}}{256}$$

$$\overline{\phantom{- \frac{x^6}{8} + \frac{x^8}{16} + \frac{x^{10}}{64} + \frac{x^{12}}{256}}}$$

$$* \qquad \&c.$$

PROBLEM III.

To reduce any surd or fractional quantity into an infinite series, by the celebrated Binomial Theorem, invented by that Prince of Mathematicians, the illustrious Sir ISAAC NEWTON, which is as follows.

Binomial

Binomial Theorem.

$$\overline{P + PQ}|^{\frac{m}{n}} = P^{\frac{m}{n}} + \frac{m}{n} AQ + \frac{m-n}{2n} BQ + \frac{m-2n}{3n} CQ$$

$$+ \frac{m-3n}{4n} DQ + \frac{m-4n}{5n} EQ + \frac{m-5n}{6n} FQ + \&c.$$

Wherein it is to be obferved, that $P + PQ$ is the quantity whofe power is to be thrown into an infinite feries ; P reprefents the firft term of the propofed quantity ; Q the other terms divided by the firft ; $\frac{m}{n}$ the index of the power, whether it be affimative or negative : And A = firft term of the feries ; B the fecond ; C the third ; D the fourth ; E the fifth ; F the fixth, &c. that is, the feveral terms of the feries, are $A = P^{\frac{m}{n}}$, $B = \frac{m}{n} AQ$, $C = \frac{m-n}{2n} BQ$, D $= \frac{m-2n}{3n} CQ$, &c.

EXAMPLES.

Reduce $\overline{a^2 + x^2}|^{\frac{1}{2}}$ into an infinite feries.

Here $a^2 = P$, $\frac{x^2}{a^2} = Q$, *m* $= 1$, *and n* $= 2$:

Therefore, $A = P^{\frac{m}{n}} = a$, $B = \frac{m}{n} AQ = \frac{x^2}{2a}$, $C =$

$\frac{m-n}{2n} BQ = -\frac{x^4}{8a^3}$, $D = \frac{m-3n}{4n} CQ = \frac{x^6}{16a^4}$, *&c.*

That is, $a + \frac{x^2}{2a} - \frac{x^4}{8a^3} + \frac{x^6}{16a^4}$, *&c. is the feries required.*

Expand

Expand $\dfrac{1}{1+z} = \overline{1+z}\,^{-1}$ into an infinite series.

Here $\overline{z+1}\,^{-1} = \overline{1+z}\,^{-1}$; *therefore,* $m = -1$, $n = 1$, $P = 1$, *and* $Q = \dfrac{z}{1}$: *Consequently,* $A = \left(P^{\frac{m}{n}}\right)$ 1, $B = \left(\dfrac{m}{n}AQ\right) = -z$, $C = \left(\dfrac{m-n}{2n}BQ\right)z^2$, $D = \left(\dfrac{m-2n}{3n}CQ\right) = -z^3$, $E = \left(\dfrac{m-3n}{4n}DQ\right)z^4$.

That is, $\overline{1+z}\,^{-1} = 1 - z + z^2 - z^3 + z^4$, &c.

Find the value of $\dfrac{v}{a+y}$ in an infinite series.

Here $\dfrac{v}{a+y} = v \times \overline{a+y}\,^{-1}$; *Wherefore,* $P = a$, $Q = \dfrac{y}{a}$, $m = -1$, *and* $n = 1$: *Then,* $A = a^{-1}$, *or* $\dfrac{1}{a}$, $B = -\dfrac{y}{a^2}$, $C = \dfrac{y^2}{a^3}$, $D = -\dfrac{y^3}{a^4}$.

That is, $v \times \overline{a+y}\,^{-1} = v \times \dfrac{1}{a} - \dfrac{y}{a^2} + \dfrac{y^2}{a^3} - \dfrac{y^3}{a^4}$, &c.

Consequently, $\dfrac{v}{a+y} = \dfrac{v}{a} - \dfrac{vy}{a^2} + \dfrac{vy^2}{a^3} - \dfrac{vy^3}{a^4}$, &c.

PROBLEM IV.

To find the sum of an infinite series, geometrically decreasing.

RULE.

Divide the square of the first term by the difference between the first and second, and the quotient will be the sum required. Thus,

THUS, the sum of the infinite series $v - a + \dfrac{a^2}{v}$

$- \dfrac{a^3}{v^2}$, &c. $= v^2 \div v + a$; and the sum of $v +$

$\dfrac{v^2}{a} + \dfrac{v^3}{a^2}$, &c. $= \dfrac{v^2}{av - v^2 \div a} = av \div \overline{a - v}$; for if v^2

be divided by $v + a$, and av by $a - v$, the quotients will be the series propofed. Therefore, the rule is manifeſt.

EXAMPLES.

Given $1 + \frac{1}{2} + \frac{1}{4} + \frac{1}{8}$, &c. *ad infinitum*, to find their ſum.

Thus, $1^2 \div 1 - \frac{1}{2} = 2$ *the ſum required.*
Given $\frac{6}{10} + \frac{6}{100} + \frac{6}{1000}$, &c. *ad infinitum*, to find their ſum.

Thus, $\left.\dfrac{6}{10}\right|^2 \div \overline{\dfrac{6}{10} - \dfrac{6}{100}} = \frac{2}{3}$ *the ſum required.*

Given $2 - \frac{2}{3} + \frac{2}{9} - \frac{2}{27}$, &c. *ad infinitum*, to find their ſum.
Thus, $4 \div 2 + \frac{2}{3} = 1\frac{5}{7} = $ *ſum required.*

CHAP. XII.

Of *PROPORTION* or *ANALOGY* ALGEBRAICALLY CONSIDERED.

WHEN quantities are compared together with regard to their differences, or quotients, their relations are expreſſed by their ratios. The relation of quantities, ariſing from the firſt compa-
riſon

rifon, is expreffed by an arithmetical ratio, that of the fecond, by a geometrical ratio; and the quantities themfelves are faid to be in arithmetical, or geometrical proportion, as the ratios of their comparifon are arithmetical, or geometrical : Which proportions, together with fuch others as arife from the alternation, converfion, &c. of thofe proportions that are of any confiderable ufe in Mathematics, will be noticed in the following order.

SECT. I.

Of ARITHMETICAL PROPORTION.

WHEN quantities increafe by addition or fubtraction of the fame quantity, thofe quantities are in arithmetical proportion : Thus, a, $a + d$, $a + 2d$, $a + 3d$, &c. or x, $x - d$, $x - 2d$, $x - 3d$, &c. are quantities in arithmetical proportion ; wherein the quantity d, which is continually added or fubtracted, is the common difference of the feries ; therefore, when in any four quantities, the difference between the firft and fecond, is equal to the difference between the third and fourth, thofe quantities are in arithmetical proportion ; as in thefe, y, $y - n$, $y - 2n$, $y - 3n$; where $y - \overline{y - n} = n$; and $y - 2n - \overline{y - 3n} = n$. Therefore, &c.

THEOREM I.

If three quantities be in arithmetical proportion, the fum of the two extremes will be double the mean.

Thus if a, $a + d$, $a + 2d$ are in arithmetical proportion, then will $a + \overline{a + 2d} = a + d + \overline{a + d}$.

THEO.

THEOREM II.

If four quantities be in arithmetical proportion, the sum of the two extremes will be equal to the sum of the two means.

Thus, if a, $a + d$, $a + 2d$, $a + 3d$ are quantities in arithmetical proportion, then will $\overline{a + a + 3d} = \overline{a + d} + \overline{a + 2d}$.

THEOREM III.

In a series of arithmetical proportionals, the sum of the two extreme terms, is equal to the sum of any two terms equally distant from the extremes.

Let the series be a, $a + d$, $a + 2d$, $a + 3d$, $a + 4d$, &c. to z: Under which write the same series with their order inverted; then adding those terms together which stand directly opposite each other, and the sum of any two such terms, will be equal to the sum of the first and last terms, as plainly appears by the following

EXAMPLE.

Proposed series, a, $a + d$, $a + 2d$, $a + 3d$, $a + 4d$, &c. to z
Series inverted, z, $z - d$, $z - 2d$, $z - 3d$, $z - 4d$, &c. to a

$$a + z, \quad a + z, \quad a + z, \quad a + z, \quad a + z, \&c. =$$

the sum of every two terms.

Now from this example, a rule for finding the sum of all the terms of any arithmetical series, may be easily deduced; for it is plain, that the sum $\overline{a + z} + \overline{a + z} + \overline{a + z}$, &c. or $\overline{a + z}$, taken as many times as there are number of terms, is double the sum of the series a, $a + d$, $a + 2d$, &c. Consequently, that sum

divided

divided by 2, will be equal to the fum of the feries; that is, (puting $n =$ number of terms, and $s =$ fum of the feries) $\dfrac{\overline{a + z} \times n}{2} = \dfrac{na + nz}{2} = s$: Or in words, the fum of the firft and laft terms multiplied with half the number of terms, will give the fum of the feries.

But in any arithmetical feries, the co-efficient of the common difference (d) in any term, is 1 lefs than the number of terms to that place; confequently, its co-efficient in the laft term, is equal to the number of terms lefs 1; and therefore, the laft term $z = a + \overline{n - 1} \times d = a + dn - d$. Confequently, $s = \overline{a + a + dn - d} \times \dfrac{n}{2} = \dfrac{na + na + dn^2 - dn}{2}$
$= \dfrac{2na + dn^2 - dn}{2}$, which is a theorem for finding the fum of any arithmetical feries, when the firft term, common difference, and number of terms are given. And univerfally, puting

$a =$ *firft term of an arithmetical feries,*
$d =$ *common difference,*
$l =$ *laft term,*
$n =$ *number of terms,*
$s =$ *fum of all the feries.*

Then having given any three of thofe five quantities, the reft may be found by the following theorems.

Theorem 1. $\dfrac{na + nl}{2} = s.$ Theorem 2. $\dfrac{2s}{l + a} = n.$

Theorem 3. $\dfrac{l - a}{n - 1} = d.$ Theorem 4. $\dfrac{2s - na}{n} = l.$

R r

Theorem

Theorem 5. $\dfrac{2s - nl}{n} = a$. Or, $n = \dfrac{l - a}{d} + 1$. $l = nd - d + a$. $a = l + d - nd$.

SECT. II.

Of GEOMETRICAL PROPORTION.

WHEN of four quantities, the product of the two extremes is equal to the product of the two means; thofe quantities are in geometrical proportion: As, a, ar, b, br; where $a \times br = ar \times b$: Alfo, when quantities increafe with a common multiplier, or decreafe by a common divifor, as, a, ar, ar^2, ar^3, ar^4, &c. and a, $\dfrac{a}{r}$, $\dfrac{a}{r^2}$, $\dfrac{a}{r^3}$, $\dfrac{a}{r^4}$, &c. thofe quantities are faid to be in geometrical proportion continued, where the common multiplier or divifor r is the common ratio.

THEOREM I.

In any feries of quantities in geometrical proportion continued, the firft term hath the fame ratio to the fecond, as the fecond hath to the third, and as the third to the fourth, &c.

THUS, in a, ar, ar^2, ar^3, ar^4, &c. and a, $\dfrac{a}{r}$, $\dfrac{a}{r^2}$, $\dfrac{a}{r^3}$, $\dfrac{a}{r^4}$, &c. $a : ar :: ar : ar^2 :: ar^2 : ar^3 :: ar^3 : ar^4 ::$ &c. and $a : \dfrac{a}{r} :: \dfrac{a}{r} : \dfrac{a}{r^2} :: \dfrac{a}{r^2} : \dfrac{a}{r^3} :: \dfrac{a}{r^3} : \dfrac{a}{r^4} ::$ &c. For, $a \times ar^2 = ar \times ar$, and $a \times ar^4 = ar \times ar^3$; alfo, $a \times \dfrac{a}{r^2} = \dfrac{a}{r} \times \dfrac{a}{r}$, and fo on for the reft.

THEO.

THEOREM II.

In a series of geometrical proportionals continued, the product of the two extremes, is equal to the product of any two terms equally distant from the extremes.

Thus, in the series a, ar, ar^2, ar^3, ar^4, &c. If x be the last term, then will $\frac{x}{r}$ be the last term but one, and $\frac{x}{r^2}$ the last term but two; wherefore, $a \times x = ax$, the product of the two extremes, and $ar \times \frac{x}{r} = \frac{arx}{r} = ax$ the product of the second and last term but one : That is, $a \times x = ar \times \frac{x}{r}$; in like manner, $a \times x = ar^2 \times \frac{x}{r^2}$, and so on for the rest.

THEOREM III.

The sum of any series of quantities in geometrical proportion continued, is obtained by multiplying the last term by the ratio, and dividing the difference between that product and the first term, by the ratio less 1.

Thus, let the series whose sum is required, be $a + ar + ar^2 + ar^3 + ar^4$, which multiplied with r, gives $ar + ar^2 + ar^3 + ar^4 + ar^5$, from which subtract the former.

Thus, $\begin{cases} ar + ar^2 + ar^3 + ar^4 + ar^5 \\ a + ar + ar^2 + ar^3 + ar^4 \end{cases}$

$$-a \quad * \quad * \quad * \quad * \quad + ar^5$$

Now

Now it is plain, that the difference $ar^s - a$ is equal to the sum of the propofed feries multiplied by $r-1$; confequently, the fame divided by $r-1$, will give the fum of the feries required: That is, (puting $s =$ fum)

$$\frac{ar^s - a}{r - 1} = s.$$

Or, generally $ar + ar^2 + ar^3 + ar^4,$ &c. $+ \frac{x}{r^4} + \frac{x}{r^3}$

$+ \frac{x}{r^2} + \frac{x}{r} + x = r \times a + ar + ar^2 \ ar^3,$ &c. $+ \frac{x}{r^5} + \frac{x}{r^4}$

$+ \frac{x}{r^3} + \frac{x}{r^2} + \frac{x}{r}.$ That is, the fum of any geometrical feries wanting the firft term, is equal to the fum of the fame feries wanting the laft term, multiplied with the ratio. Wherefore, $s - a = \overline{s - x} \times r$; that is, $s - a = sr - rx,$ and $sr - s = rx - a$: Hence, $s = \frac{rx - a}{r - 1}.$ And fince r is not in the firft term of the feries, it follows, that in the laft term, its exponent will be 1 lefs than the number of terms; and therefore, (puting $n =$ number of terms) $x = ar^{n-1}$: Confequently, $s =$ (by writing for x its equal ar^{n-1})

$$\frac{ar^{n-1} \times r - a}{r - 1} = \frac{ar^{n} - a}{r - 1}: \text{ And univerfally, puting}$$

$a =$ firft term of a geometrical feries,
$r =$ ratio,
$l =$ laft term,
$s =$ fum of the feries.

THEN having given any three of the aforefaid quantities, the reft may be readily found by the following theorems, which are deduced from the above equation.

Theorem

Theorem 1. $\dfrac{rl - a}{r - 1} = s.$

2. $rl + s - sr = a.$

3. $\dfrac{s - a}{s - l} = r.$

4. $\dfrac{sr - s + a}{r} = l.$

THEOREM IV.

If four quantities are proportional, as $a:b::c:d$, then will any of the following forms, also be proportional. viz.

Directly,	$a:b::c:d.$
Alternately,	$a:c::b:d.$
Inverfely,	$b:a::d:c.$
Compoundedly,	$\overline{a+b}:b::\overline{c+d}:d.$
Dividedly,	$a:\overline{b-a}::c:\overline{d-c}.$
Mixtly,	$\overline{b+a}:\overline{b-a}::\overline{d+c}:\overline{d-c}.$

· S E C T. III.

Of HARMONICAL PROPORTION.

HARMONICAL proportion arifes from the comparifon of mufical intervals, or the relation of thofe numbers which affign the lengths of ftrings founding mufical notes.

THE moft ufeful part of this proportion in practical Mathematics, is contained in the following theorems.

THEO.

THEOREM I.

If three quantities be in harmonical proportion, the first will be to the third, as the difference between the first and second, to the difference between the second and third.

THUS, if a, b and c, be in harmonical proportion, then, as $a : c :: \overline{b - a} : \overline{c - b}$: Confequently, $ac - ab = cb - ca$, by multiplying means and extremes: From which equation is deduced the following theorems.

Theorem 1. $\dfrac{cb}{2c - b} = a$. Theorem 2. $\dfrac{2ac}{a + c} = b$.

Theorem 3. $\dfrac{ab}{2a - b} = c$.

THEOREM II.

If four quantities be in harmonical proportion, the first will be to the fourth, as the difference between the first and second, is to the difference between the third and fourth.

THUS, if the quantities a, b, c, d, are harmonical proportionals, it will be, $a : d :: b - a : d - c$: Wherefore, $ad - ac = db - da$. From which equation, we get the following theorems.

1. $a = \dfrac{db}{2d - c}$.

2. $b = \dfrac{2da - ac}{d}$.

3. $c = \dfrac{2da - db}{a}$.

$$4. \quad d = \frac{ac}{2a-b}.$$

CHAP. XIII.

Of SIMPLE EQUATIONS.

AN equation is an expression, asserting the equality of two quantities, which are compared together by writing the quantities with the sign of equality between them. Thus, if $x+3$ is equal to $2x-1$, the equation is formed thus, $x+3=2x-1$: Also, $8-3=15-10$.

A simple equation, is an equation which involves one unknown quantity, without including its powers. Thus, $3x-2=2x+2$ is a simple equation which expresses the value of the unknown quantity; when that quantity stands alone on one side of the equation, the rest being on the other side, which if known, we then have a determined value of the unknown quantity in known terms. And the business of bringing the unknown quantity to stand alone on one side of a simple equation, is called reduction of simple equations : To effect which purpose, we have the following rules.

RULE I.

ANY quantity may be taken from one side of an equation and placed on the other, if you change its sign. Or which is the same thing, subtract the quantity from both sides.

For,

For, if from thofe quantities which are equal, there be taken the fame quantity, what remains will be equal.

EXAMPLES.

Given $x - 6 = 20$, to find the value of x.

Thus, $x = 20 + 6$, per rule, and $x = 26$ by addition.

For, — 6 taken from x — 6, leaves x, and —6 taken from 20, leaves 20 + 6, or 26, by the nature of fubtraction. Therefore, &c.

Given $x + 4 = 30 - 5$, to find the value of x.

Thus, $x = 30 - 5 - 4$ by tranfpofition :
Or, $x = 30 - 9 = 21$ by addition and fubtraction.

If $x - 3 + 1 = 21$:

Then will $x = 21 + 3 - 1$ by tranfpofition :
Or, $x = 23$ by addition and fubtraction.

R U L E II.

When the unknown quantity is multiplied with any number, it may be taken away by dividing all the reft of the terms in the equation by it.

For if thofe quantities which are equal, be divided by the fame quantity, their quotients will be equal.

EXAMPLES.

Given $4y - 12 = 2y + 4$, to find the value of y.

Firft, $4y - 2y = 12 + 4$ by tranfpofition :
Then, $2y = 16$ by addition and fubtraction :
Or, $y = \dfrac{16}{2} = 8$, per rule.

If

If $6y + 3 = y + 18$, then will $6y - y = 18 - 3$ *by transposition ; and* $5y = 15$ *by subtraction.*

Whence, $y = \dfrac{15}{3} = 5$ *by division.*

Let $3x - 10 = 20 - x + 6$, be given to find x.
First, $3x + x = 20 + 6 + 10$ *by transposition :*
Or, $4x = 36$, *and therefore,* $x = \dfrac{36}{4} = 9$.

R U L E III.

WHEN any part of the equation is divided by any quantity, that quantity may be taken away by multiplying all the rest of the terms by it ; which is the same as to multiply all the terms in the equation by that quantity. And if those quantities which are equal, be multiplied with the same quantity, their products will be equal.

EXAMPLES.

Given, $\dfrac{v}{6} + 2 = 10$, to find the value of v.

Thus, $v + 12 = 60$, *per rule :*
And $v = 60 - 12 = 48$ *by transposition and subtraction.*

Let $\dfrac{y}{2} + \dfrac{2y}{4} + \dfrac{3}{4} = 16$, be given to find y.

First, $\dfrac{16y}{32} + \dfrac{16y}{32} + \dfrac{24}{32} = 16$ *by reduction :*

Then, $\dfrac{32y + 24}{32} = 16$ *by addition :*

And $32y + 24 = 512$ *by multiplication :*

Whence,

Whence, $y = \dfrac{512 - 24}{32} = 15\frac{8}{32}.$

Alfo, if $\dfrac{3y}{2} + 6 = 2y + 4,$ then will $3y + 12 = 4y + 8$ *per rule ;*

And $4y - 3y = 12 - 8$ *by tranfpofition.*

Whence, $y = 4.$

R U L E IV.

If any quantity be found on both fides of the equation, having the fame fign, it may be expunged from both. Alfo, if all the terms of an equation be multiplied with the fame quantity, it may be ftruck out of them all.

EXAMPLES.

If $2x + 4a = x + 4a + 2;$ then will $2x = x + 2$ *per rule :*

And $2x - x = 2 ;$ *or,* $x = 2:$

Alfo, if $6x + c = b + c,$ then will $6x = b,$ *and* $x = \dfrac{b}{6}.$

Moreover, if $\dfrac{3xa}{c} + \dfrac{2xa}{c} - \dfrac{xa}{c} = \dfrac{da}{c},$ then will $3x + 2x - x = d :$

And $4x = d$ *by addition and fubtraction :*

Whence, $x = \dfrac{d}{4}.$

R U L E V.

If that part of the equation which involves the unknown quantity be a radical expreffion, it may be

made

made free from furds by tranfpofing the reft of the terms by the preceding rules, fo that the furd may ftand alone on one fide of the equation : Then take away the radical fign, and involve the other fide of the equation to the power whofe index is equal to the denominator of the radical fign.

EXAMPLES.

If $\sqrt{x+3}+4=20$:

Then will $\sqrt{x+3}=20-4=16$ by tranfpofition :

And $x+3=16\times16=256$ by involution :

Or, $x=256-3=253$.

And, if $4+\sqrt{2x+6}=9$; then will $\sqrt{2x+6}=9-4=5$ by tranfpofition :

And $2x+6=25$ by involution :

Whence, $x=\dfrac{19}{2}=9\frac{1}{2}$.

In like manner, if $\sqrt[3]{ax+3}=10$; then will $\sqrt[3]{ax}=10-3=7$; and $ax=343$ by involution ; or, $x=\dfrac{343}{a}$.

RULE VI.

IF both fides of an equation be a complete power, or can be made fo by the preceding rules, it may be reduced to more fimple terms, by extracting the root of both fides.

EXAMPLES.

Given, $y^2+6y+9-57=87$, to find the value of y.

Firft,

First, $y^2 + 6y + 9 = 87 + 57 = 144$ by transf.
Then, $y + 3 = 12$ by extracting the root :
Or, $y = 12 - 3 = 9$ by transposition.

Given, $9y^2 + 24y + 16 = 4y^2 + 32y + 64$, to find the value of y.

First, $3y + 4 = 2y + 8$ by extracting the root :
And $3y - 2y = 8 - 4$ by transposition :
That is, $y = 4$.

RULE VII.

ANY analogy may be converted into an equation, by asserting the product of the two extremes equal to the product of the two means.

EXAMPLES.

If $6 + x : 10 :: 4 : 6$; then will $36 + 6x = 40$, *by multiplying means and extremes, and $6x = 4$; or,* $x = \frac{4}{6}$.

And, if $\frac{2x}{3} : a :: 10 : 2$; then will $\frac{4x}{3} = 10a$; *and* $4x = 30a$; *or* $x = \frac{30a}{4}$.

And in like manner, if $6 : x - 2 :: 4 : 5$; then will $30 = 4x - 8$:

And $4x = 30 + 8 = 38$; or, $x = \frac{38}{4} = 9\frac{2}{4}$.

COROLLARY.

HENCE it follows, that an equation may be turned into an analogy, by dividing either side of it into

two

two such parts, which if multiplied together, would produce the same side again ; making those parts, either the two means or extremes ; then dividing the other side in like manner for the other two terms.

CHAP. XIV.

CONCERNING the extermination of unknown quantities, and reducing those equations which contain them, to a single one.

PROBLEM I.

To exterminate two unknown quantities, or reduce two equations containing them, to a single one.

RULE I.

FIND the value of one of the unknown quantities in each of the given equations, by the rules of the preceding chapter. And puting these two values equal to each other, you will have an equation involving only one unknown quantity ; which equation if a simple one, is to be resolved as in the last chapter.

EXAMPLES.

Given, $\left\{ \begin{array}{l} 2x+y=14 \\ 6x-3y=30 \end{array} \right\}$ to find x and y.

From the first equation, we have $x = \dfrac{14-y}{2}$:

And

And from the second, $x=\dfrac{30+3y}{6}:$

Therefore, $\dfrac{14-y}{2}=\dfrac{30+3y}{6}:$

And $84-6y=60+6y$ *by multiplication :*

Whence, $84-60=12y:$

Or, $12y=24:$

And therefore, $y=\dfrac{24}{2}=2,$ *and* $x=\dfrac{14-y}{2}=$ *(by*

writing 2 for y its equal) $\dfrac{14-2}{2}=6.$

Given, $\left\{\begin{array}{l}3v+y=22\\v:y::2:5\end{array}\right\}$ to find *v and y.*

From the first equation, $v=\dfrac{22-y}{3},$ *and the analo-*

gy turned into an equation, gives $5v=2y,$ *or* $v=$

$\dfrac{2y}{5},$ *and therefore,* $\dfrac{22-y}{3}=\dfrac{2y}{5}.$

Whence we get, $110-5y=6y$ *by multiplication :*

And $11y=110:$

Or, $y=\dfrac{110}{11}=10:$

And $v=\dfrac{2y}{5}=$ *(by writing 10 for y its equal)* $\dfrac{20}{5}$

$=4.$

R U L E II.

FIND the value of one of the unknown quantities in either of the given equations ; and inſtead of the unknown quantity in the other equation, ſubſtitute its value thus found, and there will ariſe a new e- quation having only one unknown quantity, whoſe value is to be found as before.

EXAMPLES.

EXAMPLES.

Given, $\left\{ \begin{array}{l} z + y = 10 \\ z - y = 7 \end{array} \right\}$ to find z and y.

From the first equation, we have $z = 10 - y$, which substituted for z in the second equation,

Gives $10 - y - y = 7$, or $10 - 2y = 7$:

And $2y = 10 - 7 = 3$:

Or, $y = 1.5$:

Whence, $z =$ (by writing 1.5 for y its equal) $10 - 1.5 = 8.5$:

Given, $\left\{ \begin{array}{l} 2z - 2y = 10 \\ 3y + z = 65 \end{array} \right\}$ to find z and y.

From the first equation $z = \dfrac{10 + 2y}{2}$, *and this value substituted in the second equation, gives* $3y + \dfrac{10 + 2y}{2} = 65$:

Or, $6y + 10 + 2y = 130$; whence, $8y = 120$:

Or, $y = \dfrac{120}{8} = 15$; and $z = \dfrac{10 + 2y}{2} = 5 + y = 5 + 15 = 20.$

R U L E III.

IF the unknown quantity is of lower dimension in one of the given equations than in the other ; find the value of the unknown quantity in the equation where it is of least dimension, and raise this value to the same height as the unknown quantity in the other equation ; or on the contrary. Then compare this value with the value of the unknown quantity

found

found from the other equation ; and you will have a new equation, with which proceed as before.

EXAMPLES.

Given, $\left\{\begin{array}{l} v + y = 10 \\ v^2 - y^2 = 60 \end{array}\right\}$ to find v and y.

From the first equation $v = 10 - y$;

And therefore, $v^2 = \overline{10 - y}\,|^2 = 100 - 20y + y^2$:

Then, $100 - 20y + y^2 = 60 + y^2$ by rule 1st.

Whence, $y = 2$ by reduction :

Or, $100 - 20y + y^2 - y^2 = 60$ by rule 2d.

Whence, $40 = 20y$:

Or, $y = \dfrac{40}{20} = 2$ as before ;

And $v = 10 - y = 10 - 2 = 8$:

Given, $\left\{\begin{array}{l} z^2 + y^2 = 25 \\ z^2 : yz :: 4 : 3 \end{array}\right\}$ to find z and y.

The analogy turned into an equation, gives $3z^2 = 4zy$, which divided by z, gives $3z = 4y$, or, $z = \dfrac{4y}{3}$:

Whence, $z^2 = \dfrac{16y^2}{9}$:

And therefore, $\dfrac{16y^2}{9} + y^2 = 25$:

Or, $16y^2 + 9y^2 = 225$:

Whence we get, $y^2 = 9$; or, $y = \sqrt{9} = 3$:

And $z = \dfrac{4y}{3} = \dfrac{12}{3} = 4$.

P R O B.

PROBLEM II.

To exterminate any three unknown quantities, x, y, and z, or to reduce three simple equations that involve them, to a single one.

RULE.

FIND the value of x in the three given equations; then compare the firſt value of x with the ſecond, and there will ariſe a new equation involving only y and z. Again compare the firſt, or ſecond value of x with the third, and there will ariſe another equation involving only y and z; then proceed with theſe two equations as directed in the laſt problem.

EXAMPLE.

Given, $\begin{cases} 2x + y + 2z = 15 \\ x + 6y - z = 29 \\ 4x - 2z + 2y = 12 \end{cases}$ to find x, y and z.

From the firſt equation, we have, $x = \dfrac{15 - 2z - y}{2}$

From the ſecond, $x = 29 + z - 6y$:

From the third, $x = \dfrac{12 + 2z - 2y}{4}$:

Whence, $\dfrac{15 - 2z - y}{2} = 29 + z - 6y$:

And $29 + z - 6y = \dfrac{12 + 2z - 2y}{4}$:

From the firſt of theſe equations, we get $15 - 2z - y = 58 + 2z - 12y$; or, $11y = 58 - 15 + 4z$:

T t

Whence,

Whence, $y = \dfrac{43 + 4z}{11}$:

From the second, we have $116 + 4z - 24y = 12 + 2z - 2y$:

That is, $22y = 116 - 12 + 2z$; *or,* $y = \dfrac{104 + 2z}{22}$

Consequently, $\dfrac{104 + 2z}{22} = \dfrac{43 + 4z}{11}$:

Whence, $1144 + 22z = 946 + 88z$:

And $88z - 22z = 198$:

That is, $66z = 198$:

Or, $z = \dfrac{198}{66} = 3$:

Whence, $y = \dfrac{43 + 4z}{11} = \dfrac{43 + 12}{11} = 5$, *and* $x =$

$\dfrac{15 - 2z - y}{2} = \dfrac{15 - 6 - 5}{2} = 2$.

AND nearly in the fame manner, may be exterminated any number of unknown quantities; but there are often much fhorter methods for their extermination, which are beft learned by practice ; yet fome of them may be thus generally given.

R U L E.

LET the given equations be multiplied or divided by fuch numbers, or quantities, that by addition, fubtraction, multiplication, divifion, involution or evolution of any two, or more of the equations, one or more of the unknown quantities may vanifh. Then taking the refult and the other equations, and proceed as before, until you have an equation in-

volving

volving only one unknown quantity, whose value may be found by the foregoing rules.

EXAMPLES.

Given, $\left\{\begin{array}{l} 2x + 3y = 29 \\ 3x + 2y = 31 \end{array}\right\}$ to find x and y.

Multiply the first equation with 2, and it will give $4x + 6y = 58$, *and the second with 3, gives* $9x + 6y = 93$, *from which subtract,* $4x + 6y = 58$; *and you will have*

$5x = 35$; *or,* $x = \dfrac{35}{5} = 7$, *and* $3y = 29 - 2x$; *or,* $y =$

$$\frac{29 - 2x}{3} = \frac{29 - 14}{3} = 5.$$

Given, $\left\{\begin{array}{l} 2x + 4y + 3z = 38 \\ 3x + 5y + 6z = 63 \\ 4x + 7y + 12z = 109 \end{array}\right\}$ to find $x, y,$ and z.

From double the first equation subtract the second, and from double the second, subtract the third, and the

results will be, $\left\{\begin{array}{l} x + 3y = 13 \\ 2x + 3y = 17. \end{array}\right.$

Again, from the second of these equations, subtract the first, and the result will be $x = 4$; *and from double the first subtract the second, and it will give* $3y = 9$; *or,*

$y = \dfrac{9}{3} = 3.$ *And from the first of the given equations,*

we have $3z = 38 - 2x - 4y$; *or,* $z = \dfrac{38 - 2x - 4y}{3}$

$$= \frac{38 - 8 - 12}{3} = 6.$$

Miscellaneous

Miscellaneous Examples.

Given, $\left\{ \begin{array}{l} v + y = 12 \\ vy = 32 \end{array} \right\}$ to find v and y.

The first equation involved to a square, gives $v^2 + 2vy + y^2 = 144$; *and* $v^2 - 2vy + y^2 = 16$ *by subtracting* $4vy\ (= 128)$ *from the last equation ; or,* $v - y = 4$ *by evolution :*

And therefore, $\overline{v + y} + \overline{v - y} = 12 + 4 :$

Or, $2v = 16$; *and* $v = \dfrac{16}{2} = 8 :$

Again, $\overline{v + y} - \overline{v - y} = 12 - 4 :$

That is, $2y = 8$; *or,* $y = \dfrac{8}{2} = 4.$

Given, $\left\{ \begin{array}{l} vy = 144 \\ \dfrac{v}{y} = 9 \end{array} \right\}$ to find v and y.

First, $v = 9y$ *by multiplication :*
Consequently, $vy = 9y \times y = 144 :$

That is, $9y^2 = 144$; *or,* $y^2 = \dfrac{144}{9} = 16.$

Whence, $y = \sqrt{16} = 4$; *and* $v = 9y = 36.$

Given, $\left\{ \begin{array}{l} v - y = 56 \\ \dfrac{v}{y} = 8 \end{array} \right\}$ to find v and y.

First, $v = 56 + y$; *and therefore,* $\dfrac{56 + y}{y} = 8$;

or, $56 + y = 8y$; *whence,* $y = \dfrac{56}{7} = 8$, *and* $v = 8y = 64.$

Given,

Given, $\left\{ v + \sqrt{16 + v^2} = \dfrac{32}{\sqrt{16 + v^2}} \right\}$ to find v.

First, $v \times \sqrt{16 + v^2} + \sqrt{16 + v^2} \times \sqrt{16 + v^2} = 32$.

That is, $v\sqrt{16 + v^2} + 16 + v^2 = 32$:

Then, $v\sqrt{16 + v^2} = 16 - v^2$:

And by involution, $v^2 \times \overline{16 + v^2} = \overline{16 - v^2}\,|^2 = 256 - 32v^2 + v^4$:

That is, $16v^2 + v^4 = 256 - 32v^2 + v^4$:

Or, $16v^2 = 256 - 32v^2$; *and* $16v^2 + 32v^2 = 256$:

Whence, $v^2 = \dfrac{256}{48}$; *or*, $v = \sqrt{\dfrac{256}{48}} = \sqrt{\dfrac{256 \times 1}{16 \times 3}}$

$= \dfrac{16}{4}\sqrt{\dfrac{1}{3}} = 4\sqrt{\dfrac{1}{3}}.$

Given, $\left\{ \begin{matrix} x^2 + y^2 = a \\ xy = b \end{matrix} \right\}$ to find x and y.

First, $x^2 + 2xy + y^2 = a + 2b$:

Then, $x + y = \sqrt{a + 2b}.$

Again, $x^2 - 2xy + y^2 = a - 2b$:

Then, $x - y = \sqrt{a - 2b}$:

Therefore, $x + y + x - y = \sqrt{a + 2b} + \sqrt{a - 2b}$

That is, $2x = \sqrt{a + 2b} + \sqrt{a - 2b}$:

Or, $x = \dfrac{\sqrt{a + 2b} + \sqrt{a - 2b}}{2}$:

And $x + y - x - y = 2y = \sqrt{a + 2b} - \sqrt{a - 2b}$

Whence, $y = \dfrac{\sqrt{a + 2b} - \sqrt{a - 2b}}{2}.$

CHAP.

CHAP. XV.

Of the SOLUTION of a variety of QUES-TIONS, that produce SIMPLE EQUA-TIONS.

AFTER forming a clear and diftinct idea of the queftion propofed ; the unknown quantities muft be expreffed by letters, which muft be ordered in fuch a manner, as to exprefs the conditions given in the queftion concerning thofe quantities. Thus, if the fum (s) of two quantities (x and y) are requir-ed ; then is $x + y = s$, an expreffion anfwering that condition. Alfo, if the difference (d) of thofe quantities is required ; that condition muft be ex-preffed thus, $x - y = d$ (x being the greater) Their product (p) is expreffed thus, $xy = p$. Their quo-tient (q) is $\frac{x}{y} = q$. Alfo, the fum of their fquares (a) is expreffed thus, $x^2 + y^2 = a$, and the differ-ence of their fquares (b) thus, $x^2 - y^2 = b$.

HAVING expreffed the unknown quantities in equations anfwering their relations, or properties, as given in the queftion ; you are next to confider whether your queftion is limited or not ; that is, whe-ther the quantities fought, are each of them capable of more known values than one ; which may always be difcovered in the following manner. If the equations that arife from expreffing the conditions of the queftion, are in number equal to the quantities fought, then is the queftion truly limited : That is, each of the quantities fought, cannot have more val-ues than one in giving the anfwer : But, if the equa-

tions

tions expreſſing the conditions of the queſtion, are fewer in number than the quantities ſought, then the queſtion is an unlimited one ; that is, the quantities ſought, are each of them of an indeterminate value, and conſequently, the queſtion propoſed, capable of innumerable anſwers.

AFTER you have diſcovered that the propoſed queſtion is limited ; you muſt then proceed to exterminate the unknown quantities by the rules already given, or other methods, which you may learn by practice ; to which we now proceed.

1. What number is that, from which if you take 40, the remainder will be 115 ?

Call the number ſought v :
Then will v — 40 = 115 by the queſtion :
Or, v = 115 + 40 = 155 the number ſought.

2. What number is that, from which if you take 10, and multiply the remainder with 4, the product will be 30 ?

Call the number ſought v :
Then will v — 10 be the remainder :
And v — 10 × 4 = 30 by the queſtion :
That is, 4v — 40 = 30 :
Or, 4v = 30 + 40 = 70 ; or, v = $\frac{70}{4}$ = 17½.

3. To find two numbers whoſe ſum is 80, and their difference 16.

Let v = the leaſt of the required numbers :
Then will v + 16 = the greater by the nature of ſubtraction :
And v + v + 16 = 80 by the queſtion :
That is, 2v = 80 — 16 = 64 :
Or, v = $\frac{64}{2}$ = 32 ; and v + 16 = 32 + 16 = 48,
the greater number required.

4. What number is that, which if multiplied with one third of itself, will produce the number sought?

If you call the number sought v:

Then will $\dfrac{v}{3}$ be one third part of v:

And $v \times \dfrac{v}{3} = v$ by the question:

That is, $\dfrac{v^2}{3} = v$; or, $v^2 = 3v$, and $v = 3$ the number sought.

5. Suppose the distance between Boston and York, to be 150 miles; and that a traveller sets out from Boston, and travels at the rate of 5 miles an hour; another sets out at the same time from York, and travels at the rate of 8 miles an hour: It is required to know how far each will travel before they meet.

If you put v for the distance that must be travelled by the one which sets out from Boston, and y the distance travelled by the other before they meet:

Then will $v + y = 150$, the distance travelled by both, and $v : y :: 5 : 8$ by the question:

That is, $8v = 5y$; or, $v = \dfrac{5y}{8}$.

Also, $v = 150 - y$; consequently, $\dfrac{5y}{8} = 150 - y$:

That is, $5y = 1200 - 8y$:
Whence, $y = 1200 \div 13 = 92\frac{4}{13}$.
And $v = 150 - y = 57\frac{9}{13}$.

6. What fraction is that, if you add 1 to the numerator, the value will be $\frac{1}{2}$; but if you add 1 to the denominator, the value will be $\frac{1}{3}$:

Put $\dfrac{v}{y}$ for the fraction sought:

Then

Then will, $\dfrac{v+1}{y}=\dfrac{1}{2}$

And $\dfrac{v}{y+1}=\dfrac{1}{3}$ $\Bigg\}$ by the question.

That is, $2v+2=y$; or, $v=\dfrac{y-2}{2}$:

And $3v=y+1$; or, $v=\dfrac{y+1}{3}$:

Consequently, $\dfrac{y-2}{2}=\dfrac{y+1}{3}$:

Or, $3y-6=2y+2$:

Whence, $y=8$, the denominator:

And $v=\dfrac{y-2}{2}=\dfrac{8-2}{2}=3$ the numerator:

Therefore, $\frac{3}{8}$ is the fraction required.

7. What two numbers are those whose sum is 60, and the sum of their squares 2250?

Call one of the numbers w, and the other y:

Then will, $w+y=60$

And $w^2+y^2=2250$ $\Bigg\}$ by the question.

First, $w^2+2wy+y^2=60^2=3600$:

And $w^2+2wy+y^2-\overline{w^2+y^2}=2wy=1350$:

Therefore, $4wy=2700$:

Then, $w^2+2wy+y^2-4wy=w^2-2wy+y^2=900$:

Whence, $w-y=\sqrt{900}=30$:

And $2w=60+30=90$, or $w=45$:

And $y=60-w=60-45=15$.

8. There are three numbers in arithmetical progreſsion, the firſt added to the ſecond will make 15, and the ſecond added to the third, 21 : What are thoſe numbers?

U u

Let

Let x, y and z reprefent the three numbers :
Then will x + y = 15, the fum of the firft and fe-
cond :
And y + z = 21, the fum of the fecond and third :
Alfo, x + z = 2y by the nature of the proportion.
Whence, x + y + y + z = 15 + 21 = 36 :
That is, x + 2y + z = 36 ; or, x + z = 36 — 2y :
But x + z = 2y ; therefore, 2y = 36 — 2y ; or,
4y = 36 :
Whence, y = 9 ; and x = 15 — y = 15 — 9 = 6 :
And z = 21 — y = 21 — 9 = 12.

9. Two merchants traded in partnerfhip ; the fum of their ftocks was 600 dollars ; one's ftock was in company 8 months, but the other drew out his at the end of 6 months, when they fettled their accounts, and divided the gain equally between them : What was each man's ftock ?

Call one of the ftocks x ; then 600 — x = the other :
But, x : 600 — x :: 6 : 8 by the queftion :
Confequently, 8x = 3600 — 6 x ; or, 14x = 3600 :

$$\text{Whence, } x = \frac{3600}{14} = 257\tfrac{1}{7} ; \text{ and } 600 — x = 600$$

— 257$\tfrac{1}{7}$ = 342$\tfrac{6}{7}$ the others ftock.

10. To find three numbers, fuch that if the firft be added to the fecond, their fum will be 12 ; and the fecond added to the third, their fum will be 20 ; alfo, if the firft be added to the third, their fum will be 16.

Call the firft number x, the fecond y, and the third z :

$$\left. \begin{array}{l} \text{Then will } x + y = 12 \\ \text{And } y + z = 20 \\ \text{Alfo, } x + z = 16 \end{array} \right\} \text{ by the queftion.}$$

Therefore, x + y + x + z = 12 + 16 = 28 :

That

That is, $2x + y + z = 28$: *But* $y + z = 20$:
Consequently, $2x + 20 = 28$; *or,* $2x = 8$:
Whence, $x = 4$, *and* $y = 12 - x = 12 - 4 = 8$:
And $z = 20 - y = 20 - 8 = 12$.

11. There are four numbers in arithmetical progreffion ; whereof the product of the two extremes is 112, and the product of the two means 130 ; alfo, the fum of the firft and fecond terms is 17 : What are thofe numbers ?

Put x for the leaft term, and y the common difference ; then will x, $x + y$, $x + 2y$, $x + 3y$ be the four numbers required :

$$\begin{aligned} And \; & x \times \overline{x + 3y} = 112 \\ Alfo, \; & \overline{x + y} \times \overline{x + 2y} = 130 \\ And \; & x + \overline{x + y} = 17 \end{aligned} \Big\} \; by \; the \; queftion.$$

That is, $x^2 + 3xy = 112$:
And $x^2 + 3xy + 2y^2 = 130$:

Whence, $\overline{x^2 + 3xy + 2y^2} - \overline{x^2 + 3xy} = 130 - 112 = 18$:

That is, $2y^2 = 18$; *or,* $y^2 = \frac{18}{2} = 9$, *and* $y = \sqrt{9} = 3$:

But, $x + \overline{x + y} = 17$; *that is,* $2x + 3 = 17$:
Or, $2x = 17 - 3 = 14$:
Confequently, $x = \frac{14}{2} = 7$, *the firft term of the progreffion ; and therefore, $x + y = 10$, the fecond term ; and $x + 2y = 13$, the third term ; alfo, $x + 3y = 16$, the fourth term.*

So that 7, 10, 13, and 16, are the numbers required.

12. There are three numbers in arithmetical progreffion ; the product of the two extremes, is 128, and the product of the leaft extreme with the mean, is 96: What are thofe numbers ?

Call

Call the numbers required, v, y and z ; v and z be-ing the extremes, whereof v is the least.

Then will $\left.\begin{array}{l} vz = 128 \\ vy = 96 \end{array}\right\}$ *by the question.*

And $v + z = 2y$ *by the nature of the proportion :*

$z = \dfrac{128}{v}$ *from the first equation :*

And $z = 2y - v$ *from the third :*

Consequently, $\dfrac{128}{v} = 2y - v$ *by equality :*

That is, $128 = 2yv - v^2$: *But* $2yv = 96 \times 2 = 192$:

Therefore, $128 = 192 - v^2$ *by substitution :*

And $v^2 = 192 - 128 = 64$; *or,* $v = \sqrt{64} = 8$:

Also, $z = \dfrac{128}{v} = \dfrac{128}{8} = 16$; *and* $v + z = 2y$;

or, $y = \dfrac{v + z}{2} = \dfrac{8 + 16}{2} = 12$; *and therefore the num-bers sought are* 8, 12, 16.

13. To find a fraction, such that the square of the numerator, added to the denominator, shall make 30 ; and if 2 be added to the denominator, the value of the fraction will be equal to the reciprocal of the numerator.

Put $\dfrac{v}{y}$ *for the fraction sought.*

Then will $\left.\begin{array}{l} v^2 + y = 30 \\ \text{And } \dfrac{v}{y+2} = \dfrac{1}{v} \end{array}\right\}$ *by the question.*

First, $v^2 = 30 - y$:

And $v^2 = y + 2 \times 1 = y + 2$:

Consequently, $y + 2 = 30 - y$; *that is,* $2y = 28$:

Or,

$$Or, \; y = \tfrac{28}{2} = 14 ; \quad and \;\; v^2 = 30 - y = 30 - 14$$
$$= 16 ; \; or, \; v = \sqrt{16} = 4.$$

So that the fraction sought, is $\dfrac{4}{14}$ *; for,* $\dfrac{4}{14 + 2} =$

$\dfrac{4}{16} = \dfrac{1}{4} = \dfrac{1}{v}$ *; Therefore, &c.*

14. To find a number confisting of two places, fuch that the fum of its digits fhall be 5, and if 9 be fubtracted from it, the digits will be inverted.

Let v and y reprefent the two digits, v that which ftands in the tenth's place.

Then by the nature of notation, we have $10v + y =$ *the number fought.*

$$\left.\begin{array}{l} Therefore, \; v + y = 5 \\ And \;\; 10v + y - 9 = 10y + v \end{array}\right\} by\ the\ queftion.$$

Whence, $9v = 9y + 9$ *; or,* $v = \dfrac{9y + 9}{9} = (by\ di$-*vifion)* $y + 1$:

Alfo, $v = 5 - y$ *; and therefore,* $y + 1 = 5 - y$ *; or,* $2y = 4$:

And $y = \tfrac{4}{2} = 2$ *; and* $v = y + 1 = 2 + 1 = 3$: *So that 32 is the number required.*

15. A certain company at an inn ; when they came to pay their reckoning, found that if there had been two perfons lefs in company, they would have paid a dollar a man more ; but if there had been three perfons more in company, they would each of them paid a dollar lefs : What was their reckoning, and the number of perfons to pay it ?

Put v = the number of perfons, and y the number of dollars each paid ; then will vy = the whole reconing.

Whence,

Whence, $\dfrac{vy}{v-2} = y + 1$
And $\dfrac{vy}{v+3} = y - 1$ $\Bigg\}$ *by the question.*

That is, $vy = vy + v - 2y - 2$ *from the first equation:*

Or, $2y + 2 = v$:

And $vy = vy - v + 3y - 3$ *from the second equation:*

Or, $v = 3y - 3$:

Consequently, $3y - 3 = 2y + 2$; *or,* $3y - 2y = 2 + 3$:

Whence, $y = 5$, *the number of dollars each paid:*

And $v = 2y + 2 = 12$, *the number of persons:* *Consequently,* $vy = 60$ *dollars, the whole reckoning.*

16. To find three numbers v, y and w, the product of each with the sum of the other two being given, viz. $v \times \overline{y + w} = 930$; $y \times \overline{v + w} = 1300$, and $w \times \overline{v + y} = 1480$:

Or, $\begin{cases} vy + vw = 930 = a \\ vy + wy = 1300 = b \\ vw + wy = 1480 = c \end{cases}$

Then, $vy + vw + vw + wy = a + c$. *But* $vy + wy = b$:

And therefore, $2vw = a + c - b$; *or,* $vw = \dfrac{a + c - b}{2}$

Also, $vy + vw + vy + wy = a + b$: *But* $vw + wy = c$:

Wherefore, $2vy = a + b - c$; *or,* $vy = \dfrac{a + b - c}{2}$:

Again, $vy + wy + vw + wy = b + c$: *But* $vy + vw = a$:

And therefore, we have $2wy = b + c - a$; *or,* $wy = \dfrac{b + c - a}{2}$

$$\frac{b + c - a}{2}.$$

But $y = \dfrac{a + b - c}{2v}$; *and by writing this value for y*

in the equation, $wy = \dfrac{b + c - a}{2}$, *we have* $wy =$

$\dfrac{aw + bw - cw}{2v} = \dfrac{b + c - a}{2}$; *whence by reduction,*

$v = \dfrac{aw + bw - cw}{b + c - a}$: *Also,* $vw = \dfrac{a + c - b}{2}$; *or,* v

$= \dfrac{a + c - b}{2w}$; *and therefore by equality,* $\dfrac{aw + bw - cw}{b + c - a}$

$= \dfrac{a + c - b}{2w}$:

Or, $2aw^2 + 2bw^2 - 2cw^2 = 2ab + c^2 - b^2 - a^2$:

Whence, $w^2 = \dfrac{2ab + c^2 - b^2 - a^2}{2a + 2b - 2c}$:

Or, $w = \sqrt{\dfrac{2ab + c^2 - b^2 - a^2}{2a + 2b - 2c}}$: *Which expression*

*turned into numbers, and the root extracted, w will
be found* $= 37$; *whence the other numbers are readily*

found ; for $v = \dfrac{a + c - b}{2w} = 15$, *and* $y = \dfrac{a + b - c}{2v}$

$= 25$:

17. Two women went to market with 42 eggs,
for which they received equal fums of money ; afterwards fays one to the other, if I had fold as many
eggs as you, I fhould have received 350 cents ; fays
the other, if I had fold no more than you, I fhould
have received but 14 cents. Query, the number of
eggs each fold, and the particular prices fold at ; alfo the number of cents each received.

Let

Let v = number of eggs fold by one, and y the num-ber fold by the other ; alfo, u = price which v eggs were fold at per egg, and w the price that y eggs were fold per egg.

$$\text{Then will} \begin{cases} v + y = 42 \\ vu = yw \\ vw = 350 \\ yu = 14 \end{cases} \text{ by the queftion.}$$

From the third equation we have, $v = \dfrac{350}{w}$: *From the fourth equation,* $u = \dfrac{14}{y}$; *and therefore,* $vu = \dfrac{350}{w} \times \dfrac{14}{y} = \dfrac{4900}{yw}$: *But* $vu = yw$ *from the fecond equation ; wherefore,* $\dfrac{4900}{yw} = yw$; *or* $4900 = y^2 w^2$, *and* $yw = \sqrt{4900} = 70$; *whence,* $y = \dfrac{70}{w}$: *But* $y = \dfrac{14}{u}$ *from the fourth equation ; confequently,* $\dfrac{70}{w} = \dfrac{14}{u}$; *or,* $70u = 14w$; *or,* $5u = w$: *And by writing* $5u$ *for* w *in the fecond equation, we have* $vu = 5uy$, *or dividing both fides by* u, *we fhall have* $v = 5y$: *But* $v = 42 - y$ *from the firft equation ; therefore,* $5y = 42 - y$; *or,* $6y = 42$; *whence,* $y = \dfrac{42}{6} = 7$, $v = 5y = 35$, $u = \dfrac{14}{y} = 2$, *and* $w = 5u = 10$.

18. Given the fum *(s)* and product *(p)* of two quantities, to find the fum of their fquares, cubes, biquadrates, &c.

Let v and w reprefent the two quantities :

$$\text{Then will} \begin{cases} v + w = s \\ vw = p \end{cases} \text{ by the queftion.}$$

And

And $\overline{x+y}|^2 = x^2 + 2xy + y^2 = s^2$ *by involution* :
Or, $x^2 + 2xy + y^2 - 2xy = s^2 - 2p$ *by subtract.*
That is, $x^2 + y^2 = s^2 - 2p =$ *sum of the squares.*

Again, $\overline{x^2 + y^2} \times \overline{x + y} = \overline{s^2 - 2p} \times s$:
That is, $x^3 + xy \times \overline{x + y} + y^3 = s^3 - 2sp$:
Or, $x^3 + sp + y^3 = s^3 - 2sp$ *by writing sp for its equal,* $xy \times \overline{x + y}$; *whence,* $\overline{x^3 + y^3} = s^3 - 2sp - sp = s^3 - 3sp =$ *sum of their cubes.*

Also, $\overline{x^3 + y^3} \times \overline{x + y} = \overline{s^3 - 3sp} \times s$:
That is, $x^4 + xy \times \overline{x^2 + y^2} + y^4 = s^4 - 3s^2p$; *or, (by writing for* $xy \times \overline{x^2 + y^2}$ *its equal,* $s^2p - 2p^2$ *)* $x^4 + s^2p - 2p^2 + y^4 = s^4 - 3s^2p$; *whence,* $x^4 + y^4 = s^4 - 4s^2p + 2p^2 =$ *sum of their fourth powers.*

And $\overline{x^4 + y^4} \times \overline{x + y} = \overline{s^4 - 4s^2p + 2p^2} \times s$:
That is, $x^5 + xy \times \overline{x^3 + y^3} + y^5 = s^5 - 4s^3p + 2p^2s$; *and therefore, (by writing for* $xy \times \overline{x^3 + y^3}$ *its equal* $s^3p - 3sp^2$ *) we have,* $x^5 + \overline{s^3p - 3sp^2} + y^5 = s^5 - 4s^3p + 2sp^2$; *and by transposition, we get* $\overline{x^5 + y^5} = s^5 - 5s^3 + 5sp^2$ *for the sum of their fifth powers ; and so on for the rest.*

C H A P. XVI.

OF QUADRATIC EQUATIONS.

A QUADRATIC EQUATION, is an e-
quation of two dimensions involving only one
unknown quantity ; and is either simple or adfected.

A simple quadratic, is an equation which involves only the square of the unknown quantity. Thus, $v^2 = a^2$ is a simple quadratic equation.

But when you have an equation which involves the square of the unknown quantity, together with its product with some known co-efficient, you have what is called an adfected quadratic equation. Thus, $v^2 + av = bc$, is an adfected quadratic equation.

All adfected quadratic equations, fall under the three following forms :

$$\text{viz.} \begin{cases} v^2 + av = bc \\ v^2 - av = bc \\ v^2 - av = -bc \end{cases}$$

The solution of adfected quadratic equations, or finding the value of the unknown quantity in those equations, is performed by the following

R U L E.

1. Transpose all the terms that involve the unknown quantity to one side of the equation, and all the terms that are known to the other side.

2. If the square of the unknown quantity is multiplied with any co-efficient, you must cast off that co-efficient, by dividing all the terms in the equation by it, that the co-efficient of the highest dimension of the unknown quantity may be unity.

3. Add the square of half the co-efficient prefixed to the unknown quantity, to both sides of the equation ; and that side which involves the unknown quantity will then become a complete square.

4. Extract the root from both sides of the equation, which will consist of the unknown quantity connected with half the aforesaid co-efficient ; and therefore by transposing this half, the value of the unknown quantity will be determined.   *SOL.*

SOLUTION of the THREE FORMS OF QUADRATICS ILLUSTRATED.

Let it be required to determine the value of v, in the form $v^2 + av = bc$.

First, $v^2 + av + \dfrac{a^2}{4} = bc + \dfrac{a^2}{4}$ *by adding the sqr.*

of $\dfrac{a}{2}$ *to both sides of the equation: Then* $v + \dfrac{a}{2} = \sqrt{bc + \dfrac{a^2}{4}}$ *by extracting the root of both sides; or,* $v = \sqrt{bc + \dfrac{a^2}{4}} - \dfrac{a}{2}$ *by transposition. But the square root of any positive quantity, may be either positive, or negative; that is, the square root of* $+ n^2$ *may be either* $+ n$ *or* $- n$ *; for* $+ n \times + n$ *; or,* $- n \times - n$ *, are respectively equal to* $+ n^2$. *It follows therefore, that all quadratic equations admit of two solutions, that is, the unknown quantity has two values in the given equation. Thus, in the foregoing example, where* $v^2 + av + \dfrac{a^2}{4} = bc + \dfrac{a^2}{4}$, *we may infer, that* $v + \dfrac{a}{2} = \sqrt{bc + \dfrac{a^2}{4}}$ *or,* $- \sqrt{bc + \dfrac{a^2}{4}}$ *; for,* $+ \sqrt{bc + \dfrac{a^2}{4}} \times + \sqrt{bc + \dfrac{a^2}{4}}$ *or,* $- \sqrt{bc + \dfrac{a^2}{4}} \times - \sqrt{bc + \dfrac{a^2}{4}}$ *are each equal to* $bc + \dfrac{a^2}{4}$ *; and therefore the two values of* v, *are* $v = \sqrt{bc + \dfrac{a^2}{4}} - \dfrac{a}{2}$, *and* $v = - \sqrt{bc + \dfrac{a^2}{4}} - \dfrac{a}{2}$: *which*

ambiguity

ambiguity is expressed by writing the uncertain sign $\pm$ before $\sqrt{bc + \frac{a^2}{4}}$: Thus, $v + \frac{a}{2} = \pm \sqrt{bc + \frac{a^2}{4}}$, or

$$v = \pm \sqrt{bc + \frac{a^2}{4}} - \frac{a}{2}.$$

In the first expression for the value of v, viz. $\sqrt{bc + \frac{a^2}{4}} - \frac{a}{2}$, the only negative quantity is $\frac{a}{2} = \sqrt{\frac{a^2}{4}}$ which is evidently less than $\sqrt{bc + \frac{a^2}{4}}$; and consequently, the value of v is positive: But in the second expression, viz. $v = -\sqrt{bc + \frac{a^2}{4}} - \frac{a}{2}$, having $\sqrt{bc + \frac{a^2}{4}}$, and $\frac{a}{2}$ both negative; it follows, that the value of v must also be negative.

Again, if $z^2 - az = bc$:

Then will $z^2 - az + \frac{a^2}{4} = bc + \frac{a^2}{4}$, by adding the square of $\frac{a}{2}$ to both sides, and $z - \frac{a}{2} = \pm \sqrt{bc + \frac{a^2}{4}}$ by extracting the root; and therefore, $z = \sqrt{bc + \frac{a^2}{4}} + \frac{a}{2}$ for the positive value of z, and $z = -\sqrt{bc + \frac{a^2}{4}} + \frac{a}{2}$ the negative one; for since $bc + \frac{a^2}{4}$ is greater than $\frac{a^2}{4}$; consequently, $\sqrt{bc + \frac{a^2}{4}}$ is greater than $\sqrt{\frac{a^2}{4}}$;

and

and therefore, $z = -\sqrt{bc + \dfrac{a^2}{4}} + \dfrac{a}{2}$ is always a negative quantity.

And in like manner, the value of z determined in the third form, viz. $z^2 - az = -bc$, is $z = \pm\sqrt{\dfrac{a^2}{4} - bc} + \dfrac{a}{2}$, where both the values of z will be positive, if $\dfrac{a^2}{4}$ is greater than bc; for then $z = \sqrt{\dfrac{a^2}{4} - bc} + \dfrac{a}{2}$ is evidently a positive quantity; and in the second value of z, viz. $z = -\sqrt{\dfrac{a^2}{4} - bc} + \dfrac{a}{2}$, it is plain, that $\dfrac{a^2}{4}$ is greater than $\dfrac{a^2}{4} - bc$, since $\dfrac{a^2}{4}$ is greater than bc; and therefore, the $\sqrt{\dfrac{a^2}{4}}$ is greater than $\sqrt{\dfrac{a^2}{4} - bc}$; consequently, $z = -\sqrt{\dfrac{a^2}{4} - bc} + \sqrt{\dfrac{a^2}{4}}\left(= \dfrac{a}{2}\right)$ is a positive quantity: But when bc is greater than $\dfrac{a^2}{4}$ then $\dfrac{a^2}{4} - bc$ is a negative quantity; and since the square of any quantity (whether positive or negative) is always positive; it follows, that $\sqrt{\dfrac{a^2}{4} - bc}$ is impossible, or imaginary; and consequently, $z = \pm\sqrt{\dfrac{a^2}{4} - bc} + \dfrac{a}{2}$ is imaginary. Therefore, in the third

form,

form, when bc is greater than $\dfrac{a^2}{4}$ the solution of the equation will be impossible.

EXAMPLES

Of determining the value of the unknown quantity in quadratic equations.

Given, $x^2 + 4x = 32$, to find the value of x.

First, $x^2 + 4x + 4 = 32 + 4$, *by adding the square of half the co-efficient to both sides :*

Then, $\sqrt{x^2 + 4x + 4} = \pm \sqrt{36}$:

That is, $x + 2 = \pm 6$; *or,* $x = \pm 6 - 2 = 4$, *or* -8 : *Either of which substituted for x, will produce the given equation.*

Given, $3x^2 - 9x = -6$, to find x.

First, $x^2 - 3x = -2$ *by dividing the whole by 3 :*

Then, $x^2 - 3x + \dfrac{9}{4} = \dfrac{9}{4} - 2$ *by completing the square :*

And therefore, $x - \dfrac{3}{2} = \pm \sqrt{\dfrac{9}{4} - 2}$ *by extracting the root :*

Or, $x = \dfrac{3}{2} \pm \sqrt{\dfrac{9}{4} - 2} = \dfrac{3}{2} + \dfrac{1}{2} = \dfrac{4}{2} = 2.$

Given, $av^2 - bv - c = d$, to find v.

First, $av^2 - bv = d - c$ *by transposition :*

And $v^2 - \dfrac{b}{a}v = \dfrac{d - c}{a}$ *by division :*

Therefore,

Therefore, $v^2 - \dfrac{b}{a}v + \dfrac{b^2}{4a^2} = \dfrac{d-c}{a} + \dfrac{b^2}{4a^2}$ *by completing the square :*

Whence, $v - \dfrac{b}{2a} = \pm \sqrt{\dfrac{d-c}{a} + \dfrac{b^2}{4a^2}}$ *by evolution :*

Or, $v = \dfrac{b}{2a} \pm \sqrt{\dfrac{d-c}{a} + \dfrac{b^2}{4a^2}}$ *by transposition.*

ALL equations, wherein there are two terms which involve the unknown quantity, whose index in one term, is just double its index in the other, are reduced to equations of lower dimensions, in the same manner as quadratics.

THUS, $v^6 + bv^3 = d$; and $v^n + bv^{\frac{n}{2}} = c$, are reduced by completing the square, and extracting the root, as in quadratics ; and the value of the unknown quantity determined by extracting the root of the resulting equation ; as in the following

EXAMPLES.

Given, $v^4 - 2v^2 = 224$, to find the value of v.

First, $v^4 - 2v^2 + 1 = 224 + 1 = 225$ *by completing the square :*

And $v^2 - 1 = \sqrt{225}$ *by evolution :*

Or, $v^2 = \sqrt{225} + 1$ *by transposition :*

Whence, $v = \overline{\sqrt{225} + 1}\,|^{\frac{1}{2}} = 4.$

Given, $bv^n + cv^{\frac{n}{2}} - d = e$, to find v.

First, $bv^n + cv^{\frac{n}{2}} = e + d$ *by transposition.*

Then, $v^n + \dfrac{c}{b}v^{\frac{n}{2}} = \dfrac{e+d}{b}$ *by division :*

And

And $v^n + \dfrac{c}{b}v^{\frac{n}{2}} + \dfrac{c^2}{4b^2} = \dfrac{e+d}{b} + \dfrac{c^2}{4b^2}$ *by completing the square:*

Therefore, $v^{\frac{n}{2}} + \dfrac{c}{2b} = \pm\sqrt{\dfrac{e+d}{b} + \dfrac{c^2}{4b^2}}$ *by evolution.*

Whence, $v = \overline{\pm\sqrt{\dfrac{e+d}{b} + \dfrac{c^2}{4b^2}} - \dfrac{c}{2b}}\Big|^{\frac{n}{2}}.$

C H A P. XVII.

The SOLUTION of a Variety of QUESTIONS, Producing QUADRATIC EQUATIONS.

1. WHAT two numbers are those, whose sum is 20, and their product 96?

Call one of the numbers w; then will 20 — w be the other:

And $w \times \overline{20 - w} = 96$ *by the question:*
That is, $20w - w^2 = 96$:
Or, $w^2 - 20w = -96$ *by transposition:*
And $w^2 - 20w + 100 = 100 - 96$ *by completing the square:*
Therefore, $w - 10 = \pm\sqrt{100 - 96} = \pm\sqrt{4} = \pm 2$ *by evolution:*
Or, $w = \pm 2 + 10 = 12$ *or* 8, *and* $20 - w = 20 - 12 = 8$ *the other number.*

2. What two numbers are those, whose sum is 36, and the sum of their squares 720?
Put w for the greater number:
Then will $36 - w =$ *the other:*

And

And $w^2 + \overline{36 - w}|^2 = 720$ by the question :
That is, $w^2 + 1296 - 72w + w^2 = 720$:
Or, $2w^2 - 72w = -576$ by transposition :
And $w^2 - 36w = -288$ by division :
Wherefore, $w^2 - 36w + 324 = 324 - 288 = 36$
by completing the square :
Consequently, $w - 18 = \pm \sqrt{36} = 6$ by evolution :
Or, $w = 6 + 18 = 24$, and $36 - w = 36 - 24 = 12$:

3. What number being divided by the product of its two digits, the quotient will be 2 ; and if 27 be added to it, the digits will be inverted ?

Put w and y for the two digits :
Then will $10w + y$ be the number sought, by the nature of notation :

$$\left. \begin{array}{l} And \quad \dfrac{10w + y}{wy} = 2 \\ And\ 10w + y + 27 = 10y + w \end{array} \right\} by\ the\ question :$$

Or, $9w = 9y - 27$ by transposition :
And $w = \dfrac{9y - 27}{9} = y - 3$:
But $10w + y = 2wy$; whence, (by writing for w its equal $y - 3$, in the equation $10w + y = 2wy$) we get $10y - 30 + y = 2y^2 - 6y$:
Or, $17y - 2y^2 = 30$; or, $2y^2 - 17y = -30$ by transposition :
Whence, $y^2 - 8\frac{1}{2}y = -15$ by division :
And $y^2 - 8\frac{1}{2}y + \dfrac{289}{16} = \dfrac{289}{16} - 15 = \dfrac{49}{16}$ by completing the square :
Or, $y - \dfrac{17}{4} = \pm \sqrt{\dfrac{49}{16}} = \dfrac{7}{4}$ by evolution :

Y y

Consequently,

Consequently, $y = \dfrac{17}{4} + \dfrac{7}{4} = \dfrac{24}{4} = 6$, *and* $w = y - 3 = 3$:

Therefore 36 is the number required.

4. To find three numbers in geometrical proportion continued, whofe fum is 78; and if the fum of the extremes be multiplied with the mean, the product will be 1080.

Put $v = $ *leaft extreme, and* z *the greater ; alfo,* $y = $ *mean :*

 Then will $v + y + z = 78$ } *by the queftion.*
  And $v + z \times y = 1080$ }

That is, $vy + zy = 1080$; *and* $vy + y^2 + zy = 78y$ *by multiplying the firft equation with* y ;

Whence, $y^2 = ($ *by writing for* $vy + zy$ *its equal* 1080 *)* $78y - 1080$,

Or, $y^2 - 78y = - 1080$:

And $y^2 - 78y + 1521 = 1521 - 1080 = 441$ *by completing the fquare :*

And therefore, $y - 39 = \pm \sqrt{441} = \pm 21$ *by evolution :*

Or, $y = 39 \pm 21 = ($ *becaufe* $39 + 21 = 60$, *is greater than the fum of the extremes, which is abfurd)* $39 - 21 = 18$:

But, $vz = y^2 = 324$ *by the nature of the proportion :*

Confequently, $v = \dfrac{324}{z}$, *which wrote for* v *in the equation* $vy + zy = 1080$, *gives* $\dfrac{324y}{z} + zy = 1080$:

That is, $5932 + 18z^2 = 1080z$:

Or, $18z^2 - 1080z = - 5932$ *by tranfpofition :*

And $z^2 - 60z = - 324$ *by divifion :*

Therefore, $z^2 - 60z + 900 = 900 - 324 = 576$ *by completing the fquare :*   *Whence,*

Whence, z — 30 $=\pm\sqrt{576}=\pm$ 24 *by evolution :*
Or, z = 30 + 24 = 54, *and v =* 78 — z — y = 78
— 54 — 18 = 6. *Therefore,* 6, 18, *and* 54, *are the
numbers required.*

5. There are three numbers in geometrical progreſſion, whoſe ſum is 117, and the ſum oi their
ſquares 7371 : What are thoſe numbers ?

Call the numbers x, y and v :

Then will x + y + v = 117 $\Big\}$ *by the queſtion.*
And x² + y² + v² = 7371

Alſo, xv = y² *by the nature of the proportion :*
And x + v = 117 — y *by the firſt equation :*
Whence, x² + 2xv + v² = 13689 — 234y + y²
by involution :

But, 2xv = 2y², *which ſubſtituted for* 2xv *in the
laſt equation, gives x²* + 2y + v² = 13689 — 234y +
y² :

Or, x² + v² = 13689 — 234y — y² :
But, x² + v² = 7371 — y² *by the ſecond equation :*
Conſequently, 7371 — y² = 13689 — 234y — y² :
Or, 234y = 13689 — 7371 = 6310 :

Whence, y = $\dfrac{6310}{234}$ = 27, *and xv =* y² = 729 :

Or, x = $\dfrac{729}{v}$, *which ſubſtituted in the equation x* +

y + v = 117, *gives* $\dfrac{729}{v}$ + 27 + v = 117 ; *or,* $\dfrac{729}{v}$
+ v = 117 — 27 = 90 :

Whence, 729 + v² = 90v *by multiplication :*
Or, v² — 90v = — 729 *by tranſpoſition :*
And therefore, v² — 90v + 2025 = 2025 — 729
= 1296 *by completing the ſquare :*

Conſequently,

Confequently, $v - 45 = \pm \sqrt{1296} = 36$ *by evolution :*

Or, $v = 45 + 36 = 81$, *and* $x = \dfrac{729}{v} = 9$.

And the numbers required, are 9, 27, 81.

MISCELLANEOUS QUESTIONS, with their SOLUTIONS.

1. Suppofe two cities, A and B, whofe diftance from each other is 216 miles; and that two couriers fet out at the fame time, one from A, and the other from B; the firft travels 10 miles a day, and the other 4 miles lefs than the number of days in which they will meet. Query the number of days before they meet?

Put x = *number of days required* :

Then will $10x + \overline{x - 4} \times x = 216$ *by the queftion* :

That is, $10x + x^2 - 4x = 216$; *or,* $x^2 + 6x = 216$:

And $x^2 + 6x + 9 = 216 + 9 = 225$:

Whence, $x + 3 = \pm \sqrt{225} = 15$; *or,* $x = 15 - 3 = 12$, *the number of days required.*

2. A traveller fets out from the city A, and travels at the rate of 9 miles an hour; and another at the fame time fets out from the fame city, and follows him, travelling the firft hour 4 miles; the fecond 5; the third 6, and fo on, in arithmetical progreffion : In what time will he overtake the firft?

Put x = *number of hours in which the firft will be overtaken* :

Then will $9x$ = *the diftance he travels* :

And $\overline{x - 1} \times 1 + 4 + 4 = x + 7$:

And

And $\overline{x+7} \times \frac{1}{2}x = \dfrac{x^2+7x}{2} =$ *distance the other travels before he overtakes the first, by the nature of the proportion* : Consequently, $\dfrac{x^2+7x}{2} = 9x$ *by the question* :

Or, $x^2+7x = 18x$: *Whence*, $x+7 = 18$; *or*, $x = 11$ *hours, the time required.*

3. There are four numbers in geometrical progreſſion, the ſum of the extremes is 84, and the ſum of the means 36 : What are thoſe numbers?

Put v and y for the means :

Then will $\dfrac{v^2}{y}$ *and* $\dfrac{y^2}{v}$ *be the extremes by the nature of the proportion* :

Therefore, $\left. \begin{array}{l} v+y = 36 = a \\[4pt] \dfrac{v^2}{y} + \dfrac{y^2}{v} = 84 = b \end{array} \right\}$ *by the question* :

Or, $v^3+y^3 = vy \times b =$ *(by writing p for vy)* pb.

But, $v^3+y^3 =$ *(by problem 18 of the laſt chap.)* $a^3 - 3ap$:

Conſequently, $pb = a^3 - 3ap$; *or,* $p = \dfrac{a^3}{b+3a} = c$ *by ſubſtitution* :

Therefore, $v^3+y^3 = bc$; *or,* $v^3 = bc - y^3$:

But, $v = a - y$; *therefore,* $v^3 = a^3 - 3a^2y + 3ay^2 - y^3$:

Conſequently, $a^3 - 3a^2y + 3ay^2 - y^3 = bc - y^3$; *or,* $a^3 - 3a^2y + 3ay^2 = bc$:

Or, $3ay^2 - 3a^2y = bc - a^3$:

And therefore, $y^2 - cy = \dfrac{bc - a^3}{3a}$:

And

$$And,\ y^2 - ay + \frac{a^2}{4} = \frac{bc - a^3}{3a} + \frac{a^2}{4} = \frac{4bc - a^3}{12a}:$$

$$Whence,\ y - \frac{a}{2} = \pm \overline{\left.\frac{4bc - a^3}{12a}\right|}^{\frac{1}{2}} = 9;\ or,\ y = 9 +$$

$$\frac{a}{2} = 27,\ and\ v = 36 - y = 9;\ therefore,\ \frac{v^2}{y} = 3,$$

$$and\ \frac{y^2}{v} = 81,$$

Confequently, 3, 9, 27 and 81, are the nnmbers required.

4. Suppofe two cities, A and B, whofe diftance from each other is 152 miles; and that two men fet out at the fame time from thofe cities to meet each ether; the one which goes from A, travels the firft day 1 mile, the fecond day 2, the third day 3, and fo on; and the one which fets out from B, goes the firft day 4 miles, the fecond day 7, and the third 10, and fo on. Query the number of days before they meet, and the number of miles that each travels?

Put y = number of days before they meet:

Then will $\dfrac{y^2 + y}{2} + \dfrac{3y^2 + 5y}{2} = 152$ by the queftion:

That is, $\dfrac{4y^2 + 6y}{2} = 152;\ or,\ 4y^2 + 6y = 304:$

Whence, $y^2 + \dfrac{3}{2}y = 76:$

And $y^2 + \dfrac{3}{2}y + \dfrac{9}{16} = 76 + \dfrac{9}{16} = \dfrac{1225}{16}:$

Or, $y + \dfrac{3}{4} = \pm\sqrt{\dfrac{1225}{16}} = \dfrac{35}{4};\ and\ y = \dfrac{35}{4} - \dfrac{3}{4} = 8.$

Confequently,

> Confequently, $\dfrac{y^2 + y}{2} = 36$, the number of miles travelled by the one which fat out from A; and $\dfrac{3y^2 + 5y}{2} = 116$, the diftance travelled by the other.

CHAP. XVIII.

Of the GENESIS, or FORMATION of E-QUATIONS in GENERAL.

ALL equations of fuperior order, are confider-ed, as produced by the multiplication of equations of inferior orders, that involve the fame unknown quantity.

· Thus, a quadratic equation may be confidered as generated by the multiplication of two fimple equations ; a cubic equation by the multiplication of three fimple equations, or one quadratic and one fimple equation ; and a biquadratic equation by the multiplication of four fimple equations, or two quadratic equations, or one cubic and one fimple equation.

- Suppofe w to be the unknown quantity, and a, b, c, d, &c. its feveral values in any fimple equation :

That is, $w = a$, $w = b$, $w = c$, $w = d$, &c. Then by tranfpofition, $w - a = 0$, $w - b = 0$, $w - c = 0$, $w - d = 0$, &c. And the product of two of thefe equations as $\overline{w - a} \times \overline{w - b} = 0$, gives a quadratic equation, or one of two dimenfions.

The product of any three ; as $\overline{w - a} \times \overline{w - b} \times \overline{w - c} = 0$, produces a cubic equation, or one of three dimenfions.　　　　　　　　The

The product of any four of them; as $\overline{w-a} \times \overline{w-b} \times \overline{w-c} \times \overline{w-d} = 0$, produces a biquadratic equation, or one of four dimensions.

Hence it appears, that in every equation, the higeſt dimenſion of the unknown quantity, is equal to the number of ſimple equations that generate that equation; and therefore it follows, that every equation has as many roots, or values of the unknown quantity, as there are units in the higheſt dimenſion of that unknown quantity. For ſuppoſe an equation $= \overline{w-a} \times \overline{w-b} \times \overline{w-c} = 0$; and that for w you ſubſtitute any of its values (a, b or c) in the given equation, then all the terms of an equation will vaniſh; for if $w=a, w=b$, and $w=c$, then $\overline{w-a} \times \overline{w-b} \times \overline{w-c} = 0$, becauſe each of the factors are equal to nothing. And after the ſame manner, it appears, that there are three ſuppoſitions that give $\overline{w-a} \times \overline{w-b} \times \overline{w-c} = 0$: But ſince there are no other quantities beſides theſe a, b, c, which ſubſtituted for w in the equation $\overline{w-a} \times \overline{w-b} \times \overline{w-c} = 0$, will make all the terms vaniſh; it follows, that the equation $\overline{w-a} \times \overline{w-b} \times \overline{w-c} = 0$, can have no more than theſe three roots, or admit of more than three ſolutions. For if you ſubſtitute for w in the propoſed equation, any other quantity e, which is neither equal to a, b, nor c; then neither $\overline{e-a}$, $\overline{e-b}$, $\overline{e-c}$, is equal to nothing; and conſequently their product $\overline{e-a} \times \overline{e-b} \times \overline{e-c}$, cannot be equal to nothing, but muſt be ſome real product: So that no other quantity, beſides one of thoſe before-mentioned, will give a true value of w in the propoſed equation. And therefore, no equation can have more roots than it contains dimenſions of the unknown quantity. To

To be more plain: Suppose that $x^4 - 10x^3 + 35x^2 - 50x + 24 = 0$, is the equation to be resolved; and that you find it to be the same as the product of $x - 1 \times x - 2 \times x - 3 \times x - 4$: Then you will infer, that the four roots or values of x, are 1, 2, 3, and 4; for any of these numbers substituted for x, will make that product, and consequently, $x^4 - 10x^3 + 35x^2 - 50x + 24$ equal to nothing, according to the proposed equation.

The roots of equations are either positive or negative, according as the roots or values of the unknown quantity in the simple equations which produce them, are positive or negative. Thus, if $v = -a$, $v = -b$, $v = -c$, $v = -d$; then will $v + a = 0$, $v + b = 0$, $v + c = 0$, and $v + d = 0$; and consequently, $v + a \times v + b \times v + c \times v + d = 0$, will be an equation whose roots $-a$, $-b$, $-c$, $-d$, are all negative. And after the same manner, if $v = a$, $v = -b$, $v = c$, the equation $v - a \times v + b \times v - c$, will have its roots $+a$, $-b$, $+c$.

But to discover when the roots of an equation are positive, and when negative, and how many there are of each kind, it will be necessary to consider the signs and co-efficients of equations, generated from the multiplication of those simple equations that produce them; which will be best understood by considering the following table, where the simple equations $v - a$, $v - b$, $v - c$, &c. are multiplied continually with one another, and produce successively the higher equations.

$v - a$

$$v - a$$
$$\times\, v - b$$

$$= v^2 \left.\begin{array}{l} - av \\ - bv \end{array}\right\} + ab = 0,\ \textit{a quadratic}$$

$$\times\, v - c$$

$$= v^3 \left.\begin{array}{l} - a \\ - b \\ - c \end{array}\right\} \times v^2 \left.\begin{array}{l} + ab \\ + ac \\ + bc \end{array}\right\} \times v - abc = 0,\ \textit{a cubic}$$
$$[\textit{equation}$$

$$\times\, v - d$$

$$= v^4 \left.\begin{array}{l} - a \\ - b \\ - c \\ - d \end{array}\right\} \times v^3 \left.\begin{array}{l} + ab \\ + ac \\ + ad \\ + bc \\ + bd \\ + cd \end{array}\right\} \times v^2 \left.\begin{array}{l} - abc \\ - abd \\ - acd \\ - bcd \end{array}\right\} \times v + abcd = 0,\ \textit{a biquad.}$$

$$\textit{\&c.}$$

FROM the infpection of thefe equations it appears that the co-efficient of the firft term is unity or 1.

THE co-efficient of the fecond term, is the fum of all the roots (a, b, c, d) with contrary figns.

THE co-efficient of the third term, is the fum of all the products of thofe roots that can poffibly be made by multiplying any two of them together.

THE co-efficient of the fourth term, is the fum of all the products of the roots that can be made by
combining

combining them, three and three : And fo on for any other co-efficient. The laſt term is always the product of all the roots, having their ſigns changed.

NOTWITHSTANDING thoſe ſimple equations made uſe of in the foregoing table, in forming the higher e-quations, are ſuch as have poſitive roots ; yet the ſame reaſoning holds, whether the roots are poſitive or neg-ative.   Whence, if $v^4 - pv^3 + qv^2 - rv + s = 0$, repreſents a biquadratic equation ; then will p be the ſum of all the roots, q the ſum of all the products made by multiplying any two of them together, r the ſum of all the products made by multiplying any three of them together, and s the product of all four.

IT likewiſe appears from inſpection, that the ſigns of the terms in any equation in the foregoing table, are alternately $+$ and $-$: The firſt term is always ſome pure power of v, and is poſitive : The ſecond term is ſome power of v, multiplied with the quantities, $- a$, $- b$, $- c$, &c. and ſince theſe quantities are all negative, it follows, that the ſecond term muſt alſo be negative.   The third term hath for its co-efficient the product of any two of theſe quantities, $(- a, - b, - c, \&c.)$ and ſince $- \times -$ gives $+$; it follows, that the third term muſt be poſitive. For the ſame reaſon, the co-efficient of the fourth term, which is formed of the products of any three of theſe negative quantities, muſt be negative alſo, and the co-efficient of the fifth term poſitive.   But in this caſe, $v = a, v = b, v = c, v = d$, &c. that is, the roots are all poſitive : Conſequently, when the roots of an equation are all poſitive, the ſigns of the terms are $+$ and $-$ alternately.   But, when the roots are all negative ; that is, $v = - a, v = - b,$ $v = - c, v = - d,$ &c. then $\overline{v + a} \times \overline{v + b} \times$ $\overline{v + c} \times \overline{v + d} = 0$, will expreſs the equation produced

duced, whofe terms are evidently all pofitive. And therefore when the roots of an equation are all negative, there will be no change in the figns of the terms. Confequently, there will be as many pofitive roots in an equation, as there are changes in the figns of the terms of that equation, and the reft of the roots will be negative.

HENCE it follows, that the roots of a quadratic equation may be both negative, or both pofitive, or one negative and the other pofitive. Thus, in the equation

$$\left. v^2 \begin{array}{c} - a \\ - b \end{array} \right\} \times v + ab = \overline{(v-a \times \overline{v-b})}$$

o, there are two changes of the figns, viz. the firft term is pofitive, the fecond negative, and the third pofitive ; confequently, the roots are both pofitive.

BUT in the equation

$$\left. v^2 \begin{array}{c} + a \\ + b \end{array} \right\} \times v + ab = \overline{(v+a}$$

$$\times \overline{v+b}) \text{ o,}$$

there are no change in the figns, and therefore both the roots are negative.

AND in like manner, in the equation

$$\left. v^2 \begin{array}{c} + a \\ - b \end{array} \right\} \times$$

$$v - ab = \overline{(v+a \times \overline{v-b})} \text{ o,}$$

one of the roots will be pofitive, and the other negative ; for fince the firft term is pofitive, and the laft negative, it is plain, there can be but one change in the figns, whether the fecond term is pofitive or negative.

HENCE alfo it appears, how that a cubic equation may have all its roots pofitive, or all negative, or two pofitive and one negative ; or two negative and one pofitive. For fuppofe the cubic equation is

$$\left. v^3 \begin{array}{c} - a \\ - b \\ - c \end{array} \right\} \times v^2 \left. \begin{array}{c} + ab \\ + ac \\ + bc \end{array} \right\} \times v - abc = \overline{(v-a \times}$$

$$v-b$$

$\overline{v-b} \times \overline{v-c}) \; 0$, wherein there are three changes in the signs; and consequently all three of the roots positive.

AGAIN, suppose the cubic equation is of this form,

$$\left.\begin{array}{r} v^3 - a \\ -b \\ +c \end{array}\right\} \times \left.\begin{array}{r} v^2 \mp ab \\ -ac \\ \mp bc \end{array}\right\} \times v + abc = \overline{(v-a} \times$$

$\overline{v-b} \times \overline{v-c}) \; 0$, where there are two changes in the signs; for if $a + b$ is greater than c, then the second co-efficient $-a-b+c$ must be negative; if $a + b$ is less than c, then the third term will be negative; for its co-efficient $ab - ac - bc \; (= \overline{ab - c}$ $\times \overline{a+b})$ is, in this case negative, because the product $a \times b$ is always less than the square $\overline{a+b} \times \overline{a+b}$, and consequently, much less than $c \times \overline{a+b}$; and since there cannot be three changes in the signs, the first and last terms having the same sign; it follows, that two of the roots of the proposed equation are positive, and the other negative.

IN like manner, the equation $v^3 + \overline{a+b-c} \, v^2$ $+ \overline{ab - ac - bc} \, v - abc = 0$, will have two of its roots negative, and the other positive; for if $a + b$ is less than c, the second and third terms must be negative, by what was proved in the last example; and if the second term is positive, that is, $a + b$ is greater than c, it is plain there can be but one change in the signs, and consequently but one positive root, the other two being negative.

AND by parity of reason, the positive and negative roots of the other equations may be discovered;

this

this method being general, and extends to all kinds of equations whatever.

CHAP. XIX.

CONCERNING the TRANSFORMATION of EQUATIONS, and EXTERMINATING their INTERMEDIATE TERMS.

ANY equation may be transformed into another, whose roots shall be greater, or less than the roots of the proposed equation by any given difference (e) by the following

RULE.

ASSUME a new unknown quantity (y) and connect it with the given difference (e), with the sign $+$ or $-$, according as the roots of the proposed equation are to be increased, or diminished; and make this aggregate equal to the unknown quantity (x) in the proposed equation; then instead of the unknown quantity (x) and its powers in the proposed equation, substitute this aggregate, $(y \pm e)$ and its powers; and there will arise a new equation, whose roots will be greater or less than the roots of the proposed equation, as required.

EXAMPLES.

1. Let $x^3 - px^2 + qx - r = 0$, be an equation to be transformed into another whose roots shall be less than the roots of the proposed equation, by the difference e.

Assume

Assume $x = y + e$:

Then will
$$\left.\begin{array}{rl} x^3 = & y^3 + 3y^2 e + 3ye^2 + e^3 \\ -px^2 = & -py^2 - 2ye - pe^2 \\ +qx = & qy + qe \\ -r = & -r \end{array}\right\} = 0, \textit{ is the e-quation requir.}$$

2. Let $x^2 - 11x + 30 = 0$, be transformed into an equation that shall have its roots less than the roots of the proposed equation by the difference 4.

Assume $x = y + 4$:

Then,
$$\begin{array}{rl} x^2 = & y^2 + 8y + 16 \\ -11x = & -11y - 44 \\ +30 = & +30 \end{array}$$

$$y^2 - 3y + 2 = 0, \textit{ is the equation required.}$$

In the first example of the foregoing transformations, the co-efficient of the second term in the transformed equation, is $3e - p$; and if you suppose $e = \frac{1}{3}p$, and therefore, $3e - p = 0$; then the second term of the transformed equation will vanish. Let the proposed equation be of n dimensions, and the co-efficient of the second term $-p$; and suppose $x = y + \frac{p}{n}$; then if this value be substituted for x in the proposed equation, there will arise a new equation that shall want the second term. For if $p =$ sum of all the roots of the proposed equation, and $x = y + \frac{p}{n}$; it follows, that each value of y in the new equation, will be less than the value of x in the proposed equation, by $\frac{p}{n}$; and since the number of roots is n, it follows, that the sum of the values of y, will

be

be lefs than p, the fum of the values of x, by $n \times \frac{p}{n}$ $= p$; that is, the fum of the values of y, is $+ p - p$ $= 0$; and fince the co-efficient of the fecond term in the equation of y, is the fum of the values of y, viz. $+ p - p$, which is equal to nothing; it follows, that in the equation of y, arifing from the fuppofi-

tion of $x = y + \frac{p}{n}$, the fecond term muft vanifh:

And therefore the fecond term of any equation may be exterminated by the following

R U L E.

DIVIDE the co-efficient of the fecond term of the propofed equation by the index of the higheft power of the unknown quantity; and affume a new unknown quantity (y) and annex to it the faid quotient with its fign changed; then put this aggregate equal to the unknown quantity (x) in the propofed equation, and inftead of x and its powers, write this aggregate and its powers, and the equation that arifes fhall want the fecond term.

EXAMPLES.

Let the equation $x^2 - 8x + 12 = 0$, be propofed to have its fecond term exterminated.

Firft, $- 8 \div 2 = - 4$:

Therefore, $x = y + 4$, *per rule:*

Then, $x^2 = y^2 + 8y + 16$

$$- 8x = \quad - 8y - 32$$

$$+ 12 = \quad\quad\quad + 12$$

$$\overline{\quad y^2 \quad * \quad - 4 = 0}$$

HENCE,

-HENCE it appears, that a quadratic equation may be refolved without completing the fquare, by ex-terminating the fecond term ; for fince $y^2 - 4 = 0$; or, $y^2 = 4$, and $y = \sqrt{4}$, we fhall have $x = y + 4 = \sqrt{4} + 4 = 6$.

Let the fecond term of the equation $x^3 - 9x^2 + 26x - 34 = 0$, be exterminated.

Firft, $x = y + (\frac{9}{3}) 3$:
Then,

$$
\begin{array}{rl}
x^3 = & y^3 + 9y^2 + 27y + 27 \\
- 9x^2 = & \quad\ - 9y^2 - 54y - 81 \\
+ 26x = & \qquad\qquad\quad + 26y + 78 \\
- 34 = & \qquad\qquad\qquad\qquad - 34 \\
\hline
y^3 \quad * & - y - 10 = 0.
\end{array}
$$

WHEN the fecond term in any equation is want-ing, it is plain, that the equation hath both pofitive and negative roots ; and fince the co-efficient of the fecond term in any equation, is the difference be-tween the fum of the pofitive, and fum of the nega-tive roots ; it follows therefore, that when the pofi-tive and negative roots are made equal to each other, that difference vanifhes. Confequently, when an e-quation has the fecond term wanting, the fum of the pofitive roots is equal to the fum of the negative ones.

HENCE, by the foregoing transformation of equa-tions and the exterminating their fecond terms, the pofitive and negative roots are reduced to an equal-ity, and the folution of the equation thereby render-ed more eafy.

IF the equation $v^3 - pv^2 + qv - r = 0$, be trans-formed into another, by affuming $v = y + e$, the co-efficient of the third term of the transformed e-quation will be $3e^2 - 2pe + q$; now if we fuppofe this

co-efficient

co-efficient equal to nothing, and refolve the quadratic $3e^2 - 2p + q = 0$ we ſhall have $e = \dfrac{p \pm \sqrt{p^2 - 3q}}{3}$ which ſubſtituted for e in the equation $v = y + e$, the third term of the transformed equation will vaniſh : Alſo, if the propoſed equation be of n dimenſions, the value of e, by which the third term is to be exterminated, is found by refolving the quadratic equation $e^2 + \dfrac{2p}{n} \times e + \dfrac{2q}{n \times \overline{n-1}} = 0$, that is, by finding the value of e in the co-efficient of the third term of the transformed equation, when that co-efficient is equal to nothing. And in like manner, the fourth term of any equation may be exterminated, by ſolving a cubic equation, which is the co-efficient of the fourth term of a transformed equation : And after the ſame manner, the other terms may be taken away.

THERE are other transformations which are of uſe in the reſolution of equations; of which the moſt uſeful, and the only one that we ſhall conſider, is, when the higheſt term of the unknown quantity is multiplied with ſome given quantity, to transform the equation into another that ſhall have the co-efficient of the higheſt term unity.

LET the propoſed equation be $av^3 - pv^2 + qv - r = 0$; and ſuppoſe $av = y$, then $v = y \div a$, and this value ſubſtituted for v in the propoſed equation, there will ariſe $\dfrac{ay^3}{a^3} - \dfrac{py^2}{a^2} + \dfrac{qy}{a} - r = 0$, or $\dfrac{y^3}{a^2} - \dfrac{py^2}{a^2} + \dfrac{qy}{a} - r = 0$, and by multiplying the whole by a^2, we ſhall have $y^3 - py^2 + qay - ra^2 = 0$; which gives the following

RULE.

R U L E.

CHANGE the unknown quantity (*v*) in the proposed equation, into another (*y*), prefix no co-efficient
to the firſt term, paſs the ſecond, multiply the third
term with the co-efficient of the higheſt term of the
unknown quantity in the propoſed equation, and the
fourth term by the ſquare of that co-efficient, the
fifth by the cube; and ſo on, and the higheſt term
of the unknown-quantity in the reſulting equation
ſhall have its co-efficient unity, as required.

EXAMPLES.

Let the equation $2v^2 + 6v - 36 = 0$, be changed
into another that will have unity for the co-efficient
of the higheſt term of the unknown quantity.

Thus, $y^2 + 6y - 36 \times 2 = 0$; *or*, $y^2 + 6y - 72$
$= 0$, *is the equation required.*

The finding the roots of the propoſed equation,
and all others of the like kind, will be very eaſy when
the roots of the transformed equation are found; ſince
$v = $ (in this caſe) $\frac{1}{2}y$.

Transform the equation $5v^3 - 10v^2 + 16v - 93$
$= 0$, into another that the higheſt term of the unknown quantity may have an unit for its co-efficient.

Thus, $y^3 - 10y + 80y - 2325 = 0$, *is the equation required.*

C H A P.

CHAP. XX.

Of the RESOLUTION of EQUATIONS by DIVISORS.

IF the laſt term of an equation is the product of all its roots; it follows, that the roots of an equation when commenſurable, will be found among the diviſors of the laſt term; which gives the following

RULE.

TRANSPOSE all the terms to one ſide of the equation. Find all the diviſors of the laſt term, and ſubſtitute them ſucceſſively for the unknown quantity in the propoſed equation; and that diviſor, which ſubſtituted as aforeſaid, gives the reſult $= 0$, is one of the roots of the equation. But if none of the diviſors ſucceed, the roots of the equation are for the moſt part, either irrational or impoſſible.

Note. If the laſt term of the propoſed equation is large, and conſequently its diviſors numerous; they may be diminiſhed, by transforming the equation into another, by the rules of the laſt chapter.

EXAMPLES.

Find the roots of the equation $x^3 - 4x^2 + 10x - 12 = 0$.

Here the diviſors of the laſt term, are $1, 2, 3, 4, 6, 12, -1, -2, -3, -4, -6, -12$, *which ſubſtituted ſucceſſively for* x,

Gives,

$$\text{Gives,} \begin{cases} 1 - 4 + 10 - 12 = -5 \\ 8 - 16 + 20 - 12 = 0 \\ 27 - 36 + 30 - 12 = 9 \\ 64 - 64 + 40 - 12 = 28 \\ 216 - 144 + 60 - 12 = 120 \end{cases}$$
$$\&c.$$

WE omit trying the negative divisors, since there are three changes in the signs of the proposed equation, and therefore none of its roots can be negative: And since none of the divisors succeed, except 2; it follows, that 2 is the only rational root of the equation, the other two being either irrational, or impossible.

Let it be required to find the roots of the equation $x^3 + 2x^2 - 40x + 64 = 0$.

Here the divisors of the last term, are 1, 2, 4, 8, 16, 32, which substituted successively for x in the proposed equation,

$$\text{Gives,} \begin{cases} 1 + 2 - 40 + 64 = 27 \\ 8 + 8 - 80 + 64 = 0 \\ 64 + 32 - 160 + 64 = 0 \end{cases}$$

WHERE the only divisors that succeed, are 2, and 4; and since there are but two changes in the signs of the proposed equation, there must be one negative root: We are therefore to substitute the divisors negatively taken, in order to discover the other value of x; and on trial, we find that -8 succeeds. Therefore the three roots of the proposed equation, are $+2$ $+4$ -8.

BUT when one of the roots of an equation is found, the rest of the roots may be found with less trouble, by dividing the proposed equation by the simple equation, deduced from the root already found, and

finding

finding the roots of the quotient, which will be an equation a degree lower than the proposed one.

THUS, in the laſt example the root $+ 2$ firſt found, gives $x = 2$; or, $x — 2 = 0$, by which dividing the proposed equation: Thus,

$$x — 2) x^3 + 2x^2 — 40x + 64 (x^2 + 4x — 32.$$
$$ x^3 — 2x^2$$

$$4x^2 — 40x$$
$$4x^2 — 8x$$

$$— 32x + 64$$
$$— 32x + 64$$

$$*\quad*$$

The quotient will be a quadratic equation $x^2 + 4x — 32 = 0$; which is the product of the other two ſimple equations, from which the propoſed cubic was generated; and whoſe two roots are conſequently, two of the roots of that cubic. But the two roots of the quadratic, are $+ 4$ and $— 8$. Therefore, the three roots of the cubic equation, are 2, 4, — 8, the ſame as before.

THE finding all the diviſors of the laſt term of an equation, eſpecially if that term be large, is much facilitated by the following

RULE.

1. DIVIDE the laſt term by its leaſt diviſor that exceeds unity, and the quotient by its leaſt diviſor; proceeding in this manner, till you have a quotient that is not farther diviſible by any number greater than an unit: And this quotient together with thoſe diviſors, are the firſt diviſors of the laſt term.

2. FIND all the products of thofe divifors which arife by combining them two and two, and all the products which arife by combining them three and three, and fo on, until the continued product of the firft divifors, is equal to the quantity to be divided; and you will have the divifors required.

EXAMPLES.

Thus, fuppofe the laft term of an equation to be 60 : Then $60 \div 2 = 30$, $30 \div 2 = 15$, $15 \div 3 = 5$; therefore, 2×2, 2×3, 2×5, and 3×5, are the combinations of the twos; and $2 \times 2 \times 3$, $2 \times 2 \times 5$, $2 \times 3 \times 5$, the combinations of the threes; alfo, $2 \times 2 \times 3 \times 5$, is the combination of the fours = their continued product, equal to the quantity to be divided. Therefore all the divifors of 60, are 2, 3, 5, 4, 6, 10, 15, 12, 20, 30, 60.

And in like manner, the divifors of $10ab$, are 2, 5, a, b, 10, $2a$, $2b$, $5a$, $5b$, ab, $10a$, $5ab$, $2ab$ and $10ab$.

BUT there is another method for the reduction of equations by divifors, which is lefs prolix, by reducing the divifors to more narrow limits, by the following

RULE.

1. INSTEAD of the unknown quantity in the propofed equation, fubftitute fucceffively the terms of the progreffion, 1, 0, — 1, &c. and find all the divifors of the fums that refult by fuch fubftitution.

2. TAKE out all the arithmetical progreffions that can be found among thofe divifors, whofe terms correfpond with the order of the terms, 1, 0, — 1,
&c.

&c. and common difference unity ; and the values of x will be found among the divisors which arise from the fubſtitution of $x = 0$, that belong to thoſe progreſſions.

Note. *When the arithmetical progreſſion is increaſing according to the order of the terms 1, 0, — 1, the value of x will be affirmative ; but when the arithmetical progreſſion is decreaſing, the value of x will be negative.*

EXAMPLES.

Let $x^3 - x^2 - 10x + 6 = 0$, be the propoſed equation ; and by fubſtituting fucceſſively for x, the terms 1, 0, — 1, the work will ſtand as follows.

Suppoſitions.	*Reſults.*		*Diviſors.*	*Ar.P.*
$x = 1$		-4	1,2,4	4
$x = 0$	$x^3 - x^2 - 10x + 6 =$	$+6$	1,2,3,6	3
$x = -1$		$+14$	1,2,7,14	2

Here the progreſſion is decreaſing, and 3, that term which ſtands againſt the ſuppoſition of $x = 0$; therefore, — 3, fubſtituted for x in the propoſed equation, gives, — 27 — 9 + 30 + 6 = 0 ; where all the terms vaniſhing, it follows, that — 3 is one of the roots of the propoſed equation ; and $2 + \sqrt{2}$, and $2 - \sqrt{2}$, the other two roots, found by dividing the propoſed equation by $x + 3$, and reſolving the quadratic quotient.

Suppoſe it be required to find the roots of the equation $v^4 + 3v^3 - 19v^2 - 27v + 90 = 0$.

Then by fubſtituting as before, the work will ſtand as follows.

Suppoſitions.

Suppositions.	Results.	Divisors.	Arith. Progref.
$v = 1$	48	1, 2, 3, 4, 6, &c.	1, 3, 2, 4, 6
$v = 0$	90	1, 2, 3, 5, 6, &c.	2, 2, 3, 3, 5
$v = -1$	96	1, 2, 3, 4, 6, &c.	3, 1, 4, 2, 4

Here are five arithmetical progreſſions; and ſubſtituting 2, 3, — 3, — 5, reſpectively for v in the propoſed equation, the whole vaniſhes; the other progreſſion being in this caſe uſeleſs, ſince the number of roots are but four. Conſequently, 2, 3, — 3, — 5, are the four roots required.

There are many other methods beſide thoſe which we have here given for the reſolution of equations; which the confined limits of our plan obliges us to omit, and proceed to diſcover the roots of equations by the method of approximation.

CHAP. XXI.

The FINDING the ROOTS of NUMERAL EQUATIONS in GENERAL, by the METHOD of APPROXIMATION.

ALTHOUGH there are other methods for the reſolution of equations, than thoſe given in the laſt chapter, yet the moſt of them are either very prolex, or confined to particular caſes; but the following method of approximation is general, and extends to numeral equations of all kinds whatever, and though not accurately true, gives the value of the root to any aſſigned degree of exactneſs you pleaſe, by the following

RULE.

R U L E.

1. FIND by trial, a number nearly equal to the root required, and call it r; and put x for the difference between the real root and that already found, then will $r \pm x = v$.

2. INSTEAD of v and its powers in the propofed equation, fubftitute $r \pm x$ and its powers; and there will arife a new equation involving x and known quantities.

3. THEN by rejecting all the terms of this new equation that involve the powers of x; and affuming the reft equal to nothing, the value of x will be determined by means of a fimple equation.

4. ADD the value of x thus found to r, and you will have a nearer value of the root required; which if not fufficiently exact, repeat the operation, by fubftituting this value for r in the formula exhibiting the value of x, and it will give a correction of the root; which if not yet exact enough, proceed to a third correction; and fo on, to any affigned degree of exactnefs.

EXAMPLES.

Given, $v^2 + 6v - 31 = 0$, to find v by approximation.

The root found by trial is nearly equal to 3:
Therefore, $r = 3$, and $r + x = v$:
Then, $v^2 = r^2 + 2rx + x^2$
$$+6v = 6r + 6x$$
$$-31 = -31$$

And, $r^2 + 2rx + 6x + 6r - 31 = 0$:

Whence,

Whence, $x = \dfrac{31 - r^2 - 6r}{2r + 6} =$ (*by writing* 3 *for* r

its equal) $\dfrac{31 - 9 - 18}{6 + 6} = \dfrac{4}{12} = \cdot 3$; *and* $v = 3.3$

And if 3.3 *be substituted for* r *in the equation,* $x = \dfrac{31 - r^2 - 6r}{2r + 6}$, *we shall have* $x = \dfrac{31 - 10.89 - 19.8}{6.6 + 6}$

$= \dfrac{\cdot 31}{12.6} = .0246$, *or rather* $x = .0245$, *and* $v = r + x = 3.3245$:

Again, if this value be substituted for r, *we shall have* $x = .000005$, *and* $v = r + x = 3.324505$, *for a nearer value of* v; *and so on, to any assigned degree of exactness.*

Given, $v^3 + 2v - 73 = 0$, *to find* v *by approximation.*

The root found by trial, is nearly equal 4 :
Therefore, $r = 4$, *and* $r + z = v$:
Then, $v^3 = r^3 + 3r^2 z + 3rz^2 + z^3.$
$+ 2v = 2r + 2z$
$- 73 = - 73$

Whence, $r^3 + 3r^2 z + 2r + 2z - 73 = 0$; *or,*
$z = \dfrac{73 - r^3 - 2r}{3r^2 + 2} =$ (*by writing* 4 *for* z) $\dfrac{73 - 64 - 8}{48 + 2}$

$= \dfrac{1}{50} = .02$; *and therefore,* $v = r + z = 4.02$; *and writing this value for* r, *in the equation* $z = \dfrac{73 - r^3 - 2r}{3r^2 + 2}$;

We shall have $z = \dfrac{73 - 64.964808 - 8.04}{48.4812 + 2}$
$=$

$$= \frac{-.004808}{50.4812} = -.000095; \quad \text{and} \quad v = r + z =$$

4.019905 *nearly.*

. And after this manner of reasoning, we may obtain theorems for approximating to the roots of pure powers.

Thus, if A be a given quantity whose n root is required, r the nearest less root in the integers, and v the difference between r and the root required: Then will $r^n +$

$$nr^{n-1}v + n \times \frac{n-1}{2} r^{n-2} v^2 + n \times \frac{n-1}{2} \times$$

$$\frac{n-2}{3} r^{n-3} v^3, \&c. = A; \quad \text{and assuming} \quad v =$$

$$\frac{A - r^n}{nr^{n-1}}; \quad \text{or, more nearly, taking the three first terms,}$$

$$v = \frac{A - r^n}{nr^{n-1} + n \times \frac{n-1}{2} r^{n-2} v^2} = \left(\text{by writing for } v \right.$$

$$its = \frac{A - r^n}{nr^{n-1}} \right) \frac{A - r^n}{nr^{n-1} + n \times \frac{n-1}{2} r^{n-2} \times \frac{A - r^n}{nr^{n-1}}}$$

$$= \frac{A - r^n}{nr^{n-1} + \frac{n^2 - nr^{n-2}}{2nr^{n-1}} \times A - r^n} =$$

$$\frac{A - r^n}{nr^{n-1} + \frac{n-1}{2r} \times A - r^n}; \quad \text{and by writing}$$

$a,$

a, for $A - r^n$, we have $v = \dfrac{a}{nr^{n-1} + \frac{n-1}{2r} \times a}$

$= (by\ reduction)\ \dfrac{ra}{nr^n + \frac{n-1}{2}a}$, the theorem for

approximating to the value of v, which added to r, will give a correction of the root; which if not fufficiently near the truth, the operation muft be repeated, by fubftituting the new r in the equation exhibiting the value of v.

Thus, for example, fuppofe the cube root of 3 is required.

Here $r = 1$, the neareft lefs root in the integers, and $r + v =$ root required.

Therefore, $v = \dfrac{ra}{nr^n + \frac{n-1}{2}a} = \dfrac{2}{2+3} = \dfrac{2}{5} = .4$, and

$r + v = 1 + .4 = 1.4$, *which fubftituted for r, and the operation repeated, v will be found $= .0397$; therefore, $r + v = 1.4 + .0397 = 1.4397 = cube\ root of 3, very near.*

CHAP. XXII.

CONCERNING UNLIMITED PROB-LEMS.

HAVING gone through, and explained the methods ufed in arguing limited problems, or fuch as admit of but one folution; it remains therefore, that we fhew the learner how to reafon about

thofe

thofe problems which are unlimited, or admit of various anfwers.

IT was obferved in Chap. xv, of this Book, that when the equations expreffing the conditions of the queftion, are lefs in number than the quantities fought, the queftion is unlimited, or capable of innumerable anfwers; yet all the poffible anfwers in whole numbers, are for the moft part limited to a determinate number.

As queftions of this nature admit of fome variations as to their general folution; we fhall therefore confider them in the following problems.

PROBLEM I.

To find the values of v and y in whole numbers, in the equation $av \pm by \pm c = o$; where a, b and c, are given quantities.

RULE.

1. REDUCE the given equation to its leaft terms, by dividing it by its greateft common divifor.

2. FIND the value of v from the given equation; and reduce the refulting expreffion, by expunging all whole numbers from it, until c be lefs than a, and the co-efficient of y becomes unity.

3. ASSUME this laft refult equal to fome known whole number, and the expreffion reduced, will give the value of y in known terms; from which the value of v may be determined in the given equation.

Note. *If after the given equation is divided by its greateft common divifor, the co-efficients of the unknown quantities, are commenfurable to each other, the queftion is impoffible.*

EXAM.

EXAMPLES.

Given, $10v - 8y - 36 = 0$, to find v and y in whole numbers.

First, $5v - 4y - 18 = 0$, by dividing the whole by 2; *or, $5v - 4y = 18$.*

Put WN for any whole number:

Then $v = \dfrac{18 + 4y}{5} = WN$ by the question:

But, $\dfrac{18 + 4y}{5} = 3 + \dfrac{3 + 4y}{5}$; therefore, $\dfrac{3 + 4y}{5}$

$= WN$, *per axiom 9. Also, $\dfrac{5y}{5} = WN$: Consequent-*

ly, $\dfrac{5y}{5} - \dfrac{3 + 4y}{5} = \dfrac{y - 3}{5} = WN$, per axiom 9;

and therefore, $\dfrac{y - 3}{5} = n$; and for the least value of

y, assume $n = 0$, and we shall have $y - 3 = 5n = 0$;

or, $y = 3$, and $v = \dfrac{18 + 4y}{5} = 6$.

Given, $26v + 18y = 140$, to find v and y in whole numbers.

First, $13v + 9y = 70$ by dividing the whole by 2:

Then $v = \dfrac{70 - 9y}{13} = WN$: But, $\dfrac{70 - 9y}{13} = 5$

$+ \dfrac{5 - 9y}{13}$;

Therefore, $\dfrac{5 - 9y}{13} = WN$, per axiom 9; also,

$\dfrac{13y}{13} = WN$; *consequently, $\dfrac{5 - 9y}{13} + \dfrac{13y}{13} = \dfrac{5 + 4y}{13}$*
$=$

$= W N$, per ax. 8 ; and $\dfrac{5 + 4y}{13} \times 3 = \dfrac{15 + 12y}{13}$

$= W N$, per ax. 7. But, $\dfrac{15 + 12y}{13} = 1 + \dfrac{2 + 12y}{13}$;

therefore, $\dfrac{2 + 12y}{13} = W N$, per ax. 9. Also, $\dfrac{13y}{13} =$

$W N$; whence, $\dfrac{13y}{13} - \dfrac{2 + 12y}{13} = \dfrac{y - 2}{13} = W N$,

per ax. 9 : And $\dfrac{y - 2}{13} = n$; or, $y = 13n + 2$; and

assuming $n = 0$, we have $y = 2$, and $x = \dfrac{70 - 9y}{13} =$

4.

I owe my friend a moidore, have nothing about me but crowns, and he has nothing but guineas : How muſt we exchange theſe pieces of money, ſo that I may acquit myſelf of the debt ? A moidore being valued at 27 ſhillings, a crown at 5 ſhillings, and a guinea at 21 ſhillings.

Put $x =$ number of crowns, and y the number of guineas :

Then $5x - 21y = 27$ by the queſtion :

Or, $x = \dfrac{27 + 21y}{5} = W N$. But, $\dfrac{27 + 21y}{5} =$

$5 + 4y + \dfrac{2 + y}{5}$; conſequently, $\dfrac{2 + y}{5} = W N$, and

$\dfrac{2 + y}{5} = n$; or, $2 + y = 5n$; and aſſuming $n = 1$, we

have $y = 3$, the number of guineas, and $x = \dfrac{27 + 21y}{5}$

$= 18$, the number of crowns. Therefore, I muſt give my friend 18 crowns, and he muſt give me three guineas.

Given,

Given, $4x + 17y = 2900$, to find all the possible values of x and y in whole numbers.

First, $y = \dfrac{2900 - 4x}{17} = WN$; but $\dfrac{2900 - 4x}{17}$

$= 170 + \dfrac{10 - 4x}{17}$; therefore, $\dfrac{10 - 4x}{17} = WN$, per

ax. 8. And $\dfrac{10 - 4x}{17} \times 4 = \dfrac{40 - 16x}{17} = WN$, per

ax. 9. Also, $\dfrac{17x}{17} = WN$: Consequently, $\dfrac{40 - 16x}{17} +$

$\dfrac{17x}{17} = \dfrac{40 + x}{17} = WN$, per ax. 7. But, $\dfrac{40 + x}{17} = 2$

$+ \dfrac{6 + x}{17}$; therefore, $\dfrac{6 + x}{17} = WN$, per ax. 8. And

assuming this last equation $= n$, we get $x = 17n - 6$, where, if n be taken $= 1$, we shall have $x = 17 - 6 =$

11 for the least value of x, and $y = \dfrac{2900 - 4x}{17} =$

168 for the greatest value of y: And since $\overline{6 + x} \div 17$ $= n$, is a whole number; it is plain, that $n + 1$ is the first augment of $\overline{6 + x} \div 17$ in whole numbers; and therefore, $x = 17n + 17 - 6$, the second value of x;

which substituted for x in the equation $y = \dfrac{2900 - 4x}{17}$

will give the second value of y: Or, by adding 17 successively to the values of x, and subtracting 4 from those of y, we shall have all the possible values of x and y in whole numbers, as follows: viz. $x = 11, 28, 45, \&c.$ to 708; and $y = 168, 164, 160, \&c.$ to 4.

PROBLEM II·

To find the least whole number x, that being divided by the given numbers, $a, b, c, d, \&c.$ shall leave given remainders, $g, k, l, m, n, \&c.$

RULE.

R U L E.

1. Subtract each of the remainders from *x*, and divide the several results by their respective divisors, *a*, *b*, *c*, *d*, &c. and the resulting quotients will equal whole numbers.

2. Assume the first equation equal *b*, and find the value of *x* in terms of *b*.

3. Substitute the value of *x* in terms of *b*, in the second equation; and proceed with the result as in the last problem, by expunging all whole numbers, until the co-efficient of *b* becomes unity, &c.

4. Put this expression equal *p*, and find the value of *x* in terms of *p*, by means of the equation of *b*.

5. Substitute the value of *x* in terms of *p*, in the third equation, with which proceed as before, and so on, through all the given equations; assuming the final result equal to some known whole number, and finding the values of the several substituted letters, *b*, *p*, &c. from which the value of *x* may be determined in known terms.

EXAMPLES.

To find the least whole number, that being divided by 7 shall leave 6 remainder; but being divided by 6 shall leave 4 remainder.

Put v = number sought.

Then, $\dfrac{v-6}{7} = W N,$ *and* $\dfrac{v-4}{6} = W N.$

Assume $\dfrac{v-6}{7} = b,$ *and we shall have* $v = 7b +$

6, which substituted for v in the second equation, gives

$$7b + 2 \div 6$$

$$\frac{7b + 2}{6} = W N: \; But, \; \frac{6b}{6} = W N: \; Consequently,$$

$$\frac{7b + 2}{6} - \frac{6b}{6} = \frac{b + 2}{6} = W N, \; and \; assuming \; \frac{b + 2}{6}$$

$= n$, *we shall have* $b = 6n - 2$ *; where if* n *be taken* $= 1$, *we shall have* $b = 4$, *and* $v = 7b + 6 = 34$, *the number required.*

To find the leaft whole number, that being divided by 18, fhall leave 14 remainder ; but being divided by 28, fhall leave 20 remainder.

Put $v =$ *number fought.*

Then, $\dfrac{v - 14}{18} = W N: \; And, \; \dfrac{v - 20}{28} = W N.$

Affume, $\dfrac{v - 14}{18} = b$ *; and we have* $v = 18b + 14$, *which fubftituted for* v *in the fecond equation, gives*

$$\frac{18b - 6}{28} = W N; \; or, \; \frac{9b - 3}{14} = W N \; by \; dividing \; all$$

the terms by 2 *; and* $\dfrac{9b - 3}{14} \times 3 = \dfrac{27b - 9}{14} = W N.$

Alfo, $\dfrac{14b}{14} \times 2 = \dfrac{28b}{14} = W N.$ *Confequently,* $\dfrac{28b}{14} -$

$$\frac{27b - 9}{14} = \frac{b + 9}{14} = W N: \; and \; affuming \; \frac{b + 9}{14} = n,$$

we have $b = 14n - 9$ *; and putting* $n = 1$, *we have* $b = 14n - 9 = 5$, *and* $v = 18b + 14 = 104$, *the number required.*

Diophantine Problems.

Diophantine Problems, fo called, from *Diophantus* their inventor, are fuch as relate to the finding of fquare and cube numbers, &c.

These

THESE problems are so exceedingly curious, that nothing less than the most refined Algebra, applied with the utmost skill and judgment, could ever surmount the difficulties which necessarily attend their solution. The peculiar artifice made use of in forming such positions as the nature of the problems require, shews the great use of Algebra, or the analytic art, in discovering those things that otherwise, would be without the reach of human understanding.

ALTHO no general rule can be given for the solution of these problems ; yet the following direction will be very serviceable on many occasions.

DIRECTION.

ASSUME one or more letters, for the root of the required square, cube, &c. such that when involved to the height of the proposed power, either the given number, or the highest term of the unknown quantity may vanish. Then if the unknown quantity in the resulting equation, be of simple dimension, find its value by reducing the equation. But if the unknown quantity be still a square, cube, or other power ; assume other letter or letters, with which proceed as before, until the highest term of the unknown quantity become of simple dimension in the equation.

EXAMPLES.

To find a square number x^2, such that $x^2 + 1$ shall be a square number.

Assume $x - 2$ *for the root of* $x^2 + 1$:

Then will $\overline{x-2}|^2 = x^2 + 1$; *that is,* $x^2 - 4x + 4 = x^2 + 1$; *or,* $4x = 4 - 1 = 3$; *whence,* $x = \frac{3}{4}$ *, and* $x^2 = \frac{9}{16}$ *, and* $x^2 + 1 = \frac{9}{16} + 1 = \frac{25}{16}$: *Therefore,* $\frac{9}{16}$

$\frac{9}{16}$, is the number required. But if we had assumed $\frac{r^4 - 2r^2 + 1}{4r^2}$ for x^2, we should have had $\frac{r^4 - 2r^2 + 1}{4r^2}$

$+ 1 = \frac{r^4 + 2r^2 + 1}{4r^2}$, which is evidently a square number; where r may be taken for any number.

To find two numbers, such that their product and quotient may be both square and cube numbers.

Assume v^9 and v^3 for the required numbers:

Then $v^9 \times v^3 = v^{12}$, and $v^9 \div v^3 = v^6$, are evidently square and cube numbers; where v may be any number taken at pleasure.

To find four square numbers in arithmetical progression.

For the sum of the two extremes, assume $2n^2$; then will the sum of the two means be also $2n^2$ by the nature of the proportion:

For the roots of the two means, assume $n + 3z$, and $n - 4z$:

Then will $\overline{n + 3z}|^2 + \overline{n - 4z}|^2 = 2n^2$:

That is, $n^2 + 6nz + 9z^2 + n^2 - 8nz + 16z^2 = 2n^2$:

Or, $25z^2 - 2nz + 2n^2 = 2n^2$:

Or, $25z^2 = 2nz$; and by dividing by z, we have $25z = 2n$:

Whence, $z = 2n \div 25$; and puting $n = 1$, we have $z = \frac{2}{25}$:

Therefore, $\overline{n + 3z}|^2$, and $\overline{n - 4z}|^2 = \frac{961}{625}$, and $\frac{289}{625}$, are the two means:

And for the roots of the two extremes, assume $n - 2z$, and $n + z$:

Then will $\overline{n - 2z}|^2 + \overline{n + z}|^2 = 2n^2$:

Or, $n^2 - 4nz + 4z + n^2 + 2nz + z^2 = 2n^2$:

And by reduction, $z = 2n \div 5 = \frac{2}{5}$:

Whence,

Whence, $\overline{n-2z}|^2$, and $\overline{n+z}|^2 = \frac{1}{25}$, and $\frac{49}{25}$, the two extremes. So that the four square numbers in arithmetical progression, are $\frac{1}{25}$, $\frac{289}{625}$, $\frac{961}{625}$, $\frac{49}{25}$.

To find a number, such that being multiplied with one tenth part of itself, and the product increased by 36, shall produce a square number.

Put v for the number sought; then $v^2 \div 10 + 36$, is to be a square number:

Assume the root of this square $= v - 6$, then will $\overline{v-6}| = v^2 \div 10 + 36$; that is, $v^2 - 12v + 36 = v^2 \div 10 + 36$:

Or, $10v^2 - 120v = v^2$; whence, by reduction $v = \frac{120}{9}$, the number required.

To divide a given number 29, consisting of two known square numbers 4 and 25, into two other square numbers.

For the root of the first square, assume $rv - 2$; and for the root of the second $nv - 5$:

Then will $\overline{rv - 2}|^2 + \overline{nv - 5}|^2 = 29$:

That is, $\overline{r^2v^2 - 4rv + 4} + \overline{n^2v^2 - 10nv + 25} = 29$:

Or, $\overline{r^2 + n^2v^2 - 4r - 10nv} + 29 = 29$; or, $r^2 + n^2v^2 = 4r + 10nv$; and by dividing by v, we have $r^2 + n^2v = 4r + 10n$:

Or, $v = \dfrac{4r + 10n}{r^2 + n^2}$; and therefore, $rv - 2 = \dfrac{4r^2 + 10nr}{r^2 + n^2} - 2 = \dfrac{2r^2 - 2n^2 + 10nr}{r^2 + n^2}$; and $nv - 5 = \dfrac{4rn + 10n^2}{r^2 + n^2} - 5 = \dfrac{4rn - 5r^2 + 5n^2}{r^2 + n^2}$; and assuming $r = 1$, and $n = 2$, we shall have $\dfrac{2r^2 - 2n^2 + 10nr}{r^2 + n^2} = \frac{14}{5}$

$\frac{14}{5}$ *for the root of the first square, and* $\dfrac{4rn - 5r^2 + 5n^2}{r^2 + n^2}$

$= \frac{25}{5}$ *for the root of the second.*

To find three square numbers in arithmetical pro-gression.

Assume n^2 *for the mean; then will* $2n^2 =$ *the sum of the extremes by the nature of the proportion.*

For the root of the greater extreme, assume $n + 2v$, *and for the root of the less* $n - 3v$:

Then will $\overline{n - 3v}|^2 + \overline{n + 2v}|^2 = 2n^2$:

That is, $n^2 - 6nv + 9v^2 + n^2 + 4vn + 4v^2 = 2n^2$:

Or, $13v^2 - 2nv + 2n^2 = 2n^2$:

Or, $13v^2 = 2nv$; *and by dividing by* v, *we have* $13v = 2n$; *whence,* $v = 2n \div 13$; *where* n *may be any number at pleasure:*

And by assuming $n = 1$, *we shall have* $v = 2 \div 13$:

Whence, $\overline{1 - \dfrac{6}{13}}\Big|^2 = \dfrac{49}{169}$ *for the least extreme:*

And $\overline{1 + \dfrac{4}{13}}\Big|^2 = \dfrac{289}{169}$ *for the greater: Wherefore,*

the numbers required, are $\dfrac{49}{169}$, 1, *and* $\dfrac{289}{169}$.

<hr>

THE END OF VOLUME I.

T A B L E OF P O W E R S.

1st. Power	1	2	3	4	5	6	7	8	9
2d. dit.	1	4	9	16	25	36	49	64	81
3d. dit.	1	8	27	64	125	216	343	512	729
4th. dit.	1	16	81	256	625	1296	2401	4096	6561
5th. dit.	1	32	243	1024	3125	7776	16807	32768	59049
6th. dit.	1	64	729	4096	15625	46656	117649	262144	531441
7th. dit.	1	128	2187	16384	78125	279936	823543	2097152	4782969
8th. dit.	1	256	6561	65536	390625	1679616	5764801	16777216	43046721
9th. dit.	1	512	19683	262144	1953125	10077696	40353607	134217728	387420489
10th. dit.	1	1024	59049	1048576	9765625	60466176	282475249	1073741824	3486784401
11th. dit.	1	2048	177147	4194304	48828125	362797056	1977326743	8589934592	31381059609
12th. dit.	1	4096	531441	16777216	244140625	2176782336	13841287201	68719476736	282429536481
13th. dit.	1	8192	1594323	67108864	1220703125	13060594016	96889010407	549755413888	2541865828329
14th. dit.	1	16384	4782969	268435456	6103515625	78364164096	678223072849	4398043311104	22876792454961

Explanation of the above Table.

WHEN the root of any number in this table, is required, look for the power at the-left hand, then casting your eye along that line towards the right hand, till you observe the number, and the figure standing at the top, is the root required.